A Siren's Song

Book Two of The Siren Series

S.R. Ruark

INDIES UNITED PUBLISHING HOUSE, LLC

INDIES UNITED PUBLISHING HOUSE, LLC
P.O. BOX 3071
QUINCY, IL 62305-3071
www.indiesunited.net

Other Book by S.R. Ruark

Coyote Laughing

The Siren Series
A Drowning World
A Siren's Song

Chapter 1

The room was opulent even by the Dead God standards. Wall hangings of natural fibers in geometric patterns were used as floor coverings. Lush paintings and more natural fiber pieces of art depicting different planetary scenes of flora and fauna hung along the grey metal walls. Metal chairs cushioned with plush foam padding covered in spider silk for the Dead God's managers, while each Dead God enjoyed lounging couches of material so soft to the touch that many would swear it was fur not woven fabric.

The table held cookware, dishes, and goblets of clay, glass, and wood. No two items the same as the other. Artisanal work, not factory made.

The silent servers were covered in natural fiber loincloths. Each server wore a different patterned material instead of a uniform color, denoting the use of material unique to each slave instead of using just one bolt for all. Several slaves had ribbons woven around arms or ankles, even in their hair. One woman with dark skin and blue tips at the ends of her braids had multiple thin strands of variegated blue ribbons woven through the rings piercing her upper and lower lips. The ribbons pulled the rings together so the woman could not open her mouth to speak or drink. The ribbons tied together at the corners of her cheek, giving her a false smile. The ends of the ribbons were done in complicated braids hanging down past her chin. Each ribbon ending in rare freshwater pearls and tiny gold and silver bells chimed cheerfully every time the woman walked or turned her head.

Chloefina watched the ribboned girl, standing next to Senodices as he reclined gracefully, her head bowed and hands clenched tightly together.

"New slave?" She asked, waving her glass goblet in the direction of the slave in question.

Senodices, smiled indulgently, a hand running down the girl's bare back, ignoring the shuddering revulsion she hadn't yet learned to hide. "Yes. A gift from Menodisces. He asked if I would find the time for training. I find that ribbons are good for silence without wastefully cutting out her tongue." His grin broadened as he dug pointed nails into her inner thigh. The girl tried to scream and back up, but the ribbons kept her pain muffled, and his fingers kept the girl in one place. "As you can see, more training is needed." Blood coated his fingers as he removed his hand from between her thighs. He held out his coated fingers to another slave, who knelt with a towel and a bowl of water to wash away the mess.

Chloefina laughed, with an edge that made her slaves unobtrusively edge away if possible from their God. "Good luck with the training. Your pens always produce the most docile yet intuitively helpful slaves I have ever had the pleasure of owning." She tugged none too gently on the honey brown braided hair of the male slave kneeling on the floor next to her couch. Only the other slaves seated on the floor saw his face pale in anticipation of what she might do next.

"You flatter me." But Senodices was not displeased with the other Undead God's assessment of his training skills. He inspected his hand for flecks of blood under the nails after the cleaning. The cleaning slave was very thorough. Once Senodices was satisfied he motioned for the ribboned slave and the floor to be cleaned. They all ignored the girl's tears and muffled sobs.

"It takes knowledge of how to tame a talking tool without breaking them," Chloefina added, admiring the ribboned slave. "I would love it if a couple of my breakers could undergo training with you."

"Breaking takes...skill. Not all breakers or Overseers have innate talent. However if you like I would be delighted to train a slave for you, or if you would like I have several who are extras in my household but excellent in all areas from managing to serving."

Chloefina blinked in surprise. "I would very much accept your generosity. I could use a couple more household slaves."

Menodisces entered the dining room with only four slaves following. His silk robes as overstated as the room.

"My apologies at my tardiness. My second wife just gave birth to a young girl." He took his place on the remaining seat at the center of the half circle. His slaves arranged themselves similarly to the other Gods slaves, one behind the seat, one at each end to serve and pour as needed. The one seated would lift any plate upwards so Menodices would not have to lean or lift, while eating. The Gods had only to talk and enjoy the meal set before them.

There were murmured congratulations. "Your dinner was precipitous. Had I known you were going to be blessed with another I would have brought a gift." Chloefina said, smiling widely, lifting her goblet towards Menodisces.

"Your company is what I craved. However, I am sure my wife would love some trinket or other."

"She favors brunettes?"

"And perfumes," Menodisces confirmed as he

accepted his goblet.

There was a general chuckle around the diners as the conversation returned to the previous discussions before Menodisces arrived.

"We heard about your world ship being attacked. Were your losses great?" Chloefina asked, a thin veneer of civility covering delight over Menodisces' misfortune.

"Luckily it was only one small battleship, fleeing from my own than an actual attack." Menodisces snapped back, lips pressed into a flat line.

"Damn runaways are getting fearless." Koarrass bemoaned, looking down into a highly carved wooden drinking goblet. "We need to bring them back to the ships. We need to remember what we are fighting!" His fingers touched the tree's trunk on the goblet as if touching a lover's face. Trees of any form were usually in growing areas or rare living spaces, hardly large enough to hide the entire six limbed animals as the carving depicted.

Menodisces looked over at his father with annoyance. More silver curls then black these days. Koarrass' days as a feared fighter had allowed his family to ascend to Gods on the world ship, displacing the former Undead God's family. Koarrass had kept the former God's wives, concubines, and daughters for his harem or kitchen slaves while killing all of the male lines of the necromancer. He stepped aside only a couple of years ago for his son, Menodisces to rule the world ship. In exchange, Menodisces kept his father for valued wisdom, though the font of wisdom was running dry as age started to take the formerly vaunted fighter's sharp mind down grey and blank corridors. Menodisces tapped long fingers on the top of his kneeling slave's head.

"He does bring up a good idea, the runaways do need to be returned, and we just can't go head to head with them," Sendices grunted, spearing a sweet green fruit in light floral syrup with a two-tined silver fork.

"Not even our gladiators can go head to head with one of those four arm monsters they keep." Choelfina shuddered. She had seen the footage from one of the mines lost to the runaways' attacks. The mines were a total loss, and only half of the minerals had been saved from ships already in route. Those being loaded into shuttles as the runaways entered the solar system; the mining colony had been either detonated remotely by the overseer in charge or his God. The slave loss from death or absorbed into the runaways had been high, but mine slaves were cheap, counting less than the loss the mineral they mined.

"Poisons would just kill our own." Chloefina mused. She nibbled on a small round pastry with a dark sweet and spicy meat filling, held at mouth height by a shaved headed petite and pale skinned slave. Her family specialties were rare plants and extracts. Everyone took care to bring tasters to one of her parties. Another slave offered her a drink from a glass goblet. The bottom of the goblet was crackled and colored with beautiful golds and greens, matching Menodisces' eyes. The comparison was not lost on Chloefina as she admired the drinking ware in her slave's hands.

"Gas jets set into hallways. Burn their damn fur off."

"Rather keep them alive long enough to skin. Those fur pelts are just gorgeous."

"I hear their own Redeyes God skins them when the mood strikes her."

"Not even we, skin our own just for amusement sake," Choelfina said indignantly, motioning for a plate of flat round biscuits with a shaving of cheese be brought closer for her selection.

"They do not understand the hardships they have on

ships, believing the lies told. They'd rather raid us for supplies than admit their ships are old and dilapidated."

"It's not like we can talk to them to negotiate their return. They just keep trying to steal our ships and developing worlds."

"We've made an attempt a few times."

"Yes, and only gained one or two ships. A severe loss by that one horrid attempt." CHloefina grumbled. "A few lost their world ships."

"The skins and slaves the rest received as gifts before they were taken were nice." Senodices murmured, into his drink as he lounged back into his seat. A slave knelt in front of him. He ran crumbed and greasy fingers through her thick blond hair before she could raise a moistened towel. He allowed her to clean both his hands when he had finished the primary wiping.

"Not being a fighter, I would seek commentary from those who supply the military with weapons, but isn't a good percentage of the ship battles hand to hand?"

"Enough of it is. Yes."

"Back to the idea of poison."

"It would kill our troops, and trained troops are expensive."

"Perhaps an antidote to our own, coating weapons and skin so that a touch would be lethal to the unwary."

"Pfft. They'd have the formula figured out in one go or two at the least."

"Poisons are like lovers. It's never good to have just one." Chloefina said, with a smile, holding her glass out for more wine. The wine was poured quickly, quietly and precisely as she liked from the slave with wide darting eyes behind her seat.

"And when they have all our poisons figured out?" Choelfina said testily, stabbing a tidbit with a two-tined fork. The force was more than the meat and fruit tidbit required.

"How many slaves and lovers can you do in a year?" Came the counter. "We can afford a few losses."

"They would lose more than us, but every loss to them is far greater than our own," Menodisces said soothingly, to keep either woman from becoming overly angry. Ships at war would hamper his plans at this juncture. Later perhaps he would flame the engine fire to blow this matter up, but for now a gentle weld along cracks would be more conducive.

"Easier then refitting our planets and ships with jet flames that are just as likely to damage our ships as their fighters."

"Perhaps traps though, of a less damaging nature."

"More steel and minerals from the mines."

"Better profit."

"Selling the remaining Gods on the idea of this shouldn't be too hard. With a well-written proposal and cost-effectiveness."

"Your dinner parties are never boring, Menodisces," Chloefina said with a smile, leaning over to lay a gentle hand on his arm.

"They can't all be blood and sex." He took her hand, saying with a smile, as he kissed her fingertips.

She favored him with another wide smile, before settling back down into her pillow filled couch. "More fun those. Though this growth plan will be more to my wife's liking." Said Senodices.

"More profit?" Menodisces asked, genuinely curious.

"More dead runaways. She still mourns her first daughter's death at their hands." Larentia's mouth turned down at the memory of the girl's death.

"A fighter, was she?"

"Yes. Well trained and well blooded. She met her death at the hands of one of those monsters."

"I think if we talked to a few others who have lost loved ones at the runaways' hands, we could present a stronger bloc with both monetary and emotional appeal."

Chapter 2

The hilt of the sword landed with a thunk, breaking at least one rib on the young God. The four-armed Wolfen didn't get the cut to her leg, as he side stepped into his opponent, but laid the sword flat on her back, splitting the skin in a long gash. Her seeping blood dried into crystals, as the wound sealed almost as quickly as it was made. Redeyes rolled with the blade slap on her back, a grunt of pain, stumbling two steps desperately getting her sword up to block the next blow. The block worked, but the Wolfen managed to land a closed fist punch to her face with his lower right hand. The sound of bone cracking accompanied the punch. He brought his sword up for an overhead blow that if it landed would have caved in her skull.

Redeyes dropped her blade, diving under his downward sword stroke, coming up under his arms and into his space. She stood face to face with him, giving him no room to position. Once there she fastened both upper hands on his throat, snarling as her broken cheekbones grated. Her hands squeezing tight, feeling his pulse quicken between her fingers. Her lower hands were trying to claw out his heart, held only an inch away from breaking skin and ripping out their target by the Wolfen's lower hands on her wrists. His lower arms bulging with the effort.

"Hold!" The General's voice boomed across the

vaulted metal room.

The Wolfen dropped his sword to grab the woman's upper set of arms at the elbows with both of his upper hands.

"Red if you kill him, you're going to have to replace him," Collins called, panting from the sidelines, wiping his face down with a synthetic towel. Iarris handed him a globe of water. Her fur as wet and matted as Collin's hair; both smelling of sweat.

"With fucking pleasure." The young God snarled or tried to, the words garbling. Her mouth sagged from the broken cheekbones and a half-healed broken jaw bone from a previous pass that morning — a gift from Iarris, re-broken sparring with Nero. Redeyes caught a sideways glimpse of Cratt swinging a metal rod down towards her arms. She moved at the last second, throwing herself backward, rolling, as the metal rod bounced off Nero's chest. The rod made a resounding thunk like hitting a hollow plastic water barrel.

Nero grunted, dropping to the mat, gasping for air like a fish. Redeyes curled her lip as she stood up slowly, hissing in pain from the broken and cracked bones. Nero's mouth formed words he didn't have the air to speak.

"Can't hear you," Redeyes said sweetly, giving a lopsided smile that didn't reach her eyes. Collin's cuff against her ear caught her by surprise, sending her stumbling to land on her ass, her arms swinging behind to catch her backward momentum with her elbows.

She looked up, tossing bangs out of her eyes, to Collins squatting in front of her. "You're getting better, but you aren't learning. And you're being an annoying bitch." He said.

"How the fuck am I not learning? You assholes beat the hell out of me every damn day." Slurring snarl.

"Broken bones tend to make me bitchy." A flash of fang in a human mouth.

"You're avoiding the blows but not learning how to fight," Iarris said, crossing her arms over her impressive chest. Her tail twitched in short sharp flicks; her lips pressed thin.

"Screw you." Redeyes snapped, scrambling up. Her head hunching low between her shoulders as her nails flexed, both set of hands loose at her side. She glared at those standing around her.

"Stop." General Cratt barked out, reaching a hand down to help Nero up. "You're not concentrating on learning how to survive, only how to win." Nero took the proffered hand, stumbling while standing up, a lower hand clutching at his sore ribs.

"And?" Redeyes snapped, not taking her eyes off of Collins. Collins gave a slow, easy smile, standing up gracefully to saunter just out of arm's reach. The lone human Guardian to the God.

"Fighting means you are looking to survive, not just kill the target in front of you." General Cratt said, with a tilt of his head and a look. The look saying she should understand the difference.

Redeyes dragged her eyes from Collins to General Cratt, with a stomp of her foot "What? Aren't you supposed to…" Collins stepped into her off side, sweeping his leg behind her and pushing her backward with his right hand.

She landed on her ass again, this time with a squawk. "Bastard!" She growled. Redeyes struggled to sit up on her lower elbows, glaring while her upper right hand brushed the sweat out of her eyes.

"Yup. Figured out why you landed on your ass?" Collins asked, leaning down with a casual smile, a gleam in his eyes.

Redeyes snorted, reaching a hand up for him to help her stand. "I took my eyes off you?" She asked, with a tilt of her head and rolled eyes.

Collins reached a hand out to help her up. "Nope, you let me get too close."

"Ahh." She said, grabbing his proffered hand. With a hard yank, she pulled him forward, piston kicking him in the stomach for all she was worth. Collins felt the yank and tried to counter by pulling back, but the kick caught him off guard. He flew to the side as she let go of his hand just as the kick landed.

"Hurts doesn't it?" Nero panted out, sagging against the General.

"You ship fucking…" Collins gasped rolling to his knees, a hand on the metal floor, the other reaching for the disc gun that wasn't there.

"And that is as far as we're getting today, cubs," Iarris said, flicking an ear at the General.

Cratt took the hint from the Guardian. "Iarris set Redeyes' bones. We're going to cover ship logistics and politics."

Iarris walked between Collins and Redeyes, neither taking their eyes off the other. Iarris thwacked Collins on the cheek with her tail as she walked by breaking his narrowed eye contact.

"Pfft…not how I wanted your tail." Collins spit fur out of his mouth, running a hand down his face to wipe off sweat-slicked skin, now with traces of Katherian hair.

"Get it how you can, but back off," Iarris said coyly, looking over her shoulder, with a wink and arching whiskers.

"Hmmph!" Collins did move back, his eyes on the Katherian's trim ass, the workout pants emphasizing the muscular roundness.

Iarris crouched in front of Redeyes, reaching a hand to touch her cheek. Redeyes flinched. Iarris waited. Redeyes took a deep breath, letting it out slowly. She pushed herself up from the floor with both sets of hands, letting Iarris work the bones.

"Sorry," Redeyes muttered, not looking the other in the eyes.

"I know this is still new to you," Iarris said softly, as if to a small child, her hand gently touching where the bones had broken. Redeyes' lips pressed tight, hunching her shoulders a little more. "This does get much easier." For everyone, was left unsaid by the Katherian fighter.

"Promise? 'Cause it's been months and I'm still getting my head handed to me daily." Redeyes mumbled, through gritted teeth.

"You're able to sucker punch Collins. That's pretty damn good." Iarris said, delicately moving Redeyes' cheekbones back together, counting to 30 under her breath.

"I heard that!" Collins grated, wheezing slightly still.

"At least you didn't say I'm not fighting fair."

"You can't fight fair. You have to fight to survive and win."

"But Cratt said survive." Redeyes heard the whine in her voice. She pressed her lips closed. Her jaw flexing in pain as Iarris pressed on the broken bones.

"You need to do both," Collins said, coming to the right side of Iarris, in front of Redeyes. "Your life is expendable." Redeyes flinched slightly but not enough to move the bones in her right cheek. Iarris held the ends together until the bones could hold their own shape.

If Redeyes moved, the bones would heal unevenly. They would need to be re-broken. A messier task than if she just held still the first time. Her bones, unlike a human's, knitted back stronger along the break line. Redeyes was doing everything she could not to re-break just knitted bones. They'd gone that route once already this month. She'd passed out when Collins had to take a metal rod to her leg at an unevenly healed break point.

"Our lives," Collins said, motioning with an open hand, taking in all of those on the ship. "Are a onetime chance. You fuck up and lose or don't see an opening, in a fight, a battle or tactics and we pay that price. You just jump bodies and timelines; the rest of us get a visit from Death."

Redeyes hung her head, clenching her fist tight enough that her nails broke skin. The sound of crystallized blood hitting the floor sounded loud in her ears, another weird difference between her and every other being on this ship. The memories of her first few lives and the deaths were still vivid.

"Fuck, I thought breaking free of the slavers was hard enough." She looked Cratt square in the face.

"You got us free Red hundreds of years ago, but now you need to learn more than just how to rip out a throat or throw a knife. You gotta see the bigger picture." Cratt motioned with his square thick fleshed hands, encompassing the whole ship, alluding to more.

"How..." She shook her head, dark blood red eyes boring into his human blue. "What am I doing wrong then?"

"You're getting the moves, but we need you to see the openings and the timing," Nero answered before the General could, as he came from the side, nails clicking on the bare metal floor. He handed her a towel and water. She accepted both, nodding her thanks. No hard feelings for either of them.

Nero patted her awkwardly on the back. "Like Iarris

said, it really will get easier for you." Iarris put her hands on Redeyes ribs feeling for bone movement.

"Holy fuck!" Redeyes yelped, squeezing her globe of water so hard water splashed over them as the globe burst.

"Think you hit the right spot," Collins said, wiping water out of his eyes. Amused, he cocked his head to the side, watching Iarris move strong hands along Redeyes' bruised skin. Blues and purples from today's hit, some already fading to a deeper yellow and greens.

"I really hate you at this moment," Redeyes said, between clenched teeth, curling her lips. She squinted her eyes close, scrunching her face from the pain.

"Don't worry. You get even with him by giving him all the shitty details when he meets an older you for the first time." General Cratt said cheerfully.

"Oh hells!" Collins' eyes widened and his mouth opened slightly as he connected the dots. "She remembered this far back?"

"Why else would she make you dive into the shit collector to search for those bodies?" Cratt said, tilting an eyebrow at him. "There are other ways to check for corpses."

"And I thought you were just being a disc eating ship rapist for the hell of it." Collins snorted, with a shake of his head, looking at the God sideways. He spun on the General "Why the rotting core engines didn't you say anything?"

"Cause I know Redeyes. She had a reason we just didn't know why she's pissing in your playpen." General Cratt gave Collins a human smile, showing all of his teeth. Predatory and amused.

"Good to know I have a sense of humor when I return to this time." Redeyes gasped out, as Iarris held the rib bones together for the initial knitting.

"It gets better Red. Now that we've broken enough bones time to learn some tactics." Cratt said briskly with a clap of his hands.

"Ship or hand to hand," Redeyes asked wearily, touching her cheek. The bones still felt fragile and wiggled a little.

"Both. Once you've taken a ship you're going to have to fight your way through it to kill the Dead Gods."

Redeyes clambered to her feet to walk to the tables, stopping for a moment frowning. "General Cratt, why do we practice with swords when we have guns? Shouldn't we be working on more than just hand to hand, sword work and the occasional use of guns?"

Cratt nodded. "You, in this life don't know this but we've tried that route. Got a couple of ships worth of people killed too. We can use guns, but only on small ship skirmishes. As near as we can figure out, on the large world ships, where there are very strong necros or necros who are willing to work together, they can combine their powers summoning ghosts to attack the power cells."

Redeyes connected the dots. "When one power cell goes, it'll explode, and if we're packed too closely, the force of one explosion can take out other power cells, causing a chain reaction."

"Aye. We do their job for them, killing ourselves. Which is why we do sword work and small guns."

"Ugh. Does this get any easier? It's been years!"

"This is the easy part."

"Shoot me now."

"Soon enough someone will," Cratt said, metal serious. Redeyes never lasted more than a few years in any body. Redeyes showed teeth in a humorless smile.

Chapter 3

"Mom! Toilets are backing up." Arie called from across the schoolroom. Lauranya looked up from her computer with a sigh of mild annoyance. Her research was at a delicate juncture. The toilet issue was unexpected and unanticipated. Jury rigging had its advantages, but reliability wasn't always one of them and the timing, irritating.

Lauranya got up from her desk to view the extent of the toilet problem in the nearest bathroom. Flooding would be a major health issue. She walked into the bathroom, surveying the damage. The first thing she noticed was that distinct smell. Lauranya made a face, taking a half step back. Instead of a slight scent of humanity, the room held a strong odor of sewage. There was no flooding, but the water sat at the rim.

"Time to pee in buckets?" Arie asked, behind Lauranya, hands on her hips jutting to the side by almost a foot, exaggeratedly. Lauranya turned to stare at her daughter for a moment, before realizing why the stance was so pronounced. Arie was mimicking her. Lauranya swallowed a laugh before answering. The child had grown so much in these years, a young woman, almost an adult now. The last years in the tower could be measured by the gardens and Arie's growth spurts.

"Probably, but we need to set up a hose to go outside," Lauranya said, tapping her lips thoughtfully. She managed to keep a straight face, though her lips kept twitching as Arie pushed out her hips in the other direction with more mimicry.

"Why not the stairwell?" Arie asked, making a broad waving motion towards the other side of their home.

"The one we get our drinking and bathing water from?" Lauranya asked, encouraging Arie to think this decision to a logical conclusion.

"No! Gross." Arie made her disgusted scrunched up face, aging her in the process before she relaxed back into her features.

Arie looked thoughtful before saying. "How about the one by the growing area?"

"We still draw water from there for the plants."

Arie looked up with a confused look and a shake of her head.

Lauranya had started to use questions that would lead to the correct answers if Arie did not respond correctly the first time, so she gave the child a few more minutes before responding, "Fecal bacteria." Lauranya answered the obvious when Arie wasn't going to get the answer quickly.

Arie's eyes widen as she made the connection. "Raw sewage is bad. Got it!" Arie nodded her head emphatically, her blond hair flying around her face in her enthusiasm. "Too bad we can't keep the solids for the compost."

Lauranya turned back to the toilet, starting to overflow, with a frown. Something niggling the back of her brain. Something important. "We...Let me look. Low water..." Lauranya muttered to herself, hurrying back to the room she used as her lab office. Arie trailed behind, used to her mother's mutters and tangent half sentences.

Lauranya tabbed to a new page. "Dry toilet. Primitive site. Two part." Muttering, she leaned over her desk typing, willing the computer to find what she needed by sheer force of will.

"Ah! Here it is!" She stood up with a wide smile, lighting up the room.

"What is it?" Arie asked, looking on with a tilted head and curious eyes.

"For a primitive base, when supplies and growing mediums have been in short supply. There are toilets made to collect urine in the front part and solids in the back, separating the two wastes.

"We could just potty in a bucket and throw it out…"

"No," Lauranya said, giving her daughter a shake of her head.

"Why not?" Arie tilted her head, puzzled.

"Do you want to be the one to clean up the drips or spills of old waste?"

Arie thought on this, before responding. "No. We already make a mess."

"I assure you, our mess is much less than if we were going in a bucket. However, we do have the issue of where to go until I can fabricate the new system."

"That means what?"

"We pee in a bucket for a short time."

Arie made a face. "Yuck!" She had to think for only a moment before asking. "So what do we do now?"

"Well, first we empty the backed-up toilets with a hose."

Arie scrunched up her nose, waving her hands as if something nasty had gotten on them.

"Yes, it is. I should stop feeding you, so you do not push out so much waste!"

"Mommy!" Arie squealed. Neither went hungry, but they talked about food all the time — growing, cooking, or new tastes.

Lauranya laughed at such young outrage. "Now I need

to find a hose long enough to dump the waste over the side. And you need to get back to your lessons."

"Okay, mommy." Arie gave her a mother a heavy sigh but scampered back to the microscope with a smile. A feather, donated from a chicken, was clipped down for viewing. Arie pulled the two sheets of paper next to her. One for writing her observations, and the other to sketch what she saw at different angles. The artwork and hypothesis were a little crude, but her work showed promise.

The hoses were found in the bottom storage rooms, with a generator for pumping. Lauranya linked the hoses together with clamps then started to drag the appropriate end to the upper deck to hang off the railing. The tail end of the exiting hose hung from the railing, swaying slightly in the breeze.

"No nothing could go wrong with a loose hose and human waste," Lauranya said, talking to herself with a roll of her eyes. "I will tie that down before pumping. Not good to teach the child lazy workarounds." Lauranya didn't head back in immediately though. She stretched in the afternoon sun, soaking up the warmth, watching the brilliant white clouds float by on deep blue skies. She let loose a pent up breath. The air smelled warm and damp, so fresh. Even after so much time, fresh air and fresh water were novelties after growing up on the world-ships or under mining domes.

Shivers ran up her spine, along arms and legs as she looked on the vastness of her new world. Lauranya felt sharp cuts of cold along her spine in fear of the open water. She ran hands over cold arms, her mouth suddenly dry.

The rains had become intermittent, making the nice days outnumber the rainy ones. The waters below were still climbing. Lauranya looked over the stone hip height balusters. Small waves lapped against the building. Her eyes saw a different set of waves. Small ripples, almost like when rain spattered on the top of the water, then a large ripple with a smooth curve of glossy grey blue scaled skin breaking the water. The water smoothed out once more.

Distance played havoc with measurement, but Lauranya did her best to calculate a possible size. The size estimated were not reassuring.

"The new water habitats filled quickly." She whispered shuddering before turning to hurry back into the perceived safety of the building.

Another round, with a different set of hose, to draw water from the stairwell into water barrels went faster than the waste hose issue. Twenty minutes at a time to fill up the four empty barrels that could last a week for showers and water needs of the people, plants, and animals.

"Mom! The fresh water hose is stuck." Arie yelled from the foyer. Her words vibrating as they echoed through the rooms.

"Stuck? Fresh water and not sewage hose? Where?" Lauranya called back, projecting her voice to match the depth and timber of Arie's. She stood, walking to the balcony from outside her lab looking down into the main room.

"Fresh water. Oops. Not stuck." Arie said, looking down and prodding the hose with her toe.

"Okay." Lauranya smiled and started to turn when Arie's next words stopped her.

"It's clogged."

"Clogged… Hmm." Lauranya walked down the stairs and past the planted flats of seedlings, just starting to push green tips through the recently made composted dirt.

"We need to inspect the hose for the clog." Lauranya

chewed her lip. "Do not borrow what is not yours, including trouble." She said, looking at the dribble of water going from the hose to the barrel. "Okay. Turn off the pump and find a few extra towels. We'll need to clear out the hose."

They walked from the hose to the stairwell, inspecting the hose every few inches. Arie carrying the towels while Lauranya crawl-walked, squeezing every few inches. Close to the stairwell, she found a lump…that wiggled. She let go with a startled yelp, landing on her rump.

Lauranya licked sweat dewing her upper lip, frowning slightly. "If it's not moving on, it probably has barbs stuck along the inner wall. Well, we can try to save the fish first, but that probably is not likely. Maybe fish for dinner?"

"Fish for dinner? Sounds yummy!" Arie stood on the tips of her toes, bouncing.

"I'm sure it does, but first let me see what I can manage here." Lauranya gently squeezed the hose to find the end of the fish or what was not pointing towards the barrel, roughly 8 inches. The squeezing caused the fish to thrash, jerking the hose from side to side. She tried to push it along gently, but the fish didn't budge with Lauranya's prodding.

"Hmmph." A little irritably.

"Going to have to splice it, mommy?"

"Unfortunately, I think so." Lauranya glowered at the hose with narrowed eyes and pursed lips. She put her hands on her hips to contemplate her choices. None of the choices were less than messy.

"I'll get the gripping tape!" Arie yelled, spinning on her heels, running excitedly for the bag of fix-it materials.

"And I will get the clamps and cutters." Lauranya rose to her feet from bent knees with shoulders straight and arms at her side, graceful in her slowness.

They returned with their supplies, Arie having added a bucket with enough water to cover the fish once they'd freed it from the hose.

"What kind of fish do you think it is mommy?" Arie stared at the hose intensely.

"I don't know dear. Do you remember from our studies which types might be this small and this lively?" Lauranya clamped behind the fish, an equal amount to its length, stopping the flow of water from even the trickle that had been flowing.

"I might. But won't it depend on if this is full grown or a juvenile? "

"Very good!" Lauranya delicately cut the hose, behind and in front of the lively fish, depositing the squirming hose occupant into the bucket. Next, she pieced the edges of the hoses together with fast setting glue. Clamps and tape holding the hose together until the glue could form a waterproof seal. A small trickle of water had flowed out, which Arie promptly mopped up with a towel, without being asked.

"We will need to let this cure for a couple of days." Lauranya sat back to admire her handy work.

Arie's attention was on the water splashing as the fish thrashed in the hose even worse than when stuck in the whole hose.

"Mommy, doesn't it know we are trying to help?"

"Thinks we are going to eat him."

"Oh. We are, aren't we?" Arie said matter factly, a child's mercurial thought from potential pet to food.

"Maybe. Some fish are too toxic to eat. We will not know until we cut it out of the hose." Lauranya stood up, observing the small wiggling bit of hose. She picked up the materials to put them back in the supply room. "Arie, take the bucket with the fish into the lab. We'll do a dissection in a moment."

"Okay!" Arie grabbed the bucket, managing to not splash on the gleaming wooden floors, by the gods own luck, as she lugged it up the stairs to the second floor lab.

Lauranya arrived at the lab a few moments after. Walking through the door, she noticed Arie crouched over the bucket staring intently down.

"Something interesting?"

"It's not moving."

"The hose, the water or the fish?"

"The fish in the hose. It's not moving at all now." Arie peered closer, reaching to touch the hose. Lauranya intercepted the hand, with a shake of her head.

"Probably dead. The water is no longer flowing over the gills, not to mention the water in the bucket is stale, not fresh." Lauranya said, sparing a glance into the bucket as she set up the counter for extraction and eventual dissection.

"Are we going to dissect it now?" Arie asked excitedly, looking up at her mother, her voice rising as she bounced slightly in anticipation.

Lauranya smiled fondly at her daughter. "Yes. We are going to dissect it now." Lauranya motioned Arie to bring the bucket over to the sink, by the window. Lauranya pulled a cutting board, various scalpels and blank slides from drawers and lower cabinets.

"Can I look at it microscope?"

"Yes, you can look through the microscope once I get the slides prepared. You will need to figure which portions are worth micro-scrutiny and which for general analysis."

Arie ignored that comment in favor of a more artistic endeavor. "Are we going to sketch?"

"If you like. We need to add to our native plants and animal book. "

"Yay!" Arie dragged a tall stool over to the counter, watching as her mother took the hose from the water, with bare hands.

"Arie if you would…" Arie had a towel ready, handing it over as soon as Lauranya placed the hose down and turned towards her. "Ahh…thank you, my dear." Lauranya placed the hose on the dissection tray, wiped her hands, and opened a drawer for her goggles. Arie followed suit, taking a few extra minutes trying to remember where she had last placed them. They were found in the bathroom. Arie had worn them while swimming and churning the dirty laundry in the tub. Soap bubbles still fascinated her. Lauranya merely smiled, hiding her giggle at Arie's unusual method for inspecting washing clothes.

Once they were both set, Lauranya slipped the industrial scissors along the edge of the hose, wishing for the 100th time for good gloves. She took care not to cut the fish inside. The black ribbed hosing took longer to cut from the thick water tight weave then from the thin flexible coating of plastic liner, and the fish wasn't quite as dead as originally presumed.

Lauranya cleared enough hose away to see the tail end of the fish; however, the hosing wasn't falling away from the fish as expected. Frowning, she tried to pull the casing away with her fingers on one side and the scissors holding the other side down. The fish's skin pulled taught almost ripping. Lauranya stopped, to chew on her lip.

"Yemoja!" Lauranya swore softly.

"What's wrong mommy?"

"I think…think the fish has barbs in its skin that are stuck in the hose."

"That's going to make getting it out harder," Arie said succinctly.

"Yes, dear. It will." Lauranya tried for bland but a little

sarcasm leaked through. Arie grinned at her mother not chastised in the least.

"I would like to keep the skin intact though that may…" Lauranya huffed in frustration gingerly poking the stuck fish with a finger. "Not be possible."

She grabbed tweezers and long pins. She pinned one side of the hose then used the tweezers to open the other side, tugging gently. As the hose opened, she tweezed each spine from the hose as gently as possible onto the dissection board. The fish, who did not agree with her ministrations, began thrashing violently. Luckily the spines were only on the back portion along both sides of the dorsal fin; however, the entire process took close to 30 minutes. The fish stopped flailing closer to the start than the end. "Done." Lauranya breathed, putting down her instruments to look at her work with satisfaction at the cutting board. There were a few tears in the skin, yet the fins and the body were extracted with minimal damage. The vivid blues and gold shimmered even as the eyes turned dull in death.

"It looks pretty!" Arie said in awe reaching a hand to touch the fish.

Lauranya caught the hand mid-way, with a gentle squeeze. "It does look beautiful. I wonder." She muttered, bending down for a closer look.

Arie leaned over to look closer as well, her hand landing on the metal tray, knocking it over.

"Arie!" Lauranya grabbed for the spilled tools. Her hand reached for two of the spilling items, but her other hand landed in a puddle of water made from the entrapped fish and sodden hose. Her hand slipped out from underneath, unbalancing her. Lauranya made a desperate grab for stability, grabbing the hose instead. Pins, spines, and tines pierced her hand as she landed on her butt, knocking Arie over as she fell. The cutting board clattered to the floor.

"Ouch! Damn it." Lauranya swore. "Arie are you ok?" She stood slowly, careful of things in her hand.

"I'm ok mommy," Arie said with a hurt voice, rubbing her butt as she stood back up. "Are you ok?"

"Oww. Think so." Lauranya pulled pins and the sliced hose from her skin, dropping the waste onto the counter. She looked down at her hand, pursing her lips. There were small pricks in the skin with red aerials surrounding a few. "Hmmm." She made another face concentrating on the skin rash. Memories of her skin contacted with the poisoned wine from the shuttle flowed through her thoughts like molasses.

"Mommy?" A quaver to Arie's voice that didn't register with Lauranya at first.

"What?" Lauranya snapped concentrating on how her hand felt, while gently running a finger over the redness. No spines could be felt. Maybe only a slight allergic reaction?

"You're bleeding…want me to grab the clean rags and alcohol?" Arie looked into her mother's face with huge eyes, the child's face pale.

Lauranya looked down. The fish had hooked into the scar tissue on Lauranya's calf. The spines were deep enough to cause small trickles of blood, painting her skin reddish pink, pooling around her heel.

Lauranya sucked in a breath. "I cannot feel the spines." She whispered her eyes as wide as her daughter's.

"Mommy?"

"Shhhh. I will need to pull the fish's spine from my skin." She gave Arie a comfortingly wide smile that didn't reach her eyes. A lying smile. "It will be fine, baby. Now go and get me those clean rags."

"Alcohol as well?"

"The cheap drinking alcohol, not the medical grade."

"Are you going to drink it?"

"I might have a sip, but mostly the alcohol will be poured over the skin. It will be almost as sterilizing as the medical stuff."

"Then why not the medical grade?"

"Because we might need the medical grade for another major surgery and not something as minor as this." Lauranya's voice held steady, calm and even. She looked down with her hands hovering just out of touching distance from the fish, twitching.

"Oh. Okay mommy!" Arie spun on her bare feet and ran to the medical room's cupboard with the alcohol.

"Well lied." A voice whispered in her ear.

"How bad is it Jacks?" Lauranya whispered, with a breath that would not have been heard past her lips.

"I don't know. We never got to study the viral and bacterial, let alone the poison applications, of the fish." Jacks took a moment before continuing. "I think you may have as much to worry about the poison in the spines causing the numbness as anything living inside you now." Neither speaking of the virus she'd been infected with from the whiskered cat years ago.

"Comforting." Lauranya wiped her cheek quickly, shaking her head.

"Comfort isn't why you asked." Jacks' voice faded as small running footsteps could be heard on the wood covered hallway floor.

"Here you go, mommy!" Arie bounced back into the room, holding a dark brown bottle with no labeling and a handful of clean rags. All but one rag wrapped around Lauranya's ankle, to catch the poured alcohol instead of letting it pool on the floor. The other rag Lauranya wrapped around her hand for protection.

Lauranya took a deep breath and releasing it slowly. "Okay. I want you to pour that over the skin. My skin, not the fish skin. And I will start pulling the fish from me."

Arie bent down, getting her face close to the wound and the fish but not close enough that Lauranya wanted to flinch back to keep Arie safe. Carefully the child tipped the bottle next to Lauranya's scar; the chartreuse colored liquid came in a trickle at first then a large spill at Arie poured more confidently.

Lauranya let out a hiss as the alcohol struck the skin where the barbs had sunk in. "Okay sweetie, stop pouring."

Arie stopped with a questioning look up.

"I need to pull the spines out then we can disinfect a bit more."

"Okay!" Arie chirped, as she put the bottle on the floor next to her mother's foot, before bouncing to grab the tweezers just out of Lauranya's reach.

Lauranya grabbed the fish gently then whispered a quick prayer to Babaluaye while pulling out the spines. The spines held her skin with less ferocity than the hose, but they did not pull out smoothly either. Lauranya's lips bruised as she pressed her teeth together using the flesh as extra padding and pain stimulation for endorphins. She was drenched in sweat as the last spine pulled free.

This time she put the fish on the cutting board, moving the board to the back of the counter away from the front edge.

"Okay love, now you may pour more of the alcohol." Lauranya grabbed the counter in anticipation. She hadn't been wrong in the strength of the alcohol's burn. Each spine prick lit up like an electric current. The pain from her hand was nothing in comparison.

"Yemoja!" Lauranya gasped a prayer to the mother of mankind.

"Mommy?" Arie stopped looking up with quivering lips and tears in her eyes, her mother's pain almost palpable.

"You are fine dear." Lauranya sucked in another breath. "I think we are good on the alcohol though. If you could put it back?"

"Sure!" Arie screwed the top on quickly. "Mommy, are we still going to look at it through the microscope?"

"Yes. We both are. I am going to take samples and many pictures. I have a vested interest in this species now. I need to know all the quirks that this fish has in life and death."

"Because it's new?"

"New to us, but no. I do not want you to get hurt if this gets pulled into the hose again." Lauranya's voice bland, leaving out the numbness of her skin from the spines.

"Should we put something over the end of the hose?"

Lauranya opened her mouth then snapped her teeth closed, pinching the bridge of her nose. "Yes, should have thought of this earlier. I will find a loose woven piece of material we can attach to the ending after I take pictures."

Chapter 4

The fever set in later that night. They had gotten the theater projector working that week and were watching an aria. They settled on the leather couch, with colorful cushions scattered about them. Arie sprawled next to Lauranya, her head in her mother's lap, with hair still wet from their shower. Both were listening raptly as the singer's incredible voice hit note after note.

Arie listened to her mother sing along softly, hitting the notes better than the singer. She felt a thrum from both her mother and the other singer, racing along her spine and in her head. The aria made her chest bones vibrate, but mommy's song was in her head, making her want to sing along. So she hummed, while Lauranya petted her hair, fingers teasing out small knots from the washing.

"Mommy, your skin is hot!" Arie said, lifting her head from her mother's bare leg, putting a cool hand where her head had just rested.

Lauranya looked down at her blond haired child, with a frown. She placed a hand on her forehead then Arie's, then back to her forehead.

"Oh." Lauranya got up swiftly, heading to medical.

"Mommy?" Arie trailed behind, keeping up with her fast-paced mother.

"I need to take my temperature." Lauranya stopped in the doorway. "Arie." She shook her head before starting again. "Arie, if something happens to me you'll have to take over."

"Like when you were injured from the whiskered cat." Arie's eyes started to glisten with unshed tears, her voice rising a little higher.

Lauranya only hesitated a second but confirmed Arie's fear with a firm nod. "Just like that." She found the drawer with the thermometer. Her hands shaking, she placed the small circular pad behind her ear, then pulling the sensor pad's connecting wire over her shoulder — the fever spiking at 102.4.

"Mommy?" Arie stood at the door, with hunched shoulders and her hands behind her back, like a toddler getting caught with a stolen cookie.

"It is ok, love." Lauranya took a deep breath, keeping her tone light. "I am running a bit of a fever. What would you prescribe?" She pulled the sensor pad from her skin, clearing the monitor before putting both back in the drawer with a soft thump.

Arie looked to the ceiling, tilting her chin up before speaking. "Hmm…cold water, rest and the red fever stuff? Like the stuff you gave me when I got fevers."

"Very good. I," Lauranya motioned to herself "am going to go to bed. I would like you to keep a close eye on me, but do not neglect your homework or the animals please."

"What about the plants?"

"This should not be anything more than a ship day of fever, so the plants should" The "should" rattled through Lauranya's brain, like a warning claxon of Babaluaye laughter. "be ok. If this does not run the projected course, then you will have to take over the plants on top of all else."

"Do you think you will want anything to eat while sick? I know when I'm sick, I usually don't like foods."

Arie's second favorite place, the kitchen.

Lauranya had to think about this for a moment. "Noni would make an excellent rabbit soup. Not a lot in it but broth and meat. Just broth for someone too sick to chew." Lauranya didn't finish the thought on what happened to those who couldn't eat after a week on the ships. Arie already had more nightmares than a child her age should.

"I can make a great rabbit soup! Those sweet white roots and some of the peas. Both…" Arie ready to start on a new adventure in the kitchen.

"Arie. Arie." Lauranya leaned forward while speaking. The motion and the intensity of the words got the child's attention. "Whatever you make will be good. Just remember I may not be able…" Lauranya's voice caught for just a second. So slight, that she didn't think Arie had caught the hesitation. "be able to eat. I need you to keep it simple."

"No white root? You love those."

"I do! Go with the sweet roots, well chopped, and the peas. Those both cook down soft enough that not much chewing will be necessary."

"I'll cut the meat up into very small pieces too!"

"A good idea." Lauranya felt a chill run down her spine, raising bumps along her arms and legs. Her teeth started to chatter. "I am going to take a shower and then crawl into bed."

"Mommy?" Arie's eyes were bright with tears. One trickled down her cheek, hastily wiped away with the back of a hand, run haphazardly over a young cheek.

Lauranya rushed forward kneeling, ignoring the dizziness for the moment. "Oh, baby. I am just having a small reaction to the fish's spine toxin. Hopefully, it is nothing major, just an inconvenience. Do not worry." touching the wet smear on Arie's cheek. "I just need you to do a little extra please." She gave Arie her best reassuring smile "Your soup sounds delicious. It will be just what I need."

"You sure, mommy?" Arie wasn't talking about the soup.

"Positive." Lauranya nodded firmly but staggered slightly getting to her feet as she began to shiver. "Time for that shower though!"

"I'll get it running for you!" Arie gave her mother a quick hug, before running out of the lab office, bounding a flight of stairs to their rooms.

"Thank you, Yemoja, for a quick-witted child." Lauranya breathed, standing up, to a wave of dizziness. Lauranya contemplated the walk to the shower. "One step then another." She muttered carefully matching footsteps to the words — her bed seemingly miles from where she stood.

The fever-wracked her with chills, then a burning so intense she threw off the blankets piled deep, sweat soaking into the bedding. The dreams though, those were the worst. Tine and the boys, laughing as they were floating through space, burning even in the vacuum, their skin flaking into dust with bright smiles and brighter eyes. Maison caught the dust to fling at the faceless men and women who danced on the wires between the apartments of her family home. Blood scattering on the floor and walls as the wires cut into the dancing bare feet. Arie squatted on the bottom floor of the apartments, drenched in red, as water began to seep in. Lauranya couldn't reach Arie, as the water filled over the child's head. Arie continued to calmly plant the seedlings in metal floor tiles. The seedlings looked eerily like the dead scientist and their children. Their small green bodies waving like seaweeds to and fro in an underwater garden.

Lauranya jerked awake when Arie's seedlings grew to the size of toddlers and started to walk out of the ship apartments. The sheets and her sleep shirt, drenched in sweat. The shirt so salt encrusted and clinging, it was making her itchy. "Stop it." She whispered fiercely to herself. "The dead are gone." Her throat burned and scratched, hurting with every attempt to swallow.

Lauranya tried to get out of bed. Sitting up made her whimper as her joints caught on fire. Any movement, no matter how small, hurt like a whipping wheel 15 seconds after the first lash hit. A hiss and a roll to her side, she tried to get her legs over the side of the bed.

"No, love. Stay in bed. I'll get Arie to come to you." Maison's deep voice resounded through her head. She felt his large hand on her fevered brow.

"You are dead, Maison. You died on the world-ship." Lauranya said querulously. "You are not here." Lauranya brushed a hand through empty air to move his hand. The voice so resounding, she half expected to feel the resistance of flesh.

"True. Yet here I am, and you, my little mouse, need to stay in bed." Maison laughed, flicking the tip of her nose as he had done. "Stay in bed, love, and I will get Arie."

Lauranya could not budge from the weight of his ghostly hand. She glared up at him. More of a squint as light filtered through the curtains, causing more pain.

"Gods love Maison, move, please. I cannot stay and dream." She whispered, looking into Maison's dark eyes, shattered with the bright flecks. Beautiful and full of love those eyes.

"I'll stay with you, so your dreams are better."

"You are not here." This time Lauranya managed to sit

up, throwing one leg over the edge of the bed. She promptly fell on her face when the floor rushed up to meet her. The motion of the leg over the bed rolled her faster than she could compensate for.

"Oww!" Lauranya felt her face gingerly, her right hand running over her face searching for pain or blood. Pain yes, blood no. She climbed slowly and painfully back into bed.

"Stubborn woman," Maison said fondly, as he helped her back up. He pulled the covers over her, putting a cool cloth on her brow.

"Still not here." She whispered but didn't take her eyes off of him.

"Do you really want me to leave?" That smile, a flash of white teeth through soft velvet black skin, warm to the touch, her treacherous memory whispered. Her heart squeezed in heartache.

Lauranya pushed herself up to her knees. Maison hunched in front of her, wearing his training loincloth. His skin looked sweat-slicked, with the occasional patch of sand, from the training ground. Grandfather had been so proud of being able to have an actual sand training ground, instead of hard metal flooring. "Less injuries." He said, framing the cost beneficially.

Lauranya's hand shook as she reached over to brush sand from his broad shoulder. The sand flecked off with the touch of her hand. His dark skin, warm under her touch, covered muscles that bunched and released like silk over steel.

"I did not want to marry your brother," Lauranya whispered, ignoring what reality had already dictated. Believing in this moment was a need stronger than the pain.

"I'm sorry, love. That's history now. I'm only here for

a short while." Maison kissed her on the forehead.

"No. Please. Stay, do not leave me." Pleadingly, she leaned forward wrapping both arms around her lover's chest, so broad that her hands could barely reach all the way around.

Maison rocked her back and forth, comfortingly. Much the way she had rocked all of her children when they were sick or in need of comfort. Lauranya melted into his arms, refusing to contemplate anything other than this moment. Lauranya drifted back to sleep.

"Mommy. Mommy." Arie's hand on Lauranya's brow roused her from dreams of her love. Lauranya felt her child's touch, as electric pulses to the skin. Painful. The pulses racing along her nerves. Maison was a dream, she realized. He died, never to return to her. The pain of loss, from his second leaving, cut through her, almost as sharp as the first time she lost him. Lauranya shook her head trying and failing, to stop the flow of tears.

"I'm sorry, mommy! I didn't mean to hurt you!" Arie's face scrunched, at her mother's obvious pain.

"No, baby. I had bad dreams." Lauranya croaked. "Dreams of loss and pain. It's not you." She gently touched Arie's cheek, giving the child a wan smile.

"I love you, mommy." Arie tried to hug her mother. Lauranya accepted the hug weakly, loving her child but wishing for her dreams. Lauranya looked away for a moment with that thought. She knew not even Ori, the god of destiny could have changed her life course after she had fallen in love with Maison.

"I love you, too," Lauranya whispered, tasting salt. "What have you brought me?" She asked, sniffing the air as a fragrant smell cut through the pain and dreaming fogginess.

"I brought you some soup. Mostly broth but I also have

some tea, sweetened with honey." Arie said, vibrating in place. She pointed carefully to the soup and cup she had set on the stand, before waking her mother.

"They smell divine." Lauranya tried to sit up, but the pain of her joints had not been a dream. The burning ripping pain felt all too real, causing her to whimper as she struggled upright.

"Don't sit up, mommy! Jacks said you were hurting a lot and I should try for with a straw." Arie scolded gently as she pulled the blankets back over her mother's chilled body.

"There are straws?" Lauranya panted, from the brief effort of sitting up.

"Reed straws…and plastic ones. But I thought you would want to try out the reed ones first!" Arie gave a conspiratorial whisper. Real plant or animal items were still a novelty to them both.

Lauranya gave a delighted ghost of a laugh, at the idea of trying an item of a God. Arie lifted the soup first, for her mother to taste. The bowl was filled halfway, with a clear slightly green tinged soup. A large wooden reed, as thick as a man's pinky with many joints along the length, within reach for easy sipping. Lauranya took a cautious sip. The soup tasted amazingly rich with flavor and fat slipping across her tongue.

Arie moved the soup after a few sips, to bring the mug within her mother's reach. A second straw for the tea. Lauranya sipped slowly. The tea tasted sweet, yet floral with spicy taste rolling from the tongue to the back of the throat. The honey coating in a soothing wave, easing her swollen throat. Her stomach did a slow roil with the first few sips, causing her to waive off any more.

"That's not a lot, mommy." Arie gave her mother a stern frown. The exact same one Lauranya had given her on those times Arie felt she didn't have to try new foods or pick up her room.

"You will be cleaning up the contents of my stomach, off the bed and floor if I take any more," Lauranya said with a ghost of laughter, at her strong-willed child.

"Yuck!" Arie had to think for a moment. "Would you like some cold water? Would that help more?"

Lauranya closed her eyes, letting out a tired breath. "It might, baby, but later. I just need more sleep." Her voice a whisper, as an uneasy sleep claimed her again.

Arie tiptoed out with the bowl and cup. She left the door open in case her mother might call for her.

Lauranya dreamed the surreal again. She watched herself move the covers aside, her hands flexing and lengthening. Her nails extended into sharp crescent claws, shredding the bedding as she pulled herself into a more comfortable position. Dark hair sprouted along her skin. She rubbed her cheek along her bare shoulder. The fur felt warm and soft against her skin.

The fur felt even better than the one and only spider silk dress she had owned when living on the ship. The one she traded for higher favor, for consideration to be on this assignment with Tine, when she had still cared, her dream-she thought, enjoying the feeling of stretching muscles. The next thought was that she should have kept the dress and left Tine to his own devices on this Gods cursed planet.

She watched as her feet lengthened, changing in ways only dreams could. Good for dancing, she thought admiring the incredibly high arches. Her toenails emerged as she flexed her toes. Crescent nails like her hands. She felt herself smile, thinking how nice the nails would be for climbing trees with Arie.

There had been one world, where Lauranya had worked on for a short while, where indoor parks held huge blue-skinned trees. Her dream saw her curled up in the trunk of a tree, her dark fur brilliant against the blue tree trunks with a tail flicking lazily in the warm evening air. Arie's laughter infections, as she jumped and skipped along the low branches, alight with soft incandescent lights. Mother and daughter enjoying life.

The fever lingered as did the pain in her joints and muscles over the next week. Lauranya got out of bed, but only for a few minutes at a time. Her stomach took more time to settle than the swelling in her joints.

Her dreams were far more mundane after the initial fever. Dreaming of life in the old apartments. Plain plastic and grey tiled walls with metal doors. Sterile. The brightest colors where Arie's colored childish pictures were on the walls.

She went to knock on Tine's bedroom door. The dream providing vivid details she would rather have forgotten like the rhythmic grunting, telling her he was busy with Micha. Lauranya's dream self-noted she had not thanked Tine's mother for the body slave. Anything to keep him from her, a blessing from Oba, for marital bliss. A thought wound its way that Tine could have used the training body slaves received to help with his singular lack of skills in bed with her, but he never bothered learning only receiving. Selfish man.

Lauranya shrugged, cracked open the door so that her voice could be heard, but she didn't interrupt. "Tine, we need to get to your lab for closing procedures, while Micha packs."

"Be…done…moment…arily." The grunting reply.

Lauranya saw herself roll her eyes as she moved on to the twin's room. The boys only a few inches shorter than their mother, yelling in their room with crashing sounds, creating havoc again. She walked in as they were jumping on and over their beds, slamming into walls as they tried to tag one another. Blankets and clothes were strewn about the room, as if looters had torn through looking for anything precious but finding only dross.

"You two need to pack clothes. Any items you want to take on the shuttle today." Lauranya said, ignoring the room's mess as an unnecessary fight anymore.

"That's what Micha is for!" One snapped, evading his brother's tagging hand slap, only to slip on a pillow, falling between the twin sized beds with a thud. Both boys' shrieks of laughter, grating even in the dream.

"Micha is packing your father's clothing and mine. If you want anything to go with you, you will need to bestir yourself and get it done." Lauranya snapped, eyes flashing as she put hands on her hips. The boys had long since gone from precocious to stupidly dangerous in what they said.

"We'll tell dad!" They shouted in unison.

"Yeah, dad said we aren't sand piss so don't need to do anything you say!" The closer one sneered at his mother, with the age-old insult for a slave born pit fighter.

Lauranya moved with speed, catching the boys unaware. She caught the closer son by surprise. Her slap hit his cheek with an open palm, hitting hard enough to stagger him against his twin. "You will pack, and you will start now. Anything you do not pack will not go with you nor will I bring it. You can wear slave tunics for all I give to the void." Lauranya chewed out, through gritted teeth. Her voice dropped a few degrees as she stood straight, looking down at her two unmanageable children.

Their eyes narrowed dangerously, like a pack of hunting dogs. They saw their mother as prey outnumbered, one to two odds. Lauranya saw that look, meeting it with narrowed eyes of her own. She may not have been trained to fight, but she knew the basics, something Tine had forbidden his sons from learning.

Lauranya shifted her stance, altering her hands and arms slightly. The boys looked at each other. They had charged their mother once a few months back, thinking their father would protect them and their mother soft. Lauranya had given them the physical punishment she saw fit. Neither had been able to sit for a day. The bruises stood out, even on their dark skin, for four days more.

The lesson had sunk in. "Yes, mother." Their sullen reply. The boys pouted, looking at the floor. They would mutter more insults when she left; however, Lauranya felt pretty sure they would have (badly) packed bags for the shuttle. That was all Lauranya cared about, too tired to fight to keep them from trouble anymore.

She turned on her heels, heading back into the living room, where she bumped into her half-dressed and livid husband.

"Why are you yelling at the boys?" His chin stuck out, as he pulled up his pants, tightening his belt. His hands caressed the metal buckle.

Lauranya tilted her head, with narrowed eyes at the implied threat. "Your sons seem to think themselves Gods. They are now packing." She continued towards the bedrooms, moving past him, flinching in distaste as skin touched skin.

Tine snagged her arm on the way past, with one hand still on his belt. "Damn it, Lauranya! We aren't arena slaves. The boys are only being…"

Dream-Lauranya did not let him finish. "Dangerous.

They can and will be collared if they slack on their exams. Oh wait, they already are!" She faced him with clenched fists. "When they realize how important those tests are, it will be too late! They are one outburst in class from being reevaluated and downgraded. You" She poked a finger in his thin bare chest. "have given them an inflated self of importance. I wash my hands of them, on the next assignment. Their training and behavior are now on you." She poked him in the chest again, her voice low and barely controlled. "Just you! You may explain to your family how you let the pride and joy of your loins become menial slaves." She turned her back on him, walking into the split bedrooms, gently closing the door. No need to advertise to the other occupants on the same hallway level that another fight was occurring.

Tine didn't let the argument go. He poked his head into her bedroom. "Yes, I do spoil them, but then again you spoil Arie." His voice went softer, mellower. Conciliatory.

"Arie is just a baby!" Lauranya snapped her head up from her drawer of clothes, looking him in the face.

"And what did your vaunted and scary grandfathers doing at her size?" Tine's lips quirked as his eyes bored into hers. He walked into her space, taking up the small area with arms akimbo.

Lauranya said grudgingly, turning to face him with arms crossed. "Studying katas and using small daggers for the children fights." She let out a sigh. "I hate it when you bring up facts.

Tine chuckled. "I will try to spoil the boys less if you try with Arie."

Lauranya thought on this for only a moment. The best deal of a bad situation, better than the whipping stocks for the boys. "Deal." She said, tilting her head slightly in acknowledgment of his win. Tine gave her a quick hug, trying for minimal goodwill. Lauranya tried not to shudder.

She waited until hearing the showerhead startup, before moving to Tine's room, seeing how much still needed to be packed.

Micha had rolled out of the bed as Lauranya entered, struggling into her plain gray shift. Her thin arms were trembling hard enough that finding the arm holes in the light shift was proving elusive.

"Stop. Stop, Micha." Lauranya said, in a soothing voice, stepping next to the girl. Micha turned huge eyes to her owner's wife. Lauranya remembered frowning at how thin the girl had gotten. Cheekbones standing out starkly against pale skin. The shaved head didn't lessen the impact of skin covering bones.

The teeth marks on the slave's skin made Lauranya hiss in sympathy. The girl's arms, neck, and chest bore Tine's ardor. Some were only red, fading, while others were bruising. Some were new bites on top of old bites. Tine had only bitten Lauranya once. She regretted her family not being able to afford to get the marriage contract nullified at the time. Tine's mother stepped in with the body slave, to deal with his sexual proclivities and enjoyment, which his wife was unwilling to provide. Gods hell she would not, her dreaming self-thought with a snort of annoyance.

Lauranya helped Micha get into the shift, saying only "At least his teeth didn't break skin this time."

Micha nodded, looking to the floor. Lauranya stifled her sigh. Neither of them could do much more, but Lauranya would do what she could to alleviate some of the pain. Tine had never learned to treat his slaves like thinking tools who felt or as real people. A short sight of his upbringing as a free man.

"Okay, girl. When Tine has left with the boys, shower and clean up, put the bruise ointment on. That should help ease some of the pain. Then pack the basics into the travel bags for him. When I have left with Arie for the day, there are leftovers from last night. Eat all that you want and need."

"The master has told me no food today." The girl's voice was as soft as her skin, eyes on the floor.

"Are you planning on telling him?" Lauranya asked, with a smile to take out the tartness of her rebuke. Tine abused the girl enough. No sense adding more. Micha gave a shy shake of her head and a tiny smile.

"Shall I pack for the boys as well?" Micha asked, looking nervously towards the shower.

"Those two are to pack themselves. Do not let them tell you differently. Hear me?" Lauranya said, waspishly with a glare towards the boys' room. She shook her head, breathing through her nose to calm down.

"Yes, Lady." Micha went still. Lauranya pinched the bridge of her nose, knowing she had startled the girl again.

The sound of the shower stopping woke Lauranya up, to her bedroom and the sound of rain pounding on the window. Arie hummed happily in the bathroom.

"Home. No more Tine." Lauranya whispered. She snuggled into her covers enjoying the sounds of her happy child.

Chapter 5

The next few days alternated between rough and recovering. Lauranya's stomach would rebel at water occasionally, but be fine after the initial vomiting. Standing was not always the wisest choice. Dizzy spells were common, tapering off as the days went on. Lauranya's dreams no longer were of Tine (a relief) or Maison (heartbreaking), but she would dream of fur and four legs occasionally. Those dreams made her smile for no particular reason.

Routine re-established. The early morning for the livestock and gardens with the mid-morning and early afternoons for the lab. Arie had frozen the fish body for Lauranya to study at her leisure. Lauranya spent hours on slides and notes. There were naps, but they became fewer and fewer. The days passed as Lauranya's stomach settled down and her joints became less inflamed.

The fish yielded information Lauranya hadn't realized she'd been searching for. When she connected the dots, she sat back on her stool. Arie sitting across from her, making sketches on the other side of the table. She chewed her lower lip. The information could make the patronage of safety she would need for her and Arie back on the ships, or it could get them both shot out of hand. Their lives depended on how well their work might be judged, worthy or dangerous. Lauranya compromised with herself. The notes on the fish and its unusual viral interaction, written in encrypted notes. Only she would be able to open the notes.

The evenings both Lauranya and Arie would spend watching various tapes of famous singers. Sometimes Lauranya would sing along. Arie would attempt to join in but would fumble some of the higher or lower notes, causing them both to giggle.

Singing wasn't the only new thing; Arie had discovered personal pleasure which needed the occasional discretionary comment.

"Arie, we do not play with our vulva while watching the projector. If you want quiet time please go to your room until you are finished."

Arie stopped masturbating, sitting up. With a yawn and a stretch, she gave her mother a sleepy smile. "Okay." Arie swung her feet off the couch, heading to her room. Lauranya returned her attention to the singer, singing along.

Part way through the door, Arie stopped. "Mommy?"

Lauranya blinked a couple of times, only partially taking her eyes away from the screen. "Yes, dear?"

"You and dad had sex to have kids, right?"

"Ah…you have been reading the reproduction section of your studies." Lauranya gave Arie her full attention, with a smile.

"Yes." Arie twisted a toe on the wood floor, looking down.

"Then the answer, as you know, is yes."

"What happens when I want to have sex with someone?" She looked up at her mom, through long blond tousled hair.

Lauranya stopped the projector, with a flick of the remote. "I am sorry, love. There is almost no way you will ever meet someone here unless the ships come back." The question deserved a full answer.

"Which would be bad," Arie said, with a firm nod. The recordings made ship life, with slaves and Gods, unappealing.

Lauranya didn't answer for a moment. "The ships, coming back to the world, would mean the reinstatement of rules that I have been lax in enforcing." She frowned at a new thought. "Why do you ask?"

"You asked me to tell you when I heard voices again."

"And you are hearing the dead now?" Lauranya asked cautiously, swallowing a lump in her throat. The bitter copper taste of fear.

"Yes, a woman from the water. She knows she's dead, but mourns her husbands." Arie's mouth turned down as she blinked her eyes from excess moisture.

"From the water?"

"Yes. A shark killed her." Arie said, tilting her head a moment listening. "A flat head shark."

Lauranya hesitated but pushed ahead. "Have you animated the body?'

"Animated?"

"Is the body moving under your direction?"

"It's next to the lobby door."

"How long?"

"Since lunch."

"When I was throwing up?"

Arie nodded, her hands fluttering nervously. "I forgot, just heard the voice and asked her to wait until you were better." She looked at her mother anxiously.

"You are going to have to release her soul, my dear," Lauranya said, with a heavy sigh, cautiously moving to her feet.

"And lay the body to rest?"

"She should animate it and use it for a guard on the

building." Jacks' voice hung in the air for both to hear.

Lauranya rolled her eyes. "Hanging around like the family banshee I see." She muttered. The idea was solid, and Arie could use the practice.

"How do I animate the body but let the soul go?" Arie asked confused, walking back to her mother, her head moving from her mother to Jacks' ghost.

"Can you feel the body now? Sense it in the water?" Lauranya asked, flaring her nostrils releasing a pent up breath.

"Yeesss?" Arie stuttered, concentrating with a furrowed brow.

"Do you feel the soul as well?"

"Yes!" Arie said emphatically. As if summoned by the question, a form coalesced in front of them, a woman with long dark hair floating in a dark halo around her as if in deep but slow-moving water. The woman's bottom half looked like a scaled fish, beautiful in coloration. Lauranya walked slowly forward from the couch to look at the woman's ghost closer, studying the scales on the woman's tail. The front, a dark red while the back scales were whorled in blues and green. The scales ranged from one inch to a quarter inch in width. There were dorsal fins and side fins. Lauranya could not say if the fins were overly large or small on a mer. The woman flared her fins for Lauranya's observation. The fins flowed lusciously like crimson silk in a hidden current, with streaks of deeper burgundy along the thick caudal fin veins. Lauranya could feel her hands itching to touch the woman and study her. The mer-woman was just as intense with her looks at both Lauranya and Arie.

The woman wore a necklace of smooth stones that shifted between pearl with flashes of blue/green/red, complimenting her natural fin coloration.

Lauranya didn't have to ask. The ghost's soul self-image saw herself as a warrior. Her chest and arms were covered in thick leather armor, leather but not of a hide Lauranya knew or was familiar with. Grey in color, probably the natural leather coloration as dyed leather did not last long in the water. The armor fitted to the mer's body, yet was in several horizontal pieces, the width of Lauranya's hand, which would move with her, not made from one singular piece. Lauranya caught glimpses of red and green tying the armor together, as the woman floated in front of them.

"How did you die?" Lauranya asked, after a moment of surprised silence.

"The flatheads are thick in this area. They may not always be as the water grows deeper." The woman's voice oddly accented. The ghost didn't seem to mind talking to the two of them, more bemused than upset.

"They can't get in through the doors," Lauranya said, off handily admiring the symmetry of the woman's unusual body build.

"Not all the lower windows have survived. At least one cephalopod can climb steep hills for a few feet in search of prey." The woman's voice was laconic as she looked, not at them but at the foyer of the building. "Gorgeous in here." She breathed, motioning with a slow wave of her hand. The motion spoke of a lifetime moving in water.

Lauranya blanched, clutching Arie close at this unexpected news. "That would answer our question about needing a guard."

The mer-woman grimaced, changing her features from lovely to fierce. "I can feel Death calling, but something is keeping me here."

"Do you have family that you need to say goodbye to?" Lauranya asked, reaching a hand out solicitously than dropping it, the dead rarely needed comforting.

The mer-woman opened her mouth then closed it, with a shake of her head. "My husbands." She tapped a sharp triangular fingernail against a bracer. "They will find another wife or others that make them happy." A shrug. Death robbing most heat from her anger or sorrow.

"Arie, we are going to release her spirit."

"Will she hurt us like Tass did?" Arie's eyes grew huge, her chin started to quiver.

Lauranya hugged Arie tight. "No, baby. We are going to release her spirit back to Obatala so that she will find her way to her next life."

Arie swiped back a tear, returning her mother's tight hug. "Okay." Her voice only quivered a little.

Lauranya turned to the mer-woman's ghost. The ghost's head tilted with a sad smile. "I had wanted a daughter."

"You have only boys?"

"Not even that. We aren't prolific breeders, shifting from water to legs takes a toll on the reproduction."

"I am sorry to hear that." Lauranya had no other words to offer.

The woman gave a slight shrug. "Nothing you could do to help."

Lauranya opened her mouth, then closed it. She couldn't help at this point, but she would definitely get tissue samples to study, now that there was a body close. A thought occurred.

"Is this part of your usual area or were you exploring?" Lauranya asked cautiously.

"Sister sent out an observer when the rains were coming. She asked if we would keep an eye on the tower when our hunting took us in this area." The woman shrugged. "I became curious about the interior and didn't pay attention."

"I am sorry for your loss. Do you know if others will venture to the tower?"

"Maybe but not for a few months. This isn't a prime hunting spot yet." A slow shrug, moving the drifting hair in a slight swirl.

"Who is Sister?" Lauranya asked, turning her head slightly questioningly.

"The Torch, who sees some of the future." The mer-woman said, continuing to gaze around the room.

Lauranya blanched at the mention of an unfettered Power, but there was nothing more she could do for them or the dead woman.

Lauranya took a deep breath. "I need your name for us to send you on."

"Sachiko."

"Ready, Arie?" a quick hug to her daughter.

"Yes, mommy." Arie looked up to her mother with an eager smile.

"Okay, repeat after me." Lauranya took a deep breath. "Sachiko, may you find peace in your next life. Back to Obatala. Leave this plane."

Arie repeated the words verbatim, her voice growing in depth and timber as she spoke. Lauranya felt the hair on her arms raise from the power Arie commanded, setting this one soul free. A strong child would grow to be a strong necromancer.

Sachiko's ghost glowed softly, haloed for a brief moment before her ghost faded away. Arie's shoulders slumped as she leaned against her mother heavily.

"Is she gone?" Arie asked softly, with a tilted head listening.

"I do believe so." Lauranya gave Arie another quick hug.

Brother stood at the newly formed beach, his feet squelching through the mud, the smell of rotting vegetation and ocean air distinctive, mildly revolting during low tide. Crabs and shallow tidal creatures were in heaven, with the rich feeding grounds. Decaying plants and the occasional bit of animal protein mixed in made for good tidal flats. Sand would be carried onto the shores, but for the next few years, there would be only mud.

Brother walked out into the water, where he knew the old rock outcroppings had been. The night sky holding the stars high above, brilliant pinpoints forming patterns in the heavens. He stared upwards, as the water moved around his calves.

"Someone is a cat in water." A sultry voice caught him off guard as he star gazed.

"Good evening to you, Keyma." Brother flashed a tired but warm smile, recognizing the voice floating through the air.

Keyma frowned as she undulated closer through the high tide water. She swam over dull rocks and mud. Pulling herself out of the water, she sat on a flattish rock next to the standing Brother.

"So what brings you out to the new beachhead?" Keyma asked.

Brother looked up into the night sky, with its distant stars. "The stars and the quiet." His voice almost wistful.

"Ah. I will leave you in peace then." Keyma started to push off with her tail, when Brother rested his hand on her shoulder, stopping her.

"I like your company. I didn't mean for it to sound like you weren't welcome."

She quirked a smile at him with a tilt of her head. "So

you do want company."

His eyes crinkling at the edges, in warmth and humor. "Possibly." He smiled back at her with a lilt of his lips. She leaned forward to kiss. Her teeth catching his lower lip, tugging gently playfully. Brother sucked in his breath, tasting her lips. His arm reached around her waist, snagging her closer, kissing her hard with want.

"So what did bring you to the islands tonight? Not that I would pass up on such a lovely time gazing at the… stars." Brother leaned on his elbow, running his free hand over her lovely rounding breast, catching a nipple between forefinger and thumb, eliciting a gasp.

"Keep doing that, and I won't tell you anytime soon!" Keyma gave a shuddering laugh.

"My bad." Brother replaced his fingers with his mouth, flicking the nipple against his upper teeth with his tongue, his hand moved lower down her belly.

"Oh, nova!"

"Well, that was lovely. Again!" Keyma rested her head on Brother's chest.

"So why did you come by again?"

"Hmm? Oh, right." Keyma sat up with a sigh. "Sachiko has gone missing, and Chehreh wants to know if Sister could "See" if she is still alive."

Brother rolled over, facing Keyma, with a frown. "She's an excellent hunter. I've never seen better. Why would Chehreh think she's missing?"

"Besides being a controlling, jealous dick?" Keyma snapped, with a flip of her blond hair. "Bastard likes to bite fins for fun and not in good fun."

"To be fair, they are married. And he doesn't like it when she flirts with others." Brother trailed his hand along the soft skin of her belly.

"Miok isn't that worried. Yet. Willing to say she might be chasing an elusive opal Kraken hunting the edges of our fishing grounds." Keyma shook her head, erasing Chehreh from her thoughts, damp hair clinging to warm skin in tangled locks.

"Valuable. And Miok isn't prone to jealousy fits like Chehreh." Brother said, distracted by the way Keyma's stomach fluttered under his touch than her actual words.

Keyma's breath caught. "Very." Her breathless reply. "Still don't see how those three formed up. Miok's the better husband."

"So why is Chehreh so concerned?" Brother asked, idly running nails along the side of her belly.

Keyma shuddered, gasping her answer."He said he saw her ghost." Her left-hand flexing over Brother's bare thigh.

"Chehreh? Said he saw a ghost?" Brother stopped, looking at her with his jaw open, his hands stilled.

"Yes. And not just any ghost. Sachiko's. Said she kissed him on the cheek, told him her body was by the tower where the flathead shark that killed her left it, but not to retrieve it. She was on her way with Death, but the body stood guarding the child and her mother." Keyma shook her head, rolling her eyes at the story. Her tail slapped the water in derision. "Seriously how unbelievable can you get to check if your wife might be seeing another."

Brother scrabbled to his feet, grabbing his clothes, spilling Keyma from his chest in his rush.

"Hey! Where are you going?" Keyma looked up startled, her hand half raised reaching for him.

"The deadhead scientists had a large building. There were two survivors. A woman and a child." Brother looked down grimly, as he hurriedly donned his pants, the shirt he slung over his shoulder.

It took a moment for this to sink in. "Oh, void!" Keyma whispered, her eyes growing huge.

Brother looked grim. "If Chehreh said he saw Sachiko's ghost…"

"Then one of them is a deadhead!" Keyma whispered in fear.

"They are both deadheads, but one of them can raise the dead," Brother said, lips pressed together in a thin line.

She swallowed hard. "I need to wait for an answer," Keyma said, in a small voice. She could imagine Chehreh's reaction already. Her hands started to shake ever so slightly.

"You'll need to shift and come with me then, but I'm pretty sure Sachiko is dead." No more star gazing or relaxing company for this night.

Keyma nodded. She scrunched up her face, concentrating on the shift. The bones didn't rearrange as painfully as when Brother shifted, but muscles flowed and bones in the tail did rearrange. Painful enough to leave her gasping for minutes afterward.

Brother picked her up, carefully walking along the rocks, heading back to the village.

"I can walk!" She protested weakly, as she clung to his neck, the quivering in her legs belying the words.

"Yep, but we need to get moving now, and these rocks are sharp. The skin on the bottom of your feet is tender. I'll put you down once we hit sand. Sooner you ask Sister, the sooner you can be back with the bad news to Chehreh."

"Fuck. I'd rather not be the one to tell him his wife is a zombie now." Keyma leaned against Brother's solid warm chest.

"Better you than me," Brother said, kissing her forehead.

"He doesn't hate you anymore." Keyma chuckled, her

breath warm against his sweat-soaked skin. "He does have other worries now."

"But he hasn't forgiven me for beating him." Brother gave a laughing huff as he made it to the muck of the new beach. His footsteps making slurping sounds with each step, as he trotted towards the village.

Chapter 6

The Guardians and Redeyes walked into the suite of rooms, like the returning dead. Bedraggled, bloodstained and starving. Roar looked up from the counter, with full hands. He was pulling various protein and hydroponic vegetable dishes out of the oven.

"Practice went well I see." He said blandly, running the side of his face along his forearm to push the bone mask back into place, over sweat slicked fur. He flicked an ear towards the various towels and clean clothes he'd laid out earlier — medical kits with bandages and pain hypos at the ready.

"Rads, you anticipated us." Nero almost whimpered, grabbing the hypo on his towel set. He mainlined the pain med into his neck. "Ahhh!"

"You should take those easy, Nero." Roar let disapproval show with a flick of his ears and snapping of his tail.

"Oh hells, no. She's not dreaming and damned if I don't hurt!" Nero's eyes were already glazing over, as his muzzle sagged in an open half dreamy smile. "Going to enjoy this while I can."

Roar's eyes narrowed at the lack of care Nero showed. Collins and Iarris walked in, grabbing their towels before heading to the shower-head together. Collins' arm draped along Iarris' hips. Her tail's fluffy tip touching the back of his neck affectionately.

"Those two won't be out for a while," Redeyes mumbled, through a slightly swollen and healing jaw. Her eyes crinkled with amusement on the couples' disappearing backs.

"They shouldn't be allowed to form a couple." Roar looked down his broad muzzle at the God. The front of his mane fell over the eyes of his mask, but not quite touching the arch where his muzzle extended from. The back of his mane touched his shoulders, shaggy glory framing what would normally be considered a handsome male if it weren't for the mask.

"Because they're not the same?" Redeyes said bitingly, tilting her head to the fourth Guardian.

"One or the other might hesitate to do a job if the other is in jeopardy." Roar countered, shaking his head to clear the longer hair.

"Iarris maybe. But that's a long maybe." Nero shambled over to the kitchen bar, reaching for a handful of raw peeled sweet white root. The drugs taking affect fast, leaving him less coordinated and hungrier. "Collins. Never. Especially if it's killing someone." He munched on the finger length white roots with evident delight. The crunching almost sounding like bones, wet and breaking.

"See. Nothing to worry about or be a snob on, Rawwwwr." Redeyes shook her head vexatiously to Roar.

"It's Roar." A stronger tail twitch.

"No, it's not," Redeyes said offhandedly, grabbing for a dark purple fruit. She took a bite, dribbling blue. "Damn it. I know it's not a plum, but I never expect strawberries." She said, annoyed at the dark sweet fruit in her hand. Her brain and taste buds in disagreement, throwing off the enjoyment of said fruit.

"What do you mean? It's not?" Nero said, fork halfway to his mouth with a human-sized bite of meat in a red sauce. Dainty and petite in such large hands.

Roar went still. "Roar is my name." He could feel heat rising through his cheeks and chills running down his spine, causing the fur on his spine to rise.

"Oh, it may be what we call you, but it's not the name you were given." Redeyes looked at Roar briefly, before grabbing a plate for some of the meat in a sweet, spicy sauce. The sauce made from the same fruit she had just bitten into, turning the tough meat into a sweet and sour delight.

"How can you say that?" Nero asked, cocking his head to her as he used a large Wolfen fork to delicately pull each piece off the tines, with sharp white teeth.

"I…don't know. But I do know Roar isn't his name. He's lying." Redeyes waived a more modestly sized human fork, filled with meat and fruit with sauce dripping down the handle, at the Katherian in front of them.

"I do not lie!" Roar snarled, with flattened ears, his hands flat on the counter as he leaned forward almost within arm's reach.

"But you aren't telling me your real name either." Redeyes grinned up at him, ignoring the threat as she chomped down on the bite sized piece of meat, from the long three tined fork.

"It's not important." He pulled back, crossing his arms looking away first, unable to maintain eye contact.

"I don't like lying pieces of shit on my team either. I may only know how to be a back alley brawler prior to this, but I've seen too many people killed by secretive lying sacks. Either you tell me or you'll never leave these rooms." Redeyes stabbed her fork at him, emphasizing her decision. "The first three deaths were on the slaver ships. I trusted the wrong people, believed the wrong things." She took a deep breath, her eyes going human green. "Good people died because of that. You, can't even give me your name, no reason to fucking trust you."

"I can't." Roar looked at the floor, fur slicked down tight with hunched shoulders.

"You mean you won't," Redeyes said succinctly, taking another bite, dismissing Roar and his name.

Roar licked his lower lip, the fur along his spine starting to rise. "You'll kill me."

Redeyes delicately licked fallen sauce from her fingers. "I doubt that. I don't know any of you well enough to want to kill you." She shrugged, being realistic. She touched her purple/yellow bruised but healed jaw, continuing with a muttered: "even if I could."

His ears flat, he hung his head. "Roland." In an almost strangled whisper.

Collins and Iarris walked in from their quick shower to sate one hunger before moving to the next at just the wrong moment. Roland survived the next few minutes by luck and divine intervention.

"Dead Gods raping a ship." Collins had a towel over his wet hair and nothing else reached for his disc gun that wasn't on his hip. Again.

Iarris wasn't so eloquent; she launched herself at Roland with a hunter's scream and a mouth full of sharp teeth, with hands outstretched, claws extended, for his throat.

"Iarris stop!" Redeyes screamed, throwing out a hand as if a human could stop a full- grown battle trained Katherian in a killing rage. Redeyes felt something move in her, a mental muscle never used before. The battle steel floor responded to that mental command. A hand formed on a long metal arm, shooting up catching Iarris around the throat, holding her firm. Iarris threw herself forwards and backward trying to reach Roland and shred him with the claws, aimed fixedly at his neck. She tried to claw through the battle steel hand holding her, causing a teeth grinding squeal as claws scraped down metal instead of flesh.

Collins turned to run back for his gun on the pants left in the shower area when the door to the shower room slammed shut in his face. Collins turned with a snarl to find another projectile to launch, thwarted from using his favorite tool.

Nero continued to eat, placidly reaching for another few chunks of meat and watching the drama unfold, with a total lack of concern.

"Stop moving!" Redeyes yelled. Her voice bounced off the walls of the front rooms. The threat from her previous lives and powers counting more than this young reincarnation. Collins and Iarris gave her almost identical snarls, showing full teeth. Iarris had the scary set of predatory teeth, but Collins had a scarier look in his eyes.

Roland had spun around to face Iarris and Collins, grabbing a hot dish cover with his bare hand for a shield and a carving knife as his primary weapon. The lid scorching his palm but making an effective shield or throwing weapon if needed. He ignored the forming blisters. Roland bared his teeth with an audible growl at the attacking Guardians.

"Everyone stand the fuck down!" Redeyes shouted again. This time everyone looked at her, but they stopped moving to attack or defend. She took a deep breath before continuing, marshaling her thoughts.

"Okay. The name doesn't mean anything to me, but it obviously means something to everyone else." Redeyes met the glares with a bland look of her own, reaching for another bite of savory meat.

"Oh yeah. We should kill him and you would too if you were a different you." Nero said, opening his mouth wide in a tongue curling yawn. He slurped on a water glob.

Roland backed himself further into the corner. He couldn't go over the counter with Redeyes and Nero to his left or forward with Iarris and Collins held at bay only by the threat of Redeyes' command in front of him. Battle steel walls behind and to his right. Trapped.

"No one is killing anyone." Redeyes snapped. She pointed her fork at Iarris and Collins. "You two go and sit down. Over there!" She moved her fork to the couches, with a stab. The hand released Iarris, flowing back into the floor as smoothly as it had ever been. Iarris stood with lashing tail and fur sticking straight out, growls rising and falling with each breath.

"Go." Redeyes locked eyes with her Guardian. The floor rippled — the promise of something worse than a hand very real. Collins moved first, stiff-backed, walking jerkily. Iarris followed but stopped every couple of feet, showing teeth and growling at the other Katherian over her shoulder.

"You." She poked Nero in the ribs with a finger from her lower left hand. "Can take a plate and sit on the other side of those two." She was grateful that one of three was so malleable at this moment. Tomorrow, they would talk on his inability to fight or think with the drugs.

She turned to Roland "You can come out from behind there and tell me why they want to kill you and why I shouldn't."

"Give it time and you will." Collins snarled, from his vantage point on the couch, his hands clenching and unclenching on his bare muscular thighs. The towel now wrapped around his lap. Iarris hadn't bothered with hers. Redeyes noted that she had a human-like body that would have been naked except for the shorter fur in front and only slightly longer on her back, legs and arms. Her mane extended lovely and thick past the small of her back in damp tendrils.

"I can see from your frothing reaction I should want to kill him, but I don't know what he did." Redeyes followed Nero, swaying between the various couches and chairs. Nero managed to navigate the furniture and floor without tripping over his own feet or spilling the plate in his hands. Impressive.

Nero sat in a chair facing Iarris and Collins, so close Nero's knees were almost touching Iarris'. Redeyes sat down closest to the kitchen where Roland stood, still backed in, leaving empty seats between her and the Guardians. She could keep an eye on her three, while still talking to the fourth.

"Roland, come out here and tell me why your name is evoking this sort of reaction." Redeyes raised her voice to carry to the kitchen, without taking her eyes from Iarris or Collins.

She heard his footsteps, claws clicking on the metal floor, approach the living area. A hasty glance showed he still carried the dish cover and knife. Iarris bunched her muscles to launch an attack, but one look at Redeyes stopped her. She licked her whiskers once but curled her lips, flashing fang. Not tamed or cowed, but under control for the moment. Redeyes could ask for more but didn't push any more than she had to on this little nova party waiting to happen.

Roland approached the group slowly, one foot placed precisely for maximum advantage of weight and momentum should he need.

He stopped several yards from the couch where Iarris growled and several feet from the young God he would betray, years in her future but years in his past. His pupils were wide, showing little of the gold and green iris.

"37 years ago, I stole a world-ship, with mostly Katherian but some humans and Wolfen. And I went to the Dead Gods." Roland said, swallowing hard coughing a whispered response.

Redeyes stood so explosively, the chair she had been sitting in moved four feet behind her from the momentum, slamming into the wall hard enough to bounce back, almost to her knees. "You took, our people, to those slavers?! Are you fucking insane?" Do you fucking know what they do to people?" Redeyes had to look up at Roland, her feet touching the ground. The God's anger so palatable the walls began to warp in and out as if breathing in time with her own breath.

"Oh, void," Iarris whispered. Her eyes huge as she curled into herself, her tail bushed out to its fullest. Her anger paling in comparison to the God's reaction. Collins' eyes darted around for the closest weapon, knowing the gesture was futile when the metal walls started to move. He wanted the guns as a child wanted a blanket to hide from monsters. If he shot Redeyes now, the walls might not continue to warp. Maybe.

"Yes. I do know. I watched them skin 81 of my kith and kin alive in front of me. My wives, daughters, sisters underwent medical experiments I wouldn't wish on anyone. I FELT every death they felt from knife, whip or on their sand covered arenas as we were hunted for entertainment. Treated like animals." Roland staggered against the wall, throwing his right hand out to brace himself, the knife dropping with a clunk on the floor.

"Why did you do it?" Redeyes let out a low savage growl. Her short white hair rose to its fullest extent, moving in a nonexistent wind.

"We were promised a world of our own. No humans, no Wolfen, no genetic anomalies. In exchange, we would train them on how to fight, Wolfen and Katherian." Roland said, this time meeting her eyes squarely, aggressively.

Redeyes looked at him with intensity, unnerving them all, as her eyes bled from human green back to their normal dark red. The question she asked unexpectedly.

"No one can just steal a ship without a lot of planning. You had help. You were contacted by someone to facilitate this?" She stared at the floor for a moment, clenching and unclenching her fist.

"Yes, one of the former slaves brought back from a freed ship. Farming ship, I think." Roland frowned, confused at this line of questioning, tilting his head to the left.

"I thought it wasn't possible for our ships to contact theirs? Per Cratt in training, we have a hell of a time even finding them."

"I..I don't know. He had ways to get in touch with someone on a Dead Gods ship to broker the deal."

"How?" Redeyes pierced him with human green eyes.

"Communications." Came his cautious reply, one foot moving slightly backward.

"Those require special permissions if you're not on the radio team," Nero said, between long licks, cleaning his dinner plate. The drama unfolding in the room almost as good as the meat skewers previously in front of him.

"How much special permissions?"

"General or higher." Nero supplied, with another slurp as he spilled on his wrist, licking up the mess.

"What's higher than a General?" Redeyes looked to her stoned Guardian

"A God," Nero said with a shrug. Collins and Iarris following the conversation and the line of inquiry.

"So a general or a God was allowing communications to happen." Redeyes looked back to Roland. "Is that a fair guess? Or someone on communications."

Roland gave a slow nod. "That's my guess."

"But you didn't think to say anything?"

"You and I butted heads on this for years." Roland's lips pulled back with a glare that could cut through battle steel. "We..." He stopped, shaking out his growing mane. "I. I wanted us to have a place, a planet even if it's a metal one, that held nothing but Katherian."

Redeyes tapped her foot for a second then started to pace from Roland to the back wall. Eighteen steps to the wall and back. Her mind focused on what the Katherian said, not what he had done. The walls having calmed down from pulsing to slow undulations.

She stopped, turning to him. "What did I say to you every time this happened? Every time we fought?"

Roland frowned, his ears flattening. "That everything would work out the way it's supposed to." His lips turned down in annoyance. "No more no less, no matter the how or when I would try pushing the subject."

"Iarris." Redeyes had to call twice. Iarris sat watching the walls, with wide eyes and clenched hands, hunched so low she was smaller than Collins.

"What?" Iarris said, with wide-eyed and slicked fur.

"How did things change when Roland left?"

"They didn't. Not until he came back." Iarris said, startled.

"Came back?" Redeyes spun on a barefoot facing Roland fast enough; the steel floor would have a foot induced whorl until the ship's decommissioning 800 years later.

"All the Katherians were scattered among two ships as pets. Shock collars and leashes." Angry bitterness in his gold-green eyes. Roland couldn't meet Redeyes' own. "I could still reach most of them telepathically." He hesitated.

"I played the pet. Tame. Broken. Show me the whip, and I cringed on cue. The Dead Gods ate it up." He sat down with a thump, legs, and arms akimbo, his tail listless on the metal floor. "I wasn't left unsupervised but they didn't think there was any truth to the rumors of telepathy — only good reading of body language. Padmavathi managed to keep a level head. Telling us to play along until we could break free and take back a ship."

"Who the hells is Padmavathi?" Redeyes snapped, lower hands on her hips while her upper arms crossed over her chest.

"My first wife." A slightly sad smile at a fond memory.

"You have a second wife? I thought you were pariah?"

"I had four wives. Padmavathi, Zainae, Nanez and Pren." He ran a hand along his cheek as if smoothing fur except for a suspicious trail of water, his eyes bleak.

"What did Padmavathi do, that got you back?" Redeyes said, her eyes boring into his skull as if trying to read his mind.

"She was a pet to a God, who liked his women docile but exotic. Padmavathi was as beautiful as you could get. Long gold mane to her tail and dancer's hips." Roland gave a sad smile. "She could charm a beserking Wolfen down, and she used every trick to seem the walking sex pet, no threat. Pet her and feed her occasionally and she would love on you like no human slave would. They believed the act." His voice sounding gruff from lost love and guilt, chasing through his voice.

"I saw them rape anything vaguely female or not." He looked up into her eyes, the horror of watching them being degraded sorted and beaten into submission, flashing so strongly through his mind the others 'saw' it.

"Infinity fucks!" Collins whispered. Iarris hid her face in his hair for a moment, shivering. Her great aunt had been on the stolen ship. She hadn't returned with the survivors.

Redeyes nodded. "The Gods don't like anything they can't control." Redeyes ran fingers along her wrists, the ghost of a chained memory, still fresh.

"Not like you would know anything about how they treat them."

"This is my fourth incarnation. The first three were on those hell holes. Slaves, whips, and rapes. I ate, slept and shit that for…" Redeyes did a count on fingers. "Three lives more than I ever want to remember again." She shook her head, dismissing that image. The time is here and now. This life mattered. These lives mattered. Broken, scared, and angry, she was learning they were the key to meaning everything going forward.

"Padmavathi." Redeyes prompted.

"She convinced them that the ship we brought should be kept with their ship and with most of us who came over. We would teach them how our technologies differed."

"You saw this?"

"Padmavathi managed to subliminally prompt the God who took Zainae and Nanez, that he could trust them. Those two, with Padmavathi, worked the Gods into ignoring the Katherians as dangerous. He put them to work in sensitive areas, communication, engineering, food, and shuttle. Within fifteen weeks, everyone, who was still alive, was put on the two tethered ships and in position to engineer our escape."

"Nanez was human, so didn't rank special attention. She was the one who slipped in and out when we were locked down. When we were all in place and ready, Nanez was serving at the banquet where all the Gods gathered. She was responsible for slipping strong drugs into the drinks and food. Padmavathi and Zainae were the main floor entertainment, dancing."

"How many died?"

"Every God, free and slave born, that ate what Nanez slipped into the meal."

"Guards?"

"We shredded them." Roland smiled, showing teeth as his claws flexed. The feel of skin ripping under his hands after months of watching the torture of his family and friends still a fresh memory.

"Then what?" Redeyes prompted.

"We brought both ships, with as many as were left originally and every slave," Roland said, with a simple shrug, belying the simple part.

"Obviously you weren't welcomed back with joy."

"No. I stood up to you and said I had coerced three of my four wives, along with all the dead males into hijacking the ship." He looked Redeyes dead in the eyes. Almost Challenging, but not quite.

"You took the blame." Redeyes tapped her lips with one finger. Green eyed, thinking.

"It was my idea and my design for getting a ship." An eloquent shrug.

"How was it taken when you came back?" Redeyes asked. Curiously. Her head tilted to the side as she regarded the pariah of a Katherian.

"I was thrown into a jail cell to be executed. By skinning. It was going to be broad-banded to every ship." Roland's claw tips cut into his hands, his voice strangled.

"Obviously that didn't happen."

"Sanctuary came to my cell. The doors opened, and I walked in." Roland took a deep shivery breath at the close call.

"And here you are now."

"Here I am." He raised his head. Redeyes didn't

mistake that look as anything but proud, even if a God did abandon him to her tender treatment.

Redeyes tapped her teeth. "Cratt said something today that has me thinking I remember things from this incarnation many lives later. What happens after you return that is so important? Iarris?" She turned to the other Katherian.

Iarris blinked, sitting up straight to respond. "Male Katherians are no longer head of households. The males that returned with the ships said they commanded their wives and children to follow them. You deemed that the females would lead their families. Having more common sense than any flea bit hormone-addled male. And that in each generation there would be one male named Roland in hopes that one day, some male from the original line, would be able to redeem the name."

Redeyes' brows furled at this. "I can see having the women lead, but the name thing?"

Iarris shrugged. "You don't always tell us why but when it works, it works."

"So if Roland is known as the real Roland…"

"He would be mobbed and shredded," Nero said with a slurp, licking the sauce off of his plate with a large tongue and a larger smile. He still managed to dribble a little onto his chest fur. "This generation's Roland committed suicide three years ago." He said with a frown, staring down at the sauce on his chest confusedly.

"None of you recognized him?"

Collins gave a slight shrug. "Sanctuary has taken the good with the bad. Criminals and Godlings. Everything in between. We," he motioned to the three other Guardians, "know of Roland because we learned of him. We weren't there, but we know of him from our lessons."

"No one speaks of him other than with the angry fury

of a nova." Iarris snapped her ears flat as she glared at Roland, the fur along her spine starting to rise again.

"At least he's not offering to get you with kittens as a favor," Nero said, with a sloppy grin, draping an upper arm over Iarris' shoulder.

"Frag off." She growled, fending him off with a controlled punch to the ribs. Nero yelped with sad puppy eyes wondering how Iarris could be so mean to him.

Redeyes looked at Nero with pressed lips. She snapped her fingers at him irritated. "You, go take a shower and sleep this off. Tomorrow you're going to hate life when I wean you off of these damn drugs."

Nero leaned over, putting his cleaned plate in Iarris' lap. He gave her a quick lick on the cheek. She fended him off with a hiss, and a light graze of nails to his nose. He jerked back with a giggle.

He nodded to Redeyes "Its ok. I can just go down to the pit and trade food for more." He said, his tongue lolling out as he staggered off the couch, heading to the showers. Full belly and numbed with drugs; the evening left him feeling good.

Redeyes watched him leave. "Is it true he can get more?" She asked to the room in general, floating three inches off the floor again, her toe-tapping restlessly with no sound produced.

"Yes, stronger and with impurities that will fuck his brain up even more," Collins said, watching the Wolfen walk unsteadily to his sleeping nook.

"We're going to address this situation." Redeyes sucked in an angry breath, putting both sets of hands on her hips, exasperated by the almost indifference to Nero's drug problem.

"But not tonight." Roar said, his shoulders pulled down and tail wrapped tightly around his feet, head falling to his knees.

"No, not tonight. Roland, Roar, you are going to be on training duty tomorrow. Iarris, I need to know how to keep Nero from getting drugs."

"Can't," Came Collins succinct statement. He gave Redeyes a flat stare, promising many things and none of them good at this line of inquiry.

Redeyes spun towards him. "Why the hell not?" Her voice sounding like a deep-chested Wolfen, vibrating down spines.

"Drugs are easy, even needed, you once said." Iarris stepped in touching Collin's shoulder with her own, forming a formidable wall. "If you want to wean Nero from the drugs, you need to address why he needs the drugs."

"Can he be weaned?"

Iarris licked her lips with a pink tongue. "I wouldn't suggest it." She said, with a shake of her head, tossing her damp mane for emphasis.

"Medical advice or personal insight?" Redeyes asked, with a raised eyebrow.

Collins and Iarris looked at each other, Iarris thumped her tail twice. Redeyes couldn't read the message.

"Both." Roar said, from the sidelines, lifting his head from his hands. "He needs the cushion from your dreams."

"Why from dreams? Am I screaming that much? Keeping him awake?" She looked between the three of them in confusion

"They will be." Roland looked at her with bleak eyes before putting his head in his hands again. He didn't elaborate further.

Redeyes glared at the top of his long mane head, before turning back to the other two in the room. "Do you think he's right?"

Collins and Iarris didn't even exchange glances this time but nodded as one. "Yes."

"Is he fit for duty?"

"When he has to be." Collins shrugged, tying his towel tightly at the waist. "He's good when he's on. He wants to be one of those who survives being a Guardian." Collins picked up Nero's discarded plate, heading to the kitchen. His gliding steps faltered for a moment, as he skirted around Roland, but he continued without engaging. He did pull back lips in a silent snarl.

"Hush, pup. I've been down this road already." Roland said quietly, twitching an ear towards Collins and his glare burning a hole into the Katherian's back. Roland's shoulder's hunched with the weight of a thousand deaths. Detente at its worst, but the peace would hold long enough.

Chapter 7

Lauranya flicked grain towards the chickens including bits of leftover bread and vegetable from yesterday's dinner. Several birds had fluffy chicks running under the wings and bellies. The chickens making happy clucking sounds at the offerings provided when the lights in the garden room started flickering.

Lauranya looked up with a frown. Her gaze lifted to the ceiling watching as the ceiling fans began slowing noticeably, realizing there were no more lights coming from the bulbs overhead. The only light came from the windows behind her, weak sunlight breaking between dark veils of clouds.

The growing room still held light with shadows cast behind the tall planters. She looked towards the balconies with open doors to the office and their rooms; only her office lab had any light.

Lauranya dumped the remaining feed into a pile, to the delight of the birds that flocked to her feet in a frenzy of feathers and clucking.

"Arie!" Lauranya called out. No sound. Lauranya took a deep breath putting a hand to her mouth and tightening her diaphragm. "Arie!" The sound pitched deeper, carrying further, a rolling sound through the hallways. The chickens behind Lauranya stopped midbite, closing their eyes while pitching their clucks in the same note as Lauranya's call. Lauranya looked over her shoulder at the birds' unusual behavior. The birds fluffed their feathers and went back to their food messily, the sunlight shining over glossy feathers with long shadows behind them. The shadows reminded Lauranya of a more pressing issue pushing the birds' odd behavior out of her thoughts.

Arie's head popped out of a doorway on the second floor. "Yes, mom?" She called down. The rich treble bounced resoundingly in the growing room.

"Electric generator is down."

"Flooding or worn out part?"

"I would say flooding at this point," Lauranya said thoughtfully.

"How can they flood? They're on the roof."

"Throw enough water on something for enough years and water will work its way in."

Arie had to think a moment. "Water is a universal solvent. Natural solvent even. Able to move through most substances, given enough time."

"Very good. Now we will need to hook up the remaining solar generators and check the wiring just to be sure."

"Space! I've been studying some of the wiring schematics." Ari came diving out of the room to fly headlong down the water stained staircase, blond hair levitating off her shoulders. Usually surefooted, Ari had navigated the stairs at a run many times, this time Arie's foot slipped on the smooth wood stairs, pitching her forward at high speeds. Arie, on instinct alone and Ibeji's love for children, survived with a tuck and roll on the last eight steps with nominal thudding.

Lauranya rushed to her child's side, dropping to her knees, as Arie slowly uncurled with a muted "Owwww." Lauranya ran shaking hands over her daughter's arms, legs and head.

Arie began to sit up under her mother's ministration, with the profound assertion of a teenager's voice "I'm fine mom." She shrugged, trying to break from her mother's touch.

"And if you broke something or are hemorrhaging, I only have moments to ascertain this before you could die." Lauranya snapped, her voice shaking. A wild-eyed look Arie hadn't seen since the ships had left. Lauranya snapped her hands closed into fists against her bent legs. Lauranya took several deep breaths closing her eyes.

"Mom!"

"If it helps you to think that you are indulging me do that, but I cannot lose you!" Lauranya grasped Arie by the shoulders tightly, unshed tears in her eyes. "I cannot lose you!"

Arie started crying at the fear she saw in her mother's eyes. "Okay, mommy." She said meekly, hugging her mother, snuffling against the soft, worn tunic fabric. Lauranya gave a tight squeeze, kissing the top of Arie's head.

"Promise me you will not go running down the stairs at such speeds again," Lauranya asked softly into Arie's floral smelling hair.

"I promise, mommy. Unless I absolutely hafta I won't go running down the stairs again." Arie gave a squeeze.

Lauranya gave a ghost of a laugh, knowing the promise would last for the next hour, maybe two before she forgot, yet that one hour felt good enough for the moment. Lauranya finished running hands over Arie's back, checking the child's eyes for a possible concussion, before letting her stand.

"Let us go and check the generator now that you are confirmed to be in one piece," Lauranya suggested, ruffling her hair.

Arie bounced on her toes, her head coming to Lauranya's shoulder. "I'll get the tool bag!" she ran up the stairs ready for the next adventure. Lauranya touched the air where Arie's head had been at shoulder height.

She smiled softly. "They grow so fast!" Lauranya went to find her laptop. She needed to check the generator parts against what might be needed in case a new replacement was the next step. Most importantly were the parts on hand.

The generator on the roof was stardust. Water had gotten in, causing a short in the electronics.

"Can we fix it?" Arie looked down with concern, as the open panel showed corrosion along the metal gears and wires.

Lauranya huffed out a breath, pushing sweaty strands of long hair from her face. "No." She glared at the innards knowing she had no spare parts. "We'll have to hook up the solar generators inside."

"Is there enough sunlight to do that?" Arie looked up, with wrinkled brows. Electricity powered everything, keeping their food growing and keeping them fed. She was starting to worry.

Lauranya sat back on her heels, brushing the wayward damp strands away. Arie handed her a headband from her hair. Lauranya nodded her thanks, pulling her hair up into a messy ponytail. "Mostly. We have only enough power to cover 1/3 of the growing area lights."

"We need all the food though." The frown grew tighter, drawing young skin into harsh lines.

"We do. Though we could learn to fish." Lauranya vaguely waved a hand towards the water. "It would help supplement the protein of the poultry and rabbits. A smaller pool of genetic material though if we continue with just the poultry and rabbits."

"Doesn't a smaller genetic pool lead to more problems?"

"It does, though the issues will not show up for a few generations. About the time we need them to be more stable not less in our old age." Lauranya grimaced at the thought of genetically deficient fowl.

"What are you remembering mommy?"

Lauranya swallowed hard. "I was once sent to a ship to help with the euthanizing of the cattle stock that had been kept in a tiny genetic pool. Too much inbreeding. There were severe skeletal, respiratory, mental and...other medical issues." The breeding pens had been horrific, with twisted blind and wheezing cattle held up in slings, unable to walk or breed on their own any more. The slaves had to wade through three feet of muck to reach the cattle, causing various maladies in the slaves, which the Gods on that ship did not care to treat. Eventually, the cattle and affected slaves had to be put down. The beef inedible. A true waste of resources. New breeding stock for both cattle and slaves were brought in under different Overseers. The body count had been...high.

"So culling the stock isn't a good idea," Arie said firmly.

"Not at this time, but we will not have enough fruit or grain to sustain what we have if we have less light." Lauranya dusted off her hands, picking up her tools before standing back up, the fresh air running playful fingers through tousled blond hair.

"Isn't there a way we can multiply the lights? Like candles?" Arie jumped down from the bench, walking back with her mother.

"Candles run out, and the sun only reaches so much." Lauranya stepped through the propped open door, letting Arie walk ahead of her. Lauranya scanned the sky, looking to see if they could afford to leave the door open a little while longer or if a storm was coming in. The clouds were building into towering pillars, moving faster than Lauranya felt comfortable with. She turned and closed the door, plunging the hallway into deep twilight.

"Even if we put the lights in the center? And move some on either edge?" Arie asked, putting her right hand along the large limestone tiles. The roughness rubbed her fingers almost pleasantly, reminding her of the rabbit's tongues when they tried to groom her.

"We may have to, though it is not optimal for lighting," Lauranya answered from the shadows behind.

"How so, mommy? Lights will still be on."

But only over 1/3 of the growing area. It won't be enough light for all the plants."

"We could move 'em."

"The planters weigh several hundred pounds sweetie. The loader is not here anymore."

"It's underwater." Arie made a face.

Lauranya tried not to laugh at her daughter, settling for a grin instead. "Exactly. So no moving the planters."

"I know that, mom!" Again the tone of a confident teen, who knew everything and their parent just stated the obvious. "I meant the lights." Arie jutted her chin at her mother, widening her eyes for emphasis.

"We need more sunlight," Arie said firmly. The dark hallway causing her to stop a few feet in, letting her eyes adjust to the darkness from the midday sun they were just in.

"You cannot multiply sunlight…" Lauranya started, then stopped. "Mirrors." Bouncing off a wall from her unadjusted eyes in the dark. "Owww! Nova take that wall!"

"What?"

"Mirrors. Mirrors can reflect the light, turning even minimal light from a bulb to much brighter."

"And sunlight into a lot more than just one sunbeam!" Arie finished excitedly.

"Exactly!" Lauranya grinned up at Arie as they had just discovered the Gods secret world-ship treasure. "We need to get the solar lights up as soon as possible."

"Do we have enough wires to hang them up?"

Lauranya thought of the large growing room, chewing her lip. "I am not sure that we have enough lights or wires to give the coverage we need." Lauranya stood still, running a quick equation mid-thought. Blinking. Mirror arcing sunlight and how many mirrors they would need for maximum sunlight reflection. Her smile at Arie made the child squirm with happiness.

"Excellent child. We will need to pull every mirror from the bathrooms and living quarters. You will not be able to pose in front of them making funny faces anymore." Lauranya smiled, teasing her child, with a tickling poke to the girl's ribs.

"That's ok. I like eating more than watching myself." Giggled Arie.

They started with the mirror in their bathroom. They had a minor delay when the drill wasn't where Lauranya had put it last.

"Oops," Arie said. Lauranya just raised her eyebrows at the girl. Arie blushed. "I fixed a loose board on the chicken coop."

"And you didn't put it back?"

"I forgot. It was time for practice." Arie blushed, looking at her toes.

"Then you need to get it now my dear, and you can write out the elemental table with colors tomorrow on top of your other homework."

Arie made a face but didn't protest. She darted downstairs to the chicken coop for the roaming drill. Mom would start assigning research papers if she got really irritated or add 20 sprints to the warm-ups they did in the morning.

Once the drill was in hand, the mirrors came down relatively quick. They cushioned them on the towels to minimize breakage.

"The edges are rounded and smooth," Arie noted with a frown, fingering said edge.

Lauranya filled in the missing data for Arie. "The rounded edges will make the mirrors a little harder to hang. So we need to find something that will not slip easily."

"Torn towels are out," Arie said looking at the nubby soft towel cushioning the largest mirror. "Same for shirts." They had done the study of fabric tensile strength and cutting resistance compared to fished out plant fibers in a several week study, sessions ago.

Arie looked up from the towel. "How about tubing? We have lots in storage!" Her voice started to rise in excitement, and her hands started to wiggle, as a solution presented itself to her.

"Yes, however what we have we need for when other tubing cracks or gets clogged." Lauranya pointed out. She looked at the floor as if by sheer will she could see what the storage rooms held. One idea floated through, discarded then reexamined as the storage room supplies kept running through her brain. "However the leather couches might be the answer."

"I thought leather was skin, which can tear?" Arie asked frowning. There was no way her skin would hold any of the mirrors without her muscles helping.

"Very true, but unlike our skin, or fish skin, treated

leather is usually thicker. And leather for furniture is usually thicker than leather used for clothing."

Arie's lips turned down, considering her mother's comments. "But I like our couches! They are so comfortable when we watch the movies."

Lauranya's laugh turned into a cough. "Not those couches dear." Lauranya gesturing towards the downstairs rooms, with its many couches from the original moving. "We have several; full suites and more of leather furniture in storage. Those couches we can use, and I believe have a few left over to spare when our current couch decides to die in many ship rotations."

"Oh, yeah!" Arie perked up, bouncing on her toes.

"Oh, yes!" Lauranya corrected. "So we do not waste what we have we'll need to measure the mirrors and the lengths needed for them to hang up on the walls, then measure how much leather strapping we will need and the best widths for weaving to achieve this strength."

"Lots of math." Lauranya overlooked the rolled eyes and put upon expression for the moment. Arie preferred reading to equations.

"Not lots, but some." Lauranya smiled gently then froze.

"What's wrong Mommy?"

"I need to find out if the leather is good leather or glued bits and plastic."

"Won't either one work?"

Lauranya hesitated for a moment. "It will have to. We are not exactly running over with ways to hang the mirrors."

And that's what they did. Thirty mirrors of varying sizes from all the upper suites. The lower suites were still packed to the corners, getting to those mirrors a challenge. Lauranya ran her calculations twice, deciding that the 30 mirrors they did have would be sufficient. Pulling everything out to get to the last 8 wasn't time well used.

The first cut exposed the edge of the leather cover. Real leather not glued, bonded nor split. Lauranya felt a flash of guilt over using such an expensive material for so plebian a thing as braided strapping. She quickly swallowed her fear and guilt, cutting careful to preserve every precious piece of hide possible.

Lauranya used one of her scalpels to pull the backs off of the couches, while Arie untied the seat cushion, slipping the leather covers off the padding. Each cushion, barring the boxing piece, would yield a rectangle piece of leather, 64 inches by 40 inches. The leather back pieces were 84 inches by 60. The solid front piece was 78 inches and 26 inches.

Once all the couches within reach had been stripped of their precious leather, Lauranya set about cutting one-inch strips.

Lauranya sat up on her heels, to look at the stack of hides, wiping sweat out of her eyes. "Arie, do you know where the purple string holder is?"

"The one used for measuring?"

"That would be it."

"I think it's in a tool bag in the other room." Arie bounced out to grab the tool. "Found it!" Arie sang out, her voice rippling through the rooms, warm and light. She ran back into the hallway where Lauranya stacked the leather in various piles, handing off the snap line.

"Perfect. Now I need you to take this end...no dear the other end." Lauranya handed Arie the string tab end as Arie reached for the body. "And walk to the other end of the leather."

Arie trotted over the leather, cocking her head to look down at the laid out material."Mommy?"

"Yes, dear?" Lauranya kneeling, hand poised, ready to cut leather.

"Don't we need to have a measurement in place for the width as well as the snap line for length?"

Lauranya looked down then back up. "Esu!" a vehement curse to the God of Tricks. "I was about to make a major mistake. Thank you, child. Would you go and get the tape measure as well?"

"Yep!"

The second round of marking the width then snapped with a purple chalk line, went quickly. Lauranya took a scalpel along her marked lines with attention to each line and pressure used to slice through. She ignored the sweat on her brow and underarms, as the work took longer than originally estimated. Once cut, Arie carefully took the leather piece to drape over a metal couch frame.

The cramps in Lauranya's hands on the last leather piece, caused her to stop and flex her fingers.

"I think my hands are unhappy with this new exercise." She said to Arie, wiping perspiration from her brow with the back of her hand.

"You've been doing this for hours. I'd be tired too!" Arie said, bouncing to her toes. Her stomach made a loud gurgling sound, emphasizing the hour's remark.

"That sounds like you need food, oh growing child."

"I'd like that!"

Lauranya put her scalpel down carefully, before stretching her arms up and arching her back. The pops were audible across the room.

"Yes, we definitely need a break for a few."

Arie led the way into the kitchen for a late lunch of leftovers, from the night before. Lauranya tried never to eat too fully, just shy of that feeling; she let Ari eat until she was full. Lauranya knew Arie needed extra for her youthful energy and growing bones. Lauranya would limit food intake until absolutely necessary, or the child had stopped growing. Lauranya hopped to never reach the need to and eventually wanted them both to be able to eat well without fear of famine.

Arie and Lauranya's fruit trees were producing enough that they could enjoy fruit with their meals now. They licked the leftover juices of spiced honey fruit from sticky fingers. Arie greedy for sweets trying to catch every dribble. Lauranya was reminded mid-lick of a memorable afternoon with Maison and a stolen jar of sweet fruit preserve, with a shake of her head, she rinsed her hands instead of following the giggling example of her daughter.

By the end of lunch, her hands had stopped cramping, though the sweat made a salty itchy coating on her skin. Lauranya dismissed the feeling by promising herself a long shower when they finished the day's work. Water they still had plenty of.

After lunch, Lauranya took the time to measure each area where a mirror would be hung and the length of braiding needed. Arie wrote down the mirror position and the numbers Lauranya called out. "Mommy, why are you calling out the tape measure number than a higher number?"

"Each braiding set needs 1 1/2 times the length of the project. So if I need 8 feet of braiding, I need 12 feet of leather plus 3 to 6 inches for tying off of the ends."

"Oh. So these would be variables?"

"Yes." Lauranya nimbly stepped down from the ladder unintentionally mimicking Arie's bouncing step.

"Do we have enough strips?"

Lauranya chewed on the bottom lip as she thought. "I think so, but I'll need to count the strips."

"What happens if we don't have enough leather?"

"We'll have to use more couches and if that isn't enough, start on the bedspreads." Lauranya said ruefully.

"Poor couches." Arie's lips turned down at the thought of her favorite couch, being cut up.

"We can sit on pillows or the floor, but I doubt you would want to go without your favorite sweet yellow fruit."

"We could use the pillows from the bedrooms," Arie said excitedly. Ready to bounce upstairs to drag those pillows wherever they were needed.

Lauranya opened her mouth then closed it, mulling the thought before speaking. "Okay, let us return to the project on hand," Lauranya said, with only a moment's hesitation. Arie bounced back to the leather cutting work area. The brightly colored floor pillows tossed into a room for surplus furniture Arie described were the bed pillows or kneeling cushions for slaves. Lauranya had never told Arie the pillows were for things other than excessive decoration.

"Yemoja's blessing, we are not slaves," Lauranya whispered, following her child a little slower, hoping her prayer to the Mother would be heard.

Lauranya had to stitch some of the shorter strappings to the longer to make lengths work. She looked to how the stitches on the couch were made then triple stitched the straps together. She and Arie went through 8 different types of needles before finding one with a flat almost spear-like flaring at the tip. The needle would not punch through the leather however the same box that had the odd sturdy spear needles, myriad tools, and thick thread also had a round hammer of hard plastic and awls for punching through the leather. Or at least that is what the database told her when she turned to the computer in frustration from broken needles and two punctures to her thumb.

Once the holes were punched into the leather, the sewing went much easier.

"Mommy, can I sew this too?" Arie asked bending over Lauranya's shoulder far enough that her hair kept getting into Lauranya's eyes.

"Not this time, dear heart. My hands are barely sufficient to work the leather."

"Umm, your fingers are bleeding."

"What?" Lauranya looked down to see that her fingers were more than just sore. The needle punctured her skin a little deeper with each pass, parting the tissue as easily as the leather hide. The small holes were frequent enough that the leather showed visible streaks of red.

Putting the needle down next to her loose straps, Lauranya wiped her hands on her dusty wrap. "I guess my hands are a little weak as well and the needle is slipping," Lauranya said ruefully, holding her hands up to observe the damage.

"I'll get you bandages!" Arie ran out of the room to pelt up the stairs to medical before Lauranya could say anything. Leaving her mother on the floor of the main room surrounded by strips of leather and couch frames.

Lauranya turned back to her hands and watched as the bleeding slowed. She wiped the blood off to find the puncture wound had closed in the time it had taken to wipe her hands twice. Lauranya frowned. "Skin does not heal that quickly." Her hands ached. She flexed them to work out the cramping from cutting and sewing. Yet her fingers did not loosen up. She flattened them on her thighs to help with the stretching. Her hands began to ache more, lengthening, popping. The nails moving from flat to crescent shape.

Lauranya swallowed bile, overcome with nausea. Taking deep breaths, she fought for calm before Arie's return. Lauranya heard the patter of running bare feet on wood floors before she saw her child with flyaway blond hair round the corner at full speed. Turning back to her hands, to hide them under the strips of leather, they were already back to normal.

"A side benefit from either the whiskered cat or the fish." Jacks observed, his eyes level with her fingers.

"What other side effects might have happened to me?" Lauranya breathed in fear.

"We won't know until it happens." Jacks said, just as softly before vanishing, as Arie ran into the room.

Chapter 8

The asteroid had been a former base. The refugees from the drowning world weren't sure for which side, though. There weren't any manacle stands, which many took as a good sign it was a Runner's base and not the Undead Gods. However, there were some small rooms, in each of the main bedrooms, with fixed long rods a few inches under an upper shelf. Some argued these were sleeping chambers for body or personal slaves, whose collar chains were clipped onto the hanging rod. An argument for boring times. This wasn't the time for those debates.

The crew with three elders sat around a table in one of the few larger rooms with a twenty-foot ceiling, holding tables and chairs for 75. Overhead lights cast a sterile light down on the gleaming steel table. The chairs were also metal and very uncomfortable. They could hold a human with room to spare, giving the impression they had been made for a larger race or people with a much larger girth.

The survivors huddle around the end corner, discussing survivability. The sound of rustling fabric and scuffing shoes amplified in the hush of the meeting room.

"Light if you will give us an update on supplies." The captain asked, turning towards the dark-skinned woman to his far right. His voice echoing in the large empty concrete-walled room.

The shuttle pilot stood, her jumpsuit baggy on her

slimming frame. "We're running out of food, and we have no medicine." The pilot said, without preamble.

"What about the hydroponics? Those should be up to full production." The captain asked, frowning at the pilot. The medicine news being ignored for the more important belly filling information. "Half the hydros are infected with a bloom. Causing any seeds or plants to wilt then melt into black sludge." She said, with a slight shrug. Defeated eloquence in that small gesture.

"What the nova?! Why weren't we told?" The other six in the room started speaking over each other to be heard. The loudest from the second mate. The captain motioned for quiet.

The dark-skinned former pilot gave them a scathing look. "I did. 6 weeks ago when I said, "Hydros aren't working." What do you want me to do? A song and dance so you'll pay attention?" Her chin jutted out as if daring to be hit for speaking the truth.

"Don't you speak to the captain like that!" the second mate snapped, raising his hand. His former bulk had melted off with severe food restrictions. The reduction of his mass was proportional to his ability to bully. Now he could no longer get a child to do his bidding. The pilot gave a flick of her fingers dismissively. The second mate fumed impotently from the sidelines, ignored by all.

"Next time we'd like more information than the hydro's aren't working." The captain said calmly, motioning for the pilot to continue.

"There won't be a next time. We're running out of food." She said, with an irritated snort, sitting back down with a thump on the metal chair.

"What do you mean?" Captain Jamison asked warily, narrowing his eyes and pulling back slightly.

"We have enough food on half rations for three more

weeks. We haven't been able to clean the hydros thoroughly enough to keep the spread of the bloom, which will kill anything growing now. What seeds we have left will require more dirt than we have and more time than we have to reach harvest." She looked at the captain with the face of a woman who has seen the vacuum chamber door open and close behind her. They were dead and she knew it. The others were just catching on.

The captain paled, understanding hitting him like a gut punch. It took a couple of moments before the others understood the gravity of the situation.

"What are we going to do?"

"We're already on half rations!"

The room erupted into a cacophony of blame and recrimination. The captain let it go for a few minutes more, before putting his fingers to his lips, giving a piercing whistle.

"Enough!" He took a deep breath, climbing slowly to his feet, knowledge weighing his shoulders down until they bowed slightly. "We have choices. Not one of them is good, so we're going to go through our options now." The skin on his face sagged. Cut rations had taken any extra padding they had had, reducing them all down to just skin covering muscles. The younger children were faring somewhat better as their rations were still half of an adult's ration, but the older children were feeling the pinch. Their hollowed cheeks knowing hunger's bite well.

"Worst case first." The captain said, looking around the room. "We cut our throats and pray that Yemoja and Olorun take our souls and not throw us to Esu for the next life." This met with blank stares and mutters at his sense of humor. Only the pilot and the second knew he wasn't joking.

"Our second option is to get back in the shuttle to find

a Runner's ship before we run out of food and oxygen then hope they have mercy." There were dubious glances moving between people at this one.

"We're truly vacuumed if you think that's a good idea." One raspy-voiced person spoke up grimly.

The captain turned to the older woman, speaking. "Because our third and final option is to get into the shuttle and find a world-ship praying the entire time that not all of us will be skinned alive by our own Gods." The captain held her eyes. The old woman dropped her eyes first.

"The gods won't take us back!"

"They will kill us!"

This time the voices whispered, like children under a blanket who know the boogie man is on the other side.

"Those are our choices." He took a deep breath looking around the room. "We vote tomorrow morning, by tomorrow night whatever our solution, we leave."

He looked around the room, meeting every pair of eyes, before nodding dismissal to them. Single file they exited. Each person was absorbed in the thoughts of what tomorrow morning would bring.

That night the old woman, along with two others opted out, seeking their gods sooner rather than later. Jameson looked at the rooms of the dead. None had reanimated, so either a necro was sleeping, or there were no active Power's near. He turned to his second "Take the bodies to the kitchen and break them down into soup packs. We'll need the protein for the trip."

His second gagged but did as told. The kitchen, empty at this time of night with no others being recruited for the task, made breaking down the bodies no less horrifying, but breakfast was broth in full measure and a quarter ration of cooked grain. No one asked where the broth came from.

The council voted for the Runners. Three hours later

they packed the shuttle with all fuel, food, and other necessities. The outpost left mothballed for others, who might need at another time.

The young boy crept into his mistress' room. His owner was jealous of her privacy and sleep. Her aim, when throwing things, was as good as a whip in her hands. Accurate and painful.

His skin blended with the shadows, fear making him cautious. He wore a pair of loose baggy trousers and a collar. The intricately carved wood collar around his neck, telling anyone who looked, his owner had high status. Where the other slaves wore clothes of woven synthetics he had pants made from a pair of his mistress' silk cast offs. Not a sign of favoritism, she wanted all things in her rooms to be beautiful.

"Mistress? Mistress, time for class." The boy's voice called out lyrically six feet from her bed.

The boy's luck held as the sounds from her sheer curtained bed were anything but that of sleep as moans and sighs greeted his call to rise. He frantically searched the floor for clothing, his mistress' and her lover's.

One woman rolled out of the huge bed, her long legs sinking into cotton woven rugs "Void. Cae, we have to get going!" She didn't have to search far for her clothing, pulling on trews and tunic the young slave held out to her.

"Ugh! I would rather be in bed with you and Meldi, instead of trouncing that waste of air Daccu." The dark skinned beauty with wavy brown hair said looking up with wet lips from between her body slave's thighs. "Not that it doesn't have merits beating that snake fucking excuse up; however priorities should be upheld." Meldi moaned, pushing her hips down on Caelia's slow pumping fingers.

"Thankfully he's only my brother by adoption and not full blood kin," Hadriana said, taking the proffered brush from the boy to run through her short blond hair.

"Now you're just being a pain in my ass for reminding me of our relations." Caelia bent back down over Meldi's clit for more cunnilingus. The girl's moans reached a fevered pitch, her hips pushing faster.

Hadriana came up behind Caelia leaning over breathing into her ear, "No lover, but I can be if you really want," sliding a hand along her "sister's" tight bottom to slid a finger between her very wet lips, rubbing Caelia's swollen clit.

Caelia groaned pushing back against Hadriana, as Meldi clenched her thighs around Caelia's hand arching her hips with a muffled screaming orgasm.

Hadriana pulled fingers out licking the sweet juice, watching Caelia grind her hips into the mattress frustrated.

"Shall I complete you mistress?" Meldi asked in soft gasping breaths, her hands unclenching from the bedsheets.

Caelia kissed the girl's quivering clit causing another writhing moan. "Sadly, no. I need to get to class sometime before the noon meal today." She bit the slave's inner thigh with a lover's touch. "Tonight though, I'll want multiples from you."

"Of course, mistress!" Meldi sat up to give Caelia a deep kiss, then smaller kisses on her wet chin and cheeks.

Caelia crawled out of the bed, putting on the clothes held out by her slave. While she arranged her belt and dagger, he brought damp cotton towels scented with a floral mixture for the mistress and her lover.

"Think Daccu is going to make the final culling?" Hadriana asked worriedly. She tossed the towel onto the floor when finished wiping face, hands and armpits.

"Undead Gods, not if I keep my scores higher than his. I'd call him a real bastard but since he is my older brother, wouldn't look good for my lady mother." Caelia said, her plump lips pouting cutely.

"You're mother is nice," Hadriana said, looking up from lacing her leather sandals, enjoying the sight of Caelia undressed. "Less manipulative than your father."

"Compared to Menodisces, anyone else is nice." Caelia rolled her eyes, throwing her dirty washcloth on the floor, joining Hadriana's. "Her idea of manipulation is..." she fanned her hands out as if encompassing a world. "more long term than father's brutally direct intervention."

"Melatheandra...on the other hand" They both shuddered at Menodisces youngest wife. "She'll poison the lot of us if given a chance."

"Strong necro that one." Dressed, they walked arm in arm out of Caelia's rooms. "Heard her daughter married a man one generation off the sands."

"That pissed her off I'm sure."

"Actually, the gladiator family breeds strong necros like crazy. Mel's family has taken the long view." Their leather sandaled feet making soft whispers on metal floors.

"Waiting to see what pops from between the Lord's legs?"

"Probably." Caelia tilted her head as they walked. "Menodisces concubine, forget which one, is from the same family."

"Possibly the touched in the head, one?"

"Which one isn't?" The girls' laughter floated down the hallways, slaves scampered to get out of their way.

Chapter 9

Sister stirred the coals of her fire with a makeshift battle steel bar. The bar had been scavenged when their ship crash landed those many years ago. The metal didn't transmit heat and was narrow enough that Sister's hands, on bad days, could grip the rod. She stared at the fire broodily, watching the flames, Leah's death even after this long, still looped through her mind.

"Should have seen that." She muttered to herself, her lips tight with eyes narrowed in anger. She gave the fire a vicious poke. "Ship raping psychopath." She sat, glaring at the dancing flames as if they were Toithan reincarnate. The fire, unconcerned with her anger, danced merrily over wood.

She was startled at a knock on her door, perfunctory at best. Brother ducked inside. Sand was on his feet, sparkling like stardust in the firelight.

Sister's mood of bitter self-recrimination fueled her anger at the interruption. "Knocking isn't just for children. You could remember your manners." She snapped, gripping her metal rod a little tighter. Mostly for show. Mostly.

Brother ignored her as he sidestepped onto a reed mat, making room for the woman following him. Sister had never seen this particular woman. Wet blonde hair down her back, wearing Brother's shirt, too long at the wrist draping over the hands yet barely long enough to cover either her front or bare butt. The woman walked cautiously, an almost mincing yet rolling gait. Sister said nothing though her eyebrows rose with surprise.

She glanced at Brother for a clue on why a mer-woman was in the village. His face gave away nothing, - grim. Sister sat up, pulling the rod from the fire to sit next to her, waiting for the woman to speak first.

The woman looked hesitantly to Brother then at Sister and back to Brother. Her hands fluttered nervously between pulling the sleeves up and the shirttail down. Clothing, which draped in gravity, seemed perplexing to her.

"Sit here, Keyma," Brother said gently, taking the woman's hand, guiding her to the mat closest to Sister. The woman gave Brother another, if possible wider-eyed stare, but demurred to his judgment on where to sit.

"I take it; this isn't just a social call," Sister said, toning down the sharp edge of her tongue for company.

Brother ignored her waspish tones as he turned to the mer-woman "Keyma, please tell the Torch what you told me about Sachiko and Chehreh." The use of Sister's formal title, caused the old woman to sit up even straighter, scrutinizing a little sharper the woman across the fire from her.

Keyma looked at Brother then back to Sister, with wide eyes. Keyma took a deep breath, releasing slowly as if for a deep dive. "Chehreh had a dream…" She started.

By the time the mer-woman was finished, Sister started reaching for her bag of bones with gnarled hands and a shrewd look. "Well, this will definitely be an interesting read." She muttered, sitting on her knees to lay out the flayed God skin in front of the fire. She reached into the pouch, pulling out the bones, clearing her mind of all distractions. Again the full number of bones fit in her hand as if they belonged. She tossed the bones, waiting for them to fall and the visions to begin. Time slowed as the bones reached the apex of the toss, hanging in the air, sparks from the fire floating up and around the bones.

Brother cleared his throat after a moment's time. "Is that normal?"

"Do bones hanging in the air and not falling to the ground seem normal to you?" Sister snapped, glaring at the bones and her brother equally. Keyma's eyes were huge.

"Why…?" Keyma began.

Sister reached a hand to the hanging bones. A small spark flickered out of the bone center, brushing her questioning fingers with a zing that reached to Sister's core. An image formed from that spark as Sister hissed, yanking back her hand, sucking on the tingling digit, like a small child with a burnt finger.

"Because we need everyone here to do this reading." Sister's attention rested on the bones, glaring at them as if her will alone could command them to fall.

"The village?" Brother asked, gracefully rising to his feet to sound the horn for a gathering.

"And Chehreh with anyone he wants to bring, but the bones won't fall for a reading until then." Sister with a final glare upwards. "This is going to be a Gods spacing sideshow with everyone needing to see this display." The bones still did not fall with Sister's comment. Half plea, half annoyance.

Sister turned to Keyma, pointing a gnarled finger. "You-" The woman flinched. "...will go and fetch Chehreh. Edit the story how you want, but if he wants to hear of his wife, he needs to get his fishy butt here and today."

"Yes, Torch!" Keyma stripped the shirt off without a second's hesitation, tossing it to Brother as she stumbled out the door and down to the night cloaked beach.

"You," Sister pointed to her brother, "will get the villagers together." Brother gave her a sideways look, conveying he knew how to do his job. "And I will need helpers to take down this hut so everyone can see the bones." She reached for the fire stick to prod the fire, regarding the hanging bones with both irritation and excitement.

Brother pursed his lips but nodded. "I'll get Grenich to help me move the hut."

"You'll need more than one to help. Get Nathan and Nori as well. Don't want my hut or few possessions lost from here to the sun." She thumped her fire stick for emphasis.

"Of course, Sister." Brother's tilted head and smiled conveyed both the seriousness of the tasks and the amusement he would enjoy when the others gathered to see the floating bones.

Roland's sword thwacked against Redeyes left side, then sizzled with the returning stroke to her right side ribs. Redeyes didn't get her upper sword-hand into position fast enough. She did lessen the impact of the blunt sword stroke, a killing blow if it had landed, by sacrificing her lower right arm with a wet crunch of a broken bone. Redeyes yelped, even as she threw a sidekick, feigning for his balls but twisting at the last minute to take an exposed knee. Roland lifted his leg, giving her the calf as a target, as he kneed her in the stomach at full speed. Redeyes went down, with a huff of air, onto all six.

"Damn me. I thought her fights with Nero were rough." Collins said, with envy at the damage Roland dished out. He counted at least four broken bones this one bout alone.

"Not to worry, you're up next," Roland said, over his shoulder as he squatted by the young dry heaving God, the claws from his unshod feet making small clicking sounds on the metal floor.

"Fuck," Collins swore, running a hand through his sweat-damp hair. The large room, usually chilly with the metal walls, felt warm from the group's combined excursions.

"Careful what you admire," Cratt said, smiling slightly, as he stood cross-armed outside of from the circle's demarcation line. Nero and Iarris laughed at the other Guardian's obvious dismay and soon to be pain. Collins shrugged, running hands lovingly along his sword hilts, taking the others ribbing in good nature.

"Are you going to be ok?" Roland asked Redeyes. She looked up with a glare but nodded. "Good." He slipped a hand under her upper left arm, pulling her up, half carrying half walking her to the sidelines. "You missed the opening to the head and didn't get the blade online when you attacked." His eyes bored into her head. "You can't just rely on your speed. Clear the damn blade or blades. If you can sacrifice a limb, make it a spare arm and make sure you won't be fighting much longer because you may need that arm later." He tapped her on the head. "Listening girl?"

"Yessss." Gasping reply, as she slowly sat up, testing the extent of broken bones this round.

Roland nodded. He stood up, turning towards the Guardians. "Collins, Nero. Two on one."

Iarris stepped into the circle.

"Not you." Roland turned his back to the other Guardian with a dismissive flick of his tail.

"Yes, her," Cratt said, without being asked. "You've

been ignoring Iarris since we've started sparring this morning. It's all or nothing."

"Females…"

"Are fighting now, you spaced dark void relic. We aren't just for breeding or your entertainment." Iarris said, with a growling purr. Her fingernails flexed on her sword hilt. Roland's tail lashing as his ears went flat.

"Collins Iarris, in the circle. Two against one, isn't it Roland?" Redeyes said, in a gasping voice from the sidelines. All heads turned towards her. At least three pair of eyes were glaring.

"Space the lot of you. Do it or get the fuck out of the Guardians." She wheezed and coughed hard enough to spit up blood. "Iarris fights and you fucking train, Roland." Pain tempered any goodwill or sense of humor.

"Fine." Came Roland's low growling assent at the stinging rebuke. The only way out of Guardianship was feet first. He changed from a single two-handed sword to a brace of lighter one-handed swords. Roland took the middle of the circle, only the quiver on the tip of his tail, giving away his emotions. Nero moved to check Redeyes bones and other damages.

Collins grinned, showing teeth as he stepped into the circle, rocking back on his heels ready to move at the slightest tell. He held a training sword and dagger. Iarris moved to Collins left. She stood with soft knees, centering her weight. Her ears were flat and the hair along her spine spiked. Iarris had both throwing and stabbing daggers at the ready along with the sword in her left hand.

Roland feigned a glance to his left at Redeyes, opening his mouth as if to say something. He moved with blurring speed to bind Collins' sword with his offhand blade, bringing his dominate hand sword for a killing thrust to the inside. Collins saw the move coming, as he stepped to his right, trying to bring his sword up in response. Iarris barely saw the feign for what it was, missing her own thrust into Roland's open back as she changed her block to an attack with a twist of her wrist.

Roland turned, even as Collins moved, to the left, blocking Iarris' sword, stepping into her space. He brought his sword up and to the right for a back-handed pommel punch to the chest. Iarris pulled back her sword, skipping three steps backward to keep out of the punishing backhand move. She sidestepped setting up her attack for the next opening.

Collins tried for a lunge of his own, pulling his sword and dagger in close for the finishing blow only to be met, not with Roland's back but the incoming point. Roland pivoted his hips to the left, stepping his left foot into Collins incoming attack, using a two-handed back thrust for positioning into a forward thrust. Had Collins not been as light on his feet, he would have been skewered where he stood.

Collins grunted, managing to spin over his left shoulder, avoiding the incoming thrust. Collins felt the practice sword scrape the skin along his ribs, hard enough to leave a shallow burning cut. The maneuver got him out of Roland's blade, but into Iarris' line of attack, following her incoming blade with his body.

Roland shifted his weight to the right leg, snapping his left foot up and out from the knee, hitting Collins square in the chest. The larger Katherian sent the small Guardian slamming into Iarris. Collins and Iarris went down in a sprawl. Roland had a foot on Iarris' throat and his sword at Collins' throat before they could disentangle.

"You didn't work together but as separate killing entities. Until you can work together as one, other than in bed, you'll get each other killed." Roland said in a low rumble, ears flat and flexing claws. He took his foot off of Iarris' throat, stepping back out of range of either opponent.

"That was fun! Let's do it again." Collins huffed, looking up from Iarris well-padded chest, grinning even wider than when they started. Iarris growled in annoyance, a chest rumbling sound with flattened ears. She flicked Collins ear with her long fingers, in irritation, shoving him off her chest. Nero started to laugh on the sidelines. "You don't know when to stop, do you?" to Collins.

"If I can learn to move like that and take out more than the usual one on one, I am so for it!" Collins scrambled to his feet, offering a hand to Iarris. She slapped the hand away, her claws sheathed, getting to her feet with a lashing tail. Iarris barred her teeth with an open mouth snarl, her nose wrinkled up to the eyes at Roland. She didn't look away, but she didn't issue a challenge either. Iarris knew when she had been beaten.

"Iarris," Redeyes called from the side, sitting on her knees with her feet tucked under her butt, with both upper and lower hands resting on hips and thighs. All four of the Guardians did a double take. The sitting pose they had all seen Redeyes take on more occasions than any could count. For a moment they were seeing the God they were used to. Strong commanding, death with a weapon or just four arms, not the child God fate had given them to train.

"You'll have to do this again and again. " Redeyes looked Iarris dead in the eyes, giving a toothy grin saying. "It will get easier."

"Isn't it time for me to check your broken bones?" Iarris panted slightly, with mock angry eyes, but curling lips.

"And now we are doing ship politics." Major Cratt stepped in, breaking the spell of the God of future past.

Redeyes made a face, but she clambered to her feet, dutifully moving towards the table with the various ship units and their Gods. There were groans all the way around.

Chapter 10

Chehreh showed at the beach the next morning at sunrise, dark bruises under pale blue eyes. The water seemed to reflect his temper, with waves building to a towering height only to crash off the shores, receding with scathing roars at the newly formed un-sanded beach: mud and other things swirling into a frothing mix. The mer leader swam as close as possible, through dark muddy waters. His red-black tail undulating slower the closer he got to shore with his free hand feeling for rocks and sunken bushes or trees underneath. The unseen could tear off a scale or open skin if a mer wasn't careful.

Chehreh kept his blue coral spear gripped tightly, in his other hand warding off green snakes, shallow water sharks or other opportunistic predators. His vigilance kept his own safe. This trip all the mers were adept in both deep and shallow waters. No mer had been lost or injured, only slightly softening Chehreh's rage and sorrow at Sister's summons.

Once in shallow enough water, making swimming difficult, Chehreh sat up pushing shoulder-length dark hair from his a pale face. The soft glow of sunrise lit his cheekbones sharply while showing dark scar tissue cutting across various muscles. The scar stretched taut pale skin that rarely felt the sun's kiss.

Chehreh concentrated for a moment, shifting from tail to legs. He stood, defying gravity's pull, a water god striding onto land. The confidence, poise, and anger radiating off the land walking mer in such waves, those watching could almost feel the ground shake with each step.

Brother sat on his haunches, covered in tattered canvas pants with no shirt or weapons, waiting on a flat beach rock to welcome, or at least guide, the mers to Sister's opened hut. He had been up since pre-dawn, watching the storm-tossed oceans for the summoned guests.

Next to him, on a thick woven mat, donated clothing, should any mer wish to wear the novelty of land clothing. Nudity wasn't taboo, but the offer of clothing showed respect for the guest and helped keep the sun's harsh rays from pale skin.

Chehreh's eyes narrowed at the first sighting of Brother, a few feet from high tide edge, but the table laden with boiled eggs, fruit, grilled meats and sweet nectar for the mer-people caught his eye. Island treats, a rarity for the mers. A welcome change from a diet mainly of ocean bounty.

The table had been Mauri's idea to help the mer with both fuel needs from their swim and the shifting. Her acerbic "It's better to have something sweet to sweeten their temper at this sad summoning than having tempers snap dangerously on empty stomachs." That swayed the other islanders to help.

"Oh, my Gods! Eggs." The youngest mer, Illig let out loudly, his exclamation helped to break Chehreh from his spiking anger. Illig's tail was gone, but he wasn't willing to stand just yet. He tried to knee walk towards alluring food, instead of waiting until his body had adjusted.

Brannig smacked the second-decade hunter on the back of his head. "Legs on land, shrimp brain. Walk; don't crawl."

Brannig sighed heavily, affectionate humor for his nephew. Brannig's blond hair shone gold in the rising sun's light, just as muscled as his chief. Unlike Chehreh, Brannig leaned heavily on his spear until he got his land legs under him. Brannig didn't want to willingly tempt gravity's fickle nature with real steps for a few more moments.

"Yes, Uncle!" Illig stumbled to his feet, uncaring if he stumbled in front of others or not. Eggs were too much of a treat to care if others ridiculed him more or not.

Chehreh had included Illig because he was an excellent hunter: Sachiko had sworn he'd surpass her as being one of the best she had seen in over a generation. Chehreh honored the memory of his wife with Illig's inclusion as a last minute addition. A good hunter, but not always the brightest per the pod.

Brother rose slowly, the tattered edges of his comfortably baggy pants dangled above his ankles by several inches. "May I be of assistance to your coming ashore or offer you clothing on our sun bright island?" Brother asked with a wave of his hand, making no forward moves towards the mer, waiting for an acknowledgment. Courtesy, above all else, for their guests.

"Shirt, if you will Brother," Brannig said, straightening slowly while he took a couple of cautionary steps. "And another shirt for my nephew if you would." Motioning to Illig who had made it to the table, busily popping a boiled egg into his mouth. The young man had his eyes closed in bliss at the creamy garlic, and onion flavors chased over his tongue.

Illig swallowed hastily to ask "Why a shirt? It's going to be vent hot here." While wiping yolk flecked hands on pale naked thighs.

"That sun, bright in the sky, will burn your skin as if

poached over newly formed lava." Brannig snarled.

"Hmm…will the skin darken like it does on Brother? Would make me even more attractive." Illig mused with another egg halfway to his mouth, contemplating another way to notch his atelier.

"We don't need any more half-wits. Stop breeding, and we can stop with you as our token." Amaris said, with an indulgent smile. She had pinned her hair up for the swim, but land's gravity caused the tightly wound water-heavy mass of hair to tilt her head backward. She pulled the top knot down with much tugging and a few muttered curses. Her flame red hair thunked against her back, in a thick curly sodden mass. She wrung out what water she could from her hair, giving her a few extra minutes to acclimate to gravity, before walking to the table almost gracefully.

Amaris' parents had feared that her red tresses hinted to the fate of a seer for their child. They had been pleased when Amaris preferred the sword and never saw anything more prophetic than where shoals of fish were most likely to be found.

Brother brought her a tunic dyed the color of new leaves, emphasizing the red of Amaris' hair. The shirt fell to her knees, looking almost like a tunic on her. Amaris smiled warmly at Brother as she slid the cloth over her head.

"So soft!" She said, with real delight. Running hands along her sides, feeling the softness along her skin. Her touching the shirt helped enhance the finer points of her round hips and chest. She gave a sideways glance at Brother, whose eyes were happy to travel along with her guiding hands. He gave her a smile that touched his eyes with the heat of his appreciation. Her return smile warmed him as her eyes followed the line of his pants and the snugness in appropriate places.

"Keyma mentioned you were instrumental in saving her life from the flat head." A coy tilt to her head.

"Keyma gives me more credit than I deserve." A lilt to his voice. "She had done most of the killing, but let me have the finishing blow."

"How generous," Amaris twined a long thick strand of her hair between pale fingers. "Perhaps you can tell me more of the hunting tale later?" A not so veiled hint.

"I'd love to." Brother's slow smile widened as he quirked his eyebrows in assent.

"Amaris now would be the time to eat before we leave again." Chehreh snapped over his shoulder, his infamous temper making a show.

"Refueling my…body is what I had in mind." Amaris turned toward the table but turned her head back to Brother so that only he saw her wink. Brother kept a straight face; his grin didn't fade.

"May I offer you a shirt or sarong, Chehreh?" Brother asked blandly, but his eyes were still following Amaris as the shirt clung to her damp backside, framing lush hips.

"I don't plan to be here long enough to be burnt by the sun." Chehreh snapped. He turned toward the table for the proffered food, taking his own advice to refuel. The fact that the food was excellent helped to curb the worst edge of his tongue as he bit into a savory grilled pork chop.

Nathan walked onto the mudflat. Like Brother, he approached without weapons. His dark curly hair, tamed with a tie, holding back a frothing mass. He wore nothing more than a sarong, done in green geometrics on a red background, highlighting his dark skin and barrel-shaped form. Like Chehreh, he kept his distance from Brother, though his eyes were cold when they did touch on the peacekeeper.

He nodded to Chehreh, waving a hand, palm up toward

the village. "When you are finished with breakfast, I will take you to Sister," he said.

Chehreh let his hunters finish until full. They would have only a few minutes of rest while he talked with the seer. The swim back would be punishing through dangerous new shallows. The hunters took bites of the different dishes, exclaiming and sharing tasty parts with others.

"Hey! Share the eggs, Illig." Brannig called to his nephew. Watching as Illig popped two at a time from the dwindling supply.

"So good!" Illig said, trying to speak and swallow at the same time. He ended up inhaling bits. Amaris pounded his back as the others laughed at him.

"Try this, nephew. Swallow, don't inhale!"

"Or at least lick first," Amaris said, keeping a straight face, setting off the laughter of the others at Illig's expense again.

They enjoyed the meal companionably, even if it was over too soon. Once fed, the mer followed Nathan to the waiting village area. Brother followed behind.

The villagers, less than 150 with only a few nonhumans, were gathered around one fire pit. The roof to a hut still in place cast a round shadow on the sand, yet the walls and contents had been moved. Space had been saved around the fire pit for the mers, with soft mats woven with strips of reeds laid out. Here Nathan directed them to sit. Sister already sat on one such mat, greens and browns predominate in color, poking the fire with sharp jabs that did little to make the fire burn, but did kill time.

Chehreh frowned down at the old woman. "Why are we here? Could you not tell Keyma your news, so that we might mourn for my wife and bury her."

Sister looked up with narrowed eyes, glaring into the

bright morning light. "I'd have loved to, but the fragging bones wanted you here." She flicked fingers upward at the still hanging Seer bones. Chehreh stopped dead, looking at the floating bones. The others were just as dumbfounded.

Chehreh walked forward slowly, sinking to his knees on a mat. For the first time in 25 hours, anger didn't show on his face. "My mother would talk about Seers who could command the future to show, in lines woven together like the sun spiders, but she never mentioned something like this." He reached a hand out slowly, like a youngling seeing a stinging anemone for the first time, cautious but curious.

"That's going to…" Brother started, just as an electric spark snapped into Chehreh's hand. "hurt." He bit his tongue on any further comments.

Chehreh glared, as he sucked on his finger, saying nothing more. Still the bones hovered. Sister glared at them. "We're here now you bleeding black hole excuse for bones." Sister's temper beginning to fray from lack of response and the continued questions of newcomers to the show.

When the last of the mer sat down the bones did deign to fall on the waiting skin below. They didn't move, but laid in a pattern, waiting calmly for Sister to read.

"About time," Brother muttered. There were a few muffled laughs from those closest enough to hear. Chehreh glared up at the village's peacekeeper. Brother gave him a bland smile before looking back to Sister.

Sister placed her hand over the bones for the visions to take her. This time, the vision showed to those closest in the circle, as small blue-white electric sparks flying to those who were to be affected by the vision. The mers, Brother, Nathan, and the Silver, Grenich. They saw what she saw.

A mer-woman, Sachiko, attacked from her blind spot by a flat head shark. The body armor protected the stomach but not the tail. Wounds on both fighters many and great. Sachiko suffering from a severed major artery, her undoing. The shark fared little better as it swam off, tilting sideways with a slow-killing spear wound. Sachiko made it to the base of a large manmade building, one of the four left by the Undead Gods.

They watched her die, her eyes clouding, her body crumpled in the mud and water weeds. Time passed in fast motion. The shallow water showed sunlight flickering over her body then dimming to dark several times. Crabs flowed over her, moving abnormally fast, and then she moved, not breathing but undulating upright in the still waters. The crabs scuttled or fell off her to feast somewhere else.

Here the vision moved in closer so that her body could be seen as she stood within a few feet of the viewers. The missing pieces of skin and flesh flowed back over her bones. The holes covered, not healed but no longer gaping either. She swam to the front door, picking up the spear she had dropped fighting the shark - her positioning that of a guard.

Chehreh reached a hand forward as if to touch his wife's face for the last time. He stopped just an inch from her face. A tear tracked down his cheek, unbeknown until wetness touched his full bow lips. He pulled his hand back, touching the tear with a look of confusion, before returning back to the vision before him.

The vision paused for a moment as if giving those viewing a moment to absorb the loss of one of their own. Then shadows of other mer, no faces but dim figures, would join Sachiko though never the same shadowy person as if the future couldn't decide who would join the first mer. Sometimes the number was as high as seven, sometimes as low as three. Yet Sachiko stood guard over the years as other bodies joined her and the building's front window broke in slow motion. They watched as flat head sharks were killed for wandering into protected space. The vision faded, showing no more.

"What…" Chehreh had to clear his throat before continuing. "What is that supposed to show us, Torch?"

"It's answering a question for all of us. Yes, there is a Necromancer, but we aren't to touch." Torch bent over her knees to reach for all the bones.

"We just saw my wife and the forms of others in front of the building." Chehreh rubbed his thumb over the wet patch on his fingertip. "If the Necromancer stays, others will die."

"No. When others die in this area, they come under the influence of the Necromancer as guards." Torch gave him a glare shaking her fist full of bones at him.

"Are you senile?!" Chehreh snapped, rising to his feet, glaring down at the Torch from his superior height. Brother tried to step forward to protect Sister, but Grenich's silver-clad hand kept him from moving forward. The man stood two feet shorter than Brother, but Brother couldn't break the battle steel grip, his forward motion halted.

"Listen, you space blinded old fool!" Sister tried to get to her feet, she would never make Chehreh's height, but she would go toe to toe with him even if her head was only to his chest. As she staggered to her feet, the bones fell from her hands; the Vision took her again. This time not for all to see.

Those surrounding saw her eyes mist over, like faceted white sand hit by moonlight. Sister's hand pointed to Chehreh's chest.

"Seek your wife, but only if you wish to join her. The mother and child will live for the final fight, calling the dead from their slumber. Should they die, the Undead Gods will enslave even the undying of this planet." Sister spoke, but her voice no longer her own, deeper and commanding, sending shivers along the spines of all who could hear.

With a jerk, the Seeing let go of Sister, she collapsed backward, where Nathan waited to catch her. Sister shivered, her eyes rolling so far back only the whites were visible. Grenich let go of Brother's wrist, handing him a wood handled knife to place between her teeth. Sister bit down on the wood, instead of clenching her teeth so hard she would've shattered teeth during the spasm.

Chehreh drew back from the Torch, swallowing hard. Grief chased fear across his face as he turned his head. His eyes landing on the faces of his own mer, showing fear, confusion, and shock. Chehreh spoke into silence so profoundly deep not even the normal tropic sounds of birds or wind could be heard.

"My grandmother spoke of a time before she had been rescued from the Undead Gods. The collar and the whip. The humiliation and lack of self. There's only the want of the Undead Gods, who took your body and soul to fulfill any desire they might have." He looked down, running a hand over the woven grass mat. "She carried whip scars with dignity but she never let us forget how those scars were made and why she learned to fight as a Marine, to free others." He dusted his hands off, looking to Sister, whose eyes were just now coming back into focus, and Brother. "I loved Sachiko, but I won't do anything to endanger our freedom. Or those of our future children."

He stood to his full height, holding his spear. "Neither I nor mine will go to the tower. The undead live there, and there they shall die." With that Chehreh turned back to the oceans. The others scrambled to stand and follow. The mer waded into the shallow, discarding their borrowed clothes on the sand above the tide line, shifting from legs to a single powerful tail to propel them through the warm sunlit waters.

"That went well." Sister's voice sounding both soft and gravelly. She started to cough, raising a weak hand to cover her lips. The hand came away with flecks of blood. Her daughter scrambled to bring her a pottery cup with cool spring water to her lips. Sister gave a weak wave.

Brother turned to Nathan with a look.

Nathan gave a nod, puckering his lips, giving a piercing whistle. "Show's over. The reading is done so let's get the Torch's house back around her." Nathan settled a pillow under Sister's head.

Brother squeezed her shoulders. "I'll put out a call on the other few islands for any others who might be potential seers."

Sister patted his hand. "Don't bother." She wheezed. "Part of that seeing is the next Torch, coming from this planet, won't be for millennials. I'm the last for a long while."

Gasps came from those closest enough to hear. Nathan licked his lips. "How are we going to see trouble coming?"

"By using the Gods-given eyes and brain you were born with." Came Sister's acerbic reply. She waved off another cup of water. "Need sleep more than water." The noise of the villagers setting her hut back around her become white noise. Sleep claimed her for the next 13 hours straight. The seeings had taken an unusually taxing amount from her.

Chapter 11

The next day Lauranya tested the viability of her braids to hold up a mirror. She looped the braid ends over and down the mid-sized mirror, forming a harness. She sewed the edges to the main strap. With the ladder moved and in place, Lauranya drilled a hook screw into the wall. Looping the braid over her shoulder, she pulled the mirror up slowly. Arie tried to help by lifting the bottom of the mirror.

"This is heavy!" Arie grunted exuberantly, standing on tiptoes with her hands under the mirror as Lauranya continued to pull upwards.

Lauranya chuckled. "You will grow into your strength, sweety." Climbing as high as the ladder allowed to the hook.

Her hands shook as the mirror came off her shoulder to be held only by the leather braid and the strength in her hands as she looped the middle of the braid over the hook. She yelped as her fingers caught between the mirror weighted braid and the wall. She wiggled them out blowing on them as tears prickled her eyes.

"Mommy?" Arie asked up in concern.

"I am ok. The braid caught my fingers wrong." Lauranya choked back watching as one finger healed the raw scraped skin before her eyes. "I am all right." She whispered to herself, shaking out her pinched fingers once more before heading down.

Lauranya looked up at the hung mirror. Clouds had parted, for a moment causing her breath to catch in her throat as light streamed in from the floor to ceiling windows. The left side window light hit the mirror, reflecting light to the other side of the main room. The room brightened, reflecting the sun's glory in living green and warm wood. The planters' paint and glass decoration illuminated, showing off the work of skilled artisans, making even the most mundane item glorious.

"Wow!" Arie slid her hand cautiously through the beam of light. She giggled, as the light warmed her skin on contact.

"Sixteen of these and you can dance through light all day," Lauranya said, wiping sweat out of her eyes with the back of one hand.

"That's going to be a long day!" Arie said, with a nod, moving out of the light to help reposition the ladder.

"Do not think that this will get you out of your reading for the day, or your calculations."

"But I can't study if we're doing this!" Arie stated with wide eyes. The of course unstated.

Means we will have a late night tonight." Lauranya said, popping the ladder open four feet from the other mirror. "However if you like, we can do calculations while watching an opera tonight." Lauranya offered casually.

"That sounds perfect!" Arie bounced on the tips of her toes, to rock back on her heels.

"Good, because we have a long day." Lauranya grinned, grabbing more woven leather to wrap around a mirror.

The clouds hid the sun once more, floating over the bright face with grey and black fluff. Rain started, streaking the windows in runnels, leaving the mirrors to reflect only the light from regular light bulbs. The effect wasn't nearly so dazzling, but the plants would grow, and the solar chargers would charge.

The sun played amongst the clouds for the remainder of the day with the clouds weeping on and off, yet they did not let down the deluge of prior days. The rains were finally starting to slacken. Both Lauranya and Arie admired their work, the sun showing through the clouds for a brief moment, before continuing the tasks at hand.

Lauranya got 12 more mirrors hung up quickly before Arie started to get unusually whiny, asking for lunch. Lauranya glanced down at her daughter, noticing her pinched expression and tired eyes. Arie's shirt was two inches shorter than the last time she had worn it. She climbed down the ladder to give her tired and growing child a quick hug.

"This looks to be a good time for a rest," Lauranya said, thinking on how much Arie had grown these years, tall enough to almost look Lauranya in the eyes now.

They ate leftovers from the night before, sweet root with savory yellow roots, roasted in rabbit fat. Arie gave a belch after her last bite. Lauranya frowned. Arie ducked her head with a sheepish "Sorry!"

"Well now that you have demonstrated you are full, we will need to put a slow cook meal on for tonight while we finish up the mirrors." Lauranya picked up the dishes, while Arie went to get a pot. "I am pretty sure we will be too tired from hanging to do much cooking."

Arie gathered her vegetables and grains together to make a slow stew with chicken stock. An extra rooster roasted a few nights before made his second contribution to their meals. The division of kitchen labor had changed from those first few frenetic days. They had found over the last years that Lauranya was only moderate in cooking if there was a recipe; however Arie could make a meal fit for an Undead God from the least ingredients, so the cooking fell to her while Lauranya did the dishes.

At the last moment, Arie decided on one more main ingredient. "I'm going to add hen to tonight's stew."

"Do we have the meat to spare?" Lauranya asked, looking up with sudsy hands, the hunger of those first few days still a sharp memory.

"Yep! All the birds and rabbits have hatched or birthed decent sized broods. So we can take one from the freezer without worry." She pulled from the fridge a hen that had been aging for four days.

"Okay, sweety. You are the cook." Lauranya ran water over the plates, adding a drop of soap to each before running a washing rag over each.

Arie set the deep metal pot, with sloping sides and a lid into the oven, setting the temperature low with the oven set to automatically turn off in four hours. Lauranya rinsed off their plates and silverware, drying them before laying the plates back onto the countertop for tonight's dinner.

With the chores done, they went back to hanging the mirrors. The sixteenth broke on the way down the stairs. Lauranya stepped wrong; she felt her foot slide out from under her, as she stepped on the edge of the wooden riser, her grip slipping on the towel wrapped around the mirror. The mirror dipped, striking on the bottom edge of the wooden step. Lauranya fell on her butt, her left knee bent under her at an unusual angle, as she made a desperate grab to re-grip the mirror but not fast enough. The sound of a ringing crackle clearly heard through the main floor. The mirror rested next to Lauranya's right, with a jagged crack splitting the mirror in two. An ugly spider web crawling along the bottom start of the break.

Arie came from around the corner of the kitchen, unable to do more than watch the damage unfold before her.

"Mommy!" She started to run toward her mother.

"Stop!" Lauranya cried out, hearing her child's footsteps on the tile floor. "I do not know if there are glass shards, so I need you to get the broom but not come closer." She said through clenched teeth, trying for a calmer tone. The adrenaline starting to wear off and the pain from the knee building to a crescendo.

Arie nodded, spinning to run back to the kitchen. Lauranya let out a soft sob as she rested the broken mirror against the banister. She then leaned back, pulling her thigh up to release the lower leg. Her leg straightened. Lauranya bit back a scream. She saw stars shooting across her vision.

"Can we save the mirror?" Arie yelled, rounding the corner again, this time with broom and dustpan in hand. She skittered to a stop seeing her mother's face twisted in pain, her mouth open in a silent scream.

"Mommy?" Arie put a foot hesitantly on the wooden staircase.

"Ye…Yes?" Lauranya had to push the words out, the pain receding slower than she could wish for.

"You're not okay. What can I do?" Arie leaned the broom against the staircase, coming to the foot once more.

"Sweep each step before walking up, and then take the largest pieces down to the main floor."

"I can do that!" Arie made sure to sweep each step, cleaning up every glittering piece before it could lodge in their feet or a greedy chicken could peck at a lethal shard. Once the pieces were cleaned into the dustpan, Arie took the shards to the trash bin slowly and carefully. With the pan cleaned, she ran back to her mother, who had not moved from her supine position on the stairs.

Arie studied the problem for just a second before

running upstairs for another towel and some tape. This towel she positioned under the mirror. She picked up the largest piece using the towel her mother had originally wrapped around it. Arie carefully used a corner to wipe down the cracked portion. Small slivers fell onto the extra towel underneath. She taped up the edges, preventing any more pieces from flaking off and protecting the edges, Arie then removed the mirror to their work station with the ladder and woven leather before going back for the next piece.

Arie took the towel with the shards, upstairs, going to the balcony area and dumping the glittering shards over the edge. The glass looked like diamonds falling into the water. The prismatic pieces didn't rest long on the water surface. Small fish bubbled up around the debris, conditioned to the daily food offerings that the chickens and rabbits wouldn't or couldn't eat.

Arie bounced back inside, closing the door with a slam, as she ran to her mother's side. She found Lauranya grabbing the railing, standing, both hands on the banister with a white knuckle grip.

"Mom! Your knee. You shouldn't be putting any weight on it." Arie looked on in horror as her mother did exactly the opposite of what she had trained Arie to do.

"Aye. If it were a break or a tear, you would be absolutely right." Lauranya said, with a pained smile. "I seemed to have just popped my knee cap, not dislocated." She took one step slowly, shifting her weight from her good leg to the injured. The knee didn't buckle but the pain radiating spiked enough to cause a gasp. "However I think I need to sit for a little bit." Lauranya amended with a grimace.

Arie came to her mother's side, sliding an arm underneath to help steady her as Lauranya limped down the stairs. Lauranya sat on the third from the bottom step, letting the injured leg rest in a mostly straight position.

"I'll grab the anti-flammation." Arie ran back up the stairs to the medical room. Lauranya could hear her bustling through the cabinets.

"The knee was dislocated." Jacks said, appearing next to Lauranya, his ghostly hands touching the slowly swelling skin. He looked up frowning in worry, curly hair wispy white and fading at the end into nothing.

"Yes. And now it is back in place without too much swelling." She touched the puffing tissue. Warm but only a degree or two above normal.

"The viruses in your body are definitely helping you." Jacks said critically, looking over the injury and the unusually fast healing.

"Glad those scars were worth something," Lauranya said, with a ghost of a smile to her old friend.

"You should take a sample and see how the viruses are working to heal you."

"There is no way I am making it up those steps, and I am not going to have Arie do this." Lauranya pressed her lips together. "I am not going to tell her until I absolutely have to." She growled softly through gritted teeth. "I will put blood on slides next week."

Lauranya won the fight with Jacks, only by the fact that he faded just as they heard Arie's footsteps on the inner balcony coming towards the steps.

"Stubborn woman," Lauranya heard Jacks whisper in her ear. The ghostly brush of air on her ear caused her to give a soft if pained, chuckle.

Chapter 12

Actaeon sat up with a groan. The bed was warm. His body slave warmer. The young man snuggled closer as the warm spot next to him moved.

"Come back to bed." Carmin murmured, reaching a hand out for the graying gladiator and tracing a thin scar on the man's back.

"Can't, Godlings are training today." The man's mouth turned down in sour smile, his thinning hair bed-tousled.

"Your lips look better when they're kissing me, not frowning." the younger man said playfully, with a beautiful smile.

Actaeon leaned over, kissing Carmin slowly. "Have a hot tub and oil ready for me when I return. This day's going to fuck snakes," he said with a sigh, leveraging himself up. He motioned for his two other household slaves to approach.

The two female slaves, gifts from his younger brother Menodisces, were older with shaved heads and no tongues. One had his breakfast grain in a carved highly polished wooden bowl. The other was ready with a damp towel and folded clothes. Both wore synthetic rough spun tunic and pants — plain, frayed, hand-me-downs from others.

The master trainer ate without relish, handing back the bowl before wiping face, hands, pits, and crotch with the towel. The slave with the clothes held out two tunics, both of dyed silk. One was blue, and the other white but both were plain. Actaeon had no use for adornments other than his armor. He chose the blue one, before sliding into his armor of boiled leather. With the women's helped, all the silk laces were cinched tight, fitting him like a worn leather glove. Each piece from the chest, shoulder, and leg articulated for movement. The women kept it well-oiled and cleaned after every wear. He could have worn the articulated steel battle armor, but this was only training, not an actual ship battle. He tied his leather sandals on without help. The women never got the sandals tied just right, no matter how many times he cuffed them. Everything else they did acceptably well, but never the shoes.

"Another day of snot nose godlings. How can this day not get better?" He said, pulling back a sneering lip, giving himself a once-over in the polished steel mirror. Carmin slid out of the silk covered bed, walking with a sway to his hips to the weapons stand. Carmin picked out a whip made of leather wrapped around a steel core, with only his fingertips. Kneeling, he lifted the whip to his master with a bowed head. With a nod, Actaeon accepted the whip and strode out of his suite of rooms.

"Listen up!" Actaeon's voice reached the 15 trainees and the soldiers behind them. "You will each command a unit of 40. There are several ways to win today's scenario. Capture the enemy's aquila." He pointed to the sidelines where crudely drown battered banners hung from metal poles. "You can unite all teams to fight for you or you may kill all teams to be the last one standing. Last, but not least, you can make it to the other side of the city to be the first one through...." Murmurs met this announcement. A win wasn't usually outlined so. "Marking on your map all 30 control points. There is a metal stamp at each one that is different from each other. You must use the stamps to mark on your map to win." Here he paused giving a piercing look to the young godlings. "And the enemy is each other. You may team up, as you choose, but only one commander will be earning top ranking today." There were looks to either side. Some nervous, some gleeful, none surprised.

"If you lose 40% of your men, you may withdraw your team from this unless you are challenged. If a challenge is issued, each Commander must face off without the help of their 40. Understood?"

"Yes, Hastiliarius!" They'd all done these before, one version or the other, but never all three at once. Today was going to be interesting.

"If you feel you would do better commanding undead and listed as Necromancer instead of Commander, step up now."

Three stepped forward. Actaeon looked over the three. Felix, Moss and Hadriana. Nothing surprising that they would take Necromancer instead of Commander. "Step to the side. I'll assign you to a Commander in a moment." Before any of them could say anything, he continued. "No, this is war. You don't get to pick who you work with. You work with who you're assigned to, and you will do your job. They fail, you fail. Understood?"

"Yes, Hastiliarius!" The three chorused together. They moved to the side where a pile of 40 bodies had been randomly stacked, without regard to sex, size or age. The necros faced off in a three way silent battle, each vying for the best preserved corpse and the most. Only the strong survived on the ships. The bodies moved, sorting themselves out, and arranging themselves next to the necro who had summoned them. Hadriana pulled 19. 4 gladiators with the remaining best preserved of the men and women.

Leaving the other two to fight over the remaining bodies. Moss took 13, asserting his strength, leaving Felix to control the last 8, the corpses of children and the broken tottering old.

The other 12 commanders arranged themselves, waiting for Hastiliarius Actaeon to assign them their 40 soldiers. Their personal slaves bringing armor to put on over simple tunics and stools to sit while waiting. The slaves chatted quietly more amongst themselves then the godlings did with each other. This was training and training was always serious.

"Daccu, Cnaeu, Jacintha, Sorria. You four pick your first 40. From there I'll assign you your sub commanders and their 40. Again, this is war. You will work with whoever I assign you." Daccu went first. Cnaeu second. Jacintha then Sorria. They each choose their 40 based on the stats each group had shown in prior training. No one group was strong in just one thing.

None of the weapons were edged though, except their personal daggers which were always kept flesh-cutting sharp. Killing would take real close up work or sheer brute force with blunted weapons.

Once the first four had their 40, Actaeon pinned them all with a look. "Caelia and Senca with Daccu, Felix and Aelia with Cnaeu, Moss you're with Jacintha. The rest of you are on your own."

Cnaeu stepped forward, earning a narrow eyed glare from Actaeon. "Sir, aren't you giving Daccu, Jacintha, Sorria and myself an edge over the others?"

"What do you think war is?" Actaeon snapped out, tapping fingers against his whip. "Do you think the enemy is going to let you have the same numbers? The same weapons? The same ships as themselves? Do you think every alliance ends in beer, sex and dancing? You take the best and worst, overcome, conquer and survive. If you can't do that…" He smiled evilly, "Tell me now and I'll save my brother the trouble of testing you. I'll slit your throat and let one of the necro's play with you until they're bored." He unrolled his whip, letting it hiss along the metal floor. "Any further questions?"

Cnaeu bowed his head, kneeling to the ground. "No sir! Thank you for the education!" His deep voice loud in the hush.

"Get back in line." Actaeon snapped. Cnaeu turned, not hurrying to the line, his shoulders high but tight. Actaeon snapped the whip against the young warrior's thigh, where the armor didn't cover. The tip just cut a two inch line into the boy's dark skin. Cnaeu hissed but didn't stop until back in his original spot. Actaeon rolled the whip back up. The lesson delivered.

The training ground covered three square miles of interior ship space. The metal halls and open areas were populated with random furniture, mock dining and multi-tiered civilian areas. Hallways dead ended into walls or small six way connections with no cover provided. There were several bay hangers with decommissioned troop ships. The ships were derelict hulks, showing years of wear with dark blast scars, not yet assigned to reclamation. Good for cover, but not much else.

"Four doors. Every team will go through a door at random times. This lasts until there is one team leader left." Actaeon raised his hand, four doors as promised opened behind the twelve teams. "Daccu, Sorria, Nicon and Quique. Go now!" The four leaders, with their teams behind them, sprinted for separate doors.

Actaeon sent in another four groups after a five minute wait. From one door came yelling with screamed commands as an ambush took place at the entrance.

Actaeon tilted his head, lips turned down he nodded. "Early for such treachery, but not unexpected." He said.

Three more rounds went through when Actaeon signaled. The Hastiliarius sent Aelia, Cnaeu second in command in without Cnaeu support. She gave a nod to Cnaeu as she and her 40 passed. Cnaeu knew Aelia would do all she could to win now that she stood as a Commander and not just support. She was a good second but second received little glory or praise.

Actaeon held Cnaeu until the very end. "In you go, sand piss," Actaeon said, sneering down his straight nose at the final trainee. With only one necro and no support, Cnaeu would come out on bottom of scoring unless he could pull off the impossible.

Cnaeu saluted with the correct amount of crispness and precision, before spinning on his heels and motioning to his 40 to follow. Both knew Cnaeu wasn't good enough to challenge the Hastiliarius. Yet…

Cnaeu took the far right door. The one Daccu had entered and set up at the entrance.

"We want to go through that door? Daccu will eat us alive!" Felix hissed at Cnaeu's elbow.

"Daccu has 11 other problems now. He can't defend this door without getting trapped himself. After the first attack, he had to move or be boxed in. No one's going to align with him; they know he breaks his word as fast as it's safe for him to backstab. This is the ONE door I know is safe at this point." Cnaeu motioned for his group to move into the corridor.

Felix opened and closed his mouth a couple of times. "He'll try and take my dead." He whined, a child wailing in the dark at the loss of his stuffed toy.

Cnaeu gave a slight roll of his eyes. "Daccu is a God in his mind. He's not nearly as strong as you. And both of us know you're as strong as Hadriana, possibly even better. Almost a threat to Menodisces."

"I am not!" Felix yelped, clenching fists and screwing his face up to glare at his current "commander".

"Pfft. I saw the bone pit when no one else was looking two weeks ago. You made almost fresh corpses from those piles."

"I...it wasn't me," Felix whispered, his voice thready with fear, as blood draining from his already pale face. His hands fumbled to touch the hilt of a small dagger on his woven cord belt. Not threatening, just comforting.

Cnaeu grabbed his shoulder, leaning close. "I won't tell Menodisces, but I need all you have. Your secret would get me killed if he knew what I know about you." He whispered. The dark skinned man's words reaching only Felix's ears.

"He'd lobotomize me and use me for breeding." He stammered. The fear didn't abate, tremors taking over Felix's body.

Cnaeu snorted. "We both know that's the easiest he'd be on a necro as powerful as himself and young. Not to mention not one of his "sons". I promise you, when we take a Runner ship, you will be my right hand necromancer. I need you, but I need all of you. I will give you my protection. Understand?"

It was the promise of protection that finally broke through the fear. Felix refocused his eyes on Cnaeu. "Safety? No more hiding?" He asked cautiously.

"Anything and anyone you want," Cnaeu said, tapping his chin with a thoughtful finger. "Within reason."

Felix leaned back, looking at the warrior as if for the first time. Cnaeu stood in his plastic and metal coat of mail, carrying the heavy battle metal training shield with a blunted metal sword, twice the thickness but none of the elegance of a true battle sword. Cnaeu wore the armor as if it were nothing more than a cloth tunic. The shield and sword carried as easily as if they were ⅛ inch rods not twice the heft of true battle shields or swords. Felix looked at the 40 around him. They knew Cnaeu. They had worked with him before. Felix realized that they would follow him without question; they trusted him to lead them into and out of any situation.

Felix nodded quickly, gulping air. Sometimes, reason and need were entangled lovers. "I just need the occasional body. Not every day or every week." A junkie looking for his next fix. "Just...fresh."

"That, I'm very sure can be arranged." Cnaeu smiled, unconsciously echoing his adoptive father. "Everything?" He stepped back, offering his right arm for Felix to take.

Felix looked at the arm then back to Cnaeu. Felix grabbed Cnaeu' arm with his hand, unable to span the muscled forearm. Cnaeu grasped Felix's thinner arm, squeezing firmly.

"Mutatis mutandis," Cnaeu said with a nod, sealing their deal. "We will get a ship of our own."

"Mutatis mutandis." Felix echoed, a slight flush returning to ghostly pale cheeks.

"Now tell me what to expect ahead from the dead," Cnaeu said, stepping back from Felix and the undead, into his living fighters. "What can you see?"

Felix let his eyes cross slightly searching for the non-living in the training situation. "Two undead ahead."

Cnaeu frowned. "We're not supposed to kill anyone on these."

Felix gave him a look.

"Yes, I know what Daccu is like. Doesn't mean he's stupid enough to just kill."

"His necro ability is stronger than he's told his dad,"

Felix said blandly. "He's got a score to settle with a few of us Godlings, and he's strong enough to dismiss the spirits after killing."

"Usable?"

"No. Brains were pierced by blades, scrambling the grey matter, but their eyes still work." Felix frowned, tilting his head as if listening. "No ghosts. They've been sent on."

"Godlings?" Cnaeu could hope that he would be facing fewer than the other eleven now.

"No. Of the 40. Both from Jacintha's though."

Cnaeu growled at his 'brother's' temerity. "I wonder if we can help Jacinth and hinder Daccu at the same time."

"If Daccu doesn't get rid of Jacintha, she'll be the one to get a mission not him. He'll never be a God, just a breeder until his dad can't tolerate his screw ups." Aelia said from the side corridor. "A dead trainee in a dangerous final testing, is the perfect place to hide a corpse."

Felix let out a scream, ducking behind 40 other warriors, all startled except Cnaeu.

"Good to see you," Cnaeu said, with a wide grin, walking over to give his second an arm clasp.

"About time that old man let you come in." Aelia returned his grin. The 80 other warriors letting out pent up breaths before beginning to chat quietly among themselves. Cnaeu's 40 taking ribbing from Aelia's at being so unwary.

"And I am very glad you're my second in command."

"Can't let that shit eater win, now can I? And we both know you're stronger than me." Aelia returned the clasp with her own smile.

"What are we looking at?" Cnaeu asked as they stepped apart.

"Daccu at his usual. Screaming and spacing everything

in his way. He's hunting Jacintha right now. Her 40 have been sacrificing everything to keep her alive."

"Felix said he could feel two of them around here."

Aelia nodded. "He's shredding ships and fighters to get to her. The spirits…" Aelia shuddered. "He's just dismissing them screaming into the void. Nothing is sacred." Murmurs around them at Daccu's lack of faith.

"Obatala won't like Daccu keeping souls from him."

"Then let's be like Esu and put star dust in Daccu's bed," Cnaeu said, slamming his sword against his shield. "Ehs-Rha!" Came the chant, as Cnaeu's band grew.

"Voiding nova!" Jacintha swore softly. Her voice carrying no further than the hearing of the warriors next to her.

"He's going to box us in here unless we can go up and over."

"He's got that blocked off with the undead from Sorria's and our 40."

"Hadriana…"

"She can't do anything." Jacintha cut her second off. "Daccu would know if she did and he would be in the right to cut her throat after throwing her to his 40."

"You could Challenge him."

Jacintha stopped, opened her mouth then closed it. "I could, but I would need a safe spot to Challenge from. He'll just cut me down if he finds us in the open."

"Have to embarrass him to follow the rules."

"I swear Esu put that metal burr brain in my life to make things difficult," Jacintha swore softly, curling her lip in distaste.

A rattling sigh interrupted anything Jacintha was going to say next. The fighter closest to him, put her fingers to his neck feeling for a pulse. "Attue's gone." The woman closed the dead man's eyes before wiping her cheek from a trail of "sweat" leaking from her eyes.

"Void!" Jacintha swore. She shook her head, grabbing the woman's hand. "I'm sorry, Vesta. I'll do what I can to save us." Jacintha said grimly. They all knew she wasn't in a position to do much in the maze. Maybe outside, they might have had a chance, but inside they were dead.

She looked at their current position. They could scale the walls to make the upper decks of "living quarters". Daccu didn't have any way to scale the walls.

"Metal brain!" Jacintha snarled at herself. If he was smart, and she knew he wasn't a lack wit sand pisser, he'd have stolen the gear and kept as many of the dead bodies as possible, with either himself or Hadriana commanding them. Meaning Daccu had all the scaling equipment he needed after picking off her 40. They needed to go somewhere he wasn't. She tasted bright hot copper, her anger flaring. She'd lose points but she and her remaining five would be alive to go at this again. If she wasn't demoted to just a sub-commander or worse a body slave.

Attue's body sat up, startling them all. Jacintha pulled her sword up for an overhand strike, ready to brain the zombie, pulling her downward motion when Attu spoke.

"Jacinth, hide in the ducts. I'll come for you, but you need to vanish so Daccu stops chasing you. Cnaeu."

The dead man's brown eyes, so fresh they hadn't dried, bore into her own. Jacinth didn't hesitate. "Safety for all of us. Not just me." She demanded, a trickle of sweat running between her shoulder blades. Fear. Daccu was bad enough to hide from, but Cnaeu would find her. He could strike a deal with Esu and come out ahead.

"For all of your people who remain alive. I promise my protection."

"Personam in personam," Jacintha said.

The dead man's chuckle was...disconcerting, but the words heaven sent. "Witnessed on this end as well. Personam in personam." Attu's head nodded then slumped down as Cnaeu's necro Felix let the body go.

"Grate's two feet ahead on the left."

"Where?"

"Behind the partitions and obstacle crap."

"Let's disappear people. Yemoja forgot mercy when she made Daccu, and that sand licker is hot on our tails." Jacintha said, her knees shaking in relief. Vesta took a moment to render Attu's body useless as a zombie before joining the others.

Vesta and Torro unscrewed the vent; while everyone else slid quietly out of their armor to wiggle through the narrow metal shafts. Their armor bundled up and pushed in front of them. Vesta was the last one through, being the most flexible, able to slide in then pull the grate behind before following. The gloom turning to darkness when the grate clicked close behind.

"It's black as voiding space in here."

"Use your hands to guide you."

"Like he can do anything with his hands."

"His wife prefers his tongue."

"So does her lover."

"I'm not following a slime trail left by that duster's tongue."

Attu's ghost, commanded by Felix provided a glimmer of light at the head of the slow moving line.

"Looks like we have our guide." Relief.

"Think he could fix Marrion's foot odor as well?"

"Come closer, I'll break your nose so you don't have to worry."

"Better than Torro's farting."

"Shut it. Don't think Daccu heard you, three rooms over." Jacintha hissed.

"Yes, Commander."

"Sorry, Commander."

Daccu wiped his fist clean. The luckless man had kept his feet, turning his head into the punch. He turned back to face Daccu, licking the blood trickling over his lips from a busted nose.

"I said I wanted her dead. Not chasing her through this sand pissing maze."

"Yes, Lord. We lost her by the living quarters. We found a dead body, but someone shoved a dagger through the eye socket."

Daccu drummed his fingers on his belt for a moment. "How many other commanders are there?"

The men and women didn't exchange glances but they shifted from foot to foot. "Cnaeu is still out. We've taken most of Jacintha's. We have all of Sorria's. The rest are sub-commanders who have either scattered through the maze or we've taken their fighters."

"I don't think any have a full force." Not one was willing to bring up Cnaeu. Daccu had a fast fist.

"Our own numbers?"

"We've absorbed all the fighters with an extra 5 dead." No one mentioned the other Godling Daccu had cut down before she could issue a challenge. Daccu didn't let rules get in the way of winning.

"I need to face Cnaeu then."

"We could just make a run for the final flag, and ignore him. We have over half of the aquilas; all we need to win is the final portal." Hadriana said. Daccu turned with a snarl to his necro. Three undead stepped forward to shield her — the other eighteen...twitched. Daccu glared at the undead. They didn't waiver.

"These are mine. Get your own dead to play with." Hadriana said, through gritted teeth.

"Kill me and you go down too, sweet sister."

"That's the only reason you're still alive." She hissed, with eyes colder than her mother's.

"Don't think I don't know how you benefit from this. One less necro to take father's attention away from you. And we all know Felix is..." Daccu laughed, thinking of Cnaeu's having to use Felix for help. "Touched in the head."

Hadriana gave him a half smile, that didn't reach her eyes. "So which option will you take?"

Daccu sucked on his lower lip. A leftover childhood habit. "We'll go to the end portal. No need to waste more time here." Or to face Cnaeu, who would challenge if they came face to face. A risk Daccu couldn't afford remained unsaid.

"Sister, if you would?" Daccu gave a sarcastically deferential bow to Hadriana. She swept past him with her head held high, her zombies marching in front of her double time. They out stripped the main body by yards. Hadriana motioned one of the uninjured 40 to her side. The older man came next to her, placing an arm out for her to grasp while guiding. Hadriana looked through her zombie's eyes to see which corridors were clear. Two always at her side with 19 views returning.

"Well?" Daccu said impatiently from behind the first line of his fighters.

"Only dead bodies," Hadriana said, tilting her head.

"Useful?"

"No. Can't get a "feel" for them. Brain damaged before they were left behind."

"Great. You're on point." He turned to his own. "Let's go people! We're leaving the maze now!"

The three sets of mixed 40 stood with groans. Those not injured, helping those with injuries to stand. They moved up through the corridors, passing a double handful of corpses lying in heaps. The fighters following Hadriana's zombies moved slowly, but steadily. The corridors were quiet. Nothing moved except Daccu's fighters. Their shield line, three across always even, in perfect formation. Four spearmen behind them, ready to thrust at anything or anyone attempting to break the forward shields. Sweat dripped in eyes, yet none dared to wipe the moisture away. Blink yes, even a quick shake, but nothing broke formation. Nothing.

Those in back kept shields up with their blunted swords at the ready. The injured followed behind, holding or leaning on spears for canes. No one paid attention to the corpses. Bodies were plentiful, expected even. Why watch for usual?

A woman with a cracked ankle fell behind. Sha'artru didn't call out for help. Daccu would have her throat cut if she lagged too far behind. So she limped as best as she could, gritting teeth to make the end of this space dusting exercise, where a medic would bandage the ankle, and she would be able to smoke something relaxing.

The sound of cloth whispering against metal made her turn, with a frown. Sha'artru was sure no one was behind her. She was right, except for an unseen zombie who was upright and moving fast. She opened her mouth to scream when a second zombie covered her mouth with a three finger hand, grabbing her shoulder with the other hand, and then pulling the hands in opposite directions. Her neck twisted with a crack. All three bodies dropping to the ground unnoticed.

Two fighters leaning on each other, like drunks on a three day bender, were yanked into a hallway by two more rotting corpses. Their falling bodies cushioned by the already dead made no sound. More and more of the stragglers fell to their undead assassins.

"How many more, Felix?" Cnaeu asked. From their vantage point in the "living quarters," they could hear Daccu's force moving through the area while still hidden.

"I've gotten all the easy ones. You're going to have to actually fight him or run, now." Felix's naturally pale complexion grew more so with each heartbeat until the pulse in his blue veins showed clearly under his increasingly translucent skin. His hands were shaking violently like a dancer's hip to a fast beat.

"What? You mean you can't take him out all on your own?"

"I've got 30 different zombies doing multiple tasks. Including keeping up with all the other commanders and sub commanders. Until you can do this too, stop touching my chin and let me concentrate!"

"The marks?"

Felix's eyes crossed as he touched the five zombies spread out to the roaming 2 man teams. "28 so far. The last two can't be found."

"Ok...tell Aelia we're ready for her to block all but one path."

Felix nodded, relaying this to sub-commander. "She says "Don't teach your grandmother to wear scarves and get your ass in position. Daccu's going to go beserk the more they block him.""

Cnaeu snorted. "Like that's news." He made a circling motion with his hand. His 40 moved back to the hallways. They knew where to go to next.

Hadriana stopped, tilting her head. Daccu was so close; he had to do a little jig to keep from bouncing into her dead bodyguard. "What the void is the problem?" he hissed. The silence and lack of attacks, making him jumpy.

"I'm "seeing" two destroyed hallways with a few dead scattered around," Hadriana said.

Daccu pulled out his tablet to look at the map. "Which hallways?" he demanded thrusting the device over to his sister.

Hadriana blinked to orient the dead views with her current position. "These." She said pointing at the two blocked areas about 120 feet ahead.

Daccu chewed a lower lip, studying what was left. "That leaves us one open path, going through the hold area and the transport equipment."

"Trap?" One man asked from behind him.

"Of course it's a nova blowing trap." He glared at his sub-commander. "Cnaeu thinks he can push me through the transport to pick us off with his javelins while he runs and hides from our swords." Daccu's fingers traced the two different blocked hallways to the exit.

"This one."

"That one's longer than the other one."

"Yep. If Cnaeu were going to set traps it would be along the shorter one. So we're taking the slightly longer one." There was a glint in Daccus' eyes as he barred his teeth at his sub-commander. "Hadriana, move a third of your zombies up. Septus get her some back up with 20 fighters. The rest of us will be around the corner. We'll move up on your all clear."

Septus nodded. "One dick driven belly thrust coming up." He turned to his fighters, picking out a mix of shields and javelins for the beginning thrust into unknown territory.

Daccu turned to the sub-commander who had asked if it were a trap. "Nicco, send 15 of your fighters through the short path. I want a convincing feint. Don't commit, just keep 'em busy."

Nicco paled slightly. "Absolutely." Was all he said, licking his upper lip free of dripping perspiration. A trap known was still a steel jawed voiding killer with too many walking in whom would never walk back out.

"We have undead here." A javelin carry scout said, looking around the corner. "The hallway is stacked about three feet high. Looks like debris from rooms and torn apart walls. Gotta slight ramp we'll have to climb over to get to the other side. Three feet tops but enough to hide twenty undead and living fighters if the living don't mind rotting corpses on top of them."

"How fresh are the dead?" Nicco whispered back.

"Looks to be from this morning's choosing. Old folks and kids." The fighter's voice held a slight hitch as she looked at the bodies of the crumpled dead kids, laid like rag dolls tossed aside. Their legs buckled under withered torsos. Heads and visible arms at odd angles. The cracked skin around their eyes with milky coverings seemed to follow their every move.

Nicco wiggled an eye tooth with his tongue. Felix had probably collected other undead during the fighting, leaving these bodies as useless to anyone. They'd probably see better bodies on the other side and maybe Felix. The closer they got to the necro, the nastier the undead would get if there weren't' too many living fighters. Fuck Daccu for not having an extra necro to work with.

"Hate going into this blind."

"Welcome to our hell." One fighter muttered behind him. Nicco whipped his head around to glare at the smartass, but all he saw were blank faces. He pressed his lips tightly together. "We go in three by three formation. Shields up front."

"We only have two shields."

"Then put them up front." Nicco gritted out through clenched teeth. "Ad aciem!"

Everyone quickly fell into position. Nicco may have been a rotating commander, but all fighters knew the basic formations, having been drilled since they could carry their first "spear and shields".

"Parati! Oppugnare!" Nicco yelled.

The first line charged the small hill. Every person 18 inches behind the person running in front.

"Nova, is he ever going to attack!" Jacintha swore softly. She and the other positioned reserves waited for the word from dead lips to attack. The waiting for Daccu to walk into Cnaeu's trap frayed everyone's nerves just a little.

"They'll come. Keep them on the rise." The crumbled dead woman groaned, dead tissue forcing air over dried larynx.

"Stop touching my chin, Cnaeu!" She hissed at the collapsed corpse next to her. To her 40, more of a mixed bag of leftovers, "Parati!" There was subtle shifting as each fighter readied themselves for the coming attack. They heard the clanking of metal and plastic armor approaching at quick time.

Jacintha's muscles tightened in anticipation. "Cresting now!" The dead woman called. Her dry scratchy voice just reaching Jacintha's ears.

"Attack! Impetus! Attack!" Jacintha called, standing from her crouched position five feet from the rise. Four in her front row clashed with a row of three. Two shields with a javelin between. More javelins behind. The noise of shield hitting shield and shield hitting flesh. Curses and cries of pain sounding loudly in the metal hallways.

"Drive them back to the main hallway. Repulsus!" Jacintha yelled, matching words with action as she slammed her shield into the man in front of her. He tried to counter with his javelin, only to be parried with one of her javelin fighters cutting the attackers down. Jacintha's shield slammed full force into his face and chest, forcing him into the ranks behind. Nicco's force fell back step by bloody swearing step.

"Cut! Cut! Cut!" Jacintha yelled.

The crumpled forgotten bodies on Nicco's side of the hallway, animated, pulling out small shivs or broken swords hidden underneath collapsed bodies. They attacked Nicco's diminishing force's feet and legs. Stabbing through plastic hobbed sandals, or cutting the back of calves, where armor didn't meet in back. The screaming took on a decidedly desperate, higher pitch as Nicco's fighters found themselves facing a frontal attack and a mobile rotting ground attack.

"Quarter! Stop!" Nicco bellowed into the din, fending off the corpses of two small children and living shield man with a wicked counter thrust. All three working in scary unison.

"Sheath your swords!" Jacintha called out, her voice cutting through the noise of battle. Most of the hallway stopped on her voice. One pair had to be broken up with shields thrust between the pair.

"You give?"

"Safety for us." Nicco panted, leaning over his shield

as he looked up to the godling. "Daccu will kill me, us," he pointed to his battered men and women, "because we didn't fight to the death."

"As much safety as I can, and Cnaeu's willing." Jacintha offered her arm.

Nicco didn't have to think for more than a second. "Better than I'd get from Daccu." Nicco took her hand up, clasping her forearm, sealing the deal.

Jacintha looked around, doing a quick count. "Where are the rest?"

"Running to the exit. Daccu leading from the front, just behind Hadriana's undead."

"Space me! This wasn't a real push." Jacintha swore. She ran to the old woman's corpse, pushing through her fighters. She shook the body, yelling. "Felix! Felix! It was a feint! Daccu isn't here!" The head flopped back and forth. Boneless, unseeing, unhearing.

"Voiding space humping father fucker!" She pulled the corpse up with her, pushing the dead woman to one of her javelin carriers. "Take that. Everyone else, we're leaving now! Move it!"

There was a scramble to adjust loosened armor and swig from bottles of water before falling into formation, plastic sandals slapping on blood slicked floor.

"Felix?" Cnaeu asked, crouching behind a derelict piece of transport in the "cargo" area. The hallway across from the randomly scattered equipment the only open path in. All of Cnaeu' fighters were hidden to maximize the element of surprise when Daccu came trotting in.

"Nothing. Same as the last time, three minutes ago!" The necro hissed back at his commanding officer. His thin hands clenching and unclenching like he was strangling something or someone.

Cnaeu's lips twitched. "Jacintha?"

Felix rolled his eyes slightly before reaching out to Jacintha's undead. "Nova!" His voice barely a whisper. "Daccu took the middle path. The push to Jacintha was a feint. He's running to the exit now."

"He's going to bend us all over the grading if he gets there first!" Cnaeu stood up, yelling for his fighters. "Let's catch us a commander! Aelia, gather yours up. We're running for the exit now!"

His fighters headed to the door in a running formation falling in. Nothing so crass as a riot, more controlled chaos. Cnaeu led from the front. Felix in the middle of the formation, holding onto the arm of an assigned fighter, as he kept up with those around him, gathering the usable dead as he was towed to the fight.

A roar went up, from the throat of Daccu's 70, as the exit came into view. They saw the Hastiliarius Actaeon watching from a balcony two stories above the open room. Medical with their assisting slaves, with stretchers at the ready, waiting to help once a winner declared.

Daccu puffed out his chest, smiling. "Parade formation! Salute the Hastiliarius as we go bye!" He bellowed to those who followed. Minimal shuffling as lines were dressed, swords banging against shields and javelins raised. All eyes left on the Godling trainer. He never saw the Cnaeu.

Cnaeu hit the line from the right, bowling through Daccu's center. Those carrying shields, punching those in front of them in the sides. Blunted swords hitting forearms, helms and armored backs with pent up fury of the driven.

"Turn them!" Cnaeu yelled. "Roll them in!" His

fighters trying to surround and roll Daccu's own back on themselves, cutting down their mobility and fighting capacity by trapping part of their forces on the inner ring.

"Form up! Form up," Daccu screamed, trying to keep his own together. "Hadriana!"

"I'm on it!" She snapped, pulling her undead from the front, throwing them into the melee. This would give Daccu's a better fighting chance. Daccu couldn't fight and control undead at the same time.

Felix stood back pulling Hadriana's undead from the edges. Dropping one who was about to make a stabbing back thrust to Aelia. Taking another who was thwarting a wedge between Daccu and Hadriana. Nothing showy or large. He could stand there and fighter her for control of all twenty she had, but that would paint a bullseye on his back with her. He whittled her down to 10 in the space of 20 heartbeats.

Cnaeu parried an incoming blow to the side, shield punching Septus in the face. Aelia used the haft of her sword to punch him in the temp of his helmet hard enough the sub commander stumbled, falling to his knees. The press of fighters pushing him to the floor. He had to turtle under his shield for protection from the stomping hobnailed sandals.

Daccu's fighters managed to form up and form a wall. The back of their formation only slightly occupied with the twenty of Cnaeu behind them.

"Hold the line!" Daccu screamed, red faced under his helmet. He turned, grabbing Hadriana by the arm.

"What the first space are you doing?" She yelled as he dragged her away from the fight.

"Getting the win!" He snarled through gritted teeth. "Just have to make the exit! Keep your undead on Cnaeu!"

"I need…" She tried yanking her arm away.

"To keep your feet under you. I can't win unless my pet necro comes with me!" Daccu pulled harder, causing Hadriana's feet to skitter from underneath her.

"Fall on me sister dear and I will beat you unconscious and pull you by your hair over this line!" Daccu snarled, yanking Hadriana up hard against him. His face contorting in rage. "And when daddy dear gives me my ship, you'll be my first sacrifice to whichever general pleases me the most."

Hadriana gained her feet, stumbling along behind Daccu. She looked over her shoulder catching sight of a tall, dark skinned female fighter looking towards them. She gave a slight smile. Jacintha had made it. Daccu hadn't killed her.

Cnaeu didn't know of Daccu's escape through the meleeing living and dead until an air horn blaring from the second tier balcony sounded. Actaeon sounded the horn as Daccu with Hadriana in tow, crossed the exit line winning the contest. All fighting stopping, with fighters pulling blows, helping their one time "foe" to their feet. Everyone looking upwards to see who won.

Actaeon motioned towards the exit, pointing to a grinning Daccu. "The prime winner is Daccu with the winning score. Everyone now may fall out. Judgment tomorrow."

Cnaeu barred his teeth in frustration, glaring at his brother. Aelia bumped his shoulder. "Stop feeding his ego. Esu will have his say yet."

"Survival of the fittest eh?"

"And those who can blend in." She gave him a saucy wink before helping her own up and calling for a healer.

"Here's to a surviving score." Cnaeu let out a heavy sigh. He reached down to help Septus from the metal floor. Septus accepted the hand with a nod of thanks.

Chapter 13

"General, a freighter is incoming."

Mesan took a sip of his hot tea, setting his mug down carefully in the wide base holder, nails clicking against the thick insulated metal. "Which ship is it from?" An almost sigh.

"That's just it. It's not one of ours," Torri said, looking back at his communication boards. "And they're hailing on all frequencies."

The Wolfen put down his mug of strong, dark green tea, looking at the screen. "Spacing snakes. You'd think they'd know we were Runners or something." He tapped highly polished black nails on his metal armrest. An odd staccato click sounding for a couple of seconds.

"Send a squad to take the ship. Make sure they check for Gods and Overseers after they check for explosives." He ran an upper hand through a thick but short spiky mane. "Put Sunshine and Leaf on this." Mesan nodded. "Yes, those two. Their squad can take a few punches." He gave a slight roll of his shoulder, thinking about that motley crew.

"Aye!" Torri turned back to his screen, punching keys with the efficiency of long practice.

The call down to the Marines was met with enthusiasm. Things had been boring since Redeyes had resurrected on another ship.

"Hey Sunshine, when are we moving out?" A large

scarred and scruffy Katherian whined while cleaning her disc gun for the third time today. She wasn't looking at her superior officer, concentrating on smoothing out a microscopic metal burr on the inside of her barrel. Complaining for something to do, more than actually voicing dissatisfaction.

"Do I look like a Gods voiding timepiece to you? How the screaming stars do I know when we're getting our happy butts out the airlock?" The human sergeant, Sunshine, snapped. His voice a slight raspy tenor coming out of a barrel chest, always throwing those first meeting him for a spin expecting a baritone instead. "Lucky for you, what I do have is our orders."

Leaf swiveled her ears at him, her pupils narrowing to thin lines as she gave him her full attention. The other Marines stopped playing tiles and throwing knives.

Sunshine threw a hand over his heart with a look upwards at the squad ship's ceiling. "The powers that be, and our General," He pinned every being in the room with pale grey eyes, "said as soon as you get your Gods soft butts in those seats we are out and taking a ship for our own." He turned to Leaf. "That good enough for you?"

"So good, I'm almost ready to take a smoke break."

"Glad that you got your fur slicked down. Now let's get moving!"

"Any time you are, Sunshine." Leaf replied, showing teeth from a greying muzzle, putting her gun back together with rapidity.

"Glad I can make your day, sweetheart." Sunshine pulled back lips from flat teeth, more in humor than domination. Leaf was damn good, trusted to cover a retreat or his back. And Sunshine relied on that trait more than following the rules.

"You're my one and only." Leaf gave the stump of her

tail a slight wag. Her gold eyes glowed eerily in the barrack's light, her whiskers arching as she gave a curling lip smile. She was ready for this hunt!

The Marines were used to the ball busting between their Sergeant and his second in command Leaf. The Katherian, Leaf, had been disciplined for more drunken bar brawls than the top ten other brawlers. She'd been disciplined so much that she was never going to be more than a private, ever; however she and Sunshine made a team that not even the General could explain. They always returned with most of their crew.

Several times they'd run with Redeyes and twice their ship had been classified as lost in space. Beyond expectations and betting percentages, Sunshine and Leaf had brought the ship back with vital intel or supplies. Their squad of marines trusted these two to bring them back safely every time.

"What are the rest of you father fuckers waiting for? Engraved invitations from Zoooooorax and his toy Tilu to get your asses in the place?" Leaf raised her voice, to echo through the metal-walled room.

The remaining marines standing, grabbed their armor with an accelerated fervor.

Leaf gave a final look over. "Good!" She gave a growling almost yowl. Her fingers reaching for her holster. She liked big guns, and her fingers were itchy.

"Get your armor on, and then you can shoot something," Sunshine said, with a look at the private. Leaf gave an annoyed growl and a thump with her tail stub but did as she was told, grabbing her armor bag, sorting out needed pieces from extra bits. The large room echoed with the sounds of thumps as plastic, and metal armor hit floor or fists hitting armor, confirming a good fit. Twenty minutes and the marines were pounding their way down to their ship, rubber-soled boots and clicking nails from barefooted Wolfen and Katherian, striding over metal floor plates.

"Phen, get us up and going!" Sunshine yelled up to the cockpit, strapping in. The others quickly followed, not waiting for any orders. No one stood even with more standing room and all the holding straps in good conditions.

"Space, yeah! Going for the stars!" Came the barking yell as the seven-foot Wolfen folded himself into his cockpit chair, origami of flesh into a breath-stealing space. His lower arms locked in the strapping while his upper arms danced on the boards.

"Yes!" Phen rumbled, as everything showed green and gold. He moved the steering bar forward smoothly, maneuvering out the open bay door with predatory speed. Phen knew how to fly like he had been born with accelerator boosters instead of legs. When Phen was flying, he took care of the ship more than he took care of the marines. The ship got everyone home, sometimes bruised and broken, avoiding incoming plasma shot, but the ship would make it home.

The freighter saw the squad ship incoming and instead of trying to flee, angled to meet them. The deadhead pilot anticipating Phen's path and adjusting the undead ship's own to match his. The frigate turned off all propulsion once aligned, waiting for boarding.

"Too spacing easy." Leaf muttered her ears flat, her fur spiking.

Sunshine nodded. "Like a little fight, but if they are coming over to blow us up, they got the sorriest crew bending over." In a louder voice carrying through "Okay you ass rabbits, get your gear on. We're going in to kick Dead God! Let's move!"

A flurry of activity as the marines gathered guns, swords and knives. The Runner ship latched onto the frigate with a grinding clunk. The seal cut into the Undead ships' ceiling in under thirty seconds.

Leaf, dropped down, landing on soft feet, crouching with her sword raised to block, ready thrust. More marines followed, dropping in behind her, yelling and screaming. Nothing. No resistance or fighters met them. Silence from the occupants.

Leaf stood up on the balls of her toes, with slit eyes, shaking with the need to kill. The ship was populated by skeletons. Every last deadhead was flat on the floor, hands over their heads. Not one made a sound. Each person, from adult to child was skin over bones thin, stomachs swollen. They were alive, but just barely. There wasn't hope, nor curiosity in any of the eyes Leaf happened to catch.

"Nova!" Leaf sneezed, wrinkling her nose. Sunshine and Leaf moved forward, walking through the shuttle to the cockpit. It was like walking through a yeasty shit pit. The smells coming close to overwhelming her. The people only shivered a little when her foot brushed against them. Not a whimper, not a scream, no pleading for their lives as monsters walked among them.

Leaf turned to look over her shoulder at Sunshine. His face as blank as she had ever seen it. She 'pathed him.

"This isn't what I expected. Think it's a decoy with more in the hold?"

"Sending Fuma and Iggy."

"I thought…"

"Why I sent Iggy. Bastard won't let anything be tail discounted if it'll mean less for him, but Fuma finds every voided thing there is."

"She's got a talent."

"That talent is going to cost her another ear or finger if

she doesn't stop being so oxygen needy, taking from the rest of us."

Leaf snorted, making her way slowly towards the cockpit. The walk was not to intimidate but to keep a wary eye open for the hidden. An Overseer, a few guns, warriors or possibly just a plasma grenade, the usual.

The cockpit door opened three steps up. Leaf found only one being at the control bar. A dark-skinned woman with short almost shaved dark curly hair. She was on her knees, hands on her head with slumped shoulders. Her jumpsuit baggy over a stick thin body.

"You the pilot?" Leaf growled, hulking towards the dark-skinned woman to look her in space shattered iris.

"Yes." The voice was a whisper, dusty from lack of use.

"How many on the shuttle?"

"149 today."

"When you started, how many?"

"262."

Leaf swallowed hard. Those were hard numbers if true, and nothing seemed less true than this. "Right...up and into the main area with your friends." She helped the woman up with almost gentle hands. Her claws firmly sheathed.

"Sunshine." Leaf lead the pilot over to the side. There was room close to the other marines.

"Watcha got there? Anything good?" Sunshine growled, turning away from his marines, jerking his chin up and out aggressively stepping into the human's personal space. He stood so close he could see the loose wrinkles on the side of the pilot's face from starvation.

The dark-skinned woman looked at him with tired blank eyes, swaying where she stood. Leaf's arm around the woman's waist the only thing keeping her upright.

"Pilot."

Sunshine looked at the woman, making a snap judgment. Whatever it had taken to get them here, he wasn't going to be scarier than where they'd come from.

"Pilot, right. Captain or Gods?"

"Captain is on the floor. No Gods or Overseers." The woman croaked out. "We ran from a doomed colony to escape."

"Looks like you got the escape."

"Closer to our Gods and dead than the Undead Gods at least." She said, with a slight lift of her lips. Sunshine's lips lifted up in response before he could stop. He reverted back to his scowl.

"They need medical and food." Leaf 'pathed to Sunshine.

"They need a lot of things, and only a few of those are we going to be able to provide." He said out loud. "Medical! Get your slow butts down here and see what we can do to keep these people from dying on us!"

The pilot looked him in the eyes, reaching slowly with her hand. "Water, soup. Please. Master." The last a plea would have broken even Redeyes' heart(s).

"Right. Anyone strapped with bombs or other nasty surprises? 'Cause if I lose someone, it's coming out of every fucking hide that's not one of my own."

The pilot gave a huff of laughter, dusty from long disused muscles. "Nothing. What you see is what you get." She leaned hard against Leaf, before sinking to the floor, her legs folding under like brittle metal structures, giving way slowly an inch at a time.

Leaf and Sunshine looked over the human's head. "Betting this one has a few whip marks," Sunshine said.

Leaf snorted. "A few? Bet they had a post just for her."

The marines were watching the two of them and the prisoners with twitches and frowns, unsure what to do with a non-fighting deadhead crew.

"Anyone not standing guard get water bulbs and start handing them out. I want these people hydrated enough to talk to me like last hour!" Leaf bellowed towards the throng of Marines.

The marines jumped to, handing out water bulbs after rolling each person over carefully. Three adults had died while being boarded. Those still alive enough accepting with shaking hands bulbs of clean water. They sucked the water slowly; none of them had energy to spare for more than a nod of thanks.

Bralli jumped down into the ship with his medic kit in hand. He took one look at what the crew of the ship looked like, before turning back to the hold.

"Where ya going, Bralli?" Sunshine asked, frowning at the medic's back.

"You don't need me. They're almost dead. Space 'em and call it a nova day." Bralli said with a shrug, jerking his chin towards the ceiling, calling upwards. "Lower the ladder."

Sunshine put a heavy hand on the dark-skinned man's arm. "We have people here who are dying. They need your tender treatment."

"They're deadheads and can spacing die for all I care." Bralli snapped, grabbing the thrown chain link and bar ladder that clattered down. He put his right leg on the lowest rung, ready to climb up.

Sunshine yanked the medic off the ladder, spinning him around. "I don't think so, darlin'! These here are our new recruits." Making a wide gesture with the hand holding a disc gun. "These fine people need you. And you will treat them." Sunshine bellowed in Bralli's face, pulling the medic down the foot in height difference to stare him in the eyes. "You will treat them, and none of them better die in your care this time, unlike those poor vap heads on Kassi's ship."

Bralli tried yanking his arm out of Sunshine's steel grip. Sunshine kept ratcheting down harder the more the medic struggled. Sunshine didn't budge. Bralli tried to pull his arm out of Sunshine's grip before conceding he wasn't going anywhere and until he stood still the bruising was just going to get worse as Sunshine's grip got tighter.

"You are a…" Bralli hissed, spittle spraying Sunshine in the face.

"Your commanding officer. And your last chance of redemption before being sent to the pits." Sunshine smiled widely, showing all of his teeth. "So I suggest you get to medicing without killing anyone."

"For once," Leaf muttered, behind him. Bralli glared over Sunshine's shoulder, craning his neck upwards as he still hadn't been released.

"Fine." Bralli ground out, through gritted teeth, his cheek muscles bulging.

Sunshine released Bralli's arm, keeping his smile. "See, that was easy enough." Slapping the medic with an open hand on the chest a couple of times, ignoring how each slap sent Bralli backward.

Bralli coughed, nodding his consent but glaring safely at the floor.

"Good boy. Now get to work!" Sunshine spun the medic around, pushing him towards those on the floor.

"That one's going to poison your food one day." Leaf 'pathed, watching Bralli turn the nearest deadhead over with rough hands, snapping at the closest medic for sweet water not plain.

Sunshine ran his arm over his face, wiping off the spit. "You'll make sure to rip off his balls then eh?"

"Does Redeyes die more than a ship of deadheads?"

Chapter 14

Arie fussed over Lauranya for the next day. Lauranya was able to make it to the second floor with Arie's help, but not to the bedroom. Lauranya decided on the way up the stairs, as her knee threatened to buckle with every other step that she would rather watch concerts if she had to be bed bound. Equally distant, but one was less likely to cause her to go stir crazy. So Arie helped her mother limp into their movie room before Lauranya collapsed on the couch. Arie fetched pain medication and ice packs as needed.

Arie was only too happy to bring her lessons in, watching arias while working on her elemental table and chemical combinations. When Lauranya wasn't sleeping from pain meds, they sang along with the opera singers. Sometimes they would improvise the songs.

That evening after a dinner of chicken stew, Arie asked a question that made Lauranya stop mid-bite.

"Mom, could we eat outside and sing under the stars?" Arie asked, sitting cross-legged on one of the large floor pillows. Arie's hands were busy working her mid-chest length hair into various types of braids and twists. "Not tonight of course but some night when it's not raining."

Lauranya had to consider. The rain had lessened, but not stopped. The water was still rising and over ten stories. Neither of them had seen any more large predatory fish, not that any of the big fish could actually get up to the rooftop or inside their rooms. Outside. So rarely had she gone outside even before the flooding. Always she worked in the lab or went home to the apartments. Field work was done by the slaves, sometimes she went but only when a specific item was needed for research.

"I do not see why this would be a problem," Lauranya said hesitantly. The outside was so...wide. She had to hide her slight shudder at this idea from her child.

"Great! I'll get everything ready for dinner on the roof tomorrow. I'll help carry you up and set up everything too!" Arie bubbled. "Will you sing and play the floor harp?"

Lauranya smiled fuzzily through the morphine haze. "I would be happy to sing; however you might want to keep an eye on the weather first before making plans."

"Oh! That's right. I'll wait and see what happens!"

The morning came with rain. A furious lashing of water, drumming against windows. The skies wept as if there had never been a cessation of rain prior. Lauranya raised herself on her elbows at the first sound of thunder, dim through the insulated walls. She was still on the leather couch of the entertainment room; Arie had fallen asleep on a nest of brightly colored floor cushions, limp and relaxed as only a child could be in sleep.

Lauranya stared outside, watching waves through the floor to ceiling windows. She flexed her knee, wincing with the anticipation of pain, but there was only a slight twinge, feeling more as if from hitting a wall than a dislocation. She looked down to the damaged knee but saw only a fist-sized bruise with fading colors of blue/green/yellow — not even the color of a fresh bruise.

Lauranya took a deep breath, sitting up and putting

both feet on the floor, testing. Again an ache, not screaming pain. Lauranya stood slowly, one hand on the couch armrest ready to take the weight off the knee at any moment. She took a cautious step. The knee flexed and held.

"The knee healed overnight. That's a six-month injury to recover from. Possibly even requiring surgery if you were on a world-ship." Jacks whispered in her ear before fading away. Lauranya rolled her eyes but smiled at their ghostly family physician.

Lauranya moved quietly to not wake Arie, each step slow and deliberate to the window. Standing at the window, she could look down for a frame of reference. The waves were two stories high, and the water had raised another story since she had last measured less than five days ago. Lauranya chewed a lip with worry. The water had slowed in rising but not stopped. They were safe for the moment. "Another day's drumbeat. Olokun, please keep us safe from your deep waters." Lauranya whispered to herself.

Even at a whisper, Arie responded to her mother's voice. Arie stretched, making small noises as she woke slowly. She blinked sleepily, turning to where her mother had fallen asleep. "Mom!" Arie bounced out of her pillow nest.

"Here, dear child," Lauranya said with a smile, smoothing the worry from her brow at the sight of her beautiful child.

"There you are! You're supposed to be in bed! Not walking around on a hurt knee." Arie fused at her mother, pursing her lips in an exaggerated aggrieved look. One that Lauranya recognized as Tine's. The look was so put upon and so familiar on a different face that Lauranya jerked back for a moment startled. She shook her head, banishing that image of Tine, seeing only Arie with a pouty pursed lips and hands on her hips.

"The knee is fine. A little sore; however we have mirrors that need to be hung so we will have crops!" Lauranya said briskly, walking in an almost normal glide to her daughter's side, giving her a quick hug. "Let us get a quick bite before we have to get to the work before Okayo takes back his blessings on our crops." Arie's head was to Lauranya's shoulder.

Arie's eyes went wide as she sucked in a breath, "Oh! We can't have Okayo mad at us."

"Exactly. So fruit and leftover stew."

Arie's stomach rumbled at the mention of food, punctuating the need for the morning breaking of the sleep's fasting. Arie looked down with surprise, a flush of pink infused her cheeks as she looked sheepishly up at her mother.

"Food first!" Arie agreed, already dancing out of the room down to the kitchen. Lauranya followed at a more sedate pace, mostly assured that Arie wasn't going to inhale everything edible in sight.

Chapter 15

The God was lounging on a low slung chair, contemplating reports on his screen when a tongue less slave bowed in Menodisces' Quartermaster, Refhar.

The position had entailed tracking supplies on the ship; however, it had evolved into including the God's own. Refhar had risen through the ranks with skill and only a little bribery before being noticed by Menodisces for his talent for keeping accurate accounts of things and people.

Refhar bowed deeply before his capricious but cruel God. He wore a cotton chiton that whispered against bare legs every time he stepped. The cerussite white of the material contrasted starkly against his blue-black skin. A gift from Menodisces after the last culling, the quality of servants picked had been superb. Refhar's hair was pulled into loose woven braids gathered at the crown, nape, and shoulders; he was unadorned other than a wide tooled leather belt at his waist. Should he want, Refhar could trade the belt for 3 of the best body slaves the ship had to offer. Menodisces rewarded good service well.

"Your children are ready for your judgment." His voice rumbled deeply as if pulled through metal air shafts sunk deep within the ship.

Menodisces waived for him to continue, sipping on a tea fragrant with honey and spice. Refhar bowed a little shallower this time, motioning for those waiting to file in.

Menodisces' wives were first, three of them lining the

left-hand side of the metal grey walled chamber. Leather sandaled feet slapped metal flooring with a soft staccato, almost dance-like. Their long peplos and stolas in various prismatic hues, sounding like blown air through the garden vines. The silk gifted to them, from their husband Menodisces or petitioners who wanted a moment to bend the Undead God's ear. Gems gleamed from pins stuck into complex braids, rings on fingers and toes, with hints of color flashing from studded trim on the hems of their garb. They were beautiful women, venomous snakes with dark kohl and gold powdered, rimmed eyes. They joined him on his couch and the heavily carved rainbow wood chairs provided.

The concubines entered next. These women were adorned in silks provided by their master or if favored by a wife, a former chiton of hers. The trim done in geometric designs, woven only from threads, gems weren't included for so trivial a decoration. The occasional flash of gifted jewelry could be seen on a finger, or a small pendant hung from a hairpin. These women were graceful in movement, slow arms, and swaying hips.

The concubines composed themselves with pleasant expressions to give no offense to Menodisces or his wives. They knew their place. If any offense were given, the concubine would be gifted to another noble or even sent to the pens as a common sex slave. Smiling brightly, they hid all feelings behind lying lips and bright eyes.

Their personal slaves brought pillows for them to kneel on. One was pregnant, to the point of bursting at any moment. She needed help lowering onto the pillow laid out for her. The help was given by her slaves, not her sister concubines. The concubines fed the weakest and the gullible to the wives. Only the strong and smart survived in this rarified atmosphere.

Lastly, the slaves, who had become pregnant by the God, entered. These women, as beautiful as the wives or concubines, dressed in gifted plain silks hemmed neatly, but unadorned. The God liked his women decorative. The slaves wore their hair loose or tied into knots at the back of their neck, emphasizing the carved rare wood collars, an inch high and a quarter-inch thick around their necks. These women knelt on bare floors, calloused knees, and bent toes the only flesh touching the cold metal. Two of the five slaves held infants, one newborn, and the other child under four months. These small children held close. All eyes cast to the floor.

The children came next. Their mother's ranking of no matter as they lined up by age. The youngest to the back as the oldest, 18 to 22, lined up facing their formidable father. There were over a hundred. The oldest of his children thinned down to fourteen, through training games and arbitration of the fittest.

"The youngest may join their mothers," Menodisces said with languorous hand waive to Refhar, as his other hand trailed down the back of his current favorite wife. She was a tall willowy dark-haired woman whose dark skin contrasted against his paleness, like dark space showing the beauty of passing suns.

Those under seven scattered, sitting next to their mothers or on laps if able. All the children released from judgment were held close. The only weakness any of them were willing to show. Children were treasures. Menodisces had killed one wife and a score of concubines early in his ownership of the world-ship. The women had thought harming another's child to advance their own was acceptable. They had misjudged their new lord and master. The lesson had been taken to heart by the survivors.

Refhar brought a tablet to Menodisces. Scores, both

physical and mental, tallied over the children's lives. Not all the children were Menodisces. A few he had adopted when talent or testing showed higher than average, in the top percentage. Some of the children were adopted as young as five, others as late as twelve. The exceptional ones Menodisces brought under his wing as his own; however blood or adopted, none of that matter when they were given their final scoring.

The second youngest line wer brought forward. There were twenty-nine from the ages of 10 to 17. They varied in height, but all were coltish, long legs with strong muscles even at so young an age. Menodisces placed a hand on his head of the lone ten-year-old. The child gave a shy smile, looking through long pale lashes.

"You are showing great promise already with dead things. I am placing you with Korlah and myself." The child's smile became wider. Menodisces motioned for the child to move to the side with Refhar.

The others stared at the ground, waiting. Menodisces touched three on their heads. "These will train for the next five years on the sands. Bring them forward for final training after the three years. I'll see where they stand." Refhar made note as these three were moved to the sidelines.

Menodisces looked at the remaining. "Keep these in general training and schooling." At one girl with honey brown hair over dark skin that was almost luminescent. "This one in dance as well."

"Yes, master." The children moved to a side wall opposite their mothers. They would only see their mothers on high feast days or religious processions. All other times would be devoted to their new training regimes.

The final line was 18 to22-year-olds. All of the young men and women followed their father with eyes, blank like their faces, showing no emotion. Today they would be young godlings or slaves.

"Ahh...my favorite children. Let's see how well you did in your five years of training." Menodisces smiled widely. Cold creeping shivers slithered up more than a few spines.

He touched the curling cap of one 18year old year old, the young man's dark skin as blue-black as Refhar's. "You are showing great promise with your training on the sands however scoring in mechanical and languages exceed those. You are going into sciences." Menodisces dismissed him with a touch.

The young man nodded, letting out a rush of air, heading to stand by the others.

Menodisces pulled two out of the line. Aelia and Septus. Both pale skinned with flaxen blond hair. Lean muscles showing where their short tunics didn't cover. "Neither of you excel on the Sands or in learning. You are not at the bottom, but your scores show indifference to either." They looked at each other with wide eyes and then snapped their heads front and center. "Aelia will be trained as a body slave. A gift for Fastus." Here he turned to Refhar. "Fastus is having a birthday celebration in 3 months. Have her prepped and ready for presentation by then. He doesn't like whip marks, so the bottom of the feet is the targeted training tool should she need." Aelia's head bent, silent tears sliding down her cheek. She didn't speak out to protest. Menodisces had pulled tongues for less.

"Septus will go to Iunia, for her work on the poisons. Same training; however whip marks are acceptable."

"Do you want their reproductive organs kept intact or have them removed?"

Menodisces tapped a gold painted nail to the tablet in front of him. "Neither of their mothers were extraordinary in necromancy or fighting. So their genetics is of no gain to us. "

"Fastus does need an heir." One of his wives offered from her spot on his divan. She was running fingers through her husband's newest acquisition's dark, loosely curling hair, trailing over pale skin. The young woman leaned into the petting.

"True." Mendoices gave a slight smile, enjoying the sight of his wife and her amusement. "We do want him to be favorable to us. Aelia will keep her ovaries. Septus will keep his balls and penis. I'll let Iunia decide on whether or not she wants a eunuch or not." He waved a dismissive hand to the two.

Both had tears streaking down their faces as they turned and stumbled to the wall where their year mates stood. The others moved away, avoiding touching either as if they were irradiated and leaking. Refhar's fingers danced over his tablet, making notations.

Three were left standing. Mendoices took his time reading through the scores. Again his fingers clicked on the tablet.

"Daccu, while your scores excel in maneuvers, your intellectual scores are only a little above average." Daccu's spine stiffened. Septus' punishment was not the worst he had seen his father mete out. "However you seem to have certain cunning." Menodisces looked up from the screen. "Did you know that Caelia blames you for her death? Her ghost was quite...angry. The small burst I saw before her ghost was...dismissed. A full poltergeist emerging." Menodisces nodded thoughtfully. "Though there is no evidence that you killed her."

Tapping a finger on the edge of the screen, Menodisces regarded Daccu as one would an amusing pet. "Did you really kill her over her breaking your favorite body slave or because she was out scoring you on testing?"

Daccu tilted his head in acknowledgment at the death of his full blooded younger sister. "My sister had problems, father. I would never do anything to harm the family!" Opening his blue eyes wide, the vision of innocence. Silence from the others profound.

Refhar snorted. Menodisces lips twitched. "Good. That bonding to familia will serve you well." Menodisces stepped into Daccu's personal space, wrapping his right hand around the Godling's throat, applying just enough pressure to choke but not cut off the airways. He lifted the young fighter up to his tiptoes. "I will personally feed you to the Gotta if I ever think you are jeopardizing us."

He shook Daccu once, twice, three times viciously, before releasing him. Daccu collapsed to his knees, wheezing one hand to his bruised throat the other on the floor to keep from falling face first on the metal surface.

"Yes, father." Daccu coughed out, through purple lips. The glare he focused on the floor, not his father. He took a moment before standing, climbing heavily to his feet, the muscles in his jaws bunching and releasing.

"Good." Menodisces patted Daccu on the arm before looking at the remaining two. "Hadriana, you will attend with me for continued training in necromancy. Your skills are becoming quite exceptional." He motioned to Refhar. "Give her rooms in the main household along with an entourage of 10. Let her pick the slaves she needs."

"Guidance?"

"She should be able to capably stock her own household." Menodisces gave his singular child with strong necromancy a nod.

Hadriana bowed to her father, understanding his gift was double-edged. A household was built on the quality of those under you. Any slave or free she acquired could and would be used against her.

"Cnaeu." Cnaeu looked to Menodisces with liquid brown eyes. A hand-sized patch of black skin the size of a man's palm covered his left eye and cheek. The patch of skin was dark enough to stand out on Cnaeu's dark skin. It was the only mar to perfection in looks and body of a young god. "Your skills on the sand have been nothing less than amazing." The young man flushed, his dark skin hiding the rush of blood to his cheeks under his adopted father's praise. "You and Daccu will be given a task benefiting our family."

Both Daccu and Cnaeu looked at each other with sharp smiles and hooded eyes before centering on Menodisces.

With a nod of his head, Menodisces continued with their full attention. "Gods are made, slaves born. And to be my God Son, you will prove which you are. I am going to give you both fighters and ships. You can take a world or a world-ship. Come back with either or both and you will be given everything a God has."

Both looked at their father, showing teeth in predatory smiles.

Hadriana spoke behind him, falling to one knee, patting the ground to get her father's attention. "Father, may I ask a small boon?"

Menodisces turned with a slight frown. "You may ask but granting is not guaranteed."

"I would like to donate two from my current household to Daccu. He has been a great help in my studies and in training."

"Two is a generous amount."

"I have four already. Mother has continued gifting me with one or two over the years. I fear 14 will be a strain on my new budget."

"As you wish."

Hadriana bowed her head, short blond hair falling over her face hiding any expression she might have. Daccu looked at his older full blooded sister with narrowed eyes. He wouldn't be able to refuse the slaves, but he could always kill them. Dead, alive. He was a necro as well as a fighter; it didn't matter how his toys came to him.

Chapter 16

The rest of the morning was slow, as they put up another round of mirrors. Two more mirrors were broken. One cracked into two pieces with one piece much larger than the other. The second mirror broke along the corner, still useable as a large mirror minus an edge. The only mirrors left at the end of the day to hand were those that were in large pieces.

The shards were cleaned but not quick enough to keep a few of the chickens from greedily gobbling a few of the glittering shards. Lauranya looked down as the birds started to droop towards the end of the day.

Arie, more sanguine than her mother, said. "Looks like we'll be having roasted chicken tomorrow."

Lauranya blew a stray strand of hair from her face, before bending to pick up a bird. "True; however this one was one of our best layers." The bird let out a strangled squawk, making no real effort to escape capturing hands.

"It's ok, mom, we have enough." Arie was already thinking towards tomorrow's dinner and future generations of potential dinners.

"I know, sweetie, I just hate randomly losing birds we might need." Lauranya sighed, giving the bird's neck a quick twist. The dead bird flapped ineffectual wings, clawing at the world without recourse. Lauranya let the bird fall to the ground, as she quickly wrung the necks of the two other affected birds.

Arie gathered the chickens up, after their nervous system quiet trying to cheat death. She turned to her mother, her arms full of grey and gold fluffs of feather, with a frown. "Mom, why is it I can see and hear dead people, but not animals?"

Lauranya stood up from her obsessive sweeping. "My mother explained to me that those who spoke during life were the only ones who wanted to speak after death." Here she took a deep breath, gathering her thoughts. "I think it is because those who were in our life, or the dead who come to us, have a hard time accepting they are no longer physical and needed. So their ghosts try to keep touching our lives."

"Animals are ready to move on to the next life, while humans aren't?" Arie asked, heading into the kitchen to start cleaning the birds.

"Possibly." Lauranya shrugged slightly, grabbing the dustpan following Arie. "We will not know until we are dead ourselves and can answer that question."

Arie tilted her head for a second, thinking. "There might be more to it." She mused, dumping the limp birds on the counter, grabbing a large pot to fill halfway with water.

"Or there might be less," Lauranya said, pouring the glass into the dump box. The conversation continued, comparing human to non-human, including the mer-woman. Some scientist had theorized that the shifter phenomenon just meant Runners had given up their souls when they took the form of beasts. Lauranya had always believed a soul that thought could always become a ghost. Both she and Arie enjoyed coming up with various theories of how ghosts evolved that turned to talk about farming, as the birds were dunked into hot water then plucked of all feathers. Once plucked, the birds were then gutted, the best parts being saved, and hung up to age for a couple of days in the cooler.

Lauranya cleaned her hands with a final comment. "The conversation of souls and ghosts can wait for dinner; we, however, have broken mirrors to hang for maximum lighting."

"Too short for the main wall space," Arie said, cocking her head to this side and that while looking into the mirror making funny faces.

Lauranya looked around the room. "But they are perfect for the corners by the stairs."She said, after considering then discarding the other options.

"Oh! Extra light from the rays bouncing," Arie stood up, twisting towards her mother in her excitement, her grip slipping slightly, causing the mirror to drop an inch in small hands.

"Mirror!" Lauranya exclaimed, rushing with outreached hands to save the large piece.

Arie's grip tightened, as she ducked her head guiltily. "Got it mom."

Lauranya pinched the bridge of her nose, closing her eyes, yet all she said was "Thank you, child. We need all the light we can generate." She looked up, considering the other corners. "Hmmm. Maybe smaller mirrors in all the corners would work to the best instead of just along the walls." She turned to Arie with a gleam in her eye that Arie had come to know all too well.

"Another research paper, mom?"

"Of course."

Arie heaved a heavy sigh, as only the young could do so well, putting down the mirror piece. "Yes, mommy!"

"Just an outline. Pros vs. Cons."

"Oh. An easy one!"

"And the ratio of light each corner will reflect. I will

help you with the equations if you need."

"Drat!" Arie snapped her fingers, vexed.

"You must work the brain…" Lauranya started.

"To keep atrophy at bay," Arie finished.

Chapter 17

Zorax looked down from the catwalk, into the ship bay where all the deadheads had been brought. Observing, as long thin fingers moved restlessly over the catwalk bar.

"Tilu."

"Sir!"

"I'm told this lot had a captain and a second in command." Zorax let his eyes narrow, regarding the soon to be dismantled undead ship disgorging slow-moving passengers.

"Yes, sir. Do you want me to get Sunshine to confirm this again?" Tilu asked, with an almost servile hunch of his shoulders. This shortened his height, so his head was lower than Zorax as he stared wide-eyed up into the God's face.

"No. I want you to bring those two to me." Zorax said, impatience creeping into his voice. He gave his servant a sideways glance.

Tilu hesitated. "Sir? I...I don't think the survivors can walk yet." he hunching more, not wanting to disappoint and ward off any blows.

"No matter, bring them on a gurney." Zorax gave a slight smile, touching thin lips with the tip of his pink tongue. "They'll be leaving by one as it is."

"Yes, sir!" Tilu hesitated for only a moment. "Will you need help with your questioning?"

"I haven't decided who I intend to invite, but there will be a couple." Zorax touched Tilu on the arm absently. Tilu shivered, smiling wider. "Would you like to watch?"

"Always," Tilu breathed as if he had been kissed, his eyes bright with desire.

"Then consider yourself one of the few," Zorax said, giving Tilu a broken tooth smile before strolling back to his apartments. Presentation was everything and a good host always made sure to put forth his best side.

Sergeant Sunshine entered the God's apartment at 19 hundred hours, as his message pad directed. The door slid open, letting weak screams drift out like smoke, tainting the air he breathed. Sunshine tightened his spine before stepping through. He marked both his direct superior Captain Daffer, a rather non-descript human, and General Mesan sitting on a leather couch. Both were sipping from glass cups, while the God Zorax was in the midst of telling an amusing antidote. Tilu was busy applying a small hot curling wand to one of the two of the deadheads.

Zorax was the first to notice the Sergeants entrance. "Ahhh, Sunshine. It's good to see you!" Zorax took small flouncing steps over a floor painted in yellows and pinks. Zorax vibrantly colored silk over-robe floated behind the God, as he sashed towards Sunshine. Zorax pulled him into the middle of the room. "General Meran was just extolling your...virtues and how you were the man for a rather hush-hush project." Zorax giggled at another scream, with a slight shiver. Sunshine swallowed bile, keeping his face empty.

"Could mean a bump in your calories and living quarters," Daffer said, taking another sip, barely giving the Sergeant a once over, his eyes followed Zorax's every move.

"Well, he'd have to get the task done, with a few

others. They'd need a bump as well." General Mehan said, giving Sunshine an open mouth grin, his tongue almost lolling out, his hand weaving his drink through the air almost randomly as he gestured.

"Yes, yes. Such unpleasantness. I think that's behind us, now that all the information is gotten." Zorax said, fluttering a hand quickly as if waving away noxious fumes. He moved his robe to the side, slumping into an overstuffed chair, covered in a material Sunshine had never seen. The fibers seemed to shimmer like silk, absorbing more light than reflecting. Sunshine wanted to run his hands over that chair like he would a woman's hips. Slow and long, nothing hurried.

"Sir?" Sunshine asked, realizing his staring at the chair had been construed as staring at Zorax while missing part of the conversation.

Zorax pursed lips together, looking down his elongated nose. Sunshine didn't think it wise to tell the God he looked more cross-eyed than cross when doing that.

"I said...I need your discretion in taking care of the extras we can't afford on the ship."

"Discretion, sir?"

"Mesan, I thought you said he was the man for this job?" Zorax huffed, turning to pout at the General. "He's not as sharp, as I was lead to expect. I need good men for this job, not...marine mental fluff." His hand waved towards Sunshine, vaguely dismissive.

"Oh, he is," Mesan said. "The man for the job, that is. He just needs to be told what you want, and he'll figure out the rest." Mesan took another sip. "You just have to be...blunt." The large Wolfen stood unsteadily, putting his glass cup firmly down in empty air. The cup shattered in an almost melodic tinkling on the painted metal floor.

Zorax glared at the General, ready to yell at Mesan,

when Daffer got up, bent over the mess, sweeping the glass shards into his hands. Everyone stared at the Captain. Glass, being rarer than a surviving Redeyes' Guardian, still deserved respect for sharp edges. However, the shards melted together in a swirl in the Captain's hand, catching the room's light before reforming into another glass.

"For you." Daffer presented, with a flourish, to the God.

"Daffer, I never knew you could do this!" Zorax said with delight, examining the new glass. It was a little heavier than the last but just as beautifully wrought, with a wider base to hold a curling stem and slightly larger, if thinner, bulb.

"A small power," Daffer said, with an effacing shrug. "I usually use only when my guns or armor break. The ability to fix something so precious to you is my pleasure." Captain Daffer gave the God a wide smile as he sat down, taking his plain glass back in hand, sipping the contents.

Daffer took up the commentary thread General Mesan had tried to start. "Sunshine, Zorax is asking you to take the deadheads from the ship and make sure they aren't here." He said, holding up his glass for a refill. Tilu put down the heated irons, pouring the Captain another drink from a small glass bottle set on the side of the table.

The Captain nodded his thanks. Tilu blushed in pleasure, before putting the bottle back and heading over towards the deadheads once more. Zorax grabbed Tilu's hand as he passed by, pulling the plump young man to sit at his feet. Tilu leaned his head against the God's leg, as Zorax ran fingers through dirty blond hair.

"Esactly!" General Mesan said, his words slurring as he flung a large hand with thick black nails outwards. "Space is their home not here. Understand?"

"General, I do understand." Sunshine nodded his head

firmly, finally catching all the implication of what was said and what wasn't.

"Good. You'll need a dedicated crew while Daffer, here, gets everyone loaded back up." Mesan ambled over to Sunshine, resting his top arms on Sunshine's shoulders, while still gesturing with his lower arms. "This is up to you!" He belched into the Sergeant's face. "Oh. Damn, bad manners." He wavered on his feet.

He turned to Zorax. "Think I'm done for the night. Sunshine here knows his new job and can escort me home." with another belch, this time much more prodigious than the last. "Oh, excuse me! My manners are fragged." Mesan wobbled a little more, looking down at the floor sheepishly

"Yes, yes. You are done." Zorax looked at Sunshine, whose stunned eyes were on his General. This night couldn't get worse. "Sunshine, we can count on you for this delicate task, yes?"

"Of course sir!" Sunshine stood up straighter, looking the God in his eyes.

"Good." Zorax purred, touching his pointed chin again with thin almost nervous fingers. "We will have the ships ready to leave in a day. Will that give you enough time?"

"Time?"

"Crew boy. Crew." Mesan pounded Sunshine on the back, emphasizing his point. Sunshine staggered a little under the pounding, Mesan staggering with him.

"Yes, sir! I think I can get the right crew to take on this task." Sunshine said, standing in a slightly wider stance taking on Mesan's pronounced slumping weight. "Those two on the cross, sir? Will they be with the other…" a brief hesitation as he wasn't sure how to name them "deadheads sir?"

"Oh, yes. We can't have any extra bodies lying around;

now can we." Zorax said, wrinkling his nose at a stench that only he could smell.

"Whoa. Thinking it's time to get me to my bed." The Wolfen started staggering again.

"Out, out. We won't talk of this again." Zorax waved him away with one hand, turning his attention back to the young man leaning against his leg.

Mesan draped both right arms over Sunshine as they headed out the door. Mesan staggering threw Sunshine's normal wide stride off, making the walk to the General's room longer than necessary.

Sunshine waited until outside the General's door before speaking.

"Sir…"

"Ah, Sunshine, we need to keep this quiet and to ourselves. No sense in worrying anyone else or any of our shipmates, that the God doesn't want added burdens. Yes?"

"Umm…Yes, sir." Sunshine kept his face still.

"Good man! I always knew you could do the job the God gave you." Mesan stuck a wide hand out for Sunshine to grasp. Mesan placed his free hand on top, pushing both his and Sunshine's hand close together. "Remember, this is for the God, and you are the only one to do the job…right. Understand?"

Sunshine blinked but nodded slowly, their hands parting. "I do. I'll make sure the crew are assembled tonight, and we are good to leave by morning."

"Excellent. Have a great night Sunshine and safe travels." Mesan opened his door, with a final nod to the sergeant.

"You also, General."

Sunshine waited until he was several levels lower, before pulling out the thumb-sized object from between his fingers the General had palmed him. It was a teardrop shaped crystal, faceted to catch even the dimmest light, reflecting a deep red inner fire. A blood drop from Redeyes, large enough she had probably died from whatever wound that this had formed from. Message received.

"Sunshine!" Leaf said, from her barstool, as the sergeant walked through the bar doors. "You going to join us for a drink or five?" She had a metal tumbler in front of her that would have dwarfed human hands.

"Nope, just here to tell you we've got a job in the morning." He touched her hand, thinking hard "MIND WALK WITH ME!" as loudly as he could hoping her shields weren't fully in place after a couple of drinks.

"Space me; stop yelling." Leaf flicked an ear at him, as she 'pathed. "Lorren! A drink for my Sergeant! He needs a few."

The Wolfen behind the bar waved a lower hand at her, as his other three hands were busy with a louder party at the other end.

"Got a job for us in the morning, so don't go drinking what wits you have away." Sunshine started. Mentally he gave Leaf the rundown of the job.

Leaf started taking a big swallow of her drink, choked as she reviewed the God meeting and the General's message.

"It's a one-way trip," Sunshine added, in case the message had been lost in the background.

"Push me out an airlock, why don't you! I got the message." Leaf sputtered, Sunshine pounded her on the back. The Wolfen bartender handed him a drink. "You ok, girl?" He asked the sputtering Katherian.

"Do I voiding look ok to you?" Leaf wiped spittle from

her chin, shaking her hand of the excess moisture. "Gah."

"Nope. I think I've seen happier corpses." Lorren said, refilling her glass, before turning to Sunshine. Sunshine held up one finger. Lorren nodded, getting him the same as Leaf.

"I'll be a corpse once I've finished drinking this engine fluid." She said, chugging the mug, slamming it down with a metal on metal thunk.

"You wanted cheap and plentiful, engine fluid is that." Lorren gave her an open jaw laugh, picking up the mug, tossing it into the wash bin with another metal clatter.

"Yeah, it was that."

"Refill for you, Sunshine."

"Not done yet and no." Sunshine took another sip. "Ball busting job to gear up for tomorrow. Can't afford the headache; that'll give me."

"Can understand that." Lorren gave him a nod, wandering down the length of the bar for the next person needing a drink.

"Who do you trust? Not just trust to do the job but with your life." Sunshine asked her.

"Probably the same as you." Leaf licked her broad nose, smoothing her whiskers with a hand.

"Let's compare notes then and start rounding 'em up," Sunshine said grimly, finishing off his drink. He pushed the cup to the back of the bar for Lorran to pick it up, leaving a generous tip.

Chapter 18

The next morning came, with sun shedding his harem of clouds, bringing a glow to the sky and the water below. The growing room glowed with light. Arie let out a whoop of excitement as the dawn light hit the first mirror then the others. Each mirror reflecting the sun back into the room. The only mirrors that weren't glowing gold were the ones Lauranya had set above and between the windows up high to catch the setting sun's reflection through the windows on the opposite side. Lauranya allowed herself a smile of satisfaction for work well done.

The solar charge had the main generator up and running within three hours. The clouds rolled in during the afternoon, yet the generator kept working and the regular lights running. The mirrors reflections made the day bright inside even with the gloomy weather out.

Lauranya measured the time needed to charge the generator, planning on the use for two other generators with two held as back up. Arie danced and twirled in the light, laughing.

"I think this calls for a treat," Lauranya said smiling at her boisterous child. "Peaches? Well peaches in a crust that is." Sweet dishes were one of the few things Lauranya was good at cooking.

"Cumin and honey peaches?" Arie stopped with one hip out and her head and torso bent to the side, so it appeared she was looking almost upside down at her mother. Arie stood up with a flip of her hair, running to give her mother a quick hug.

Arie was almost her own height and no longer a child. A quick count of the years, Lauranya realized that Arie was almost 16 ship years. A lump formed in her throat. Lauranya cleared her throat before giving her daughter another quick hug.

"Sounds perfect!" Lauranya said with only a slight hitch in her voice, as they walked into the kitchen arm and arm.

Menodisces lounged on the wide low slung couch surrounded by bright pillows, rich food and sumptuous dancers. He motioned for a slave to bring him a tan finger length fruit on a burnished blue green plate. The slave was efficiently silent and unobtrusive, offering the fruit to Menodisces and his guests, before melting back along the sides.

"How goes the poisoning of the weapons?"

The woman made a face. Her male counterpart gave a heavy sigh, taking a sip of his sweet red wine. "The first few months' trial was just a disaster. We lost more stock than we care to admit." He held up his glass to the dim light, making the red wine much darker and more viscous than it would normally look.

"We gained valuable insight, though." The woman insisted, almost testily, picking up the strands to an old argument.

"Such as? I don't wish to fund a project without a return of investment." Menodisces asked smoothly before the scientist could become locked into their verbal dancing spar.

"Poisoning each weapon uniquely, then giving a

counter poison is a gamble that there aren't going to be side effects and death; however poisoning the weapon with a generic poison and giving the antidote seemed to work better."

"Well since we weeded out a lot of weak stock while keeping the strongest."

"Will this poisoning affect breeding or intelligence?"

The two exchanged glances.

"I take that as a yes."

"We haven't seen a decline in intelligence; if anything the reverse with a couple of extra points for a select few. As for breeding, we have no clue. There hasn't been enough time to follow the sperm and ovum."

"That would be an excellent line of inquiry though." The man said thoughtfully, before sipping slowly a wine he would never be able to enjoy outside of his patron's indulgences. "Perhaps we could adjust the poison levels. We don't have to kill the runaways, just incapacitate their fighters."

"Expelling all stomach content for the next few hours would certainly incapacitate most fighters." The woman mused thoughtfully, taking another sip of the excellent wine.

"One experiment at a time, please," Menodisces said with a smile as the two scientists talked. Their enthusiasm contagious.

"We could see if they breed exclusively to produce their own antidote or if they can only breed with non-poisoned due to a break down due to the poison."

"Both of those sound fascinating, yet how are they going to work with our long term goals for regaining the runaways?" Menodisces motioned towards another plate on a table within arm's reach. "And having slaves that can't be touched by the masters would be... problematic."

A willowy slave knelt smoothly, to lift and offer the tray of delicacies for his God's selection.

"We have a trial run ready to go on your approval."

"A trial run?" Menodisces made his selection before turning his attention back to the conversation. The small bite sized piece of thinly shaved beef, so rare the center was deep red, on a toasted crisp of bread with a savory spread of creamy cheese he popped into his mouth chewing slowly, savoring the salt and savory flavors.

"We plan on using a quarter of the fighters we've been working on."

"This gives a good assessment with enough held back for further work or modulation of the poisons."

Menodisces held out his hand for a slave to wipe down with a damp cotton towel. "I will give the approval, but I do want to see how breeding is affected." He took a cup from another.

"Of course."

"No reason to continue if we can't keep the main stock from dying." Menodisces sipped his wine, a drier red that blended seamlessly with the thinly shaved beef and cheese.

The willowy slave offered the tray of tidbits to the guests. The man took a tidbit while the woman ran her hand over the slave's back, an unconscious gesture of touch, absent mindedly judging breeding potential. The boy was too well trained to shudder, holding his poise while making an offering. The woman's hand continued fondling both muscular and soft sensitive parts, as she made her selection.

"We can take the most robust stocks ovum and sperm and transplant that into breeders."

"That might kill the breeder if the fetus is rejected due to changes in the basic cellular structure."

"Then we need to know that now and not later if this is

to be a continued project. Do you have enough breeders?"

The woman gave a heavy sigh, patting the slave on the head like a favored rabbit. "Unfortunately we could use another dozen or so for the first round." An eloquent shrug. "We have been given fighters, not breeders."

"I have a few breeders I can spare. Nothing prized mind you, but as they need to only carry to term, they should be more than adequate. Perhaps if you optimized the egg placement for more than one viable fetus, we can increase the output with less stock needed?"

"We could take six eggs at a time from the female fighters to implant in the breeders, then sterilize the less robust fetuses so only 2 or 3 are delivered at a time."

"That would double our production, but we still have a slow lead time needed for full growth potential."

"This leads to another question. Could the poison be administered orally so that the subject could exude their own poison?"

"Yes, we had thought of this. It's possible, just not viable in the long term due to the need for intervention for breeding. Fighting stock could breed with fighting stock but then we would never be able to send them out on kill missions we would be building up stock for generations without actually seeing a return on the investment."

"So we need to test the generic poisons, which the fighters can handle, and the antidote as well as their continued breeding viability. Is that where we stand?"

"Exactly!"

"Then let us have a test to see if this is the start of something we need to turn the edge."

Cnaeu stopped Felix with a hand to the shorter necro's shoulder, pulling him into the side corridor. Felix let out a high pitched scream; Cnaeu covered his mouth with a broad hand, stopping the sound before it could travel far.

"Felix, stop. It's me and Jacintha." Cnaeu hissed into the terrified young man's ear.

Felix stopped screaming, but he didn't stop shivering, as Cnaeu let him go.

"What's wrong with you?" Jacintha hissed into his ear.

"I'm terrified to end up in the bone pit! I can't find any of my ghosts that... Never mind." Felix pressed his lips firmly together, wrapping thin arms around his thin torso.

Jacintha and Cnaeu looked at each other. "I need a favor Felix. One that you and only you can do."

"And for me?" Felix's eyes shifted from one fighter to the other.

"What do you want?" Jacintha asked with an annoyed huff.

"Cnaeu takes me with him when he goes off ship. Nothing else."

"Not even a fresh body." Cnaeu asked, tilting his head slightly with a smile. Felix licked pale lips. Cnaeu could see the internal war chase across the necro's face.

"Fresh won't do me any good if I'm dead."

Cnaeu turned to Jacintha, giving a wider grin. "I win. Pay up."

"Father fucking ass biter," Jacintha said without heat, pulling a small silk purse from her belt pouch. It was so full of wooden coins the seams were almost bursting. She passed it to Cnaeu, sticking out her tongue only slightly aggrieved at losing the bet.

Felix looked between the two, eyes narrowing in heat as the two looked to be making fun of him.

Cnaeu took the purse from Jacintha, holding up to Felix. "I need you to get Aelia out of the slave pens. She'll have her own cell so..."

"So you want me to just walk in and pull her out? How voiding stupid do you think I am?" Felix put hands on his hips. "There is no way Renfra is going to sell me Aelia. She's been tagged for sale to a Lord."

"That's why we need you," Jacintha said. "And the ghosts Hadriana is going to provide you with."

"Why? Why Aelia? What's she to you?" Felix asked suspiciously, ignoring the bag Cnaeu held up at eye level swinging slightly from his fingers.

"I promised her my protection." Cnaeu simply. Felix opened his mouth then closed it. Cnaeu had promised him similarly, and Jacintha. Felix looked sideways at the other Godling. He didn't miss her hand on the belt dagger.

"I go with you on the ship hunt?"

"And the occasional fresh body." Cnaeu nodded solemnly, looking Felix in the eyes.

Felix nodded slowly. "Tell me what you have in mind."

The Godlings smiled at each other, showing teeth. "First you'll need to acquire a blond that looks mostly like Aelia…"

Chapter 19

Redeyes was awakened from troubling dreams, where a small imp stared at her with sharpened teeth in a forest glade, waiting to eat her if she strayed from the path to a cottage. The ship siren at first mistaken as the imp scream as it slowly opened its mouth filled with sharp teeth, before Redeyes sleep muddled brain recognized the sound as a siren and not a nightmare. It took her a moment to clear her head from waking in the middle of REM sleep. When she became more cognizant in thought, she dropped like a rock to the bed she'd been hovering a few inches over.

"Fuck me. Keep forgetting to tie a foot down." She muttered, pushing aside blankets to get to her clothes, only to fall on her face as the tossed aside blankets tangled her feet.

"Mother fucker!" She snarled, loud enough for the others in the next room to hear. She looked up to see Roar slam the door open, a disc gun the size of a small cannon at the ready, teeth bared as he rushed into her bedroom. Collins and Iarris hung back slightly, blank faces with wide eyes and sweating brow. Nero was behind them with ears flat and hands shaking so hard his guns, snaked from side to side in both his lower and upper grips, unable to remain still.

Roar careened to a halt when no one and nothing jumped out at him. The claws of his feet digging into the metal, hard enough Redeyes could swear she almost saw sparks from her floor side view. Collins and Iarris edged in behind Roar's line breaking rush, covering the corners. Nero didn't even try to make the door.

Redeyes pushed herself up from the floor, wiping small drops of crystallized blood from her nose. Collins and Iarris exchanged glances, while Roar tilted his head to look at her.

"What? You can't tell me that has never happened before." She snapped, sitting in her tangle of blankets, looking up.

"No." Roar huffed, sliding his pistol back into the shoulder holster, trying not to laugh.

"Nope," Iarris said, with a tilted head contemplating her prone god.

"Can't say as I've ever seen you fall flat on your face, well I should say, not getting out of bed that is." Collins grinned, squatting down to get a better eyes view.

"Thanks, assholes." She glared up at her towering Guardians. It was Iarris who laughed first, then Collins, a shaking of the shoulders at first then laughter doubling the human over. Roar tried hard to keep a straight face, as he offered a hand to help her up.

"You people suck today." Redeyes glared, gaining her footing.

"It's a good day," Collins said, the laughter in his voice reflecting in his eyes, as he flashed her a broad smile.

Redeyes' narrowed her eyes, taking in Collins jovial attitude. "That smile makes me think you have someone in mind to kill."

"You do tend to pick sociopaths for Guardians on occasion." Roar said laconically.

"Frigate has been spotted." Was all Collins said eagerly, quirked an eyebrow at the tall Katherian.

"Ore transport. Few guns and fewer people on the inside." Nero called from behind at the doorway.

"And we need the ore for ships and supplies." Redeyes sighed remembering Cratt's lessons. She scissored her legs, kicking the blankets aside, moving towards her clothing once more. "Let's go kick ass and steal some ore."

"Yes!" Collins grinned, as he slowly slid his pistols into hip holsters, hands touching the well-oiled leather lovingly.

"Try not to shoot the people on our side Collins," Redeyes said, running an upper hand through her hair. The hair spiked up even more, standing out in all directions.

"What not even..." Collins stood smoothly from his low crouch, eyeing Redeyes' naked body with admiration.

"No, not even anyone." Redeyes pulled back her lips, exposing her elongated teeth in a silent snarl. Collins backed away with his hands up but didn't stop looking.

"That Redeyes doesn't authorize you shooting." Roar amended, flicking an ear at their God.

Both of them glared at Roar who looked blandly back.

"Fine. But if she says I get to shoot 'em, I get to pick the area." Collins said smugly.

"Sure. You keep that in mind when I authorize shooting you." Redeyes said mildly, heading to the shower, throwing random pieces of clothing from the dresser onto the bed.

High Sarge had the marines in place and strapped in when Redeyes and all four of her Guardians showed up. The normal chatter stopped as the ship's crew looked over the new Redeyes and the new Guardian. The tale of how he arrived from sanctuary the day the other Redeyes died, still circulating in the lower bars over a couple of pints.

High Sarge's nails clicked on the metal flooring. She looked Roar over, growling. "Looks like you survived." With lowered ears and a not quite curled lip.

Roar gave her a smile, dropping his jaw slightly, with a slight head tilt as he answered. "This Redeyes at least. I may not be so lucky with the next one." Spoken with aplomb, causing High Sarge to blink several times in surprise.

High Sarge just grunted, turning her back to the taller Katherian, dismissing him for the moment, as she 'pathed the pilot about the five extra on board

"You doing ok, Red?" High Sarge asked out loud, running her eyes over the short god as she chewed an inner cheek. Redeyes was never the same from one body to the next, but she did like the odd if sometimes bloodthirsty God.

Redeyes' eyes flashed human green, then back to red. High Sarge pulled back for just a moment. "Yeah. So far, so good. Ready for this." High Sarge was about to ask about the new Guardian when the pilot came over the speaker.

"Need to know if you are going through the floor or do we need to do this old school." The man's voice crackled on the com. "This'll affect how we approach the ship." There was nervous shifting among the marines who had seen Redeyes ghost through walls.

"Old school." Came Iarris' reply, pitching loud enough to carry to the com and through the ship. She flicked an ear with an almost smile, the relief in her voice almost palatable. Chuckles from those close enough to hear.

"Going through the walls is just freaky," Collins said, grimacing. Echoing the unspoken words the marines were thinking. The marines closest to the door moved down towards the pilots giving the five newcomers choice of seats.

"Could be worse." Roar said with a grimace, his pupils' hunter wide.

"I don't wanna know," Nero said, flopping down on the recently vacated seat. His eyes were almost sleepy, echoing his relaxed posture. Anywhere but in the Gods' apartment, seemed to suit him, even if he was on his way to dying, it seemed. Redeyes sat next to him with Roar, Iarris and Collins across.

"You'll need to get us armor." Iarris sent a private 'path to Redeyes, a slight tilt of her head to High Sarge.

"High Sarge. Armor for us when you can." Was all Redeyes asked, still looking around absorbing the ship. She didn't raise her voice or even look at the Katherian in command.

High Sarge's frowned briefly before she smoothed her brow. "Jupe, get 'em dressed and let's get this going. A ship needs plundering and won't wait forever!"

A young Wolfen, barely out of his teens, bolted towards the lockers where the extra armor was held. In moments, he came stumbling back with armfuls of vests, helmets, and leg gear.

Redeyes examined the armor curiously. It was made of various articulating plates, tied together along the inner edges of the armor. The vests were both puncture and cut resistant to damage at close range, covering from the neck to a rounded v shape coverage over the groin, and along the upper arms, with protection to the major veins in the neck, arms and legs. There were Velcro straps for stability. Nero's had ties for the extra arm coverings for his. Redeyes helped him with the adjustments before donning her vest. The legs covered from ankle to hip with double webbing at the hips to hold them up and add extra protection. The legs were strapped onto a belt under the main breastplate, the inner thigh, either with Velcro or ties depending on the amount of personal modifications into their armor. General armor is what Redeyes and the Guardians wore from the common stores and therefor lots of Velcro.

Redeyes looked to Iarris while pulling fur from the Velcro sending a query. "Why general armor for us? Why not specialized or at least less metal grey?"

"You insisted that if you or your own stood out, you'd be targeted. Mostly by the Undead Gods but sometimes by those holding grudges on the ship."

"Shipmates would do that?!" Redeyes head snapped up, eyes flashing human green.

"You've killed more than a few people with your dreams or as Guardians, not to mention these raids aren't always successful." Iarris said with a shrug, flipping one of her daggers slowly, watching the spin, catching the handle by two claws, tossing the dagger up again, making sure the armor fit snugly without impeding her aim or throwing ability.

"Fuck me!"

"Pfft. Wrong toys." Iarris gave a wide toothy grin, through her flips.

"Thanks for the heads up and waaay too much information." Redeyes said, with the verbal equivalent of an eye roll.

"Any time. Keep your head down and your cool. Stick next to Roar. Let us do the thinking and don't get us killed!" Iarris narrowed her eyes, with the last bit of 'pathing, trying to get her point across.

"Wasn't planning to." Redeyes muttered, re-adjusting her gun belt over the armor. One of the marines reached over to help her with the armor. Redeyes gave a grateful smile.

"New to this ship?" Iarris asked, watching her knife spin and not the woman. Her tone curious as she looked over the marine's well worn, obviously personally tailored and acid etched decorations but not recognizing the face or the armor.

"Yes, from Nekole's ship." She cleared her throat. "We've got an excess of population and this ship put a request for 500 plus."

"Welcome to the pack," Nero said, thumping his own chest armor into place. A quick twist of the torso and arms for fit and he was ready to go.

"So how many Guardians survive their sentence with you?" The marine asked, a little too casually.

Redeyes cocked her head. "So far they've all survived." She jutted her chin, motioning to the four with her.

"In the last 100 years or so?" the woman clarified, tugging on lacings, before giving the tied on armor a tug and smack assuring it settled correctly.

Collins looked at the small knot of his world and the slightly larger knot of those not listening in from the marines. "About one so far."

The woman swallowed thickly. "Nekole's Guardians usually only have to worry about him wanting to shoot or fuck 'em, not much else. Still sounds like a better deal."

Iarris looked at the woman a little closer. Tall, on the prettier side for a human with round cheeks and large eyes. "Why you transferred over?"

"Yes." Clipped answer from thinned lips. She wouldn't meet the Guardian's eyes. Her hands froze mid strap pull on Redeyes' upper leg, her head jerking up hard. "Those are low odds." the newcomer said, clearing her throat a couple of times to get the words out, going back to the main conversation. She finished tightening the strap before sitting back, a little further away than before.

"Not really." Roar said, at the same time, with a flick of his ear towards High Sarge who was about to say something cutting. "Unlike the marines, we see weekly action. And training isn't until the person taps out. While we use practice weapons, claws are uncapped and we don't pull punches."

"Why?!" A marine blurted out three down. The Wolfen's stripes solid with a few gray hairs around his muzzle showing him to be in his 8th decade.

"The deadheads don't pull their punches or use blunted tools," Redeyes said without looking up from testing her leg armor's tightness. "I'll heal and they," she motioned with her lower right hand "wear lots of armor. Unlike me." She muttered around strapping held between her teeth as she attempted to tighten her upper left vambrace.

Iarris was getting ready to make a comment when her head snapped to the right, her nose flaring at a familiar scent. Her ears went flat, as her fur spiked. A deep growling rumbling in her chest. Collins glanced at his partner, following her concentrated gaze. His eyes widening as he saw the other Katherian who just walked onto the Marine deck. Collins didn't even try to holster his gun, dropping it to the deck, making a grab for Iarris.

"Iarris?" Redeyes asked, looking up at her normally calm guardian.

"Iarris, don't!" Collins wrapped his hands around the Katherian's arm, jamming his feet against the deck to give him some leverage, as Iarris tried to unhook her seat harness. "Redeyes will shoot you, or I'll have to if you go after her." Collins' kept his hands locked on her bicep, as Iarris tried to yank her arm away from his grip. She pulled him halfway across her lap.

"Gods tears, Roar, fucking help me!" Collins snapped grimly, holding on for both his life and Iarris. "She'll try to kill Okayzona!"

Roar slipped out of his harness, grabbing the other Guardian by her shoulders, spinning her back to the seats, slamming her down. Iarris threw a sucker punch at Roar, feigning for his stomach. He pulled his stomach back, pushing his head downward. Iarris' fist connected with the side of his muzzle. Roar yowled, dropping her arm to clutch his nose. Iarris bounced back out of her seat, dragging Collins with her, heading to the front of the shuttle with Okayzona in her sight. The sound of disc rifle cocking froze the three guardians.

"Sit the Gods ship raping down now, or so help me, Iarris, I will shoot you," Nero growled, crouching in the middle of the aisle 14 feet from the almost brawl.

Iarris curled back her lips, "You wouldn't shoot me, you…" She never finished. Nero exploded forward from a crouch, dropping the rifle to punch her in the face with the full force of lethal Wolfen strength. All four fists connecting, the upper right hit her in the jaw just below the ear. The two other fists took her in the ribs with the lower left hitting the solar plexus. Iarris dropped into a heap. A one, two three, four combo. Collins fell on top of her, the force he pulled against suddenly stopped.

"Nicely done, Nero." Roar nodded approvingly, reaching a hand down to Collins, pulling him off of Iarris.

"He should have shot the boot donor instead of just knocking her out." The other female Katherian drawled. The three Guardians turned as one to look at her, an older Katherian, with grey threading through her muzzle, with angry narrowed orange eyes, missing part of an ear. The ear scar looked recent, within the last two years. The scar was badly healed, leaving the ear twisted and knobby.

"Shut your hole sucker, Okayzona." Collins growled, bending to pick up his disc gun without giving his back to the Katherian.

"Still kitten fucking? No humans want your damaged genes?" Okayzona purred at him, her hand dropping to her holster, empty, for the moment.

"I don't know who the fuck you are...this life, but if you fuck with my Guardians any more, I will shred your other ear and cut out your tongue," Redeyes said mildly from her seat, finishing up the last of her ties, looking the other female up and down.

"You're taking sides? Now?!" The Katherian's ruff stuck out, her voice growling louder as her tail shivered and spiked.

"Like I said, I don't know you…"

"You damn well should! I'm Okayzona! The…"

Okayzona never got to finish her sentence as Redeyes pulled her disc gun out, aiming it at the Katherian's head, stopping the angry tirade mid syllable.

"High Sarge? How badly do you need this one? Because I need my Guardians stardust more than I need this shit so early in a mission. This one is bothering me." Redeyes' voice could have frozen water, in the air as she studied the older Katherian female in her sites.

High Sarge stepped between the God and the outraged Katherian. "Okayzona go up front and sit." Okayzona's ears went flat. "Yes, we all know what happened, but this isn't that Redeyes. Deal with the new one and that Iarris still lives." High Sarge said, accompanying the 'pathing she was sending. Okayzona gave a murderous glare at Iarris' collapsed on the floor, before turning with the grace only a Katherian had. She moved towards the upper seats of the shuttle, staying out of the way, her tail moving in short angry jerks. Nothing forgiven or forgotten.

High Sarge watched the stiff backed bristling Katherian walk away. "Try not to kill her if you have to please, Redeyes. I need her but the blood runs bad between the two." She turned back to Redeyes. "That's why Iarris is your Guardian, which has a short life expectancy."

Redeyes raised an eyebrow but put up her disc gun. "I'll keep that in mind."

Nero and Collins exchanged glances. "Right. Let's get our girl in her seat and strapped in before Krom's flying gets her killed." Was all Collins said.

The silence on the shuttle broke with a loud cough, then voices speaking in whispers that gradually rose to normal levels.

Chapter 20

Renfra picked up his tablet, glaring at the short thin necro in front of him. "I'm busy Felix. What do you want? I don't have any fresh bodies for you to play with." Giving a dismissive wave of his hand.

"I know. No ghosts floating around." Felix said with wide eyes and hunched shoulders. "I...I need to buy a slave. Nothing too expensive but umm…"

"Still living?" Renfra said, pulling back his upper lip. "You necros are all alike, weird in your fucking habits."

"Considering who our God is you might want to be careful what you say." Felix looked into the dark man's eyes. "Not all of us are easily swayed with just one body."

"Menodisces needs me."

"Only till he has another trained who doesn't question his...undead tastes."

Renfro glared at the Godling for another moment. Felix didn't have Menodisces' ear...that he knew of.

"This once, I will help you select from the culling stock. Next time you'll have to wait till one dies. Understand?"

"Yes!" Felix whispered, a gleam coming into his eyes as he licked pale lips. "I really appreciate your help."

"Remember that. Help goes both ways." Renfra held out his hand. Felix pulled out the usual amount of coins plus three extra, sweetening Renfra's temper.

"Always! I'm not," Here he hesitated before naming

names. "one of the others. I know my place and how to help."

Renfra nodded. They both knew what Daccu was like.

"Come on. " Renfra motioned with the tablet. "I haven't got all morning. A couple of the newer slaves need to be cataloged for training."

They walked through the corridors where the open air cages stood. Some held as many as 20 slaves, some as few as three. Past those were closed cells, with doors of glass showing small cells holding no more than one slave each for these rooms. Cells for the higher prized better trained or slaves in training.

"Fresh! There's a ghost!" Felix gasped, his hands reaching forward, shaking slightly.

"What?!" Renfra snapped, turning towards the necro, before looking down the corridor. "Screw me with a spacing snake!" He snarled, running towards an unmarked cell. Septus sat on the narrow metal cot, head in his hands. Renfra went to the one next to his. Aelia's. The blond was collapsed by the side of the metal cot. Blood pooling around her head.

Felix tried to push past Renfra. The freshness making him bold. Renfra pushed the necro back. "No. Back!" Felix pouted at him, backing up behind Renfra, but didn't go away.

Renfra knelt by the corpse, turning it over gently. The face was smashed beyond recognition, pounded against the rounded edge of the cot until a bone fragment had broken loose or enough blood let out, killing the young woman.

"Can I have it now?" Felix whined, moving into the small narrow cell. His pale hands reaching to touch the still warm corpse.

"Not this one," Renfra said with a shake of his head, choking back a gag. He'd seen a lot of bad deaths, but this one was hard. "Menodisces is going to want to know of her death."

Felix sighed. "She won't be fresh then." wringing his hands.

Renfro looked up, glaring. "You'll be lucky if I let you back in here unless you're occupying one of the cells. She was supposed to be a present."

"Just replace her. It's not like he inspects every slave going out!" Felix said almost dreamily, a hand reaching out to stroke the air near him. A ghost that Renfra couldn't see, looking down at the body, screaming silently.

"Make the ghost go away," Renfra said suddenly. "And don't say anything about this."

"I still need...someone fresh."

"I'll get you fresh but make that father fucking ghost vanish!"

"Fresh first!"

"Fine." Renfra snarled. He walked back to the caged cells pulling out a woman in her third decade. Tired eyes with slumping shoulders and sagging stomach. Worn out breeder unable to have any more children. The woman didn't protest or flinch from the rough hands. The cut throat a blessing. She slumped for only a moment before Felix rushed in, touching her still warm hand. The body twitched, standing.

"The ghosts!" Renfra hissed.

"Gone," Felix said dreamily, taking the dead woman's hand in his own, leading her out of the pens lover like.

"Space dusting necros." Renfra shuddered before turning back to the various messes that had to be cleaned up now.

Dinner was held on the roof that night, having been

delayed for a few turnings from rain. The stars shining through wisps of clouds, with the moon low on the horizon. Water lapping against the building a lulling background noise. The air smelled of water with a slight tang underneath, Lauranya was hard pressed to define. She took deep breaths, enjoying the un-recycled air of the indoors. The unenclosed space made her slightly uneasy, hurrying to get under the heavy wooden trellis of 18-inch steel beams, still standing after the initial deluge. Arie convinced Lauranya to move one of the steel harps to the rooftop. Arie loved Lauranya's harp playing, wanting to hear or mother play and sing after dinner.

"You can teach me under the stars!" Arie bounced with excitement, as her mother tried to demur gracefully. Logic was not going to be the winning point to this argument.

"We have been playing indoors since we moved the harps. Why now on the roof?" Lauranya asked with knitted brow, putting fruit and a small container of spicy sweet honey into a lidded container, along with the meal of grains and roots in a carrying bag. The root dish was warm even through the layers of cloth. Arie handed her plates and utensils to accompany the meal. Without slaves to pick up or clean, Lauranya had learned to pack things both compactly and quickly as possible.

"I want to hear the harp outside in the wind. I…it makes me tingly to think about it." Arie said, touching her head than her heart. It was the best argument Arie could express verbally, the one that Lauranya understood the best.

It was something Lauranya could do to make her daughter happy. So she said "We can move the harp to the roof for tonight."

Arie whooped loudly, the sound reverberating through the kitchen, bouncing off of the steel and stone, throwing her hands up excitedly.

"Hush. You are loud enough to wake the dead." Lauranya smiling fondly.

"Mom! They're already dead. They can't hear anything but me already." Arie said with the certainty of a teenager.

Lauranya stopped, to look at Arie, asking casually "Any new ghosts?"

Arie tilted her head, her eyes un-focusing. "Not more than the ones already here," She said, looking towards the front of the building.

"Good, then let us gather our things and have dinner on the roof while seeing this world's stars," Lauranya said firmly, concentrating on the good things.

The sunset, painted the sky in oranges, blues, golds, pinks and purples. The roof was gorgeous in stone and wood, reflecting the fading light. There were no more trees or even hills surrounding the building, only water. Lauranya found she missed the sight of green things outside.

Arie had planned for the dinner by bringing up cushions and a small round wooden table she had found in the back of the kitchen pantry. Big enough to hold their plates, cups and cooked dishes but with little room left over and light enough for her to move without help.

"An entertainment table for one," Lauranya said with little intonation. "At the most two."

"What's the difference between this table and a regular table?"

"This table is small and portable, for the Gods and Lords to be seated where they pleased not where the host might want them."

"Did you and daddy use these?" Arie ran curious fingers over dark whorl patterns in gold wood.

"No dear. I helped move the tables when the Gods

came to view the gladiators and bid at my family's compound. Let us eat and play instead of talk about tablets." Lauranya said, laying out a cloth of red intricately stitched in gold thread that would protect the wood tabletop from spills.

They sat on pillows varying from solid colored with geometric designs to designs in layers of colors, rivaling the sunset in beauty. The setting sun set the water on fire in a path leading to the tower, illuminating everything in a soft golden glow. Dinner was a joyous affair. Good food as the sunset and pinpoints of starlight peeking out through the darkening skies. The water reflected the stars like a mirror, that rippled with fish searching for small plankton or lost insects.

Twilight was upon them when Lauranya started to play the large floor harp. Her hands floated over the steel harp, plucking strings accompanying her voice. Mother and daughter sang songs from the arias as they watched the sunset. There were also songs Lauranya's grandmothers sang when she was a little girl.

Sitting on bright colored pillows neither Lauranya nor Arie could see beyond the waist high stone baluster, but their voices traveled far across the water, unhindered by obstacles. A small hunting party of mers heard Lauranya's voice. The five oriented towards the voice, water buoying them like corks. Even with the sun warmed water, chills ran along their skin as Lauranya's voice wound through their brain.

"The tower," Illig whispered when the singing stopped. He flicked his tail, moving towards the sounds as if pulled by unseen ropes.

Jord grabbed Illig's arm. "Off limits," Jord said, his vice-like grip belying the soft dreamy quality of his voice. He too stared at the building, rising from the water.

"But the song." Brushing sodden hair from his eyes, Illig looked around at the other three questioningly. "Don't you want to get closer?" They bobbed up and down in the water, moving languidly as if a slow moving riptide were pulling them towards the building.

"I want that music to roll me in the deep and never let me go," Tikka said, a sigh of yearning escaped from pale lips. She gave a slow shuddering breath.

"The deadheads are singing."

"Don't care who's singing, as long as they keep singing."

"We're leaving now!" Jord snapped, spinning to face the other four, pointing his coral spear for emphasis. "None of you are worth Chehreh ripping off my scales when he hears we were close enough to hear music." He flipped his tail, splashing them all, jolting them from the music's thrall. "Now move. We're going home!"

Jord had to prod them home, if there was a break any one or all of them would have turned back towards the tower, as if trying to catch the last refrain. Jord could feel the pull of the voice. He wanted to turn back, climb the walls and lay at the woman's feet. He couldn't get the singing out of his head. The fear of his chieftain was only slightly more powerful than the call of the music. A woman's voice calling him, Jord's dreams and days would be haunted for years. Strands of song he would hear when it was silent and calm. The song was the last thing he heard when a kraken wrapped tentacles around him in a bone crushing grip, dragging him to the cold silent bottom of the deep dark sea.

Lauranya wept over her microscope. Jacks ghosted beside her. "Cancer?" Not even the world-ships could cure all or even most cancers.

Lauranya wiped her eyes, trying for a tremulous smile but failing even that. "No." She shook her head. "I have done as much research on the mer-woman's DNA and mine. There is no cure."

"Surely you can inject some dead cells to inoculate."

"Not even that." She clenched a fist. "The cellular level of the viruses is man-made. This wasn't born in nature, yet it infects the DNA of anything it touches but only in a certain range. It's beautiful, persistent and incurable."

"Deep breath, my dear. What have you found out that might help?"

Lauranya sniffled, wiping her nose on a sleeve. Jacks grinned at her; he had heard her remonstrate Arie many times for the same thing.

"It's a two, possibly three, part virus. I have one section, the Mer had another. I combined cells from us both and the virus mutated again. I couldn't tell you into what but it was…" She took a deep breath, exhaling as a shudder "beyond anything I had ever seen before. The beauty and simplicity." She touched her microscope lovingly. "I do not have the words to describe the complexity from each simple virus when combined with another. I could spend years working on this."

"But no cure."

"The virus gets into the DNA, each cell is infected with one virus. Whatever the Whiskered cat had and the spine fish, both contributed…something." Her hands formed a globe. "There is more to this virus."

"Could you infect Arie?"

"Yes, but it would have to be a serious blood transfusion. The virus will not take just any host. The virus has very specific parameters."

"You've tried."

"I used cheek swabs. Neither virus will infect Arie. They touch her cells and bounce off."

"That is good news!" Jacks said with relief.

"Yes." Lauranya gave a wan smile. "My daughter will never worry about having to shift.

"Is it something in her genetics?"

"I am still looking."

"If she can keep from being infected, you could possibly use what she has to kill your virus."

"I have tried that." She reached for a small box of slides. "The virus ignores Arie's cell for mine. Like javelins."

"I need more time, more samples that are not just three sets of cells. Mine, Arie's and the mer's." Lauranya flexed her hands in frustration as if she could grasp the problem and make it follow the rules she knew. She shook her head, bending back down over the microscope. "Maybe this new line of inquiry with the hook fish will yield something new.

"Mom!" Arie yelled up the stairs, a rising voice that reached her mother's ears.

"Yes?" Lauranya asked, pitching her voice to carry but not looking up from her microscope. The fish cells were acting oddly when confronted with cells from the mermaid.

"Something's wrong with the rabbits. They're going in circles and crying. Not the noise but the tears." Arie's voice faded slightly as if she had turned back toward where the rabbits were housed.

Lauranya jerked up as if electrocuted, yelling in full bravata, "Do NOT touch any of the rabbits. Do not go near their pen!" Jumping down from her stool, she gathered a handful of supplies then did what she had told Arie to never do; she ran down the stairs, blond hair flying past her shoulders as she took the stairs as fast as her feet could carry her.

Arie stared up at her mother, with wide eyes and an open mouth. "But you said never..."

"Hush! Have you touched the rabbits?" Lauranya grabbed Arie's shoulders with a shake, yanking Arie's hands up where she could see them easily. No fluids. No fur.

"No. I finished with the chickens when I saw the rabbits acting oddly." Arie started to look scared. Her mother was always calm not...wild like this.

"Stand here, by the stairs," Lauranya said grimly, moving towards the rabbits with a look of determination.

"Mom?" Arie said, hesitantly taking a step to follow.

"Stay!" Fear lacing Lauranya's voice as she swallowed metallic saliva. "Do not follow me!" Lauranya's voice snapping out the words in a harsh clipped tone. Lauranya swung back, throwing a hand up, stopping Arie in her tracks.

"But why?" Arie asked, her lower lip trembling. Her mother had never spoken to her in a tone so emotionally crippling.

"If the rabbits have Black Eye, I am going to have to put every rabbit down and quarantine this area after bleaching it."

"What's...Black Eye?"

"A virus. A virus that attacks the blood. Causing uncontrolled clotting for an unspecified time." Lauranya chewed her lip, weighing the danger with information. "It can last a day or weeks. Causing bruising around the eyes first, then blindness. The clots start blocking the veins going to the extremities, lungs and the brain. Once in the brain, small aneurysms will form." Lauranya looked at

Arie intensely. The child's eyes widened. Lauranya continued with an inhaled shuddering breath. The terror of this virus could not be overstated.

"Breathing will become labored. It will not kill, not at first, just debilitating. If not stopped quickly, brain function will deteriorate beyond any chance of recovery. Limbs will rot off. Eventually a heart attack will occur. By that time the person is a little more than a painfully breathing vegetable in a skin suit."

"Won't you get it?"

"I have been inoculated. I cannot get it. You, however, are not vaccinated. The virus is highly contagious, so you could easily get infected if you came in contact with anything the rabbits might have touched or excreted. That is why I want you to stay far back."

Arie swallowed, stepping backward until her heels barked painfully on the first riser of the stairs, her elbow banging into the banister post. "Okay, mommy." Fear making her voice as loud as a ghost whispering.

Lauranya picked up each rabbit carefully by the scruff of the neck, checking the eyes and tissue around. Lauranya straightened up slowly, putting the last rabbit down. Staring at the wall, not seeing the wall but a past medical study.

"Mom?" Arie asked hesitantly.

"Yes. They are all infected, and now I have to dispose of them all."

"Where are you going to put them?"

Lauranya shook her head, coming back to now. "Arie. Love. I am not going to put them anywhere. They are all going to be disposed of as humanly as I can provide, then their bodies will have to be removed."

"Fire usually works." Jacks spoke up, next to Arie. Even in death Jacks feared Black Eye.

"Fire is the one thing I cannot provide, without cooking which would contaminate the entire kitchen or burn down our only place of residence."

"Water drowns."

"Until a damn shark eats the rabbits or the other fish eat…" She took a deep breath to calm her heart rate, finishing the sentence. "…and fish do not catch Black Eye. Only mammals, meaning we will still have chickens" Lauranya said, with a nod towards Jacks.

"Arie, go to the supply closet and get me a metal bucket. Place the bucket to the side of the coop. Once that is done, go shower with lots of soap in as hot of water as you can stand for 30 minutes, and wait in the viewing room. Do not come out until I call for you."

Arie darted out of the room to search for the metal bucket. It took her longer than expected as the bucket was at the back of the closet. She ran back into the growing room to the sound of a loud squeal and a bone cracking snap. Her mother, lifting her foot off of a rabbit's neck holding it by the back legs. Lauranya tossed the black furred rabbit to the side, away from where Arie had been standing, on top of three other rabbits. There were 22 left.

"I…I have the bucket." Arie said, digging a toe into the wood floor, her head bowed over the loss of the not-pet-rabbits. She superstitiously wiped her eyes, running damp hands down her tunic sides.

"Thank you love, put it down over there." Lauranya waived a fur and blood covered hand to the coop, before moving to catch the next rabbit.

"How? Why now?" Lauranya muttered, as she grabbed for another rabbit. "What changed that the virus suddenly pops up now?"

"Something in their food or change in the environment?" Jacks asked, he stood well away from her, even ghosts remembered fleshy fears.

"I do not know!"

"I remember reading somewhere that some viruses seemed to almost have a timer. Years after hibernation, it popped up and out of their hiding cells ready to infect."

"I… And I cannot keep blood on hand to confirm this." Lauranya stood up with a sigh, trying to block out the rabbits crying around her. If she didn't she would start to cry, then the task would be five times longer. With a deep breath she grabbed another rabbit, finishing what another virus had started.

Culling the rabbits took less than 30 minutes, cleaning up the blood and living area took 6 hours. Lauranya pulled all the rabbit bedding out, putting it on a plastic tarp. This was then carried to the upper deck outside and tossed, plastic and all over the edge along with the dead bodies. It took three trips to remove all the bodies and anything they might have come in contact with. By the second body dump the water erupted in a frenzy of feeding fish, both small and large. The larger fish swallowing both the rabbits and smaller swarming fish.

The plastic pen sides were also carried up the stairs and dumped into the waters below. Lauranya saw several large fish chase smaller fish through the wiring getting stuck between, only to be fed on by other fish.

Next came the floor. First she had to strip her clothing off, throwing that over the edge and using a bucket of water with bleach to sluice off the blood from hands arms and legs. The towel she used to dry herself, and the floor was also tossed over the edge. She headed back downstairs once dried, rinsing the bucket out then refilling with water and bleach. Where the rabbits had been kept was scrubbed with a thick bristle plastic brush, the floor wiped dry with another towel. The floor shone brightly, the grime along with any other trace of the rabbit, washed away.

Halfway through, the mop broke from the force she used pushing. Lauranya let out a slight growl, at the delay while she had to go in search of the gripping tape. Next the stairs and the path, leading to the upper deck, were cleaned, washing backward. Another sluice for herself, everything used going over the edge. Any fish still in the vicinity when the bucket of bleach water went over floated belly up would be eaten eventually, killing their cannibalistic kin from the poisonous bleach. The circle of life fickle that way.

Lauranya made her way to the shower, for one last scrubbing. When finished, she dragged into the den. A domestic scene of calm greeted her. Arie sitting cross legged on a bright pillow at the low table doing homework, while watching an aria. Lauranya sagged against the doorsill enjoying the site, before slumping onto the couch behind the child.

Arie flashed a smile. "All clean?"

"Myself, yes. The floor and area as well." Lauranya said tiredly, wanting nothing more than to lay on the couch to never move or at least not until her bladder demanded she void.

"Mom." Arie looked at her mother solemnly, a slight crease between her eyes.

"Yes?" Lauranya looked, with heavy eyelids and drooping shoulders, at her child.

"Are we going to be safe?"

"Oh, baby!" Lauranya sat up, opening her arms. Arie walked into the welcoming embrace. "As safe as I can make us." Arie snuggled deeper.

"We're going to be short on meat," Arie said, squeezing her mother's ribs a little harder, her voice not much louder than a whisper.

"We will figure something out." Lauranya took a deep breath, remembering the feeding frenzy of the fish earlier. "Perhaps we can try our hand at fishing."

Arie sat up excitedly; Lauranya put a finger over the child's lips to stall the incoming torrent of questions. "Tomorrow, we can discuss it. Tonight, I want nothing more than to enjoy the evening."

Arie grinned "Okay, mom!"

The rest of the evening, what portion Lauranya was awake for, was spent listening to arias. Aria heard her mother's slow deep breathing from behind her. Arie just smiled, pulling a soft fuzzy blanket over her mother.

Chapter 21

The transport found the slow moving ore carrier, following their ion trail. Redeyes stood in the cockpit, listening to the pilots. "Easier than stacking cubes on the children setting." Krom, a dark furred Wolfen, showing off ropey muscular arms in his modified sleeveless black uniform shirt, giving a low chuckle, his Katherian partner flashed a toothy grin, his hackles raised in anticipation.

"They must think this area safe; they aren't even trying to hide their signature!" The disapproving response from the seated human, behind the Katherian.

"Is this normal?" Redeyes asked, leaning into the screen with a frown. The screen showed a ship four times the Marines transport size. Blocky with no outward guns.

"Only when they're transporting between ships in "safe' areas," The human pilot said, reaching over to flip lower right hand switches. Redeyes followed his hand movements, knowing she would need to learn this at some point as well.

"Why are we hitting 'em this close?" She asked, distracting herself from thinking of the fighting to come.

"Easier to find," The Katherian pilot shrugged. The two pilots exchanged glances. This was not the Redeyes they had flown with before.

"Bigger payload," Krom offered.

"What are the security measures like?" Redeyes stepped forward for a closer look at the control panel and viewer.

The Wolfen shrugged. "Usually there's a bit of a dust up. Less than 20 or so dead, a few living fighters. Kill the necros and the dead and living falling quickly in line. We get the shipment and a new almost shiny ship."

"Waste not, want not." The human had a pinched look of too few calories and a slight shake to his hands. Redeyes idly wondered if he was hooked on something, and waiting to get back to the ship to shoot up.

"We'll be in position in ten, Redeyes." The Wolfen said with a firm voice, looking at Nero.

Redeyes looked at the pilot. Krom ducked his head at her stare.

"We're leaving now," Nero said with a chuckle, taking Redeyes by the upper elbow, steering her towards the others.

"I wasn't finished." She grumped, sotto voiced.

"You were making them nervous." Nero said, just as softly. His lower left arm on her upper right.

"Something…" She made a gesture with her up her hands forming a ball "Feels weird."

"At this point, you haven't been on any raids. You're just nervous." Nero waved off her concern breezily.

"Contact in three minutes. Hats and bats people!" High Sarge rumbled out. There was a flurry of activity, putting on helms, checking straps and gathering weapons.

Collins reached over, tapping Redeyes on the knee to get her attention. "Follow us in. We'll be taking the bridge for information. Let the others do the subduing." Redeyes looked over to her other Guardians, eyes flashing human green.

Redeyes nodded, swallowing bile. The pit of her stomach burning acid, hot and cold waves going up her spine. She brushed stray bits of hair from her face. Iarris and Collins exchanged looks. Collins gave a toothy grin, while Iarris fiddled with her knives.

Collins gave a quick look over Nero and Roar. "Nero. Roar" he started.

"Aye, covering the back as usual," Nero said, bending his head to pop a tight spot on the back of his neck. "Ahhh." When the neck joint released.

Roar just gave Collins a curled lip. Collins tried staring down the older Katherian. He failed, having to blink. Roar gave him a toothy grin. Collins continued on, without skipping a beat. "Ro...Roar follow Iarris and I," Collins pointed to Nero. "You, stay next to Redeyes." He looked to the sides and the listening ears. "We'd like to keep her alive if at all possible."

"I am certainly happy to keep this one from needing a new body." Roar twitched an ear towards the Godling.

"No telling which one will come back," Nero said, flexing upper and lower hands. His claws the color of polished obsidian. Nero touched his guns lightly, ready for the run down the ramp.

Roar's tail began to flick to the side, not quite vibrating in anticipation. Iarris' tail was still only by sheer force of will.

The transport locked onto the ore ship with a thunk. The drilling team already at the acid and diamond drill, cutting into the ore transport, while forming a vacuum seal. 45 seconds and they were done and sealed, pushing the cut steel down to crush anyone waiting underneath. Marines began jumping five at a time into the ore freighter. The noise wasn't deafening, but the living and possibly the dead would have heard that.

What was supposed to be an empty corridor above the ore, filling with Runner Marines ready to take over on a lightly staffed freighter with a pilot a few guards and fewer slaves, proved to be a trap. The Marines funneled into the corridor, met with a flurry of swords or stainless steel spears glinting bright silver in the low light. The swords were bouncing off the marines' armor, but the spears were being braced against planted feet or walls, as the marines rushed in without clearing the incoming blades. The spears were punching through the incoming armored fighters.

There was nowhere for the trapped Marines on the bottom to take cover, while the Marines from the top were being pushed down. The howls of pain mixed with snarling roars of anger, climbed up through the hole reaching the first rank.

Roar ignored Collins words to wait behind, shoved to the front, pushing a smaller human to the side, dropping down into a crouch. He grabbed the harness of a luckless Wolfen already skewered. "To me! Use the dead as shields!" His voice pathed through the Marines. With one hand holding the body shield and the other wielding a disc gun, Roar started to broadcast through the deadheads mind "Down! Yield to us! Yield!"

"No time like the present," Collins yelled, dropping into the pit, hitting the ground at a rolling thump over the dead and wounded. He stood behind Roar, using the larger Guardian as a living shield while aiming to the left side. Collins shot anything fleshy or penetrable, the deadheads exposed behind their shields.

Iarris and Nero grinned. "Time to earn our keep." Iarris dropped first. Nero pulled Redeyes to the edge and dropped her unceremoniously down the makeshift shaft. Nero dropped down behind her. Redeyes curled up, throwing her hands over her head as Nero stood over her, grabbing a body for a shield while pulling out his disc gun.

Roar let out a scream of pain as a spear from one of the fallen brushed his leg. A swatch of skin and fur fell off leaving behind a raw red patch of bleeding muscle. Other's started to scream as they tried to advance, only to find poisoned coated weapons and bodies making it impossible to make headway.

One telepath with a spear in her stomach "Poisoned spears! Don't touch!" before succumbing to the poison. Her dying thought broadcast to those within an eight foot radius, taken up vocally and telepathically where possible, as the fight raged around.

Iarris dropped to all fours, crawling through the bodies to Redeyes, shaking her. "Red! You have got to do something!"

Redeyes looked at her with human green eyes, wide with huge pupils, her face frozen in fear. "Get it together girl! We need you!" Iarris slapped her, not Katherian hard but human safe hard. Redeyes snapped back then forward. The eyes bled red again as Redeyes, pulled back lips over her teeth; she reached a hand out to grab Iarris by the throat.

"Not me you fucking void brain! Them!" Iarris pointed to the wall of humans in armor so minimal it was a wonder there weren't more bodies. Until she looked down seeing for every one of the Runners there were four deadheads.

Redeyes sat up, feeling the mental muscle flex she'd use to create a hand on the ship. "Hands." She whispered. The walls shivered only slightly, missed by everyone but her and Iarris in the battle flowing over them. "Hands!" She stood screaming, ripping off her helmet. Her standing wouldn't have been noticed, but the eyes gave it away.

"Kill the false God!" The cry went up from the deadheads, taken up from those behind the frontlines. They surged forward ready to sacrifice all for the chance to kill the red-eyed god.

Redeyes let out a scream of her frustration, jumping

forward with nothing but hands and extended claws of her own. The walls and floors reacted to that final push of adrenaline in her mind, with hands sprang forth from the sides, grabbing all that trampled over them.

The metal hands grabbed arms, feet, heads, shields, swords. Metal creaked, bending under the pressure of the God guided hands. Lightweight metal armor shattered, damaging the flesh underneath even as the metal hands closed, pushing metal shards deeper into vulnerable flesh, giving way in wet chunks of bone, breaking into pieces, fragmenting under the pressure. Those trapped in front were pushed to the side, trampled by those in back, and looking to the fight, screaming to kill a god. A glassy eyed madness upon them with the need for action.

As the hands grabbed, more Marines jumped down, swimming through their dead to shoot at anything not their own. Knees, heads, hands being the most open targets. Collins and Roar keeping the right side of the corridor occupied. Roar using a body shield and his great sword, while Collins shot anything remotely likely to cause death or serious harm. The reinforcements came down; strong Katherian telepaths came through echoing Roar's mental barrage at a louder setting. This sound barrage seemed to have some effect, but not as much as they had seen in past battles.

Redeyes, flexed her hands open, the metal hand echoed her motion. Eyes narrowed, she winnowed her arms, stiffing her hands into blunt edged bludgeons. Another round of screams from new throats. A warrior stepped forward from the back, dodging the deadly new Runner induced obstacle, to throw his spear at Redeyes.

The spear by luck or aim didn't hit Redeyes as she stood there moving metal hands but slid across her cheek and across a section of scalp. The spear did hit Iarris in the biceps, as the Guardian aimed her knives in deadly accuracy at those who weren't going down to the hands. She let out a screaming snarl, reaching to pull it out when another Marine, human, grabbed her hand before it could reach the spear.

"Poison coated. Don't touch or you'll lose your hand as well!" He yelled over the din. He grabbed the tunic off the dead, spinning Iarris around, yanking on the haft under the head of the spear. He pulled the entire spear through the hole. Iarris went down to her knees; blood mixed with the drool as she bit her tongue to keep from screaming again. The human ripped another tunic into strips tying the gaping, bleeding wound.

The Marines weren't able to shoot through the new shields. The discs hit and stuck. Normally the recoil would have knocked the shield holding person down if the disc hadn't gone through the shield, but this time the warriors weren't budging.

"Ricochet the damn things!" High Sarge yelled, snarling frustration, while 'pathing the same command. Shooting as fast as she could pull the trigger, High Sarge aimed at the side of the wall, bouncing the fast spinning discs into the back and sides of the deadhead warriors. The deadheads were unprotected on their flanks and backsides, High Sarge's disk causing massive shredding damage.

The deadhead warriors kept fighting, even when the remaining few were swarmed by the Marines. They asked for no quarter but kept on until the last one took a dagger between the ribs, collapsing with blood bubbling between snarling lips.

"Disc to the head so we don't get any undead coming from behind or rising up while we're patching up!" High Sarge 'pathed and yelled to her crew. There weren't any groans or bitching as bodies were rolled over and a disc planted between the eyes. A testament to how unnerved this raid had gone ship raping sideways.

"Spacing hate guts between the toes," Nero growled, mincing his way to Redeyes through the dead bodies, blood and guts squelching loudly, coating the fur up to his ankles in dark red clots. He didn't shake his foot to get rid of the goo; other globs would just adhere at the next step. So each step was a splotch over wet and firm or wet and gooey. Little of the freighter's floor could be seen through the litter of bodies.

Redeyes had sagged to her knees, head bent. Her pants coated in blood. The various cuts from sword and spear healed with teardrop crystals of blood, like glued on red jewels in odd patterns against pale skin.

Collins was besides Iarris, holding her hand while a coagulant was applied to her free bleeding wound. Roar dropped the Wolfen he had used as a shield. The young Marine who had gotten their armor, eyes open in surprise from death. Roar knew he would see the cub's face in dreams but right now he was too damn tired to do more than motion forward a medic to tend his own wounds.

"There are more where this came from." High Sarge said, shoving the bodies to the side. "We'll need to keep moving down."

"Still?" Collins asked.

High Sarge translated this. "Yes, we still need to move down to take the ship. We need the damn ore."

Redeyes looked up at Nero's furred hand on her shoulder. "Hundreds dead."

"Aye and we've got more to kill," Nero said, lifting his kilt out of the bodies as he squatted next to her. "We're going to have to do this again and again, depending on how many of the damn deadheads are left."

Redeyes raised a hand to her face, to wipe off a drop of

sweat beading down her forehead. The blood coating her hands, not hers obviously, leaving a smear across her skin, bright red on translucent skin. The smell of battle had merged during the fight, but the blood smeared on her face brought the copper scent of blood and poison too close, setting her staggering away from Nero and into the viscera coated wall. Her hands, arms and back slammed into the wall. Blood, wet and sticky, coating her.

"Redeyes?" Nero reached a hand out to her. She pulled her hands away to stare at the blood, human green eyes wide, breathing shallow of the copper scent and loosened bowls. Redeyes began to shake, her body convulsing as she dropped to her knees again on top of three dead, caught by her lower hands outstretched while her upper hands clutched her head. She raised her head letting loose a keen so piercing the Wolfens and Katherians covered their ears to block the painful sound.

"Redeyes!" Nero jumped to his feet, but didn't rush to her side. Collins alerted to Nero's voice, scrambled to his feet, pulling his pistol out, checking the discs inside. But it was Roar who pulled them both back.

"Don't!" Roar yelled, yanking them back hard enough that Nero lost his footing. He landed with an "Oof" of lost breath as he thumped into the solid Katherian. Collins didn't resist the pulling for once by Roar but kept his pistol pointed at Redeyes. Roar pulled them closer to the other Marines, who were slowly backing away from their convulsing god.

Armor bulged as skin split, muscles and bone rearranging into a much larger being than the human that had stood there. White fur, chest height on a human, six legs and dark red eyes.

"Gods love what the hell did she do?" High Sarge whispered in awe.

"Shifted."

"Looks like a Wolfen but less person like."

"She calls it her werewolf form." Roar breathed in awe. He'd only heard about this from retired fighters in his own time but had never seen the change until now.

Redeyes tried to shake the armor from her, not all of the armor was willing to let go, clinging with tenacity of velcro and ties. Where she could reach, her jaws snapped through the ties. With the chest and arm ties snapped, she squirmed out of the leg armor. Walking towards the hall doorway, blood and viscera coating her legs where she stood, streaking along her.

She sniffed at the door, standing on her hind legs to look upwards. She dropped down with a huff. Redeyes looked over her shoulder, letting out a snort. Turning back to the door and then looking over her shoulder again.

"Umm. Roar? What does she want?" Collins asked cautiously, accepting more ammunition passed over his shoulder from a Marine from behind him.

Redeyes growled, twitching an ear at her Guardians.

"She wants us to follow." Roar said grimly, ears flattening, before bending over to rip off a dead Marines tunic, pulling out his knife to cut strips. Redeyes growled again, with a little more force.

"Woman, wait. We need to fix our armor and get more ammunition. Not to mention we're light on troops." Roar snapped as he wrapped his hands in the bloodied strips. He bent down again, flipping over bodies to find guns, ammunition and non-deadhead weaponry. Redeyes grumped at him but waited, shifting from foot to foot. A small squishing sound with each shift.

The Marines moved the bodies to the side. Touching only their own, leveraging the deadheads with boots or dead Marines. Anything cloth from their own was removed and ripped into strips.

"Okay, people! Wrap what you can that's exposed and re-supply from the dead. We're backing up the Guardians." High Sarge snapped to the marines. "Let's get this black hole moving people!"

"Injured ones, High Sarge?" Nero asked mid-rip of a former Marines pants.

"If they can walk and shoot they come with. Anyone else back to the ship. Be ready to leave and pass on this data." High Sarge looked over the survivors. A quarter flat out dead and another third too injured to continue. Leaving her less than 60 to take over the ship with Gods only knew how many necro humping deadheads.

Roar approached his shifted God with slow steps, his eyes not meeting hers. Non challenging. "Gods fucking, woman, I hope to hell you know what you're doing." He muttered.

The wolf snapped at his fingers. Roar pulled back his fingers, looking down. She opened her eyes wide, and then pointed to the door, letting out a woof.

"Okaaaay. So you want through." He ran a hand through his mane, examining the grey metal door. The lock was keyed to an electronic key as well as a hand or multiple handprints. No easy exit.

Nero came up behind Roar, looking at the lock. "You'll need someone to see to that." He said blandly.

"Really?" Roar snapped, turning to the Wolfen but stopped mid-turn. His hand reached out to touch the closing seam. The door hadn't closed properly. Broken bit of metal had lodged in the door keeping it from sealing tightly.

"Too bad we don't have a telekinetic to open this eh?" Nero said, looking down at Redeyes, with an open mouth grinned.

Redeyes growled, flicking her ear dismissing him.

"Seriously, are you trying to get yourself killed or are you just irritating to be an ass?" Roar ran his hands along the seam.

"High Sarge! We need a spreader." Nero yelled over his shoulder ignoring Roar's comment for the moment.

"Manual or electronic?" She snapped back, squatting beside one Marine with a hole the size of a human fist in his thigh. "Just missed the vein on that. But you won't be fighting for a few months until it heals." She patted the Wolfen on the head as another Marine stuffed cloth into the wound, tying it off with another strip of fabric.

"Electronic if we have it...not sure how much of a ferrous comet this is going to be for manual." Nero yelled back.

"You heard the damn Wolfen! Get a spreader bar for that voiding door now!" High Sarge rose to her feet, with a soft growl.

The spreader bar came down through the hole, looking like a square wrench 10 feet long and 4 feet wide at the mouth. There were tines at the ends, hair thin that widened to the size a Wolfen's hand closer to the base. It took 5 muscle bound Marines, mixed races, on each side to steady it while Okayzona punched in the commands.

"Split the snake!" She yelled, stepping back. The spreader was eased into the narrow opening. The bars pulled while those holding the bars pushed. The wider the opening, the more the spreader was shoved in. Each inch fought for, in squealing gears and exhausted Marines.

Redeyes hovered near the doors, close enough her nose touched the back of a Wolfen Marine as he strained to keep the spreader up and pushing in.

The Marine gave a startled yelp, causing a ripple along the line as he dropped his part of the spreader, spinning in place to beat the crap out of a rising deadhead. His swinging fists barely missed Roar who stepped backward just out of range. The marine seeing it was just Redeyes didn't make him any less nervous, just more twitching with the shifted god at his heels.

"Red…" The werewolf ignored him. Roar bent down, tapping the god on her thick furry head. The wolf turned growling. Roar looked down through the bone eyes slits of his mask. "Back the hells up so they can work. You're scaring the piss out of 'em."

"More like making them drop the spreader, wasting time," Nero commented, as he looked over his pistol from a few feet away.

Redeyes chuffed at them both, but she did back up, as far as the hallway would let her, until her tail hit the cold side wall. Her eyes remained glued on the door as it inched open. Roar grabbed her scruff, as she gave a slight quiver, bending over her. "Don't even think of leaving us behind!" He growled low in her ear. She snapped wetly at his face, her teeth clicking loudly, missing his broad nose by inches. He released her ruff but kept a hand on her head, lightly. Redeyes growled but didn't shake off his hand.

The door widened to human shoulder width, when Redeyes barked sharply, heading through the door.

"Father fucking snake!" Roar and Nero took off, edging sideways through the door, Collins and Iarris bringing up the rear. The hallway was clear, bare metal with scrapes and gouges telling of a long history, a hallway T intersection ten feet from the door. No Redeyes in sight. Roar motioned Nero and Iarris to the other side, Collins with him on the left.

They approached the intersection cautiously. There were screams and a clatter of metal on metal with the sound of wet crunching, then quiet. The Guardians moved a little faster. Nero slipped a small mirrored piece of steel from his belt pouch; the size of a child's head, tiny, in his huge hands, checking around the corner without exposing his head. Roar waited for the all clear. Nero slipped the steel back into his pouch, motioning them forward. Roar had a hand on his gun, when they heard screaming further along the left-hand side of the hall.

Blood and torn bodies met them 20 feet down. Gore coated the walls, with most of the bodies unmoving. Most. One kept trying to stand missing a leg at the knee and the opposite foot. The woman turned at their approaching footsteps, her throat torn out, yet she kept trying to stand.

"Zombie," Roar whispered in disgust taking aim, as Collins beat him to the punch, blowing a disc sized hole in the middle of her forehead. The body dropped; a puppet without strings.

They moved forward, following the trail of bodies and screams. Right, straight, left, right, straight.

"Nova, you'd think she'd run out of bodies by now," Nero said softly, at the fourth pile.

"She's not saving anything for us to kill. Damn God." Collins said, annoyed at the lack of action.

"Something's just not right with you." Roar snapped, looking down at the human standing next to him.

"Yeah...I'm more ready to kill then you or Nero," Collins said, with an easy smile. "That makes me the better person here?"

"Psycho more like it." Roar replied.

"Vacuum or space. Not much difference." Iarris growled.

They continued down one of the endless worn corridors, following Redeyes' bloody footprints. They found her sitting at a door, her skin and muscles bulging in disturbing ways as she tried to shift and kept failing. She saw them and growled, pawing at the sealed door in front of them. Her claws raking against the metal, leaving lighter scored markings on the dark battle steel.

"Where do you think we are?" Nero asked.

"We've traveled, as much as possible, straight...so best guess is the bridge." Roar said, touching his sword and gun.

Collins checked the remaining discs in his guns. "Good to go here."

Iarris nodded her readiness, Nero flicked an ear, both sets of hands holding disc pistols the size of a well fed human's thigh and a bitch of a recoil.

Redeyes couldn't get her shift to complete, but she could shift into something not human and not wolf. A mockery of a Wolfen, with thin patchy fur with bones pushed against pale skin. Not quite human by any means, it was enough though. She placed all 4 sets of hands on the seam of the door, her crescent shaped nails sliding into the indentation where the doors met, pulling.

On any normal given ship, not even a werewolf would have been able to pull open the doors, Redeyes managed to put enough telekinesis in her hybrid form, moving the doors.

Roar moved to the right side, giving Redeyes more room, pulling Nero, who watched Redeyes shifting with a sick fascination, next to him. Iarris and Collins followed suit to the opposite side, not wanting to be in the middle of opening doors.

The remaining Marines came running through the corridor, double time or as double time as injured soldiers could. High Sarge took one look at the situation and started to 'path orders, splitting them in half on each side of the door. The door opened, the hydraulics squealing protest at the abuse, but open they did.

Spears thrust through the door, nailing Redeyes in the side and stomach, as the fighters attacked from inside. Roar fired his disc gun through the door, his gun arm angled awkwardly while he freed his sword, bringing the battle steel blade down on the steel spears. High Sarge and her merry band of killers shot through the door at anything that looked remotely fleshy.

Luckily for Redeyes, the cuts were only inches deep, not piercing all the way through. The werewolf form healed the cuts as they happened. However, not all spears were cut or knocked from their owners' hands. Redeyes grabbed, with clawed hands almost paws, the spears thrusting through. She ripped them out of the owner's hands or pulled the owner through the door. Once through the door, the fighter was dispatched by a variety of weapons.

The fight lasted a few minutes until nothing but screaming and moaning attacked their ears.

"Get in there and clean this up!" High Sarge roared, ducking through the door, sweeping her gun to either side clearing the corners. The troops flooded the room, finishing off the wounded. Collins followed behind, running hands over the shot up controls.

"It's a bar. There's no flying this anywhere." Collins said in disgust, pushing a chained pilot off the boards only to have the body dangle by handcuffs, still in his way. Collins gave the body a vicious kick in annoyance.

"We'll take it back and scrap what we can't recycle," Iarris said, searching through the non-fighting bodies for usable blades.

"Is there even ore on this thing?" High Sarge asked, wiping her knife blade on a dead fighter's tunic. The front of her armor painted red in sheeted blood, the freshest dripping slowly down her front and face. There was no cleaning anything at this point, except the weapons, until they were back on the ship.

"We'll need a detail to go and look," Iarris said grimly, looking up with three different types of shivs in her hands.

"With a possibility of another round of fighting," Nero commented from the side, counting his ammo, while watching Redeyes shift back to wolf form.

"Wonderful." Roar said, wiping a hand over his face, leaving red streaks in matted fur and mane, shaking off the blood with little success.

Redeyes whined at the door, shaking from head to tail. Her red streaked fur shed both hair and droplets of blood. Roar looked up tiredly from the bodies at her, wiping his blade on a not too dirty tunic. "Time to move on?" He asked of the God.

With a jerk of her chin, Redeyes moved towards the door once more.

"Fuck me," Collins growled, in fair imitation of Nero bass growl.

"Not tonight dear, I'm too tired." Nero said, standing straighter to follow their God.

Iarris snorted laughter, but moved to follow the others, when High Sarge handed her a pistol. "You might need this."

"You know I can't," Iarris said, lifting palms up, refusing the gun.

"This one doesn't know jack about your sentence." High Sarge snapped, pushing the gun at Iarris again.

"No, but the others do and a gun is a hard habit to break again."

"I'd like to not bury another of Khina's daughters." High Sarge said sliding the pistol back into her hip holster.

"I'd like to keep my skin in one piece as well." Iarris touched High Sarge's arm with two fingers, before turning back to her God.

"Anyone you can spare for this gear hunt, High Sarge?" Roar asked, looking at the others, weighing their injuries to another pitched battle.

"Take any 10 of your choice and don't get them killed." High Sarge said, grabbing her stat phone. "Need to figure how to get this rod home without flying it."

"Think we need to figure out if there are any more left first." Roar said off handedly, holding his sword to eye level checking the edge for nicks.

"Would be better if we know for sure it's carrying ore or we're just flying a rod." High Sarge snapped.

Roar pulled out three uninjured and 7 others in various states of walking wounded who could keep up. He didn't take all of High Sarge's uninjured, just enough if things got hairy down below.

"Okay, Redeyes, let's get this going." Roar pointed to his God, sitting by the door shifting from paw to paw impatiently. "Some of us need medical attention."

Redeyes tilted her head for them to follow, before sliding out the door. "Follow her. Don't get in front of or next to unless you want to lose a knee cap." Roar said, chivying the Marines through.

They followed her through the empty corridors with fading lights and dented walls. Redeyes paced a little in front of them but didn't run off as she had previously. Occasionally they would see stains along the floor or wall. Some identifiable as blood, others less easily discerned.

Redeyes stopped dead in her tracks, whining.

"What? Why are you…?" Then the smell hit Roar full on. He gagged at the smell of rot. "Stop!" he gasped. The others with acute smell started to gag and cough as well. Collins and Imma were the only two humans to not catch the smell strongly; human noses immune to scents unlike the Katherian and Wolfens.

Roar motioned them ahead.

"That's a first." Collins gave a sly smile as he glided forward, pistol held out, steadied with his off hand. He and Imma made it another 15 feet before the full strength hit them.

"Holy first ships!" Imma gagged. Collins started sucking air through his teeth, but kept moving forward. The cargo hold didn't have ore, but it did have bodies, stacked like cordwood, 5x the amount of fighters than they had actually fought.

"Looks like we were supposed to drop in on all of these."

"Can you imagine how this would have gone if we had found them earlier?"

"What killed them?" Collins asked, poking one greying corpse with the barrel of his gun.

"Whatever they are coated in that cut through us would be my guess." Roar said grimly, noting the slight greasy sheen the bodies all wore.

"Why would they poison their own?"

"They're vacuum crazy." Roar coughed, making a face at the rotting meat and shit smell. "Back to High Sarge."

Once back on the deadhead bridge, High Sarge listened closely tugging on one strand of her mane. "Take three of the bodies back, wrapped in body bags. Medical can isolate what the nova they are coated in. Maybe we can get an antidote. After that, we're going to blow the ship."

"No scavenging?"

"You want to clean the poison off every surface before we incorporate the metal on our ships?" High Sarge looked at several of the faces. "No? Good, let's give these sons of vacuum back to their undead gods."

Once back on the ship, Redeyes started to growl and

whine, her skin writhing as if something living were crawling underneath.

"Back! Get away from her!" Roar yelled, yanking High Sarge back as Redeyes shifted slowly painfully, with bones and muscles popping in weird strange ways.

"Oh Gods...I think I'm going to be sick." One of the marines whispered loudly.

"Look away then." Roar snapped, watching Redeyes carefully, High Sarge still pulled against him, both forgetting their antipathy at the horror happening in front of them.

The whine became an inhuman scream warped and undulating as the vocal cords changed with the shifting throat until a hoarse scream was all the human god could manage once fur had become naked skin.

"Medic now!" Roar yelled, pushing High Sarge to the side in his rush to get to Redeyes' side. High Sarge stumbled a step at the abruptness and her own lack of belief, leaving her too stunned to process. The screaming stopped as Redeyes arms gave way, hitting her face on the floor grill.

"Collins, hand me your shirt." Roar said, still not touching the God, keeping other hands from helping or touching. Collins started untying and pulling armor off.

"When the nova did she start doing that?!" Iarris whispered.

Roar looked up startled, his hand an inch from Redeyes' back. "She's never shifted in front of you?" Those closest all shook their head. Roar looked to the Guardians. "You either?"

Collins pulled his shirt off in one smooth motion over his head. "Never. Looked like it hurt like hell."

"She always said it hurt doing the shift but it was the shift back to human that hurt the worst." Roar said, not trying to dress Redeyes, just wrapping the shirt around her as he gently picked her up to put in Nero's larger lap. "Something about all the mass re-fitting into human."

"So this is something not new, just new to us."

"Void…" was all Roar said.

Collins leaned over to Roar in a sotto voice soft enough to carry only to the Katherian, barely a whisper. "We're going to have to talk about why she's shifting now and not before this set of Guardians."

"Agreed."

"Show's over people. Get strapped in so we can get home and get our drinking face on." High Sarge belted out to the Marines. A flurry of activity as the survivors settled in for the trip back and mourning for dead companions could start.

Chapter 22

Lauranya looked at the chickens in disgust, with hands on hip scowling. "I should let Arie cook you all up if it were not for the fact we like your eggs." Lauranya bent down, picking up the pieces to the newly hatched chicks the non-brooding hens had decided were tasty moving snacks. The cannibalistic hens watched at her expectantly for more treats, with red and gold irises. They clucked to each other every time she retrieved another bit of chick piece. A few of the bolder ones tried snatching the small globes from her hand, only to scatter when she flicked their beaks.

Arie sat on the stairs, crying inconsolably at the death of the 11 small lives. "Mom...we...we need to do something." Arie wailed, wiping her nose on the short tunic she wore.

"Yes, yes we do," Lauranya said, dumping the red bits of meat and down into a bucket. "They need more protein in their diet. We've been skimping on feeding them fish. Which means they're going after the chicks." She let out an annoyed sigh.

"But we give them rabbit scraps!" Arie wiped away another tear on the back of her hand.

"Obviously not enough to meet their dietary needs." Lauranya straightened up with a heavy sigh. "We can't let them continue eating the chicks or all chicks become food. We're going to need a nursery area, preferably closed off somewhere in here to keep these birds from eating their successors." The bucket weighed nothing, but the heaviness from the deaths was hard to bear. They needed the next generation and quickly. All but one incubator had died a ship's 10 days ago. And the remaining incubator held only 15 eggs at a time. Lauranya tried to fix the others, but Okayu was having none of it. His help was withdrawn from the machines. Protein in egg form was excellent, but the hens were laying less and less frequently. This meant a new round of hens needed to be hatched, with the older hens being cycled into a stew pot. This would keep the flock at a healthy size with the limited feed source.

"We have metal couch frames leftover from taking off the leather," Arie said meekly, watching her mother pick up another set of small bloody down chunks.

Lauranya looked at Arie for a second before the translation kicked in. "Ahh...the couches." She had to consider this for a moment. "We could...cover one to keep the chicks in and the chickens out."

"What if we wove something between? Like leather." Arie asked excitedly, brushing the last of her tears away to come and help. She took rags from the cleaning bucket to wipe up the spilled blood, her face scrunching up.

"All the leather was used my dear," Lauranya said gently, trying to forestall another round of tears. "Though we might be able to use something other than leather. Sheets?" She mused to herself out loud. "No, we will need those to sleep on. What are we not using that weaves?" She chewed a lip staring at the supply rooms mentally scrolling through items still remaining.

"We have more couches to spare other than the one in our den room."

"I do not want to denude all the leather just yet,"

Lauranya said, with a smile. A heavy sigh. "Time to feed the fish."

"They'll like the little pieces," Arie said woefully, sniffling slightly again, as her eyes started to brim over.

"If we could catch the fish we would not need to worry quite so much." Lauranya let out a heavy sigh. Raising their crops and livestock held unexpected surprises she still found frustrating at time.

"How did they do it on the ships?" Arie tilted her head to the side in curiosity.

"Large tanks with seine nets with space for the little fish to swim through, catching only the largest harvestable fish."

"Could we make nets for fishing?"

Lauranya started to say no, stopping before the words left her mouth. Nets would solve two problems. Netting over a board cage to keep the non-broody hens out and a net or nets to gather fish. Then the question of how to make such netting came full circle.

"We need to find something to make nets out of, dear. Something I do not have the knowledge for." Lauranya mused aloud.

"Who would?"

"Those who would know are either on planet or died recently for you to ask." was the crisp reply.

"The computer would," Arie said.

"True, yet you asked who." Lauranya gave her child a teasing grin.

"Mom!" The almost eye roll "You're being silly now."

"Learn to ask precisely, my dear."

During lunch, Lauranya found references to skein netting used polymer fibers which she did not have. She tapped her foot staring at the wall. "What can be used? What do we have a plentitude of that we will not need for another project?"

"You have several rolls of 2mm wire in the storage room." Jacks whispered in Lauranya's ear.

"Aiyyeee!" Lauranya squeaked at his voice. Jacks smirked at her, just as he had in life. "Damn it Jacks! You could at least give me warning next time! Giving me more grey hairs than the All Mother!"

"Your beauty is more transcendent than hers."

"Flatterer." Lauranya gave him a half smile, and then frowned at his first comment. "Would wire work? I thought the net had to be flexible."

"Depends on what you want it for. Netting over chicks would work well. For fish you could make a netted box with bait, then an opening that fed into a wider cage that the fish couldn't swim out of."

"That!" Lauranya broke into a grin. "If you were alive, I would hug you."

"I'd have preferred a kiss." He said, with an almost sad smile.

"I would not want to be on the receiving end of your wife's ire!" Lauranya turned from him, to head back downstairs to the holding room. "Will have to spend time learning to shape the wire. Thank you again, Jacks."

"And to you, love." Jacks whispered out of Lauranya's hearing, fading slowly.

Lauranya found the spools in a box of other random bits. She spent half a day stripping the stuffing from the denuded couches to just their metal frames. The frames were of lightweight aluminum, easily moved and hard to bend, or at least with bare hands. One would make a large size pen for the chicks the other a fishing trap. If this worked and there was enough wire, they could have more than one fish trap going at a time.

Here she had to visualize the games that her

grandfather trained the gladiators for. There was one where fighters or animals were funneled through a shoot but those leaving could not return. Either the door closed behind them or guards would stand with spears facing outward ready to skewer anything returning.

For the fish, a doorway wouldn't be practical, no way to control the opening and closing but an open tunnel with tines pointing outward, sharpish, would discourage swimming back out. The fish wouldn't need height but she would need depth to make a chute for the fish to get through.

Now she just had to form the netting portion.

She looked at the wire as if it would speak to her. The wire didn't speak to her, lying tightly wound waiting for her to create. She glared at the spools with pursed lips.

"Fine. I will see what can be done with you." Lauranya gathered the spools together, heading back to the lab. She stopped halfway up the stairs, throwing a hand over her mouth. "I need adult conversation, talking to inanimate objects is not healthy!" She shook her head, continuing upwards, vowing to correct this new trend of hers.

It took 30 days to make netting that wouldn't unravel or knot up while weaving into shape. Arie scavenged through the supply rooms for arm length pieces of metal. She took the pieces upstairs to the stone balustrade to sharpen one set of ends that would keep the fish from swimming out of the cage. Lauranya made the first net large enough to cover half of a couch. She and Arie sacrificed two sheets. One sheet was ripped into strips to tie the netting over the frame, while the other sheet was made into a makeshift doorway, tied into place with well-spaced pinned on ties every 6 inches. Lauranya and Arie would pick the largest three eggs every other day, placing them in the last working incubator for the next few days for a new and younger flock of layers. Most of the roosters would be eaten at a young and tender age. They would leave two roosters alive for fertilization diversity for a year, continuing the breeding cycle.

The fishing trap took a little longer to make. There were a few false starts and two complete weaving failures. Each failure spurred Lauranya on to get the weaving right.

Arie was watching her mother weave the netting, paying more attention to the weaving than her homework. "How are we going to get that into the water?" She asked as her mother's hands formed connected loops steadily.

Lauranya looked up from her silent counting of the loop in the rows. "I had planned on having one of the zombies place it or hang it off the side of the roof to dangle a few feet below the water surface." She went back to her task. "I don't know which area would be better for collecting fish."

"Should we ask one of the mer?"

"We released their souls dear. What you have are husks who obey, not thinking beings anymore."

"Oh." Arie's shoulders slumped in disappointment.

The first placement, hanging a few feet in the water next to the building, caught a much larger fish than anticipated. The fish swam into the trap, getting stuck on the prongs as it entered the much smaller opening than its body. The thrashing attracted other predators that tore into the fish and trap netting, several fish getting stuck in the netting along with the original fish.

Sachiko brought the metal frame up to the top of the stairwell, which was still in perfect shape. The netting was a little less usable as there were gaping holes the size of Arie's torso where fish had torn through the netting to get at those inside.

Lauranya breathed a prayer to the water god.

"Perhaps have it carried down to the bottom floor?" Arie said, running fingers along the large holes.

"Probably a better idea." Lauranya made a face at the damaged trap.

It didn't take Lauranya nearly as long to repair the netting. The woven netting spaced into equal sizes, the knots tighter than the previous attempts. She also found several cables, one with a connector large enough to go round one of the couch's bars that was also long enough to dangle over the side of the roof.

Arie tried cooking up the fish that they'd retrieved from the damaged trap's maiden catch. Her first attempt ended in burnt flesh and a smoky kitchen, leaving her in tears.

Lauranya gave her daughter a long hug. "Easy, easy. We have an ocean of fish. One night of not eating well will not kill us.

"But I, the fish died to feed us and I ruined…" Arie couldn't string words together.

"Hush." Lauranya stepped back, having to bend only slightly, to look her daughter in the eyes. "One failure does not the future make. We will try again tomorrow. Yes?"

Arie wiped her eyes on the back of her hand, staring at the floor, but she nodded. "Yes."

"That's my girl. Now let us eat what we can salvage."

The chickens ate well that night on burnt flaky white fish, while Lauranya and Arie had fruit in sweetened grains.

Chapter 23

Redeyes woke in her rooms, hurting in every joint. Her muscles felt like she had been the piñata at a wedding. She didn't move quickly out of bed, thinking of her home gone so many years. The mage who had brought her over had been killed when that world exploded, her first death. "God I could use a sugar powdered cookie right about now. Fuck, I'd take some dark chocolate while I'm thinking of what I can't have." She muttered to herself, pulling the covers off.

Nero walked in as she moved to sit up. No knock, the only warning the whoosh of the door opening.

"Need to put a lock on that door." She groaned, moving her legs over the side of the bed. "Why the hell do I hurt so badly."

"Nova, no locks please," Nero said, stepping to the side, holding out a hand to help her up. "We'd never be able to get here in time to take out whatever you were dreaming or shoot you if your dreams were too damn dangerous." He chose to ignore the second question, for the moment.

Redeyes looked up with a frown. Her hand in his massive hand, she had admired the blunted black nails that went well with the dark tan and black patched palm.

"How many times have you had to shoot your way in here?"

Nero pulled her up. "Three so far." Steadying her.

"Once you were already dying. Speared by something that looked like a cross between a tree and something with a water bulb for a head." His hand closed over her's with little shakes before he took a deep breath continuing. "The other two times, you woke up screaming and everything that was ghosting into reality just...evaporated."

"So you mainline, when you know there aren't going to be dreams." Redeyes finished for him.

"Yep." Flick of the ear, dismissing the past. "You need a shower, then it's time for a debrief with Cratt and the others Generals with their Gods."

"Thought Cratt was in command of the ship?"

"He is and isn't."

Redeyes gave him a frown.

"Shower while I talk. You smell like a pit whore who's been snorting 3 days straight." Nero said, waving an upper hand in front of his nose.

"Perhaps if you had better taste in company you wouldn't know that smell," Redeyes said primly, gathering her dignity around her with a lift of the chin and a straightening of her spine.

"Rough childhood and friends," Was all Nero replied, handing her into the shower column.

Six feet in circumference, stainless steel with water jetting out of square cut holes in the wall. The column showed scratches and dents on the inside like a cage match or 15 had taken place inside. She didn't ask, just grateful the hot water was working and it wasn't another cold shower day.

"So start talking," Redeyes yelled, pulling her head out of the hot water sheeting over her head.

"Every God is in charge of the world-ship they live on. The only one who can override any other God, is you."

"Convenient," Redeyes muttered, pulling a squirt of

soap from the small recess in the column. "Keeps the other Gods from inviting you over for meat and beer," Nero half yelled, scrounging for a towel in the shelving closet set into the wall.

"Can't imagine why. Do I override often?" She ducked back under the water, scrubbing sore muscles with the gritty soap, smelling lavender and leather.

"You do have a tendency to shoot other Gods when they start trying to become like the Undead Gods." Nero replied with a straight face.

Redeyes looked up and out from her shower with a frown. "Happens often?" She had an arm over her head, dripping soap while looking at Nero in disbelief.

Nero tilted his head, thinking. "Twice so far," Was all he said.

"And Cratt?"

"When a ship doesn't have a God, the acting General of the ship is in charge under your command."

Redeyes did the connections. "So Cratt is acting in the interim until I've got a better grasp of who is who and who needs to be shot."

"Pretty much," Nero handed her a towel when the water shut off.

"When is the meeting?"

"Three hours."

"Good. I have a project for you," Redeyes tossed her whiter than snow hair out of her eyes. "No mainlining until tonight please."

"Pfft," Nero snorted. "Will it actually call for all of my attention?"

"I certainly hope so!" Redeyes threw the towel over a hook before rummaging through the closet shelves for a pair of folded pants, shirt and overtunic. "Fuck...where are the damn bras and panties."

"You mean the ones that you didn't bother storing before we went snipe hunting?"

"Hey! I planned on putting those up when I got back. Not being tossed into the bed and beaten with a sack of potatoes."

"Uh huh," Nero fished through a small pile of clean laundry on the bench next to the shower, where the unfolded clothes had been dumped, tossing her the requested under garments. "You don't remember shifting into a wolf?"

Redeyes froze, her hands dribbling clothes as she just stopped moving. "I shifted?"

"Yes. Much to our surprise."

"Was anyone killed?" She asked, in a breathy voice. It took Nero a second to figure out why. Fear. Redeyes was terrified she had killed one of her own. Nero discovered two things. Redeyes could be scared of something and she cared for them. It took him a moment to find his own voice at this.

"No," Nero patted her shoulder awkwardly, trying to comfort the new God.

"Good enough then." Redeyes took a deep breath, closing green eyes. Twice more until her shoulders were no longer hunching and her feet no longer touched the floor.

Finished they headed out to the main room. Roar had laid out a lunch of grains, vegetables and a portion of meat. Roland limped to the counter, adding another dish of sweetened fruit.

"Late start," Redeyes said wryly, grabbing a plate, filing in behind Collins. Nero fell in behind her.

"We let you sleep in," Iarris said, from the living area seats, sitting down to eat her own lunch. The gauze bandage a stark white against her arm's lovely tawny fur.

Redeyes frowned, noticing the bandage was three times the size of the wound she remembered.

"The hole got bigger," Was all Iarris said, balancing the plate on her knee while using her good arm to lift the fork with.

"Meeting with Cratt later," Collins said through a fork full in his mouth, pulling Redeyes' attention back to the kitchen area. Roar growled when Collins tried to grab another bite with his fingers, flattening his ears at Collins rudeness.

"Use the damn spoons. You aren't a slave and I know you have better manners," Roar said, snapping the offending hand with the dishcloth he held. The towel landed, with enough momentum to leave a stinging red mark behind.

"This is Collins you're talking about. One too many blows to the head as a Marine," Nero said, from the relative safe spot behind Redeyes.

Collins glared but took the spoon Roar motioned to, keeping the fork in his mouth while giving a three finger salute to the Katherian with his other hand. Roland rolled his eyes, flipping his tail in irritation.

As they sat down to eat, each nursing various wounds except Nero and Collins. Redeyes spoke up. "I have a job for Nero. Roar and Iarris, you two are too wounded to wander guard at this time, Collins you're following me to the meeting with Cratt and the others."

Silence greeted this with various levels of wide eyes, flat ears and stunned disbelief. Collins choked on the bit of vegetable going down his throat. Iarris pounded him, gently on the back to clear the windpipe, humans were usually unable to handle a full Katherian pounding.

"If you take Collins into the meeting, you'll piss off three of the Gods and at least 5 of the generals," Nero said, motioning with the fork, dripping sauce on his leg fur. "Space!" he growled, moving the fork back over the plate, wiping the mess with his lower right hand.

"Roar would be a better choice," Iarris said, handing Nero an extra napkin. "As long as he doesn't open his mouth or talk about female breeders." With a flick of her ear towards the bigger male.

"Damned with faint praise?" Roar said mildly, not bothering to look up from his own plate.

"Nothing else from you Roar?" Redeyes asked curiously, pushing the food around on her plate not quite up to eating yet.

"Nope. You're going to do what you want, unless there is a major life threatening reason not to and even then, that's touch and go." Roar shrugged, taking a casual bite of food from the plate in front of him.

"Collins?"

It took Collins a moment to clear his air passage but he motioned with his fork between Iarris and Roar. "Either is better."

Redeyes nodded. "Good, we're settled. Nero and Collins with me." She took a bite of meat mixed with a savory pale blue sauce that hinted at tartness.

"Roar! Talk sense into her," Iarris growled, her tail twitching in irritation. Redeyes took a big bite, grinning.

Roar looked up from his lunch to his God. "You're doing this to see how people react, aren't you."

"Got it in one," Was all she said, saluting him with her now empty fork.

Roar looked at Collins. "Try not to get shot or in a duel." Was all he said with a shrug, before concentrating on his own food.

Collins looked glumly down at his plate. "Easy for you to say. Not your favored nephew I shot because he was a drug spaced void getting Marines killed."

"Or seriously wounding or sometimes killing Challengers just because you could. Which humiliated several captains and generals," Iarris quipped, before taking another bite of lunch.

"Hide behind Redeyes. Might help a little," Nero suggested, dropping his lower jaw in a full Wolfen grin.

"Thanks all of you for your helpful comments." Collins' sarcasm was ignored.

"So what's my project?" Nero asked as they headed to the elevator shafts. Only a few people walking by, so Nero wasn't keeping his voice low.

"You're going to take me to the bridge, or wherever it is communications are done and I want you to track any incoming or outgoing calls that look suspicious. Times and people."

"Metal, that'll take a few hours to go through all the logs for today." Nero flicked an ear at her motioning to the left hallway. "Usually you navigate the ships better than your Guardians."

"Living on the ships decades longer than we've been alive helps, I'm sure," Collins grumbled. "For the last 40 plus years. Last 2 months first then work backward by years," Redeyes responded.

Nero stopped dead in his tracks, a young human bouncing off him as the taller heavier Wolfen didn't move out of oncoming traffic. "Years. Communication in years? Do you spacing know how many communiques we do daily?!" He just stared at her, people flowing around them.

"Not a clue, but if there is a way to do this and find a shortcut you are the ma...Wolfen," Redeyes said breezily with a wave of her hand tugging on his tunic to get him moving again.

Nero dragged a hand down his broad face as he followed slowly. "Shoot me now Collins please. This is going to be worse than…"

"Not worse than her nightmares, that's for fragging sure." Most of the hallway travelers giving the God a wide berth.

"Fine. But with me doing this and not at practice you're now designated as a punching bag."

"Ugh. Trade you places?" Collins asked hopefully, a bright smile and wide charming eyes.

"Not even. Those Generals are going to eat her and you alive."

"Bastard."

"MY" Nero made the full emphasis on the word "parents were married."

Collins shrugged. "They had good sex, was all my dad would say."

Iarris ignored the older Katherian as only a female could, disdain and indifference emanating from her like heat from her fur. She gracefully folded herself onto the couch, leaning on her side, with a flat screen in her hand. Delicately chewing one nail, before scrolling to the next page.

Roar kept busy for a few moments, putting the last of the dishes up, prepping what he could for the evening meal.

"Reading?" Roar asked, trying to alleviate the oppressing silence.

"Yes." Tail twitch.

"Anything good?"

"Possibly." Another twitch of her tail.

"Ignoring me?"

"Trying to." Growling, her ears half flattened.

Roar grinned, knowing he was batting the other Guardian at this point. He didn't think she'd shoot him but only because Redeyes told her not to, but he wasn't going to push her too far. Too far being relative.

"Going to lie down." Roar said, with a yawn. "Getting old in my dotage." He headed to the closet sized room where his bunk was. A full stomach and a wounded leg made the cramped room seem appealing for once.

"Mmmhmmm." Iarris flicked an ear at him, trying to lose herself in the historical texts. Three of the books dealt with the rise of Katherian antipathy towards humans and world-ships as a disease, the other as a crowding aspect alleviated only with more space and more "outdoor" type of environments to combat the metal worlds that were unnatural for all beings trapped inside.

Iarris flipped between the four texts getting more annoyed at the dieses spouting authorities. "Who writes these pieces of scat?" Iarris grumped. The writers were no one she had heard but the fourth writer espousing more room for everyone was...Redeyes.

"Well that explains a lot," Iarris chewed a nail thoughtfully. "How many texts did she write?" She queried the ship's computer system. 31 all told, texts of various lengths and over various subjects. Some over 300 years old.

"Why am I just now reading these?" Iarris growled, under her breath. Skimming the overviews each text seemed as relevant today if not more so than at the time of their writing. "Nova, this would seriously help to get the younger God up to date with subjects she'll have to deal with later. But why have I not seen these before?"

A knock at the door distracted her; she realized the

knock had occurred a couple times prior. Cratt may be early to collect Redeyes and he didn't have authorization to just walk in.

"Death tarok ke it," She flowed off the couch to open the door. It wasn't Cratt but one of the oddities. "Redeyes isn't here." Iarris snapped to the first male. Morris and his two brothers rounded the door, pushing her aside. "Hey! Get the space out you aberrations!" Iarris snapped.

One slammed her against the wall, the other pinned her throat with a knife. "We aren't here for Redeyes, just...you." He rubbed a chin against her, burying his nose in her hair. One clawed hand sliding along her stomach, his nails scratching along her clenching muscles.

Iarris recoiled as much as possible, the centimeter in space giving her just enough room rather than feeling skin on skin slimy contact. She twisted hands to get to her daggers.

The other two put hands on her arms and hips, pinning her against the wall, waiting their turn. Iarris tried pushing back, lifting a leg to kick out a knee, when she felt a tentacle wrap around her legs tightly, moving her legs apart.

"I do like a good struggle when everyone is still fresh." The one in front purred into her ear. He tightened his hand on her hips, nails dimpling her skin. "Please keep fighting." His whisper/growled into her ear. She could feel his excitement, in his voice, in his touch and his body.

Iarris wasn't a great telepath but she could 'path short range bursts. She started to panic pathing, bursts of screams to anyone who might be close.

One of the brothers slammed a fist into the side of her head, knocking her into the sniffing brother. "No screaming," He growled, as her head swam, stars floating through her sight.

"We don't want any company but us for this little date of ours." This brother began to mentally push against her. Boxing her thoughts in, his mental pushes causing small bursts of pain as she tried to keep pathing.

Morris put a hand on her hips leaning in, the tips of his claws scratching skin through her fur. "We won't take too much of your time. Just enough to make it fun for us all." He smiled wide showing teeth, but his eyes were crinkled enjoying the pain and humiliation they were going to inflict. "Torriense will make sure that you remember enjoying it." He purred at her, a half smile lifting full human lips off Katherian sharp fangs.

Iarris' eyes showed only a thin rim of iris; her pupils dilated to their fullest.

The sound of a disc gun cocking froze the three brothers.

"There won't be any fun today or any other day," Roar growled. "Get the hells out of here or I will have Redeyes skin you alive and make boots out of your metal burr ridden hides."

"Where the fuck did you come…" Torriense started but didn't get to finish as Roar swiveled and shot him in the stomach. He went down screaming, clutching the torn skin and guts. Blood flowed through his hands, sheeting down tan furry legs onto metal flooring.

"You have 15 minutes to get him to medical before he bleeds out." Roar pointed at Morris. "I suggest you get moving before the next shot goes through the brain pan." Roar growled low and dangerously, showed a wide toothy smile, belying his flat ears and slashing tail.

The brothers half turned towards Roar, stepping away from Iarris. One smiled, holding up a hand placating, the other hand hidden by his body reaching for an illegal two shooter.

Released, Iarris' face contorted in a soundless snarl. She slipped a dagger from her hip sheath, stabbing downwards between the neck and shoulder at the closest brother. The dagger sank to the hilt, six inches deep in muscle and tendon. So sharp, severing everything touched, including the carotid artery. He went down with a scream, dropping the machine shopped pop disc gun and clawing ineffectually at the dagger as Iarris twisted it, cutting through the front of his neck to the other side. Blood gushed over her, him, the walls and floors. Iarris stepped back, pulling the dagger with her as his moans and cries got weaker. He was dead, just hadn't given death his soul yet.

Morris jumped backward, hands feeling towards the door, attempting to escape when a blade sprouted from his eye socket. Iarris threw two more. Both hit on either side of the neck, cutting through the arteries. Morris fell backward in slow motion, his head hitting the doorway as his knees gave and he went down. Iarris fur bristled out, as her tail lashed. Her growls filled the living space echoing against the walls.

"Looks like we only need medical for one," Roar said taking a step towards brother #2 who still writhed on the floor. His screams silenced by the sudden deaths of his other two brothers.

"Should've raped you after you took out Shisha," He whispered as Iarris stalked towards him with claws extended, her tail lashing, like a fur covered avenging battle goddess covered in blood and gore.

Iarris bent over, grabbing his head between her hands, twisting and pulling as hard and fast as she could. There was an audible snap. The body joined the other two, this one looking over his shoulder instead of forward. Iarris began to shake, the adrenaline and terror running their course.

"Iarris, are…" Roar started, when she bolted to the bathroom, bloody footprints marking her path. Roar heard her retching through the open door. "I guess not."

There was a knock at the door. Roar stepped over the bodies carefully before answering. The gun held at his hip ready to shoot.

Cratt stood there with a fist raised ready to knock again. He took in the scene of Roar holding a gun with a frown, and then he noticed the bodies.

"Doing some redecorating?" Cratt asked with a raised eyebrow, crossing arms over his barrel chest.

"Not by choice." Roar put the gun up, snapping on the safety before stepping back to make way for Cratt to walk in.

"Causing trouble? Or were you just short tempered?" Cratt asked, observing the carnage. He didn't step in. Blood pools were still expanding, moving towards the door and hallway.

"They came for Iarris. She wasn't interested." Roar turned his back to Cratt, surveying the damage with a small smile.

Cratt took a moment to survey the bodies. "Four knives. You take out the one with the neck?"

"Iarris took them all. I only got to gut shoot one before she broke his neck," Roar said, with real pride in his voice.

"She ok?"

"In the bathroom." He flicked an ear towards the back set of rooms.

"Roar, who's…" Iarris came out, a towel in hand as she dried off her face. The other hand held another dagger.

"Just me," Cratt said with a nod, taking in the blood spatter gore still covering her fur. "Rearranging the place I see."

"We're going to need a cleaning crew," She growled, as her fur started to spike again. She sat at the kitchen counter knowing there would be questions soon.

"Aye." Cratt pulled out a stat phone. "I'll get this taken care of now."

Roar walked to the kitchen to pull a few things out, making a fast plate of meat and sweet carbs. "Nice work." was all he said as he handed her the dish.

Iarris looked at the plate with revulsion, pulling back her lips, pushing it away.

"You just lost all of your lunch and breakfast. You're going to be hungry in 30. Shaking in 15," Roar said, leaving the plate between them with a level gaze.

"I don't need to be space fucking coddled," She snapped, claws extending scraping against the metal top as she half rose from her seat.

"Fact, not coddling," Roar motioned to the bodies Crat was walking around, speaking into the stat phone. "That was damn fine work in the killing."

"Shouldn't have happened in the first place," She grumbled, sitting down, only slightly mollified.

"Everyone gets jumped at least once." He gave her an open lower jaw grin. "Just make it once though." He flicked an ear towards the General, lowering his voice to a conspirator whisper. "Don't think Cratt approves of me killing."

"Hey those are my kills! No claiming those for yourself." Iarris gave a ghost of a smile. She speared a slice of meat with her fingers, popping into her mouth, licking her fingers clean.

"Pfft. I have my own kill count. We'll talk totals in a few more years. You might," he stressed the word with a finger against the side of his broad muzzle, letting her in on the joke, "have caught up to my younger, more indiscreet, days."

Cratt came to join them on the tag end of this sentence, raising an eyebrow looking between the two. "Cleaning crew is on their way. I'll need to take a statement but it seems pretty cut and dry what happened."He made a face. "Should get rid of the other four but they are damn useful on raids."

"Why did Redeyes have them made?" Iarris growled, around a mouthful of sweet bread.

"She didn't. Genetic anomaly with the birth mother's DNA. Ricca is working to stabilize the gene sequence when humans and Katherian have kids. One or the other, not another type of hybrid," Cratt said looking away from Roar and Iarris as well as the bodies.

"Ricca?" Roar tilted his head looking at Cratt, unfamiliar with the name.

"Chief of Medical. She's been working with Redeyes on genes and stabilization for a while." Cratt shook his head as he pursed his lips. "She and her team only answer to Redeyes. No other oversight."

"You think she's going to add some type that would be injurious." Roar's ears started to lower.

"Redeyes, never. Ricca may go overboard." Cratt waved a hand towards the bodies. "This litter was a one off. Not to be reproduced again."

"Not if Redeyes is touching Ricca's chin on every genetic piece," Iarris said, swallowing the last bite of meat, reaching for the sweets.

"True. Ricca is a fanatic but a well collard one." Cratt tugged on his left earlobe in frustration. "So the real reason I'm here, instead of cleaning up the bodies, Redeyes."

Roar and Iarris exchanged looks. Iarris took another bite, leaving the talking to Roar. He flicked an ear at her, huffing slightly in annoyance.

"She took the boys for a walk. Something about a project, with Nero doing the research and Collins as her Guardian of choice for the meeting." Roar said blandly.

"What?!" Cratt stabbed a finger at Iarris "Did you explain to her WHY this is going to go nova in just 3 minutes?"

Iarris licked her whiskers, her tail lashing before answering. "Yes. All of us. At least twice."

"Why the hells." Cratt threw up his hands, as his face went red looking between the two of them for a sane response, he wasn't going to get.

"She's a God. And will do what she thinks is best." Roar said blandly, giving the pristine metal counter another swipe.

"Fuck me with a freighter." Was all Cratt managed as Redeyes and Collins walked in.

Redeyes stopped dead in her tracks. Collins sidestepped, surveying the damage, walking over to Iarris. "Good work, darlin'. Two out of three." He touched her chin with fingertips. Iarris leaned in with a purr.

"Three out of three," Roar said, arching his whiskers.

Collins turned back with a closer look. "Damn girl. Remind me to never piss you off." He grinned back at Iarris, who ducked her head with a faint smile. Collins covered her hand with his. He frowned in concern, feeling the small tremors. Iarris shook her head, giving his hand a slight squeeze. Collins didn't ask, knowing she'd talk when she was ready.

Cratt looked over at Redeyes. "Red? You got this?" Redeyes facial bones began to flex and bulge.

Redeyes looked up through human eyes. "I need to step back. The blood...smells..." She spun and stepped back through the door, letting it shut behind her.

Frowning Cratt turned towards the Guardians.

"Shifting?"

"She's just now coming into that." Roar said, his lips pressed thin.

"Nova. Just what I need. Blood hungry young shapeshifter." Cratt groused.

"Perhaps you should explain the ups and downs, not to mention how the void to control it?" Roar said, with biting sarcasm. "Nothing like a hungry werewolf around a lot of tasty fleshy types."

"One problem at a time." Cratt snapped, moving towards the door. "Have an assembly with the other ships to attend."

"That's my cue." Collins gave Iarris hand one last squeeze before following Cratt out the door.

Chapter 24

Brother watched the swift grey clouds moving over the beach with a troubled look. His full lips thinned as their bigger siblings lumbered behind, both larger and darker, dense with rain. He let a handful of dry leaves fall from his hand, watching the slow pattern they made in the wind as they drifted downwards.

"How bad will this one be?" Nathan yelled, from the dark churning water. He twirled a skein net over his head, tossing with ease of practice. The muscles in his arms were bunching and un-bunching, showing a high level of muscle detailing. Nathan like many of the other islanders was hip deep in the warm water, keeping the pull line in hand, with his sarong pulled up high but not high enough to keep dry.

Brother looked back to the village leader. "Bad. Could wash this beach away and more than a few huts." Brother wasn't seeing Nathan; he was seeing the last huge storm 61 years past. The village had lost huts and a few lives in that storm. Nathan hadn't been born until a few years later, had only heard the stories, but he knew the risks of a major storm.

"Shelter in the caves, eh?" Nathan watched as his net settled under the waves before pulling on the line which closed the weighted ends forming a closed net around anything caught under and in the skein.

"Better hope no one is allergic to Wolfen or Kat hair." A fishing woman said, with a wink and a grin to their

Katherian.

Treasher stood on a jutting rock, the ocean breeze ruffling his buff striped fur like grass in a field. He waded further out than the skein fishers with a fist-thick reed fishing spear at the ready. "Only on your bad days, Nikka!" He grinned, flashing fang towards her before scanning deeper the waters below him for a fish to swim close enough.

"Gods, I am tired of fish." Corlin groaned from the side, pulling out a large red fish and a handful of shrimp from his skein.

"Until we find what the void has been killing off the goats, it's the best protein we've got. And we have a lot of mouths to feed." Nathan snapped, anger his response for worry.

The unlucky recipient ducked his head. "I know...I just want to eat it without it tasting so...fishy is all!"

"As much as you go down on your wife, I'd think you'd like the taste of fish!" Another jibbed, as she tossed her skein net into the water. Not as gracefully as Nathan but with competence in her well-muscled arms.

"Not the same!" He protested, to the giggles and laughter of those fishing near enough to hear the exchange. "I'd rather be eating pork anyway."

"We lost most of the damn pigs to the last deluging rain. Need to give 'em time to breed." Nathan said, trying for stern but failing as he too was laughing.

"I'll get the message out that the Grenich will be having the village cooped up with him in a couple of days and everyone should pack up the essentials." Brother commented to Nathan as he pulled in his haul.

"We'll need to get medical packed up." Another said further up along the new beach.

"Aye, I'll get Mauri moved first then pack up my

own." Nathan looked towards the clouds before speaking to Brother once more. "Any news from the Mers on any more lost members?" He motioned towards the east where the unseen tower stood, where the darkest of the clouds were heading towards them.

"Nothing more than the four they think were lost in that area already." Brother frowned with his jaw muscles clenching. Nathan knew that worried look.

"I'm sure your girls will be fine. They seem not to want anything to do with the tower."

Brother gave a shake of his head with a slight snort. "My girls," emphasizing the words with a roll of his eyes showing how much they were not his. "Would rather be hunting than exploring that tower under any circumstances. The chief's demand no one go back scared the scales off of most of the mers as is." Still, he looked at the distant horizon as if he could conjure up the tower by staring hard enough.

Brother took deep breaths trying to work out the knots in his stomach. The woman and her child still haunted his dreams. The unknown; who knew more than Brother about this world and the space above them.

Did they still live? Sister's vision seemed to point that way. How were they surviving? There had only been one report of that area since Sister's bones hovered. Singing voices floating over the water and nothing since. Even that report had been whispered into his ear, fear of the Chief's anger very real. Brother took a deep breath, letting it out slowly. Nothing he could do even if the Sight had said not to.

Chapter 25

"Sunshine!" General Mesan's voice boomed through the shuttle bay. "Your team ready?" The large Wolfen asked, pounding Sunshine on the back.

Sunshine staggered under the backslap, coughing. "Ready as we're going to be, sir." He said, coughing with lips pulled back containing the rest of his surly response.

"Good good! We're just about finished loading." Mesan nodded towards Leaf, who was overseeing the last of the deadheads shuffle on board. The men and women could barely muster more than a few tears, one glared at Sunshine when he looked over the line of humans being forced back onto the shuttle. The dark skinned pilot. She was quick to look at the floor, shuffling along with the others when he caught her eyes.

The deadheads captain and second in command were brought in by stretcher. Sunshine called in a favor. A medic came to the loading bay under the guise of gathering DNA, with cheek swabs from those moving towards the transport. He had pulled the medic to the side, where she had taken pity on their ill acquired wounds, applying pain meds surreptitiously, where none of Zorax's cronies could see, she gave Sunshine a quick nod before moving on to the last few. He palmed her the last of his ship's credits for her use when they left.

Mesan looked over the mixed crew Sunshine had assembled, loading supplies while the God's Guardians pushed and shoved the last of deadheads onto the ship.

"Light crew."

"Didn't want this to be something so large I couldn't keep it...tight."

The General nodded, "Good idea." He turned back to Sunshine, giving him a lazy two-fingered salute off his brow. "I'll leave it to you." He sauntered out the dock, calling out for the Zorax's Guardians to follow. "Leave that to the Marines. They need something to do today!"

The Guardians, mostly humans, were only too happy to leave the job to the Sunshine's crew. One gave a viscous backstroke with the butt of her gun to one deadhead moving a little slower than the rest. "Voiding deadhead. Should have shot you when there was time." She growled before joining her fellow Guardians.

The man, down on all fours, wheezed hard before, climbing to his feet unsteadily. Those next to him helped him stand up. The pilot wrapped an arm around his waist, helping him to stagger up the ramps.

Sunshine's crew watched the interaction, not interfering. They went back to loading faster. Sunshine meandered over to Leaf, touching her on the wrist. A conversation both 'pathed and spoken for those close by.

"Think they saw the extra supplies?" Sunshine thought, touching Leaf lightly on the wrist with two fingers.

"Guardians ever anything but less than helpful?" Leaf asked, with arched whiskers.

With a snort, Sunshine rolled his eyes with his response. "No, they were too busy getting their kicks in on the deadheads."

"Why the General pulled them?" Leaf responded

"We're getting into the extra extras now."

"We have a plan?" Leaf asked, her tone bored,

motioning to the passengers with her chin.

"Getting the hell away from here to finish our work," Sunshine said, hooking thumbs into his pistol belt, rocking up on his toes then down again. Nervous.

Leaf glared at him pulling lips back from sharp teeth. "Co-ordinates?" Her tail stub lashed. "Stop that; you look nervous." She gave him a mental slap before continuing. "I don't want to be spacing lost for space dusting ever."

Sunshine winced but stopped rising on his toes. "Phen has all current maps and the general location of where we need to go for this mission." Continuing in private "Check with Iggy on how much longer he needs on supplies."

With a nod, Leaf flicked an ear towards Sunshine, "Going to see what else needs to be done for this shuttle raping mission." She raised her voice, barking to the crew loading supplies. "Come on people...move it! We don't have all the ship hours just to be standing around."

Sunshine started hustling the last of the deadhead stragglers into the ship when Leaf 'pathed him an unwelcome message.

"Bralli is on his way to you."

"What does that incompetent voider want now," Sunshine muttered, but not low enough to keep from being heard as he turned around, almost into the doctor's chest.

Brallie gave Sunshine a grim tight-lipped sour look. "Should learn to keep your mouth shut, Sergeant." Bralli smacked Sunshine in the chest with a message pad. "I was told you were signing off on all the prisoners. And you specifically requested I not accompany you!"

"Get your feelings hurt?" Sunshine asked, with a roll of his eyes, turning away when Bralli grabbed him by the arm.

Sunshine looked down at Bralli's arm, then into the doctor's face. Bralli let go as if Sunshine's arm was scorching hot.

"You know, you have to sign off on my work before I can go back to the main ship offices." Bralli crossed his arms over his chest. "And to do that I need another 400 hours of ship time. With you!" This time the disdain couldn't be missed, with the look down the nose or the haughty tone.

"You'll get those hours doc. But this trip won't be needing your tender ministries."

"The deadheads," Again a sneering curl to his thin dark lips "...are about to keel over. I was told…"

"You're not coming on this trip. Go back to the main crew deck and wait until we get back."

"But…"

"Shove a nova core up your tight incompetent pissant ass." Sunshine stepped up to Bralli, toe to toe with him. "You're not coming on this mission if I have to shoot you in the leg to keep you here." Sunshine looked up with his own snarl, poking a stiff finger into the doctor's stomach. "Now get the fuck away from them and my crew." Sunshine stepped back with a glare, a hand on his disc gun.

"I plan to take this to General Mesan!" Bralli said tightly. Shame and anger causing his skin to flush even darker.

"Who the spacing do you think I asked that you stay here?" Sunshine said, with a dismissing wave of the hand. "Now get off the deck." This time he unclipped the pistol holster. Bralli glared but took the threat as it was meant. Serious. He turned and did his human best to stalk away. Stiff legged and tight shoulder.

"Looks like a teenager that got his hand slapped," Iggy said, pushing a hoverjack past Sunshine, filled with unmarked metal and plastic crates.

"As long as he gets the void away from me, I'm good." Sunshine turned his back on Bralli to give a narrow eyed look at Iggy. "You got everything loaded?"

"Yep. Last load now."

Sunshine gave the nod, taking a deep breath. No coming back from this one. "Leaf! Round 'em up. We're gone."

"You heard the Sergeant! Everyone on board. Move, move, move!" Leaf bellowed at the top of her lungs.

Phen yelled down from the cockpit as Leaf secured the door. "I need another fucking pilot or do you want me to crash this pov? Or better yet, get us voiding lost?"

Leaf and Sunshine looked at each other. Sunshine sighed. "Coming." He walked over to the deadhead pilot. "Think you can help pilot one of these."

She just looked at him blankly. "Pilot this?" She asked in confusion. "Thought you were going to kill us." In drawn breaths around her.

"Aye, we are going to die if we don't have a second pilot. And Phen is screaming for another. Think you can help?" Sunshine asked, opening his hands as he asked. Nothing to hide.

She sucked in her lips, before nodding. It was Sunshine's turn to let out a breath. He helped her unbuckle, walking her to the cockpit. "Phen this is..." Here Sunshine stopped. "I, umm...don't know your name."

"Light."

"Light?" Sunshine asked, almost gaping.

"Light in the dark of the night." She said with a ghost of a smile. "So Light."

Phen nodded. "Phen." He held out his right upper hand for her to shake, large enough to swallow her hand twice over. Light looked at him with huge pupils, but she took his hand not to shake but lacing her fingers through his.

Phen and Sunshine looked at each other.

"Did I insult you?" Light pulled back, only her shoulders shaking slightly gave away her fear.

"No, a handshake is like this." Phen demonstrated with Sunshine. "It's an introduction."

"Oh. Good to know." She said faintly, trying again when Phen stuck out his hand.

"Great, Light. Here is what I need from you…" Phen said briskly, ignoring his co-pilots fear as he started running over the controls getting his co-pilot up to speed.

Sunshine took the hint, beating a retreat back to the hold. "Leaf?"

"All strapped in."

"Phen, we're good to go back here. Take us up and out!" Sunshine grabbed his seat, buckling in quickly.

The ship eased out of the world-ship, Infinite Elysium as smooth as a newborn human. The several deadheads started weeping. "Sarge?"

"Get them food and water. Make sure we have calming meds in the water if possible."

"Their captain and second are in bad shape."

"Internal?"

"Not that medical listed."

"Pain meds and keep their bandages clean. We can't do snake raping anything at this moment." Sunshine looked around at his crew of too few and the deadheads. "Gods, I hope She's in a forgiving mood."

"Or a killing one," Leaf 'pathed back.

Chapter 26

The storm exceeded all prior established measurements, Lauranya had seen. The windows shook as thunder and waves battered their tower. Lightning replaced sunlight as the primary illumination through the shaking windows. Luckily the solar generators had been at full when the storm rolled in. The tower's top floor glowed in the dark of the storm, like a beacon even with visibility severely curtailed.

Lauranya and Arie watched the storm roll in, Arie with delight, Lauranya with concern. The clouds gathered slowly, one fluffy smoke puff at a time, darkening over the hours, wet and heavy. The homemade barometer originally gave them a few hours before the main storm hit. Everything that could be dragged to the upper hall was. All that was left were the extra fruit trees Lauranya was growing from seeds; over the last few years. An experiment, inside conditions vs. outside conditions for growing, along with a few vining vegetables that had their fruits harvested, even if green, and would be left to a watery fate.

"Can't we replant the trees?" Arie asked, pulling plums from her favorite flowering tree, wind slapping her sarong along her bare legs and back with stinging force.

"We are out of space inside, my love," Lauranya replied, pulling sweet and sour tomatoes from the vine along the north wall. "When the storm is over, we will try to pour out the excess water if the trees and vines haven't blown away."

"You don't sound hopeful, mom."

"This storm," Lauranya was not sure how to frame her reply, responded cautiously "has a dense, heavy feel. Stronger than even the first storms of the deluge." She gestured upwards to the flat roiling clouds above.

They managed to get most of the fruits in before the worst of the storm hit. Lauranya cast one look over her shoulder; lips pressed thin at the loss of the outside harvest. Time and labor lost to the storm. Nothing to do but take what they could, and pray to Oko for a chance to regrow next season. The door slammed closed with a resounding thud, muted by a window-shaking boom of thunder.

It wasn't until the storm was well established, passing directly overhead Arie realized there was a problem with the birds.

"Mom! We have a couple of birds outside!" Arie ran to the door, before being caught by Lauranya around the waist.

"They are gone, or they will be wet and waiting when the storm passes," Lauranya said firmly, looking into her child's tear-bright eyes.

"But…"

"Nothing we can do," Lauranya replied, guiding the child down the stairs by shoulders. "We will salvage what we can when the storm is over."

The storm exceeded even Lauranya's fears. The waves crashed into the building taller than the windows during the height of the storm's worst pounding. The waves would hit the windows, for a moment Lauranya and Arie would see the deep green depths brought to their eye height. The waves would occasionally be populated with occasional fish, but usually the detritus from the new ocean floor bed, bits of branches, occasional brick or former items from the now removed population. Once a large fish speared through from the trunk of a long-dead tree hit the window, only to be tossed around like the ocean's plaything, before sinking out of sight.

Water running dribbling down the stairs was Lauranya's first clue the door's exterior seal was being overloaded with the barrage of water. Her foot landed in a small puddle on the upper floor before their bedroom suite.

"Olokun! Spare us your love today!" Lauranya swore to the God of oceans, as her eyes followed the trail of pooling water to the stairs.

Lauranya took a deep breath, using her diaphragm as she called out "Arie! Grab towels and sponges." Lauranya's voice echoed throughout their living quarters, from the upper floor to the lower, bouncing off of walls. The chickens stopped to cock their heads, and then shudder as the voice resounded into their area. The bees hovered where they were before zooming up the stairs en-mass. The clump of bees stopped when Lauranya's voice stopped, falling apart into individuals once more.

Arie dropped the small fluff ball of chick she was examining, to respond in kind. Her voice was a yell instead of a lyrical projection, untrained potential still growing. "Coming!"

Lauranya heard Arie, as she made a mad dash up the dark stairs, her arms filled with towels from the bathroom, dropping a towel every few feet to absorb the trickling stream. At the door, she dropped her remaining towels in an untidy heap, except for one. That one she twisted from both ends, before laying at the edge of the door. The door wasn't spewing water; a small, steady trickle could be felt along the edges, singular drops that ran together. The remaining towels were put to the same task, absorbing the errant water as it dribbled in.

Arie climbed the stairs, slowly. She stopped, pulling the dropped towels over the stairs covering the already formed puddles. "Think I got the puddles covered, mom." handing a sponge to her mother over her shoulder.

Lauranya sat back to look at the towels on the floor accepting the sponge. "I think we are going to need to drain the towels and water the plants extra today. Well as long as the storm continues." She amended.

"How often will we need to wring out the towels?"

Lauranya chewed her lower lip. "The leak is fairly slow. I would say every 2 hours, maybe."

"When we're sleeping?"

"I'll set an alarm. I would rather wring out the towels than have warped floors with mold and mildew growing where we cannot see the damage easily."

"I can help!" Arie said, with youthful enthusiasm.

Lauranya looked back to her almost adult daughter with raised eyebrows. "Are you sure? Because this has to be done and on time."

Arie nodded, with enthusiasm. "I can!" She defended her original statement.

"Well then. Let us get a bucket and start a timer." Lauranya rose gracefully from her knees with little enthusiasm for the long task ahead.

Arie whooped in excitement, dashing to the lab to grab a bucket, not grasping the extent of work the task would require.

Lauranya had a better sense of what was going to happen. For the next three days, they would alternate who walked to the deck door, picking up sodden towels or sodden sponges, wring the saturated material into a bucket, laying each layer back down again, then proceeding to the bottom floor where the plants were to pour the filled bucket, alternating planters so as not to overwater any one section.

"This job isn't any fun," Arie said, crawling next to her mother on the couch the second day of the storm. "My back and arms hurt!"

"You could make two trips instead of one," Lauranya said, wrapping an arm around her child sleepily. The screen was playing one of their favorite singers, an opera on the goddess Yemoja. The Goddess had just blessed the last 25 of the first 100 humans with the gift of children, as the first animals found mankind to be a tasty snack.

"Then I would have to work longer." Came the muffled indigent reply.

"Yes, dear. The job is not fun, and it is hard on the back and arms. Sleep now." Lauranya adjusted the blanket to cover them both as she closed her eyes again to sleep before her turn at towel duty. Soft child snores answered her. Lauranya gave a slight chuckle, drifting back to sleep.

Chapter 27

Hunting had gotten worse due to the change in sea elevation. The mers normal area was becoming overfished, so parties were sent out for fresh habitats. Illig and his uncle struck outwards, looking for shoals of fish and new oyster and clam beds. The islanders were willing to exchange a lot for good oysters not to mention the mollusks were excellent eating anytime for anyone.

Illig kept dashing through the water, feeling the current on his skin and along his gills.

"Illig, damn it don't leave me behind, shrimp brain." His uncle groused from behind.

"Catch up old fish! We have to get your spear back eh?" Illig said, with a swish of his tail chasing the grouper through murky waters. The blood leaving a faint trail in the water, leading through drowned trees. Half the forest already down in the murky bottom, the other half swaying dangerously in the currents. They would fall soon; the bottom feeders would grow fat.

A grouper swam lazily from deeper waters. 500 pounds of prime fish, 500 pounds with barbs along the spinal ridge the dorsal fins and sides. Few would mess with this bad boy and he knew it. Fat, sassy and king of his watery domain until Illig got a look at him.

Illig let out a whoop and darted towards the grouper. The grouper paid no attention other than to slide slightly to the side to nibble on a better seaweed patch. Illig swam close with his coral head spear to stab the king grouper in the side. The hit was almost perfect. Almost. The king took offense sideswiping Illig with barbs along his side as he made a run for it in the dark waters.

"Are you spacing kidding me?" Uncle snapped, catching up to Illig. His hair a dark frothing halo, as Illig scented the water for blood. "This is a world-ship of a fish when we only needed a damn darter. No need to load ourselves down with this monster."

"It'll feed everyone tonight." Illig countered with a flashing grin and a flair of fin. "Why kill many when just one will do!"

"Damn it, boy, I'm too old and fat to be chasing grouper through new waters." his uncle grumbled, his tail pushing as strongly if not as quickly, only a meter behind his exuberant nephew.

"Old probably, but fat never. The flat heads would have eaten you already!" Illig darted right as he caught the blood scent again. The hunt was on. Illig and his uncle would harry the fish until it dropped, being too big to just spear and go.

The grouper had shot out from behind an odd outcropping, hidden by seaweed, darting towards the surface. Well as darting as a 500-pound grouper could be. Illig pushed harder, his uncle now yards behind. Illig could still see his hand on the spear when the wave pushed him down then rolled him into the curl. Spinning so hard and fast he could no longer tell up from down. Trees that were already loose from years of water at their roots were uprooted with the violence in the storm's waves. They joined Illig and Uncle in the spin.

Illig spun into rocks, fish and uprooted trees. He was slammed into sharp-edged rocks; his fingers latched onto the edging pulling him down to the stone as the wave crashed overhead. The outcropping afforded some protection from the incoming pounding, but not always from the receding edge.

Chapter 28

Collins walked three steps behind Redeyes and the General, trying to minimize the initial reaction. Redeyes could be counted on to draw the eyes to her most times, letting others fade into the background. The small room was set up like an amphitheater for 16. Four rows of four chairs. Each chair tier could accommodate one of each race. Each row had a table running the length of the chairs with inset computer screens for note taking and typed conversations. The front of the room was monopolized by an 18 x 18-foot screen.

Redeyes and Cratt walked into the meeting late. Their entry was made without fanfare, yet all side screen discussions stopped, not with Redeyes' entry but with Collins. Redeyes looked at the screens for a moment before finding her seat, center row, standing over the computer, looking over the Gods in front of her. Cratt sat two rows up and to the right. The Katherian sized chair matching his barrel-chested bulk better than the smaller human-sized chairs. He started typing as soon as he sat down, the keys tapping loud in the room's relative emptiness.

Two techs, a male Wolfen, with an almost Katherian tawny gold fur, and his shorter human female partner with dark skin but blond loosely curling hair, were setting up the screen for each ship, 8 in total. Each ship had one General and at least one God, sometimes three Gods. The screen was split so each General and the Gods had their own section on the main screen. There were 32 3x3 blocks. Four blocks were blank, showing green screen. Each screen had person and ship listed in white lettering underneath. The techs looked at each other and squared off, shaking a fist at each other chest height 3 times before making a symbol with their hand.

"Space me!" The female tech said, with a sour expression.

"Yes!" The Wolfen gave a fist pump of his upper left arm, walking out the door with only the briefest glance of pity for the woman stuck with the General and their God.

Collins looked over the remaining tech, doing a quick pat-down search, finding no guns, only the usual array of tools. He dismissed her, letting her take up her position on the other side of the chair row. She was level with Redeyes, ready to fix any computer glitch during the conference at a moment's notice. The techs eyes were glued to her tablet while one hand would occasionally touch her tool belt, a nervous habit in such august company.

Collins stood at the door, visible with his back resting against the wall, so he had to look at the screen over his left shoulder. His stance screamed bored, though his eyes moved from one side of the room to the other while taking in the screen.

Cratt's message floated across Redeyes screen. She looked down, reading Cratt's message, making a slight face. She didn't turn and stick her tongue out, by space forged steel-will alone.

The surprising silence of Redeyes' Guardian choice wore off quickly. "You bring that murdering son of a father fucking hound to this meeting…" One General started.

"Stop," Redeyes said, not taking her seat. She looked

over them her eyes touching briefly on each one. "All of my Guardians are killers. He stays, or you go. End of discussion."

There were angry mutters from several of those present. The General who had started, Nefra from the ship Starbuck, half rose from her seat. Her pupils had narrowed to slits in pale icy green eyes. She tried to bore holes through Redeyes skull but failed as the God smiled faintly at the other female's anger.

"Any of your other Guardians would have been better choices." One Katherian General said mildly, with a flick of her dark colored ears. General Gynx from the ship Troubled Skies. She tapped silver capped nails on the edge of her table. The silver capped nails contrasting with her dark furred hands, muzzle, and ears. Her fur was as silver as the nail caps otherwise.

"Not all of them," Redeyes said mildly, with a tilt of her head. "Two have been injured, and one is on assignment." She clarified to those on screen.

General Nefra narrowed her eyes, moving from the God in front of her to the General. "New Redeyes, Cratt?"

"Same as last discussion and the same for the last few years," Cratt said with a shrug hooking thumbs into his wide disc belt. "Alive, cognizant, sane, and able to lead raids."

"Pity." A man with a narrow chin and dark irises in bulging eyes said, blowing on thin pale skinned hands. A clay cup with bronze shimmer, sat to his left, an ostentatious display of luxury. The others had globes or at best metal mugs within hands reach but nothing so rare on display for just a meeting.

"Zorax, just because you'd like to shoot her every other 10 days isn't news. Perhaps you could shut the void up for a day period." An acid growl from a cinnamon furred Wolfen on the ship Celestial Navigator.

Zorax gave a slight shrug tugging on thin lips. "We'd get more done if we weren't perpetually catching her up to the new ways."

"Or when she hands you your head for being a stupid black hole of…" Nefra growled, flat-eared at the human God.

"Stop." Redeyes' voice cut through the chatter. "The agenda for the day, if you would. We all have places to be."

Again the silence and shifting of eyes. Redeyes took her seat, resting upper elbows on the chair arms and steepling her upper hands while resting the lower set of arms on the computer keyboard in front of her to take notes. Another message scrolled across from Cratt. "Good, now let them talk, just as we practiced." Redeyes, bent her left lower arm behind her chair, those on the screen couldn't see but Cratt could, when she flipped him a three finger fuck a snake sign.

The ships Generals said they needed more metal and less people. Three of the Gods didn't agree, wanting more people and more ships, but fewer explorations of planets or space. Another 9 Gods preferred to explore more planets and set up colonizes. The remaining twelve thought it was too dangerous for colonization and wanted more world-ships.

Food levels were stable, but water was becoming an issue even with reclamation of waste. The Generals brought up the need to raise calories while the Gods weren't willing to see food stores dip below set levels.

"Those levels are years out of date!"

"We need to start rewarding and expanding. Can't expand if people are on base calories!"

"Why should we have population expansions if we

don't have more ships?"

"Need to mine comets for their ice and metal."

The discussion circled back around to metal, ships and colonization.

Redeyes sent a message to Cratt. "Is this usual?"

"The fighting or the topics?"

"Yes."

"Yes."

"My past suggestions?"

"You haven't made any at this point, demurring to a future date."

"Was I brain damaged?!" Her fingers flew over the keyboard, while she faced the screens and others.

"Not on the days of the meetings that I saw." Quieter, slower clicking behind her.

"What vote count is needed?"

"None. You're the final word. You listen and take action as you deem fit. The Gods fall in line as do the Generals after you lay out your reasoning."

"So not done by a vote."

"No and yes. You listen to what those not on the council say as well as to the council. Sometimes the two don't line up."

Redeyes sat back, steepling fingers again, eyes hooded contemplating, before typing. "Reminds me of congress."

"You've said this before. Still, don't know what a congress is."

"This but larger and more dysfunctional."

On screen, Zorax stood up tapping on his desk with his cup, a hollow earthy sound emanated through the screens, signaling his need for speaking. "I'd like to take this moment to make a suggestion." There were several derisive snorts and at least one outright laugh.

Zorax glared at the screens, pulling thin pale lips back

from human teeth, banging the cup harder as if the cup would command more respect or attention. The hammering force shattered the cup into small shards, scattering over the tabletop and the floor — one of the shards embedded in his hand.

Zorax stared at his hand dumbly for a moment, as the cut began bleeding profusely. Zorax began fumbling for the edge of his silk tunic to press against the cut while the other Gods and General on hand tried to help him.

The human tech, still until now, moved towards Redeyes, her own head down as if looking over her pad. Redeyes had briefly noted the tech to her side, but her concentration was on the screens in front of her. The tech slipped a hand into her tool belt, pulling out a small wire splicing knife from one of the multiple pockets, sliding a thin knife between Redeyes ribs. The attack was swift and smooth. Expertly timed.

The knife was small but sharp, sliding between the God's ribs, cold as space yet too short to penetrate the heart. The tech pulled the knife out again, barely clearing the ribs, stabbing under the sternum to the heart. She got the knife halfway in a second time when Redeyes training took over. Redeyes lower right arm grabbed the woman's right wrist, pushing it down and away. Redeyes upper right arm shot up, her handing stiff and flat, slamming into the woman's throat, while pivoting to the right and stepping to the side and behind the woman, bringing up her left hands against the woman's right arm with the knife, slamming into the joint with enough force to break the elbow outward with a sharp crack. The woman went down with a scream of pain. The scream was cut off as a disc slammed into the woman's head ending her screams.

Redeyes looked up with a snarl, as Collins started to re-holster his gun. He gave Redeyes a fast, easy smile flashing white teeth.

"Glad someone had fun." Cratt groused, re-holstering his disc-pistol.

"All in a day's work," Collins said. "Though our girl here had it under control."

"No one to question now," Redeyes growled, looking down at the cooling corpse and puddling blood. Her lower right hand held over the cuts in her side. Blood dripped out, forming crystals as they fell off her hand.

The smell of the woman's blood overpowering everything else except the sound of her pounding heartbeat. Redeyes' upper hands clenched into fists, trying by sheer will to hold off shifting. She could feel her muscles spasm and something trying to rearrange under her skin. A shiver up her spine and a metallic taste in her mouth. A taste that wanted blood. Hot fresh ripped from still moving flesh. She swallowed sharp coppery tasting saliva, fighting the primal urge coursing through her veins.

"Give it time. Someone else will try to kill you." Collins said, with a tilt to his head, watching Redeyes fight the shift, trying to distract her. "You're going to need stitches for that side." He wasn't coming any closer to Redeyes then he had to until she got this shifting under control.

The door opened behind Collins. He turned to wave off the ship guards, as they were a ship day late and a meal short. The first shot missed him, but the second shot hit his hip, dropping him to the ground as it chewed through the muscle and bone. That was the attackers' first mistake.

The second mistake, they started shooting at Cratt instead of Redeyes, assuming the tech had done her job correctly. Redeyes loosened her hands, letting the change take her as she leaped over the chairs onto the third-row desk diving into the human attackers, half wolf half human, a bloody thirsty flesh shredding Godling.

Those watching the horror unfolding from the safety of their own ships, remembered again how and why Redeyes took the lead in battle. She went after those actively shooting. Bounding from table, to chair, to floor, bouncing from flat to horizontal surfaces as long as it got her closer to whoever was shooting. Battle steel walls and tables had claw marks gouged in surfaces by were-powered claws, as she moved from one level to another. One limb stabilizing the other five as hands, feet, and teeth gripped soft flesh, rending as she bit and tore into victim after screaming victim.

She ripped off arms and tore out throats with an abandon not even the most blood crazed Wolfen could live up to. Once an attacker was down, Redeyes moved to the next, sometimes taking on three at a time in the target rich environment. Collins would later tell of how watching Redeyes fight as a werewolf was like watching the most insane of a Wolfen in frenetic blood-crazed berserker mode yet graceful almost dancing while painting the walls in eviscerated blood. Beautiful in the gore and mayhem created.

Cratt fired from the upper deck's far back corner, out of Redeyes' rampaging reach and Collins line of sight. Cratt aimed high or low, taking out shoulders and knees, determined for at least one living prisoner.

Collins wasn't being held to such high standards. He went for the gut or headshot. Kicking out knees and ankles with his good leg, as they came within range. The sound of bursting cartilage lost in the screams of Redeyes kills. Collins wasn't above shooting them point blank in the stomach or crotch as they went over, pushing off those who fell on top of him or using them as still screaming shields. When the occasional attacker pulled their eyes from the incoming werewolf to notice one Guardian alive, causing his own mayhem from the floor, they didn't live for much longer.

"Damn it Collins! Leave one alive!" Cratt yelled, as another point-blank head shot by Collings, blew a slow-moving attacker's head into bone and brain matter covering the walls, carpet and himself in sticky red.

"Yell at the God while you're at it!" Collins screamed back, rolling left to fend off a foot to his head while shooting another in the stomach.

"You're more likely to listen!" Cratt snapped back, shooting another attacker in the neck while fending off a knife aimed at his chest. He took the knife in the arm before he could angle his pistol into the girl's chest. A hole the size of a human fist opened up on her backside. She dropped but another was there trying to shove a wavering pistol into his face, before having his head ripped off by Redeyes.

The stream of people trying to kill the trio ended as abruptly as it started. No more rushed through the door, nor were any running away. A do or die suicide attack.

Redeyes let out a screaming howl, sending chills down Collins back. She had one long boned hairy sharp nailed hand on the floor, crouching over an eviscerated human when she turned towards Cratt. Collins pulled his gun to Redeyes. Redeyes saw the motioned, spun on her long arched feet to face a new threat. Collins felt his breath come in fast pants. Those green eyes weren't human or any other species. They were in the realm of nightmares. Blood, the only thing he saw swimming in there that made sense.

"Collins! Collins, drop the void fucking gun now!" Cratt yelled, waving his hands in the air to get Redeyes attention. She spun on those odd elongated taloned feet toward the yelling man, pouncing on Cratt as Collins dropped his gun to the side. Collins swore as one hand held at chest height the other dropping the disc gun to the floor, knowing he wouldn't be able to do more than watch if Redeyes decided to shred either of them.

Redeyes slammed into the General with bone bruising force. Cratt's head hit the metal wall with a resounding thunk. His vision dimmed dark, shot with stars. Four arms pinning his two, her teeth around his throat. Cratt went limp, waiting. Teeth dimpled his skin. The teeth released and Redeyes let go, stepping back. She started changing to her human state with breaking bones and popping muscles. Whimpers, almost howls, then human cries of pain as the change finished.

"Done." She said naked, looking up from her hands and knees on the floor to Cratt, smeared in blood from head to toe.

Breathing a sigh of relief, he choked out a reply. "Yes, we're done here." Cratt leaned over to help her up with shaking hands.

Redeyes shook her head, blood wet hair slapping her cheek, splattering red gore. "I'm done." She enunciated clearly before falling to her side. Cratt could see the damage done by the attackers. Three knives had found the heart through her ribs. Two were still stuck deep. Two more were in her gut. One had cut down and across, cutting through organs and intestine. She had at least three lethal disc shots bleeding her out.

"Next time, Cratt." She whispered, closing her eyes. The last breath rattling.

"Spacing snakes!" Cratt snarled, shaking her shoulders. "You don't get to leave yet!" He fell to the floor on abused knees, feeling for a pulse. "I've put too much time training you to have you die now!"

Collins slumped for a moment, picking up his gun, before rolling to his side, trying to gain his legs and failing. "She's gone Cratt. We'll need to lay out bodies." He leaned against the wall, smearing the red as he pulled himself towards Cratt and Redeyes' corpse.

"Bleeding black holes," Cratt swore. "You'd think she would've been able to survive that."

"I count 22 bodies." Collins groaned, making his way to the General, one step at a time. "We almost didn't survive that, and she did most of the killing."

"21." A man's voice said from the side, moving from among the pile of dead. The pale skinned bearded man sat up slowly ignoring the others in favor of himself. Cratt and Collins' guns were trained on the man before he finished sitting up.

The man looked around, seemingly unconcerned by the guns. Lifting one thin hand then the other, feeling along his ribs, then grabbing his crotch with a grimace. Collins didn't know what to make of this, repositioning his gun for a clean headshot. Cratt grabbed his forearm, pushing the hand with the gun, down.

"What in Death's kiss are you doing?" Collins growled, unable to move his arm or elbow Cratt in the face so he could re-aim.

The man looked up at them both at this, asking. "Where am I? No. No, that's not the right question. No chains and no whips so not a slaver's ship. When am I?" His eyes bloodshot and getting redder, looking from one to the other.

"That's why," Cratt said, with a wide grin. "No need to lay out a body, me boyo, she's already back."

Chapter 29

The rain came to a sudden stop as if a spigot had been turned off. There was no gentle tapering. A deluge then...nothing. Clouds broke from a solid bank, heavy with water, letting their less fluffy kin trail behind them, leaving room for the sun to shine between.

Both Arie and Lauranya were working in the lab so used to the gloom of the dark skies that the influx of sunlight light to the gloomy room almost blinded them with the first rays of natural light.

"Sun!" Arie cried, bouncing off her stool, rushing to the banister to look at the light flooding through the living area windows. Exhaustion forgotten from too little sleep, trying to keep waters at bay on the stairs.

Lauranya followed, if a bit more sedately, no less eager to see the sun through the windows. The gloom had become oppressive during the last five days. Lauranya had realized how gloomy the rooms were until sunlight filtered through the windows, illuminating their downstairs living area. The generator kept up with the bare minimum of their lights, but it was barely enough to cut through the dark green of the rooms or the almost night dark at high noon of the storm. Sunlight hit leaves, reaching upwards towards the lamps and the windows from trees and vining plants, with the root and grain vegetables in shades of gold, brown and lavender brightening the room akin to a living jewel. A peaceful hum of bees flitted through the greenery, looking for untapped flowers to siphon sweet juices from. Lauranya smiled, drinking in the sight of their life, they had done well these last few turnings of the world.

"Mom, let's go see the terrace!" Arie bounced past her mother towards the upstairs door. Ready to see the world from above.

"Towels first!" Lauranya called upwards. The words vibrating off the walls and doors.

"Working!" Arie called behind her. Her words didn't reverberate the way her mother's did, but the sound traveled to all reaches in their living domain.

The first push of the door was the worst. The door stuck; long enough for Lauranya to worry it had rusted shut, before opening into a balmy bright summer day.

They blinked for a moment, letting eyes adjust to the light, before stepping onto the ankle-deep running water. The water cascaded from the pool waterfall into the overfilled pool. The excess water flowing over tiles and out the small squares openings along the roof edge.

The first look was as bad as Lauranya had feared. The trees they had left were either broken sticks or gone entirely. None of the vines had survived. The stone and wood planters that were still standing, overflowed with water, any dirt flowing with the water over the edges of the container and into the ocean. Those might be of use later, but the water would have to drain out first.

Lauranya shook her head at the sight, expressing only a small sigh of disappointment. The inside was a mass of growth, while the outside nature's destruction at its worst. "Truly a blessing we do not live from the roof harvest alone."

"The fish are still alive!" Arie exclaimed having run to the pool to check on her water pets. She bent at her waist, trailing long blond hair into the pool to look over the edge, watching the sliver and green dartings in the depths below.

Lauranya started to laugh only to choke as she saw what Arie hadn't. "Arie, come away from the pool please."

Arie turned her head to look at her mother, giving the illusion that her head sprouted from her knees. Lauranya walked slowly forward, motioning Arie back towards her. Arie frowned, as she straightened.

"What?" She said slightly peevish, ignoring her mother's command, staying poolside.

Lauranya didn't even raise an eyebrow at this behavior, asking quietly "Any new dead voices?"

"No. Why?" Arie looked back towards the pool, finally seeing what her mother was seeing. "Oh."

A mer was lying flat against the waterfall as if they had tried to climb upwards. Probably storm-tossed when one of the monster waves crested over the building. Its' back towards Lauranya and Arie, with hair mid shoulder, meaning nothing as both male and female mers had short and long hair as seen from their dead guards. The back was well-muscled with a random scaring pattern, looking like bite marks. Where the legs should have been on a man, was a gorgeous blue streaked tail fin with black flecked flashing points of gold. Lauranya had a stray thought, wondering if fin color could denote the sex. The thought was fleeting as a new problem presented.

The mer was hurt and badly so. There were open wounds along the back and scaled tail. Deep mottled bruising around the rib cage, more pronounced on the left than the right. The purple almost black was fading into a slightly lighter ring of blue. The spine looked free of bruising or cuts. A minor miracle to whatever Gods the mer prayed to. There was no telling if the front was as badly damaged as the back. The probability was high.

Arie acted without thought, while Lauranya struggled to make a decision. Arie jumped forward towards the mer, without consideration that her help could be met with danger

Lauranya tried to stop Arie, too late, with an outstretched hand. Arie bounded past her mother's hand, just brushing her arm. Lauranya's hand stayed in the air as if trying to recall her child but the words stuck in throat and the hand stayed out, frozen with indecision.

Arie nimbly clambered up the waterfall rocks, reaching the mer's side in seconds. She felt for a pulse the way she'd been taught. Arie stopped for a moment looking for the neck vein above or below the gills on the neck.

"Alive!" She crowd, turning triumphantly towards her mother.

Lauranya nodded but she followed after her daughter, unsure what she would do if the mer proved dangerous. Kneeling next to the mer, Lauranya had to revise her original estimate of sizing. He was easily ten feet in length from the crown of his head to the tips of his tail. The bottom fifth of his tail wasn't the same as the scaled upper. This part was opaque like blurry plastic of a light blue color with dark blue fin rays as thick as her wrist.

Arie and Lauranya turned him over, as gently as possible, to get a better look. He, and he was definitely a he, had a heavily armored pronounced thick line, almost tube, along his tail where a normal man's penis would be. He had a strong jawline, no protruding mammary glands, and high cheekbones. Perfect bow lips that could cause envy in almost any woman, perfectly formed and full. Lauranya was more concerned with the cuts to the upper chest and the tail where a human's knee would normally be. There was some bleeding, more like a slow leak than gushing.

Lauranya made her decision, as Arie reached out to touch those perfect bow shaped lips. "Yes, he needs care and then back to the ocean he goes, as soon as he can swim." She said firmly, with a look to Arie.

"Okay, mom! What do we need to do to get him to the lab?" Arie's concentration was still on the mer, not the next day or week after. Only the here and now.

Lauranya shook her head. "Not the lab." There was no way the Mer would fit into the lab nor the bathtub in their makeshift lab.

"His wounds?"

"We'll stitch those up first."

"That's going to hurt."

"Very much so. I will be sure to give him a sedative and pain medication before I start to stitch. Arie, take a towel and get it wet, then place it over his gills. Keep the towel wet and watch his breathing." Lauranya could see that his gills were already drying out. As far as she knew, they would be useless for air breathing.

"Yes, mom!" Arie had to dash to the kitchen for a bowl, before returning within moments. She came back with the bowl and questions for the surgery. "Antiseptic and antibiotics. Bandages, needles and silk thread. Do you want the good antiseptic or the drinking alcohol?" Arie ticked off the things they would need on her fingers.

"The good antiseptic but no bandages. They will be wasted in the water which is already free of most impurities large enough to give us any problems." Lauranya said offhand, thinking of what wound would be sewn up first. "Also bring me two of the green tipped filled syringes."

"The ones you color coded for me if I needed to put you to sleep but couldn't read?"

"Yes, those." Lauranya looked up with a smile. "You

were young when we came up with the system."

"I'll be right back!" Arie darted to the lab.

Lauranya turned her attention back to the mer with a heavy sigh. It would only take a moment, minimal effort, to form a seal over his nose and mouth. A swift if pained death before Arie returned.

Lauranya shook her head. The first living soul they had seeing in years and she was thinking like an Overseer. Arie would know if Lauranya killed the mer, when his ghost came crying on her shoulder. Another thought. One Lauranya embraced wholeheartedly. If he proved to be dangerous, the poison of the hook fish could be applied several ways to incapacitate or kill.

Grimly she checked him over, running hands over his well-defined torso. There was bruising along his ribs, probability for one or more being broken, high. She ran hands downwards, adjusting her estimation to three ribs broken. She leaned over to listen to his breath. No rattling so the lungs weren't punctured. Although with him breathing water, Lauranya wasn't sure if hearing no rattle was good or bad.

Arie brought the requested items along with clean towels and an extra bottle of antiseptic. Lauranya nodded her approval, as Arie began to lay out the supplies, before putting a water soaked towel over the mer's gills. Lauranya took the first syringe, injecting into the mer's well-developed bicep.

The merman was unconscious when she slid the not so small needle into the vein on the inside of his arm. The mer woke flailing arms and tail, sending both Lauranya and Arie to the sides as he screamed in pain, before passing back out, flopping with head bruising force back on the buff-colored wet paving stones.

Lauranya rolled to her knees, frantically looking for

Arie. "Arie! Are you ok?"

"Yes, mom," Arie said, rubbing her bruised butt, standing up slowly. Lauranya sank back to her knees, breathing a sigh of relief.

Lauranya went back to the mer's side, examining where his head thunked onto the stones. A hollow sound of ripe melon. Firm and only slightly swollen. No bone moving under her touch or blood when she examined the skin underneath a little closer. The pupils showed the same size and dilation when the lids were opened, so no concussion.

Arie frowned at her mother's lack of action towards the cuts. "Why aren't you sewing, umm...stitching him up?"

Not taking her eyes off the injection sight, "If he's allergic, I need to know. I also need to make sure if he isn't allergic that the injection is in his system before I start stitching. It will be incredibly painful and I do not want him waking halfway through."

"Oh. We'll need to move him to the deck."

"Aye, do not teach your mother how to wear a scarf." Lauranya smiled. She reached up, gathering her hair in both hands to twist and tuck the long blond strands into a tight bun at the back of her neck. Next came the lifting, Lauranya took the shoulders with Arie on the fin. The mer wasn't as heavy as Lauranya had originally thought, though Arie struggled a little with the tail. Lauranya felt she could lift the mer's torso and upper tail portion with only a little strain. Arie was sweating profusely by the time they got off the waterfall stones to the flat stones poolside

"Start watering his gills again, please."

"How long do we wait?" Arie asked, trying not to fidget in place too much while pouring water from the pool over his gills.

"Fifteen minutes is the usual time." Jacks responded, ghosting next to Lauranya.

"Good to see you Jacks," Lauranya said with humor. "We have not seen you as much lately."

"And you too, my dear. You haven't needed my wit or humor until now." He said, touching a ghostly hand to her cheek. "Time." Jacks said, looking towards the mer.

Lauranya opened the alcohol, running the needle under a briefly poured stream, before stringing the silk thread. "Arie hold his shoulders down. This will hurt even with the pain medication. I do not expect him to wake up, but I would rather not take chances."

Arie moved to the position her mother vacated, leaving a wet cloth over the mer's gills, putting hands on his shoulders pinning him down.

Lauranya moved to the eight-inch gash on the front side of the tail. She poured antiseptic over her hand then over the wound, letting it drain onto the stone, before doing an exploration as gently as possible.

"Looks like the scales ripped off when he was dragged onto the roof." Jacks commented.

"Will help as I stitch flesh, not having to go through those scales."

"Wonder how hard the scales are?"

"Sachiko said that the scales are hard enough to fend off the bite of small flat head sharks. But the older ones have enough jaw strength to cut through." Lauranya said offhandedly, as she probed the depths of the wound. Less than an inch deep, finding muscle, not organs. A good sign

"Those sharks have incredible jaw strength no matter what the size." Jacks said leaning closer with evident surprise at this new information.

"Just so," Lauranya responded, as she carefully inserted the needle into flesh pulling the two sides together then tying the knot carefully. The mer twitched. Lauranya stopped until he lay still again; however, his breathing became labored and loud.

The impromptu surgery continued. Lauranya did 34 stitches total to the wound before moving on to the next and the next. No wound was overly deep just long, both a blessing and a curse. Easier to treat, with less chance of infection but more stitches. The first wound was the worst in length. There were five more. Besides the first long one, two more on the torso and two more on the tail for a total of 97 stitches.

Lauranya poured the last of the antiseptic bottle over the final stitched wound, sitting onto her haunches on the wet paving stone, pushing the hair from her loosely tied bun plastered to her face back.

"His skin is drying out." Arie touched a non-wounded part of the mer's tail.

"Yes, now we put him into the pool and check him tomorrow." Lauranya took the last dose of pain meds, injecting into the other bicep. She took his wrist feeling his pulse with the tips of her fingers — slow, steady.

"That's not recommended." Jacks said. "Too much and you could kill him."

"I want him sleeping, not waking up to an unknown place and…"

"Until you have some sort of security in place?"

Lauranya made a face, but she lifted the mer's shoulders gently, Arie grabbing the tail once more. "What security I do not know, I…just want him to sleep for a while longer." Deferring responsibility a little longer.

"Why don't we just put him in this pond?" Arie asked, dripping wet with the watering of the mer's gills.

"We have Hook fish and Razor Mouths in the pool. They would find him a tasty morsel within minutes."

"Oh, yeah." Arie shook her head at what she had been thinking. "So if not this pond then where are we going to keep him?"

"The inside pool." Came Lauranya's reply, as she thoughtfully chewed her lip in consideration.

"We can't carry him," Arie stated, with a snort at her mother's comment. Teenager ready to question everything.

"We can if we use a sheet." Lauranya pointed out, bringing logic into the discussion.

"Why not the carry basket that we got from downstairs?"

"A good notion but I would like to keep him from bending, as much as possible with those stitches."

"Right! I'll go get a sheet!" Arie bounded off inside, to find a sheet long enough to fit the mer and strong enough that they wouldn't have to worry about it ripping in two.

Arie returned quickly. Lauranya had taken over the watering duty, pouring water over the gills and the body while she waited for Arie's return.

Lauranya positioned herself so that she could pick up the shoulder end of the sheet, motioning to Arie with her chin to tuck the sheet underneath him as far as possible. Five long minutes later they had the mer on the sheet, well-watered as Arie poured water after every tuck to keep his gills wet.

"And..ready." They lifted the sheet carefully, but the mer groaned in pain, his eyes shivered but didn't open.

"Mom?"

"We keep going," Lauranya said grimly, wondering how bad his internal injuries were if he had any. The possibility the mer would die was unknown. If he survived the next three days, he might have a chance for a full recovery. Until then, he was in the hands of the All Father, Olorun.

Lauranya and Arie took opposite ends of the sheet and lifted. The mer was manageable in the sheet, where without the sheet he had been unwieldy with floppy body parts. With some groaning and a few knocks into random walls, they got him to the inner pool on the second floor.

"Arie…" Lauranya began lowering her end of the mer gently.

"Fine, mom." Arie struggled to breathe evenly with the weight.

"Okay, love, I am going to step into the pool. Keep the sheet up so he doesn't drag on the stairs please."

Lauranya backed down the rough steps, feeling carefully where she placed her feet. Lauranya's swimming could still be called hesitant with lots of splashing. She would never be the swimmer Arie was; however, she was strong and could lift more than Arie, so in she went first. Lauranya went as deep as she could stay standing while still keeping her head out of the water, before lowering the mer down, letting him sink gently to the bottom. Arie released her end just as carefully. The Mer's tail was covered in water but just on the stairs. Lauranya gently rocked the mer from side to side, pulling the sheet out from under him, before splashing her way to the stairs, while trying to not step on their prone and sleeping guest.

Chapter 30

Medics swarmed Collins and Cratt. Redeyes had only one attending to him/her. S/he was looking more bemused than worried or concerned at the poking and prodding.

"Cratt, what's going on?" Collins whispered to the General seated next to him, motioning with his chin towards Redeyes. They were both swathed in bandages. Collins' view of his leg was being blocked after local anesthesia had been applied. He couldn't feel anything other than the occasional tug, as his leg moved a little from stitches being applied.

"The body she's in will shift back to her normal."

"Bitchy killer?"

Cratt snorted and then grunted in pain as broken rib bones rubbed together. "Space that's going to hurt for a while." He took a shallower breath. "Human female with white hair and four arms."

"Red eyes?" Collins mouth quirked up.

"Aye, those too."

Collins opened his mouth when a medic gave him an injection in his neck. Collins turned snarling, then his eyes fluttered and he went limp.

"Sorry, General, but he needs to go to surgery."

Cratt waved a hand. "Go go...take him. Maybe you can sew his mouth shut while you're at it."

The medics looked at each other. "Joke. Try to stress to the surgeon; Redeyes will want him as healed as possible so he can keep up as Guardian. Crippled is no good."

"Will do, sir!" Collins was wheeled away in a gurney with a blood bag in his arm. Cratt slumped back against the wall, watching Redeyes being tested. There were two medics now, busy peeling off h/er shirt, checking the healing stab wound on the chest, while checking the various other injuries.

"Lung's been punctured."

"No rattling, so healings began."

"Graze marks over here."

"Healed disc wounds." The other replied.

"The body seems fresh and mostly working." Redeyes interrupted, getting to h/er feet, brushing past the two medics. They froze, and then moved back towards the others, letting the God move as s/he would.

"General Cratt is it?" Redeyes came to stand by him. S/he snagged a medic, peeling her out of her outer front split tunic as if it were a dance. Slow precise, beautiful, and confusing for the medic involved. A dance that ended with Redeyes wearing a non-ripped smock and the medic wondering what the space just happened, as she stood only in her medics scrubs.

Redeyes slipped two arms into the main sleeves, h/er emerging lower arms were still forming. Pinky thin, fragile things, emerging against the abdominal skin and muscles.

"You remember me," Cratt said, his eyebrows almost reaching his hairline.

"You were never forgettable. What year is this, and who are my Guardians?"

"You met one already. Collins."

"The one on the gurney."

"Yes."

"I remember he was bloodthirsty. A real killer who thrived as a Guardian."

"He's survived longer than any other sentenced for 15 years. Whether that's good or bad I can't say, but he's lived four years so far."

Roar and Iarris came jogging into the room. Roar entered first limping hard, slamming an arm out blocking Iarris from entering. She growled, biting him in the forearm for blocking her.

"Ouch, woman!" He clutched the arm, blood welling up from the teeth marks.

"Don't ever block me." Iarris snapped her ears flat against her skull.

The bite just pierced his skin, a few drops of blood welled up. "I was only trying to keep you safe." Roar said, slanting his eyes at her in annoyance.

Iarris pulled her lips off sharp teeth, growling. "Don't." Tail snapping twice in emphasis.

"Ahh, these must be the other Guardians." Redeyes looked at the arguing Katherians with bemusement.

"Two of them," Cratt said, trying to stand, holding a hand out to Redeyes to help him up. Redeyes pulled him up smoothly. "There's one more."

"Names?"

"Iarris and...Roar." Cratt said.

Roar she looked at, nodding but Iarris she came over to place a hand to the Katherian's cheek. "I remember you well." Iarris jerked back startled by her god's physical touch. Unless they were sparring, Redeyes wasn't into physical touch.

She turned to Roar. "And I know you as well. We have a lot to discuss." She looked through the room then back to her Guardians. "You weren't here, but you're injured."

"We were trying to hijack a ship."

"Successfully?"

"No. It was a trap. The fighters used a contact poison."

"No poisonics?"

"What?"

"Too soon then." Redeyes saw past them as if contemplating the universe through battle steel walls, distracted for the moment.

"Tell me of the Sirens."

"Sirens?" Cratt and the Guardians exchanged looks at this. They had sirens to signal danger such as fire, loss of air/vacuum pending.

Redeyes frowned. "A world of water where the singular shifters landed and women who sing people to their deaths."

"We lost the ship holding that the original shifting genetics was on, but we don't have anything…" Cratt coughed, blood speckled his lips as he finished. "listed as a siren.."

"No attempt to rescue the crashed?"

"You said it wasn't time."

"And we were in the middle of losing that sector to the deadheads," Iarris said from the sidelines.

Redeyes smacked her forehead. "Damn me. How long ago? Have we gained any new world-ships?"

"We haven't fought the undead gods in a pitched battle in over 30 years. That battle was" Cratt had to think back, "Over a hundred years ago."

The others looked at him. He shrugged massive shoulders. "Had a great-great uncle who volunteered for the genetic experiment right before the ship went down."

"How many ships do we have now?" Redeyes asked, coming back to the here and now.

"We have 18 world-ships."

"Too soon. Time, we should be here." The floor squished under her toes, the bodies mostly removed, the blood would be cleaned once everyone left.

The General and the Guardians exchanged glances. Only Roar didn't seem confused by Redeyes rambling.

"Don't you want us to find out who did this?" Roar asked.

"This?" Redeyes waved a hand to the bodies, casually as if piles stacked up were an everyday occurrence. "Oh, this was the rat-faced good Zorax."

"What?! How can you know that?" Cratt wheezed, doubling over.

"I killed him years ago after an attack." Redeyes regarded Cratt steadily. "You need to lay down."

"But you need proof today for an attack that will happen in your future." Roar said, going to Cratt's side, lending an arm for the General to lean on. Iarris kept the door open as the four of them made their way out of the gore-spattered room.

"Yep!"

"Which is what Nero is doing."

"Nero. He teaches young marines how to fight." Again the look between the three.

Iarris spoke up. "No, he's a Guardian who is doing communication research for you."

Redeyes opened her mouth then closed it. "Proof before I kill him. That's right. Can't just shoot the God then come up with why." She stopped her forward motion, beginning to pace. Her toes the only thing touching the floor, as her feet were already beginning to reshape with elongated arches and flexing claws.

"I need to shower. The blood is itchy, and this penis thing is driving me nuts until it absorbs. I need to sleep to finish the change." She looked up at her staring Guardians.

"This way." Roar took the lead again, heading out of the room.

Menodisces sipped from a steaming glass carefully. The handle warm to the touch, the body still too hot to comfortably hold. Flowers from various plants and trees perfumed the terraced garden in heavenly scents. Fans sent air through the gardens, making a slight breeze. Enjoyable. Solar panels tilted away, leaving the area in comfortable shade, mimicking nightfall.

Renfra entered cautiously, bowing low to his God.

"Are both my sons away?" Menodisces asked, enjoying the view of the stars, as he stood on a stone tiled terrace underneath a vine-covered archway.

"Yes, master."

"Aelia? Septus?"

"Aelia was rescued by Cnaeu but Septus was left to rot as a slave."

Menodisces tapped his cup for only a moment. "How did Cnaeu get past your guards?"

"He had three of his 40 slip through with a blonde slave of similar height, weight and muscle tone, during shift change and slave washing. During the late night cycle. Changing her for Aelia, then killing her moments before Felix came in to get a fresh body."

"Using the chaos of change to hid his movements?"

"Yes. If you hadn't suggested this as one of the ways in, I would never have known Aelia wasn't the corpse on the floor." Renfra said, with another bow.

Menodisces smiled faintly, knowing when he was being flattered. "So, Felix is either a cat's paw or stronger than expected for Cnaeu to willingly take a risk for him."

"You're not worried Cnaeu has the loyalty of the soldiers?"

"Oh, that was going to be a problem for another date. However with him safely out chasing a Runner ship, I don't think he'll be back." Waving the hand with tea towards the black of space. One young threat is gone. "Daccu though. His lack of support will be a more serious concern."

"He wants this ship."

"And almost dangerous enough to take it."

"Almost? He is a strong fighter with necromancy to boot."

Menodisces snorted, turning to face Renfra. "Strength isn't all you need to take a ship. Loyalty is another. Daccu couldn't get anyone to follow him unless he promised them the improbable. He's burned so many allies no one is going to believe his given word."

"So...that leaves Hadriana as your heir."

Menodisces smiled again, saluting Renfra with his cup. "Just so. She'll be at the height of her power and ready for her own worldship in a handful of years. With coaching and more training, she'll be ready to be challenged at a Convening of the Gods."

"Another ship under your influence. Without threats to you remaining on the ship."

"Exactly so." Menodisces went back to contemplating the unending stars, enjoying the warmth of his tea.

Chapter 31

Illig woke groggily, pain his companion. The pain radiated from places he'd never felt this much sensation from before. He groaned, bubbles pushing out of his mouth, floating to the top. He noted those absently; he had been in the air at some point to fill his lungs. His ribs were on fire from the push of his diaphragm with the groaning. Illig took slow shallow watery breaths. There were lines along his skin that hurt more than others. He ran exploratory fingers over one on the front of his torso. His fingers encountered stitches, eliciting more pain and a gasp. He yanked his hand back.

"Not doing that again." he thought. "Or at least a bit more carefully."

He continued to follow the bursts of pain with a lighter touch, cataloging the damage and the stitched areas. He laid back, letting the slow-moving water rock him for a moment, his hands falling to the surface he laid on. His eyes snapped open as the surface touch wasn't....expected. He expected sand; what he felt was like textured rock but not in a way an island water hospital would be. There was light but no moon or sun reflecting overhead on the water surface that he could see above him.

He reached hands out in both directions. One encountered a wall, the other did not; however small eddies made from reaching bounced from a perpendicular surface close by — presumably the other wall.

Illig sat up slowly, torn muscles screaming. Illig gritted his teeth, adjusting to using arms for swimming to the surface, without the push of his tail. The pool wasn't very big, just deep. 10 feet wide and 14 feet long, maybe 14 deep. He wasn't focusing much on the pool as the room took his breath away. The room was as large as the meeting cavern the mers used, but this room had wood floors and tan fiber mats spread out in marked sections. Mostly empty except there were odd things scattered along the walls and a lone couch cast into shadow even as the moonlight filtered through breathtaking windows.

He took a deep breath, sniffing. The room smelled of...green vegetation. Odd. Only the islands smelled like this. Maybe an inner island water hospital?

The clear panel openings must be windows because doors opened and these didn't open to the night sky. The windows did let in the diffuse light of the moon. They spanned from a few inches off the floor to a domed point a few inches below the ceiling, as wide as a mer's spread arms with inches to spare. The bird's eye view was breathtaking as he looked out on the expanse of the surrounding water and sky.

A voice mumbled in the dark, yanking Illig's attention away from the novelty of windows to the couch. A dimly lit figure on the couch rolled over in sleep. An arm thrown over the head exposing bare breasts, showed the person to be a woman.

Illig could read an ocean current and eddies, telling where fish were or would be. It had taken a moment, but the clues finally clicked, the windows and the couch were the final clues. Things the Islanders hadn't bothered with and the mer didn't feel necessary. He was in the deadhead building

He slammed a hand down, hitting the water in

frustration, fear and anger chasing through his brain like minnows before a redfish. How could he have let the grouper lead him so far astray with a storm coming! The singing, his treacherous mind whispered. Illig flushed guiltily at the thought, though the tune haunting his dreams and sometimes waking thoughts.

The splash wasn't loud, but the sound carried in the hushed room. Water droplets traveled from the force of his hand to the person sleeping on the couch. The woman stirred, blinking sleepily as she rolled over, running a hand over her now damp bare chest. She sat up groggily to run a wet hand on her short sarong. She looked over to the pool and the frozen mer. She smiled, beginning to speak excitedly motioning with her hands while swinging her feet off the couch. She shook her head, laughing, only to dart out the door, speaking louder and calling for another.

Illig's heart beat faster in fear. Brother and the Torch had said only a mother and child lived here, but what if they were wrong? What if the thing the woman was calling came from space and liked the taste of mer-men. Illig sank to the deepest part of the small pool lying flat on the floor while his brain swirled with one horrible what if to the next.

It wasn't long before the woman's voice returned. Water carrying sound well, if slightly muffled. There was another voice this time. Another woman's by the sound. Illig strained to hear barking or growling of something possibly...bigger. The voices stopped for a moment then faded as if they were both walking away. Illig took a deep, ragged water filled breath. Maybe they'd let him be.

It seemed an eternity, punctuated with moments of dozing when he heard the voices return. This time the voices were closer to the pool edge, just not at the pool edge. Then the singing began. Soft. Harmonizing. The song called to him. Safety. Trust. This song promised him much and more.

Illig's eyes half closed, relaxing for the first time in longer than he could remember. He rose to the surface in a trance, pain receding as the song wound through his brain. He pulled himself to the pool edge, leaning on the rough surface, staring at the two women singing to him.

Kneeling on large puffy mats, two young blond women sang. Similar enough in looks to be sisters. The singing stopped, leaving him happy but wanting more.

The one he first saw with only a short sarong and bare-chested, sat to the left, while the other also with short sarong but wore a V inverted top, tied at the point of the V around the neck and the wider bottom around her chest. Both of them were blond, with hair down their backs. The one to the left with longer hair to her waist, while the one to the right kept hers no longer than to her shoulder blades. A closer look showed the sister on the right to be a few years older than the one on the left. Illig didn't know where the mother was but the Torch had gotten it wrong. There were two sisters and the mother hadn't shown or hadn't made it.

In front of them were several wooden plates on small one inch legs. The woman on the left had a larger plate with various fruits and vegetables. When they stopped singing, she took the nearest oblong gold and red fruit, slicing it in half then in quarters, setting the quarters to the side in a small red wood bowl.

The older sister to the right darted a hand into the large bucket at her side, pulling a snapping fish up with fingers behind the gills. The only safe spot on the mean-tempered overly aggressive fish. This sister quickly dispatched the fish with a quick clean cut to the spine, behind the head. From there she gutted, cleaned and de-skinned with the efficient motions of one who had done this a few hundred times. The refuse she placed into another smaller bucket.

The sister to the left went to squeeze a slice of gold red fruit over the filet when the right-hand sister said something, causing the other to blush. The blushing sister returned the fruit to the bowl waiting until that one plate was finished. One filet was left to the side. That one she squirted juice on adding a few of the finely minced vegetables to the side.

A small feathered bird, with glossy white, black and brown feathers, wandered into the room, clucking cheerfully. The bird made a run for the bucket, with loud squawking and flapping of wings. The right-hand sister made a disgusted noise, saying something to the other sister, making her laugh, a rich rolling sound. They both tried to shoo the bird away. The bird evaded capturing hands, trying to get into the bucket with fish skin and guts. Standing with grace, the right side sister deftly grabbed the bird, who gave a loud disgruntled squawk as it was picked up, tucking it under one arm. The woman bent low grabbing the refuse bucket in her free hand and walked out the door only to return a few minutes later without the chicken, the bucket still in hand. There was a loud, almost happy sound, of birds in another room.

She continued with the fish fillets, after sinking back to her knees with an unconscious grace and ease of long practice. Quickly, two more wooden plates were filled with filets. The first one the left-hand sister leaned over to push to him, when the other sister said something sharply, causing her to sit back as if slapped. The left-hand sister took a long wooden handle, with an unusual brush attached to one end, before pushing the plate to him with the non-brush end.

Illig was just as cautious. He eyed the food, his hunger

only a muted rumble, but made no move to eat. He stared at the women and they at him.

"Ahh." The woman to the right said. She turned to her sister speaking in a liquid tone and a slight smile. The left-hand sister laughed again, reaching for her own raw fish filets. She ate with gusto spooning finely chopped vegetables onto the filets with her fingers, licking them clean when done. The right-hand sister, shook her head in amusement at the other, before eating her own filets daintily and with less chopped vegetables but more of the squeezed fruit juice on top.

With hands shaking in pain, Illig picked up one filet, biting down cautiously. Tasty, but plain. He tried a small nibble of the juiced filet with a dabble of chopped vegetables. The flavors of tart, spicy, warm chased over his tongue with every bite. The other filets he put a little more of the vegetables. This was much better, he thought.

He finished three of the filets, unable to eat any more as pain roiled his stomach, cramping the muscles in his arms holding him up. Closing his eyes, he let go of the pool's side to sink down into the depths, breathing through the pain.

"Mom?" Arie said in concern, leaning forward as the merman slipped back under the water. "What...Where did he go?"

"Under the water," Lauranya said gently, as she stacked the dishes for easier transport to the kitchen.

"Should we do something?"

"He probably could use something to help with the pain. Blessed sleep from Erinle heals many injuries."

"We have the meds?" Arie looked to the pool, then her mother, blond hair whipping from side to side in agitation.

"We do." Lauranya stood gathering the dishes and the

pail with the live fish. Those would be returned to the holding pool for the night's dinner.

"Why aren't we giving him something?" Arie demanded, standing up in a single motion, flinging her arm towards the pool.

Lauranya stared at her child for a moment. "He is at the bottom of the pool with no way to get him."

"Yes, there is!" Arie rushed to the pool edge, sliding into the water before her mother could do more than drop the wooden dishes onto the floor with a clatter. The bucket of fish dumped over, spilling three live fish to flop over the floor in the resulting puddle of water.

"Arie! No!" Lauranya made a grab for her, feeling the silk of the sarong slide along with her fingertips as Arie dove into the pool.

Lauranya dropped to the edge of the pool with knee bruising force, peering into the churning waters unable to see either Arie or the mer.

"Arie!" Lauranya screamed.

The mer surfaced with Arie in his grip. One arm wrapped around her neck while the other arm pulled him to the opposite wall. The mer let go of Arie, pushing her towards the stairs with enough force to splash Lauranya on the side. Arie spluttered, treading water, glaring equally at her mother and the mer. The mer glared back while yelling a few words.

Lauranya, after years of being around the gladiator training pits, didn't need a translator to figure out he was unhappy with being pushed or stepped on by Arie's enthusiasm of helpfulness.

"We're trying to help you!" Arie yelled back, splashing him indignantly. "You could at least try to take some of the medication, so you'd get better!"

"Arie!" Lauranya added her voice to the cacophony

going on, sitting back on her heels, her voice reverberating off the walls.

"What?" Arie snapped, still trading glares with the mer. The mer stopped mid splash with a wild eyed look at Lauranya.

"Please, get out of the water. Now." Lauranya said through gritted teeth, exhaling to keep her voice calmer.

"But he needs…" Arie let her voice creep into a whine, turning to look at her mother with blond hair plastered around her face and shoulders. Defiant in her certainty that the mer needed their help.

"For you to not be in his pool while he's injured," Lauranya snapped. She motioned for her bedraggled daughter towards the stairs.

"But…"

"Get. Out. Now." Lauranya used a voice she had only used on the boys at their worst, never on Arie. The voice sent shivers down Arie's spine, her protest stopping as her mouth snapped shut with an audible click.

"Fine." Arie pouted, turned towards the stairs in a graceful spin that only water could provide.

The mer took that moment to lunge towards Arie, grabbing her around her waist, pulling her back towards him and the other side.

Lauranya saw the lunge but could do nothing other than raise a hand to warn him from her daughter ten feet away to be effective.

"Mom!" Arie yelped, struggling at the unfamiliar hand around her hips.

"Do not struggle! Go limp!" Lauranya called from the side, she moved towards the stairs. She had no idea what she would do but she couldn't just let him take Arie.

To the mer, she held out empty hands, slowly walking down the stairs. The mer pulled himself and Arie backward, causing Lauranya to stop halfway down the stairs. Arie went limp in his arm, moving her arms only to keep upright.

The mer spoke. Lauranya shook her head. "I...we do not understand." She spoke slowly gently as if to a small child. The mer let go of the poolside long enough to point to the windows, before flinching as a reflex to stay afloat caused his tail to flex.

Lauranya got the hint looking at him grimly. "I would love to get you back to Olokun's grace and water, but I need my daughter back."

"Mom, he's flexing his tail and flinching."

"He probably ripped out a couple of stitches."

Arie squirmed slightly, testing the mer's strength. He let go of the side, sinking down with them both.

"No!" Lauranya had taken no more than one step when he reemerged with a spluttering Arie, who turned to glare at him again.

Arie elbowed him in the chest. "Can't breathe water, you fish head!"

Lauranya was proud of her feisty daughter though at this moment she could wish that Arie be a bit more on the gentle side. More mouse than gladiator.

The mer motioned to the window again this time he lowered Arie slightly. The threat very real. Arie squeaked, panicking to turn in his arm, throwing her arms around his neck, feet and legs thumping against his tail. This caused a yowl of pain from the mer.

"Arie! Be still!" Lauranya hissed.

"He's going to drown me." Arie started to cry, her voice muffled on the mer's shoulder. "Just wanted to help him."

The mer wasn't sure what to do with the now crying young woman in his arm, but he didn't lower her any further into the pool.

Lauranya needed help with the mer and Arie was the only link. "Arie, I need you to concentrate for a moment. Do you hear any new voices?"

"Voices?" Arie sniffled, turning to look at her mother.

"The storm washed this one onto our roof with wounds deep enough to almost kill. How many more did not survive?"

"Umm…" Arie stilted her head slightly, eyes half closed. Lauranya held her breath praying to Yemoja.

"Three more new voices," Arie said softly, her powers touching the new spirits.

"Can you bring their spirits here?" Lauranya said quietly, into the suddenly hushed room, watching the mer's face and shoulders for his next move. Currently, he was patting Arie's back, as she wiped her eyes with the back of her hand. Her head only an inch lower than his. With his tail in the water, it looked as if there was only a few inches difference in height.

"Okay." Arie closed her eyes, listening.

Three ghosts showed up, two men and one woman. They all seemed slightly confused. One merman, older than the others with deep laugh lines around his eyes and a barrel chest, swam through the air to the trapped mer in the pool, smacking him on the back of the head with a ghostly hand.

"What are you doing holding a woman hostage?" The mer ghost growled at the younger.

The injured mer stared opened mouth at the ghost. He let go of Arie, who still clung to him, to touch the ghost's arm. The living hand passed through the specter. The younger mer said something to the mer ghost.

"Yes, I'm dead. How the void do you think I got here so fast?"

The mer's nostrils flared, and he let out a snarled reply.

"Illig." the ghost gave the equivalent of a deep sigh at his response, "Nephew, you'd not make it more than half a mile before the nearest flat head got you."

The mer's lips thinned to a hard line. The red-headed female mer, rolled her eyes at him. "This isn't the time to get stubborn. We all knew they raised the dead and that this area wasn't safe. Storm-driven never leaves you with good choices." She pointed a finger at him. "You're alive. Don't waste the second chance at life."

The mer, no Illig, Lauranya thought to herself, shook his head in grief, speaking to the three. "Nope. She'll let us go shortly. Or at least that's what the other spirit says. The girl, you've got clinging to you asked us here to speak with you."

Illig jerked back as if bitten by a razor mouth, baring his teeth at Arie, pushing her away from him. She returned the snarl in kind, kicking him in the chest, pushing off towards the stairs.

Illig sucked in air, going under the churning water, screaming in pain.

"Nice kick, girl. You'll make a fighter yet." The barrel chested mer said in approval.

Lauranya grabbed Arie, pulling her up the steps by an arm out of Illig's reach. "We only want to help him heal then get him out of here," Lauranya said grimly, dropping next to Arie, holding her tightly. "Can you make him understand that?"

The three looked at each other with varying degree of chagrin and amusement. The uncle ran a hand through shoulder length grizzled grey shot black hair. "Illig is a good kid, a good hunter, not always the brightest…"

"He'll listen, once he figures out you don't want to eat him." The woman with the waist length red hair said, flashing teeth in a genuine smile.

Lauranya jerked her head back looking to the three. "Why would we eat him?!" She shuddered, clutching Arie a little tighter. "We just want him gone, once he can swim!"

"We'll need a little time to convince shrimp brain of that." The uncle said, with a roll of his eyes.

"Pfft. Your nephew isn't that dense, just not quick on the right mental hunt some days." The third mer finally chimed in.

"Some days?" The female grinned.

Illig surfaced, glaring at the three of them. He snapped at them while hanging onto the side of the pool. Hands shaking and his complexion noticeably paling as he gripped the edge of the pool with white knuckles.

"He is about to lose consciousness," Lauranya said. She pressed her lips together in a tight line scowling at the ghosts. "I would like to get some pain meds in him to re-stitch him if that is something you could get through to him."

"Well nephew, you need to let the woman get something in you to take care of those wounds."

Illig said something disparaging, with a dismissive hand wave, those perfectly bow-shaped lips, pale in a thin pressed line of stubbornness. He glared at the three of them before blinking a couple of times, his eyes finally closing and he sank into the pool.

"Is he dead?" Lauranya whispered to Arie.

"Illig just passed out." His uncle's said, with little sympathy. "You can dose him now and give him a new set of stitches."

Lauranya and Arie exchanged glances. Arie stood up, kissing her mom on the cheek. "I'll pull him to the stairs mom." Taking a deep breath, she dove into the pool.

Lauranya ran cold hands over her bare arms.

"You really don't like him here." The ghostly woman commented.

"I do not want any trouble coming from helping him."

The three of them looked at each other again, inscrutable.

"Troubles not going to come from helping him." The third unnamed mer said succinctly. "It'll come from you just being you."

Arie emerged at that moment, stalling any further comments, as the two of them hauled Illig up the stairs and onto the wood floor.

"Arie." Lauranya started, as she arranged Illig on the wood flooring.

"I'll get a needle, thread and some towels," Arie said, shaking long wet hair out of her face with a flip of her head, water puddling around her bare feet.

"Good girl." Lauranya smiled, watching her child dash out of the room, her running footsteps slapping against the floor, echoing through the emptiness. Lauranya looked down at Illig, her smile turning into a frown as she examined him.

"You, however, are a pain in my arse." She let out a sigh, observing the rips in his tail needing stitches.

Illig woke this time, feeling like his head was stuffed with small flat head sharks, and his mouth had been filled with a sandbank recently. The walls weren't behaving properly either. They kept sliding closer then moving just out of reach, taunting him with their solidity.

"Ugh." He tried to sit up on his elbows only to drop back to the floor of the pool, bands of fire racing along his tail and chest. "Right. Undead women and injuries." he shook his head, remembering the last few days.

"Uncle!" This time he shot up, ignoring the pain, breaking the surface of the water looking for ghosts.

He looked around frantically, thrashing his arms to stay afloat, spinning in place twisting to view the entire room.

"Brannin!" Illig's voice bounced off the walls, echoing hollowly in the room. His uncle was nowhere to be seen. The only person in the room with him was the older sister. She sat on the couch staring intently at a piece of rectangular metal.

She jumped up at his yelling, looking around with wide eyes and slightly hunched shoulders. "Hush!" The older sister snapped, pulling her shoulders back as she stood up straight. She put the metal piece on the couch pillow, before walking towards him.

Illig moved back to the other side of the pool with narrowed eyes. The sister just sighed, before settling down on the pillow by the water edge. They stared at each other for a few moments. A sizzling lightning bolt illuminated the room in sharp relief seconds before a wall-shaking boom of thunder broke through the detente.

Illig jerked his eyes towards the window, noting how the sky was dark enough to keep the room in mid-ocean gloom.

"Where is my uncle? Where are Amaris and Miok?" He slapped the water surface — fear hidden behind anger.

The woman sat back looking at him with sympathy. She spoke slowly miming sleeping. Someone else sleeping.

"Your sister is sleeping? What does that have to do with my uncle?" He snapped, glaring at the woman. "Bring him back!" Illig demanded. His deep baritone voice keeping the demands from sounding like a tired five-year-old wailing for a favored stuffed animal.

The woman shook her head, air whistling as she puffed through her teeth hard. A ghost showed up next to her. Not a ghost he knew. This one a man, shorter than the older sister with tightly curled hair and quirking lips. The ghost glinted in his eyes. The two spoke in soft tones. The older sister laughing softly at something the ghost said, as he gestured toward Illig. He touched her cheek gently, lover-like, before vanishing again.

The sister smiled after the ghost's vanishing visage, before turning back to him. She slapped the water, splashing enough to get droplets on herself, trying to get his attention.

They locked eyes. She nodded then pointed at herself. "Lauranya." Then to him. "Illig."

Ahh. Names. That might help. He repeated her name, carefully. She sat up on her heels visibly relieved.

She mimed a hand to her mouth pointing at him. "Really? That's all you want to know is if I'm hungry?" Irritation roughing his voice to a growl, as he tossed wet hair from his eyes. "There's a whole spacing more that I need than food!" He glowered at her from the other side of the pool.

She sat back with a blank face, watching him for a moment before getting to her feet in that smooth unusual way, almost like she were in the water herself. He watched her start walking from the room. Lightening illuminating her features blank-faced but her eyes glittered, the way Chehreh's did when annoyed.

"Wait! Don't leave" He yelled at Lauranya's back as she passed through the doors. He saw her back stiffen when he yelled, and she missed a step, but she didn't turn back around. Illig's voice sounded almost desperate even to his own ears, as he continued yelling. His voice bouncing back at him riding the booming rattle of thunder, mockingly. The yelling stopped, only after his arms started to shake holding all of his weight on the pool rim. He sank back to the bottom of the pool with a pounding head and cramping triceps.

"Arie." Lauranya stepped into her daughter's dark room. "Arie." She called a little louder. Arie made a muffled noise, turning in the bed, her head buried under pillows and blankets. Lauranya picked her way carefully through the girl's room. The floor strewn with clean clothes along with various wire and metal projects. Lauranya frowned slightly at the sight. "Child, you need to pick up your things. There are no slaves to clean up behind you."

"Why does it matter? No one but us here." Arie said sleepily, pulling the blanket from her head. "How can you see the floor? I can barely see you." Lightning crackled, illuminating the room, her mother standing at the foot of the bed. "Oya and Sango's sense of humor," Arie said with a sigh, sitting up with a yawn. She reached over for a side table lamp. The light illuminated the room dimly, needing more solar charge for a brighter bulb.

"The mer-man, Illig, is talking," Lauranya said, tight-lipped, clipping her words with short tightly controlled breaths. "Could you ask the ghosts to translate, please?" Arie noticed her mother's hands clenching at her side, with shoulders unnaturally tight.

Arie frowned looking to her mother's face. "He said something to annoy you?" She stumbled out of bed, reaching for a wrap, tripping over a project next to her bed. "Ow! Esu! Fine, I'll pick up my things!" Thumping back on the bed, holding a foot to check for bleeding.

"Probably, but I can't understand what he said."

Lauranya shook her head sharp enough; her hair swung over her face.

"Then how..." Arie asked, stopping at Lauranya's narrowed eyed look.

"Speech isn't just words child," Lauranya said, opening her hands to flex the muscles held so tightly in fists.

Arie looked up with a frown. "What's wrong, mom? Why is he upsetting you, so much?" Moving a circular bit of wire with untwisted, pointy ends to the side table.

Lauranya looked towards the windows jerkily. "His voice...the tone, reminded me of your father a little too much." She took a deep breath. "Years later and I still can't keep from being angry or scared by a dead man." Turning back towards Arie, she rolled her shoulders back, releasing the anger. "He's scared and hurt. I understand this, but I would really appreciate the ghosts translating. And since I..."

"You can't summon; you need me." Arie bounced over to her mother, skipping around the scattered bits on the floor, hugging her tightly.

"I will always need you, dear," Lauranya whispered into blond hair, hugging her child back tightly.

Arie pulled back with a grin, noting she was almost even with her mother now. "Let's see if we can't get some talking done!"

Illig heard the women's voices before his uncle materialized next to him, scaring the scales off of him. "Ship raping snakes!" Illig flicked his tail, pushing him to the back of the pool and up, scraping skin on the wall, pain flaring up his tail.

"Good morning to you, nephew!" His uncle had a

gleam in his ghostly eyes and a wide smile.

"What the void is going on?" Illig could feel his heart thumping against his chest. His fingernails scraping against the wall.

"Seems you're wanting to talk, so the girl asked me to come and speak to you. Do try to make it unnecessary for them to leave you to rot."

"I can walk out of here any time!"

"Not with a tail that messed up you can't, and you know it, shrimp brain." His uncle snapped. "Those cuts are going to seriously mess with your shifting to legs. Possibly crippling you for life and not just for walking."

Illig glared at his uncle again. "You're wrong; void it!" He centered himself, letting the water soothe him as he reached for the shift. The pain he expected, but the pain of this shift jerked him out of the shift as he came screaming out of the water. Flesh tore along the cuts unable to connect and reconnect. He passed out, sinking below the surface, his tail once more a tail, this time the cuts were deeper torn open by the shift and the stitches ripped out in spots.

His uncle gave his nephew a disgusted look before rising out to Arie and Lauranya. "My nephew isn't long on brains, but he has a good heart. Please don't eat him."

Lauranya glared, while Arie giggled. The uncle went to ruffle Arie's hair his hand touching her hair, moving it slightly.

"So strange still." He mused then looked at the two of them. "Where are the other two?"

Arie straightened, but looked at the floor, before looking at the imposing ghost mer, blushing. "I sent them along, letting their souls go. The mer-man seemed to know you best. I didn't think you'd mind staying for a little bit longer."

He gave a slight smile. "My love went to the other side a long time ago. I miss him." He looked off to the distance for a moment. "I don't mind staying for a bit but I'd like to move on when my nephew, Illig, learns your language and can talk on his own."

Lauranya cleared her throat, putting hands on Arie's shoulder with a slight squeeze. "We'd like him to teach us what to say."

The mer tilted his head. "Aye, can see that. A lot more speaking our tongue then yours, though to be honest, the difference isn't that huge."

"What I thought, though the words are hard to understand."

"Shrimp brain...Illig is good at talking." The mer stopped mid-turn. "He's gone and ripped his stitches worse this time. Could you…?"

Lauranya rolled her eyes. "That have anything to do with him coming out of the pool screaming?"

Illig's uncle looked sheepish. "Probably."

Lauranya gave him a hard look. "You're doing?"

"I didn't tell him to do anything!"

"But scaring him was totally allowed, eh?"

"Hey, now!"

"I have been around ghosts all my life, and they all like scaring the living at least once if given a chance." Lauranya said with a tilt of her head, her lips twitching at the uncle's sheepish look. "Arie would you?" She motioned towards the pool.

Arie had put hands over her mouth stifling giggles at the mer ghost who was getting verbally chastised by her mother. "Sure, mom!" Arie took a running jump into the pool to find the passed out Illig. Lauranya smiled at her child's enthusiasm.

Uncle turned towards Lauranya. "Illig is a good kid

even if he is a pain to deal with sometimes when he thinks he's right."

Lauranya nodded, giving him a sideways look with a slight smile over her lips. "I have noticed the trend in young men and women who are not properly directed towards goals. They tend to have a high opinion when uninformed of reality." She turned towards the door. "Tell Arie I have gone to get towels and suturing material."

Uncle snorted as he drifted away in Arie's direction. "You'd think I was your beck and call ghost or something."

Illig woke up with a pounding head and a mouth feeling like it had been stuffed with sand. He rolled over, on the pool floor groaning. "I'm beginning to hate this place."

"Only thing keeping you alive, shrimp brain." His uncle snorted next to him. "Though I'm sure Lauranya would be happy to dump you down the stairwell, so you could find your way home again."

Illig glared for only a moment before his stomach gave a heaving rebuttal to the strong narcotics in his system. His uncle looked concerned, before swirling off with a ghostly swish of his tail. Illig was too ill to do more than hang his head over the arm propping him up.

The water changed from a slight swirl to a stronger push against him, agitating the water. He watched the bile and acid move from him towards the stairs, where a bottom grate could just be made out. Then a foot was on the bottom step, joined by two others.

"Gods, I swear I'll be nicer to women in the future and never tease Tara for preferring legs again if these two would just let me sleep," Illig begged, as his stomach roiled again setting him to heaving for the third time. Luckily the temperature began to drop, and the water filtered faster than he could heave.

The younger sister swam next to him, bracing a foot on the steps, straight legged with knees locked, reaching for his hand. The girl's hair pulled back from her face as the water pushed against her hard enough to cause her to move from side to side as she tried to reach him. Illig gave the girl a pathetic look of misery, unable to glare. Her fingers just brushing along his left hip before pulling off. The water current strong enough to propel her upwards and back. He watched as her feet flying at the mid-level stairs just covered in water. The other foot shifted and moved out of the pool.

The feet moved out of the water and the current eased to a less riptide level. The younger sister was back; this time her fingers closed in over his hand. She twined her fingers in his, tugging him towards her. Illig resisted the insistent tugging, trying to untangle his fingers, the girl hung on like an eel. He heard the other girl's voice yelling above.

"Up you go, nephew. Don't keep them waiting." Uncle's voice was in his ear, startling him enough so that the current moved him up and towards the stairs.

The girl holding his hand shot up to the surface, gasping for air, only to tumble onto the stairs when the back of his tail and side pushed into her from the water pressure. The contact pushed against his stitches causing more pain. Illig yelled loudly, water shooting from his mouth in a spectacular frothing mass, much like a water faucet, covering both the girls. He fell against the younger sister, pushing her back into the stairs.

Lauranya rushed to the lower side, slipping arms underneath him, lifting him so his back and tail cuts weren't on the stairs. She spoke rapidly to Arie. Arie bounced up, disentangling her finger, to run out of the room. Wet slapping footsteps receded out of Illig's hearing. Lauranya picked Illig up stepping back into the water; he floated in her arms. He squirmed, trying to flip out of her arms.

"Stop it." Lauranya snapped, bracing herself against the water push and the uncooperative mer-man. "If we don't give you something the vomiting will continue. Dehydration isn't likely but tearing your stitches is a good possibility and I can't give you anything more for the pain."

Uncle ghosted behind her to translate.

"Tell the Deadhead to go and dive into a black hole."

The uncle tried to slap the back of his head. "I'll be saying no such thing. They tried to take the pain away but misjudged the dosage unless you want to keep heaving out your guts until you rupture something important. Since we know the brain isn't working right in the first place."

Illig laid in Lauranya's arms stiffly, or as stiffly as he could trying not to touch her but unable to do much with his back and tail aching every time he tried to move away. She kept him low enough in the water that his gills stayed wet but not so far she was swept away with the current back up the stairs. When he started heaving, Lauranya patted his arm and crooned at him as if he were a babe, the cold water washing over him, whisking his watery stomach contents away. He laid back limp, swallowing metallic bile, he could tell the next round not far behind, aching from muscles spasming at his involuntary stomach reactions.

The other girl ran in dashing down the short steps to Illig. The two spoke briefly when the girl reached for his arm. Illig yanked it back, throwing Lauranya off balance.

Lauranya fell to one knee, taking Illig underwater with her. He heard her knee hitting the concrete bottom with a hollow pop. She clutched Illig closer, even as he threw an arm out grabbing onto the other girl, as Lauranya struggled to stand.

"Mom!" The girl called out, tugging Illig up and her mother at the same time.

"Mother?!" Illig said looking to the one holding him and the one to the other side of him.

"Oh, aye. Lauranya's the mom and Arie is the child."

Illig looked wide-eyed at the drenched older sister...no mother back to the younger, her daughter. "She's not more than three years older than the other!"

"A bit more if she's the mother," Uncle said with a shrug. "Now give the girl your arm like a good boy and let her fix you up."

Illig didn't resist Arie's tug this time. His arm out, Arie placed the device to his arm. A small rectangle of metal connected to a clear tube containing a blue liquid was pressed to a prominent vein. He felt metal against his skin that was both cold and hot. He shivered, the sensation traveling along his arm and down his spine. A light turned green then, what felt like a small puffer fish had rubbed against the inside of his arm with its spines, Arie withdrew the device. There were small spots of blood where the device had been, so small there weren't not even droplets.

Lauranya nodded her approval to the girl, moving with Illig still in her arms to the steps. She sat down, leaning against the wall, with Illig's head on a step, cushioned by her hand, his tail and chest in the pool.

"That's it?"

"Aye. They know what they're doing. And they would like to keep you alive."

"Why? Wouldn't I make a better door guard?"

Uncle snorted. "You have talents, nephew. Some well-hidden."

Lauranya spoke to the ghost. "I'm working on getting to that."

"Why is it she can understand you but I can't understand her?"

Uncle opened his mouth and closed it a few times. He asked Lauranya this. Arie blinked and said a few words. Lauranya looked at the three of them before responding slowly.

"It seems it has to do with the speech center of the brain and necromancy. Something to do with the person who raises you from the dead, needing you to understand them and they to understand you. Both of the women can talk to ghosts, only one can raise them."

"So if they couldn't talk to ghosts…"

"Neither would understand what I was saying" stopped for a moment, "by that logic though I wouldn't be here to bridge the gap."

"That hurts my brain."

"Yep, you're a good hunter just not long on the thinking there, kid."

Illig glared at his uncle.

The uncle tapped his nephew on the forehead. "Listen, Illig. I can't stay for too much longer." He raised a hand stalling the questions. "If they keep my spirit here much longer I won't be able to move on. So the girl, Arie's going to send me to…" here he just shrugged "whatever the next step is. They need you to teach them how we speak. The languages aren't that far apart but enough so they need help. You're the lucky sod to do it."

Uncle looked at him intently. "Understand, nephew?"

"Yes." A hoarse whisper.

He nodded. Then turned to Arie. "Ready to go, little

one."

Arie and Lauranya spoke a few words while Illig watched. At the end, he saw his uncle's ghost shred away into mist until nothing was left. He cried. Lauranya held him close, rocking him gently as she did for her own children when they were small. Arie twined fingers into his. They sang for him.

Chapter 32

Daccu looked over the small ship with a curled lip. "This is the best you can do?" The third hangar bay was filled with a variety of ships. The metal walls and floors scoured dull grey, entropy's encroach of oil and effluvia both by the living and dead, on the back of slave labor. Scarred from mundane wear and tear as well as a few pitched battles in the last two centuries for control of the world-ship, the hanger had seen better days. Daccu with both his personal bodyguards and a portion of his new fighters were reviewing the new to him ship gifted to him by his father.

The small party, 24 strong, stood in front of medium war class transport. Squat and broad. The whore of war, as they called it. A low slung belly and small cockpit, with a wide easy to climb ramp, meant to let a triple line of fighters in, opened into the ship bay. Slaves were busy moving materials and supplies into the open ramp, their bare feet slapping a random staccato on the bare metal floor.

"Master, all the accommodations have been upgraded just for you." The under-quartermaster said bowing low, her dark curly hair touched the floor, with her subsequence bow. Her eyes downcast as she cradled her tablet to tunic clad chest. Her plastic and cloth sandals silent on the decking.

The godling hit her with the back of his right hand,

hitting her cheek. The force slammed the woman into his guards, breaking the cheekbone if the purple bruise against pale skin was any indication. The tablet went flying from stunned hands.

"I find this to be fit for my slaves, not me." He growled, holding out his hand for a body slave to wipe away the woman's and his blood from the pale calf skin tight leather gloves.

The woman got to her feet unsteadily. One of the guards bent over, picking up her tablet before the feet of teaming many could find it first.

"What would you like for me to do to make the accommodations to your liking?" She asked, her words garbled but still understandable. She searched his face frantically, for a hint of understanding.

Daccu looked over his cleaned glove, looking for the slightest smear left behind, before answering. The glove was as spotless now as when he first put them on this morning. Nothing less would have been acceptable. The godling looked the woman in the eyes, with a wide smile showing strong teeth, yellow from his one indulged habit of the strong sweet drink of kopi. "Anything but this." he waved a negligent hand. Where it was smooth, with a touch of the dramatic on Menodisces, it looked effeminate on the son, an affectation he hadn't grown into yet.

"Yes, master. This will be done immediately." The woman bowed low again. She turned to stagger off towards the head Quarter Master. The guard, who'd picked up her tablet, handed it to her before she could leave. She gave him a broken smile with a small nod. Blood smearing down her face from split skin. The guard shook his head in pity.

"We leave in three weeks," Daccu said to her turned back.

The quartermaster turned slowly, looking at him with huge eyes, not sure she heard right. "Three weeks, Master." She didn't question or protest the timeline. She licked a blood-smeared upper lip before asking hesitantly, "How many will be accompanying you, master?"

This stopped the godling for a moment. Daccu looked to the captain of his guard. "Your father has granted you 4 cohorts." The short dark-skinned woman said, her eyes could be seen between her helmet's steel curved cheek pieces. The crest stiff horse hair as black as her skin. Her dark eyes gave no emotions away.

"How many necromancers?"

"One, master. You."

Daccu raised a hand to backhand her for the bad news. It could've been the stiffening of her shoulders or the adjustments the remaining of the guards behind their captain or the fact her helmet guarded the most vulnerable parts he liked to hit, that made him reconsider the gesture.

"I want three with me when we leave," he growled, getting nose to nose with her, smelling the garlic spread she had on cumin honey bread.

"Master." her response was as neutral as her eyes.

"I have a world to take over. I want every edge possible! Do you understand me?" His face turned red, contorting from well-formed human to angry hobgoblin. Spittle flew from his lips as he screamed in her face.

"Perfectly." She stared him directly in the eye.

They both knew she could no more requisition or steal a necro, any more than he could. He would have to petition his father for more if he had any chance of being taken seriously as a threat.

He turned back to the quartermaster. "2000. I want a room for me and three for my concubines. The best place where you can." He turned on his heel, spinning so fast he gave a small wobble off balance.

Daccu glared at those around him. All the guards looked straight ahead, not one face anything but set in steel. The quartermaster bowing low with her eyes to the ground. Snapping his fingers, the gloves muting the sound to a soft tchkkk, four guards fell in around him as he sniffed, stomping off to his rooms. He had two new body slaves to break in for this trip.

The remaining guards waited until the bulkhead doors closed, before laughing. Armor jingling as the mirth escaped in guffaws and snorts. Murmuring amongst themselves.

"Shut the snake raping fuck up!" The captain growled, rounding on her troops. "Do you want that baby rapist coming back and skinning you alive for amusement?" Not one would look her in the eye.

"Cap, there ain't no way we're getting 2000 of us on one of those transports." The guard, who had handed the quartermaster her tablet back, spoke up from two rows back.

"I...I don't know how I'll fit you all into this." The under quartermaster said, almost sobbing. Tears falling down her bruised cheek.

"How many can you fit into this and still accommodate the young master?" The captain ground out.

"1200. I could go up to 1400, but the room would be..."

"Tighter than a sewn up re-used body slave." She finished for the quartermaster. "Stick to 900. 800 fighters and 100 slaves, concubines and ship personnel."

"He's going to want all 2000."

"Think he's going to count us all?" She snapped, glaring to her taller lieutenant.

He shook his head. "Don't think he can count higher

than what he can lift his chiton for." His long blond braid jerking across his pauldrons.

"I'm not going to agree to that." She pinched the bridge of her nose, with a sword scarred hand. The scar tissue ropey pink against dark skin. "'Cause I want to retire with a few 16-year-old body slaves to ease my old bones. And none of you are making that easier."

"Sorry, captain. We got the short straw."

The under-quartermaster held up a hand hesitantly. "We might have a couple of smaller scout ships that could dock onto the transport. They'll hold an extra 300 each. But if you want room, we can go to 100 and make the accommodations more spacious?"

"Do that girl, and we'll take care of the Godling." She sighed heavily. "Shouldn't have beaten Georgia on Ludus. What a sore losing dick."

"Well, you did take his favorite boy toy when you cleaned up." One woman said. The others started to snicker. No-one laughed out loud.

"Shut it before I have to officially reprimand you." She grinned, to the snorts of the other fighters. "Let's make this work people! We have a world to conquer and whores to fuck!"

Chapter 33

Illig was slow to teach. He stayed in the water until there was food, then sank back down once he had eaten. He didn't want to talk with either Lauranya or Arie. He just couldn't face the loss of his uncle. Intellectually he knew they had not been the cause, but he still blamed them for the loss.

"Still not talking?" Arie asked when she and Lauranya had brought boiled eggs with grains and fruit for dinner.

Illig didn't look at her, just finished his last egg before pushing back from the edge, sinking under the water.

"Mom." Arie turned to Lauranya with a huff of young injured feelings.

"He lost a loved one," Lauranya said, collecting the plates, scraping the leftovers into a bucket for the chickens. "The pain cuts deep. However, we will need to get him talking soon before misery is all he knows."

"How do we do that?"

"I do not know, my dear. I have been trying foods that might tempt him, but good food is a meager consolation for the loss of a loved one."

"Have you lost someone?"

"Yes." Lauranya didn't elucidate further.

"What brought you out of it?"

"Marrying your father."

"Aww...you loved him that much."

"No, your father and I sort of existed in the same

rooms." Lauranya locked her teeth together to keep from saying any more.

"Then how did that break your sadness?"

"The best thing your father did was give me you."

"I remember having, a brother?"

"Brothers. Twins. They were not always the easiest of children to love." A shake of her head and a sigh. "They were amazing as babies, but your father spoiled them a bit."

"Illig doesn't have kids to help him out of this."

"Not that we know." Lauranya agreed.

"We can't just let him die!"

"Illig probably would not die. But he will become angry, unable to be around others without hurting them and himself."

"That would be bad."

"Very. So we should try to find something that might take his mind off of his pain."

Arie was thoughtful.

Illig laid at the bottom of the pool, watching the light move from one end of his watery room to the other side. His mind kept running over the last hunt he and his uncle did if they had gone after smaller fish instead of one big one. If he hadn't followed the wounded fish. If he had only slowed down. Illig balled up fists slamming them through the water onto the concrete bottom of the pool.

He heard thumping from topside of the pool. He ignored the noises and the women's voices. The thumping stopped while the voices went back and forth. He could sometimes tell who was talking but not always. Their voices were too similar. Then they stopped speaking. Illig took a deep breath of water, releasing the pent up shoulder muscles that had tightened with the intrusion of his solitary time.

The music filtered through the water gently, like fresh rain on the ocean. A note, then another, then a cascade. The sound flowed through him gently, but gentle wasn't what he wanted. With an annoyed growl, he pushed off the bottom, coming to the top ready to splash Arie and Lauranya into silence when the two started to sing.

Had Illig only been able to breathe air he would have drowned as he sank down, letting the water close over him. Lauranya's voice wound through his brain soft, loving, warm. Gifting him with a taste of childhood safety, even in childhood something he never had. He bobbed back up as the water muffled the voices and he wanted to catch every sound. He pulled himself to the stairs, laying on the steps, arranging so that his wounds weren't pressing into the stone steps.

Illig didn't know how long they sang, but when they stopped, his eyes popped open into a dark room. Night had come, turning the pool from a pale blue to black.

"No. Don't stop. Please."

Lauranya and Arie stood stretching. Arie said something sweetly, giving him a huge smile. Lauranya rolled her eyes even as she smiled at her daughter, heading out of the room.

"Wait! No." Illig sat up, feeling the pull of the stitches so he moved slowly to the side of the pool.

Arie came to the edge of the pool, dipping a hand into the water and pour it out. She looked at him. "What? Why aren't you singing?!" She sat back and singing a short burst, then went silent again just as a lethargic relaxation took him over. Again she put her hand in the water, pouring it out.

"Why are you playing with water? Sing! Please."

Arie tried to duplicate his words, managing to butcher the entire sentence. When she was done, she sang for a brief moment then stopped, sitting back, waiting. Illig looked at her with an almost glare, understanding.

"You're not going to sing until I start teaching you the language, are you?"

Arie smiled sweetly at him before leaning over the pool to scoop up more water. She sat back again waiting.

"Water." He said through gritted teeth, touching the water. "Lift or pick up. Lifting water. Pouring water." Each word he demonstrated. Arie stared at him intently, enunciating each word mimicking him perfectly.

"Yes, exactly." He nodded.

Arie sat back with half-closed eyes to sing for him.

Illig exhaled, melting into the music. "We aren't going to get far if you keep singing.

Lauranya walked in with food. A small sampling of several dishes he enjoyed. She set them by the edge of the pool as Arie finished singing. Arie's voice was liquid like water droplets as she sang/spoke the new words Illig had taught her, demonstrating the different verbs.

Lauranya nodded, giving a slight smile and nod to Illig, as she knelt on her pillow. Lauranya repeated the words. When she stopped, she looked at Illig expectantly. He nodded approval but did correct the verb to lift. Both of the women repeated the words back to him, perfectly this time.

Lauranya set out the plates, putting small bites of the various foods. She put one in front of Illig, Arie and herself.

"Illig." She spoke. He looked up mid-reach for half an egg and a dab of sauce. She pointed to the whole egg.

"Egg." He said. He took a whole egg, splitting it in half with his fingers. "Half an egg. Yolk."

They repeated the words. Lauranya mimed the splitting gesture.

"Split in half. To split." Illig said.

Lauranya smiled, nodding her thanks. This time Lauranya sang for him. Where Arie could relax him, Lauranya's could lure him out of the water, happy to crawl over sharp and brittle lava rock with a smile on his face. A sharp stab of pain went through him when she stopped. He sucked in a shuddering breath.

"Your voice could kill a man and he'd die happy." He whispered he shook his head, blinking rapidly to clear his eyes of tears. Arie leaned forward to wipe away a tear on his cheek that had fallen. She said something to him; concern in her voice the words unknown.

Lauranya answered her, causing Arie to look sharply at her mother, her hand still on Illig's cheek.

Illig cleared his throat, touching Arie's hand giving her a brief smile, before tapping on the plate. They did this for all the items to be eaten. Arie singing to him while Lauranya sat and listened. Illig was both relieved and disappointed. Arie's voice would grow into her mother's but not today. Today Illig was just as happy to listen to the younger singer and not the older. Keeping his soul a little longer.

By the second 10 days of Illig's language lessons, Arie and Lauranya could mostly converse. The language drift wasn't as bad as Lauranya feared yet she and Arie could speak in private if needed.

"Illig." Lauranya slapped the water lightly, to get his attention as he and Arie were going over a video on her tablet.

The mer turned to Lauranya with a startled look and a

boyish smile. Both he and Arie were smiling more these days.

"Yes, Lauranya?"

Lauranya smiled at this, with a slight downward look and shake of her head. She had missed the company of others as well. "I need to take out your stitches before skin covers the silk thread."

Illig made a face but pulled himself up the stairs to lie out on the tile. Lauranya knelt by his side, as Arie slid the tablet onto the small portable wood table set next to the pool. She took the other side of Illig, holding his hand.

Lauranya hesitated over the first stitch on his tail. She chewed her lower lip for a moment before turning to him. "This will have some pain. Would you like something to drink or a shot?"

Illig sat up, the muscles in his stomach flexed with ridges "Neither. I really don't want to puke in the pool again." This time he said it with a smile.

Lauranya nodded, understandingly.

"Though if you could tell me a story to help keep my mind off of the stitches that would help as well."

"Oh, how about the marriage story mom!" Arie said excitedly.

"Your uncle's marriage and how they took over a world-ship?"

"Yes, that one!"

"World ship? Marriage?"

"I think that one might be a little more intense than Illig will want to hear. How about how the Undead Gods came about?"

"Oh! Like in the aria!"

"Yes, just like that, as my noni told the children." Lauranya turned to Illig. "Does that sound acceptable to you?"

"Sure?" Illig didn't sound sure, but Arie's enthusiasm was contagious.

Lauranya took a deep breath as she started on the first suture. "When the world was new, the air was scented with all the flowers and water as sweet as wine. Every man was free; all cared for another. There were no plagues or wars. Life was good."

The first few stitches had skin growing over them. Lauranya began tugging gently when there was the occasional stuck stitch. Illig bit his lip or pounded on the wood floor.

"The Gods moved among us unseen but always felt. Men were the favored child, best beloved. Some children were born dark-skinned, or pale skinned, some red as the steel fresh from the foundry other's as yellow as newly turned butter. Yet as beloved as all their children were, the Gods knew that mother or father would coddle a child if the child was too full of potential. The Gods loved us, but they let us fall and fail, to pick ourselves up, learning from the mistakes."

"VOID!" Illig sat up with a not so muffled snarling curse on the third stitch.

"This is the worst of the stitches," Lauranya said, sitting back on her heels as he gasped for breath. "Do you want something to help with the pain?"

"No! Just do it." With his teeth clenched, the words came out almost as if he were chewing before spitting out each one."

Lauranya continued, teasing each stitch with slight wiggling and tugging before extracting the next set. Lauranya's voice changed pitch. Low soothing, as if she were almost singing a song of comfort while speaking of her past. Her words lulling Illig into a meditative state.

"There came a day when the skies grew dark, boiling

with clouds never seen before. Ships that floated in the air, never touching the ground, approached the villages and cities."

Illig's fists unclenched with the first few words, and his breathing evened out. Arie tilted her head, listening to her mother before adding an almost inaudible harmony meant to relax and calm.

"A new type of God came to us. Gods with skin so hard, spears bounced off and swords broke. The Gods laughed and roared as the ground shook beneath their feet. They wanted slaves, something we knew nothing about. Their demand was met with laughter."

This angered the new Gods, so they decided to steal what they had been denied. They stole the people, by the thousands, into their floating world-ships. They fed the people rotting grain and foul meat, killing over half of us in the first few ten days. The people cried and begged their gods to help on bended knee. Their cries were so piteous, the gods were moved to help.

One woman had just given birth to twins. These twins were touched by Ibeji, the protector of twins, God of vitality and youth. One child black as the night, so dark that stars could almost be seen in his skin. The other one, white as delicate bone porcelain, so pale the mother at first thought the child dead until a great cry burst forth from his lips on strong lungs.

The gods decided that they should gift these children with the tools to throw off these new usurping Gods. Every mother's child, from that day forward, would have these gifts to fight their oppression.

Olorun, our all father stepped forward with Oya and Oloosi gods of war and hunting. They granted those with dark skin the ability to blend with the shadows, stealthy as the Namiri as strong as a silver backed Nayani. These gifted children would be both spear and shield in the fight to come.

To the pale cloud child, the gift was more dangerous. Obatala reached deep from within himself, gifting with the ability to raise the dead. The dead would come when called and obey when ordered. The spirit would have to answer to the one who summoned.

Yemoja, our all mother, with Orunmila the holder of wisdom, deemed this gift dangerous even if it would save us, so they placed a warning on those who would call upon this gift. They would not deny the gift, but they set rules as one does for children and fire."

"Why was it dangerous?" Illig asked, his voice distant, trance-like.

"At some point, the gods would be defeated, but these gifts would not just vanish," Lauranya answered. She nodded to Arie, to help move him to his stomach. They turned him over, both harmonizing to keep him in the relaxed state. Lauranya waited until Illig adjusted and got comfortable.

"For the person with the gift of summoning, they would always know where the dead were, know what the dead said and for the strongest, they would feel what the dead feel. So that no-one who could raise the dead would want to kill another, for they would feel the pain and sorrow of the person who had died.

Esu, the god of tricks and surprises, added one more gift to his favored children. He gave the gift of losing one's self in the fight, able to push beyond pain or thought, to do an impossible task, even past the point of death. The one fighting could go until there was no more left, their body and soul used, completely beyond recovery. This angered the other gods. They loved their children and did not want a child to die due to lack of control or boundaries.

Ori, stepped in, proclaiming that Esu's gift would be a great boon to the people but not all of the children would grow into such powers, those who did not or could not would help bring those lost to the fight back to themselves. And so the children and every other child born to our people were gifted with necromancy or fighting. But not all powers were equal. Some children would be the intellectual.

Finally, Ibeji stepped in. He deemed that each child would be born either black or white but the gifts would not always follow the day or night. Usually, the skin and gift would match but occasionally there would be a split. The gods were pleased with their gifts. The children learned to control, overcoming the thunderous Gods taking their homes in space to live as their own."

Lauranya tugged on the final stitch, touching the alcohol-soaked cloth over the drop of blood that welled up. She and Arie stopped harmonizing letting Illig come out of the song induced daze pale and sweating. Lauranya put her scissors and cloth to the side. "Ready to rest in the pool now?"

"Space, yes!" Illig croaked, drawing in a shaky breath. Lauranya helped him to roll into a sitting position. She put arms under his tail and chest, lifting with her knees. Walking into the pool, she had to feel with her toes where the steps were, so neither took an unceremonious dive headfirst.

Illig threw an arm around her neck for balance. He didn't question her strength. Land-based people fought gravity with every step and every item lifted. Lauranya let him down gently once the water was deep enough for him to be comfortable. Illig, pulling with his arms, moved to the deeper end, letting the water soothe him to sleep.

"Mom, you're getting stronger," Arie said, with a little

worry.

"A little, I have been lifting him up and down for a couple of weeks now," Lauranya said, with a smile to ease her child. Arie gave her mother a look. A look copied from those times she herself was not always perfect.

"Not telling me everything, are you?" Hand on her hip.

"Most of what I know I try to teach," Lauranya said, put hands to the small of her back and stretching. "He is not as heavy as previous, having lost weight from the drugs as well as not eating as much as he usually does."

Arie frowned but couldn't find the holes she knew were in her mother's statement.

Chapter 34

"Master, we're approaching the old science base now." The slave pilot said melodically, over the intercom.

Daccu, growled even as his concubine sped up to finish him off. "Off, woman! I have a planet to conquer." He roughly threw her to the side, into the other two naked bodies.

"Accip, clean me off." Daccu snapped. The young man rolled off the bed to the small towel warming service next to the bed. He pulled out three towels, knee walking towards his master, lifting with both hands palms up for Daccu to choose.

Daccu used the first towel to wipe down face and hands while Accip ran the other warm towels over his chest, arms and landscaped penis and balls. Daccu dropped his used towel on top of Accip's head, before turning back to the bed. Accip removed the towel, standing up with little room, the huge bed taking most of the available space.

Meldi gave a purring stretch, making sure to accentuate her ample chest and flat stomach emphasizing her curving hips. Daccu stopped and starred, appreciating his dead sister's body slave yet again.

"The blue toga master?" She asked, rolling over to spoon with Star, run a hand down the other woman's beautiful dark skin. Meldi's porcelain skin contrasted with the other girl's exotically.

"Yes. That'll do for the moment." Daccu thought he sounded haughty, but his voice came out breathy and needy. Meldi smiled coquettishly, dipping her head to kiss Star's shoulder before rolling out of bed. Daccu found himself once again watching her lush hips moving to his walk-in closet.

Daccu turned to Accip, pushing the young man to his knees. "Finish me off, now." Accip paled only a little but accommodated his master's desire as the well-trained body slave he was.

Daccu made the bridge with two of his guards in tow. The white toga with blue stripes would have scraped along the floor if not for his gold and sapphire leather belt. He had done away with his overwrap. Walking through the ship caused the wrap to catch on chairs, corners, and soldiers as he moved about. An annoyance he got tired of within the first 10 day.

The captain of his cohorts, with the pilot and his guards made the tiny cockpit hot and crowded.

"Is that a building above the water?" Daccu leaned over the pilot, pushing her to the side, craning his neck to look down.

"Yes, master." The pilot squeaked out, pinned to the side of her panel. She fumbled to stabilize the rotors, as Daccu was pushing into her.

"I want to see it up close. Land on the roof." He commanded, turning back to his guards.

"Master, that building has been standing in water for over 14 ship turns. The stability is questionable."

"There are plants on the roof and green things seen in the upper floors."

"Yes, master probably a few potted plants have survived where water has leaked in and their roots have found such nourishment as they could." The captain stopped for a moment "All ship captains recaptured have all reiterated that there were no survivors left, all scientists and slaves were emptied into the atmosphere after takeoff."

Daccu looked at her, a twitch to his hand as if he wanted to raise his fist. She tried a different tact. "There is a very good chance it will collapse, taking us with it, if we land on the top."

That argument seemed to sink in. "We could make an expedition back to the building to check on this after we take the world and have a hand-picked team accompany you to confirm that there is nothing insect or animal that is surviving on these upper floors as well."

"Once this world is mine, we will be back."

"Of course master."

"I want to have the small scout ships explore the different areas. We can wait in space."

Chapter 35

Lauranya heard the transport before she saw it. She froze in place long enough to identify the sound before rushing to the pool room, yelling.

"Arie, get away from the windows!" Lauranya's voice reverberated off the walls. The voice held command, pulling Arie away from the pool edge and pushing her against the opposite wall without any windows. Illig felt the command reverberate through his head but the voice held no command for him, just Arie.

"Mom!" Arie wailed against the wall, waiting for her mother, her voice not as powerful held fear and confusion, collapsing into a small huddle.

"Arie! Arie, you're ok!" Illig yelled from the pool, reaching for her but unable to get out of the water.

Lauranya rushed in, looking frantically for her daughter. She rushed to Arie's side, wrapping arms around her, huddling in the shadows as a loud roaring passed overhead.

"What was that?" Arie asked meekly into her mother's shoulder.

"A transport. A fighter transport from a world-ship. They've found us." Lauranya whispered grimly. Her eyes following the sound as if she could follow the actual ship through concrete and steel. Arie huddled closer, shaking harder. Lauranya held Arie until the sound dissipated pressing her cheek into Arie's hair, tears rolling down her cheek.

Illig waited until Lauranya was no longer following a noise he had never heard before asking questions. "What was that? Why are you so scared?"

Lauranya looked up from Arie, brushing off the tears. "The Undead Gods have found us."

"Undead Gods? Void! What will they do?" Illig pushed back from the back poolside, pushing from one side to the other in agitation.

"If, if they stay true to form, they will try to recapture as many Runners as they can." Lauranya's voice emptied of all emotion, as she stared out the windows into wide blue skies. "Those they can't recapture, they kill. They will destroy any habitat, eco structures, livestock, crops, and possible hiding areas."

She looked at Illig, then away. "Those who are not human will be shot at first chance if they are lucky."

Illig had to swallow. "And if they aren't lucky?"

"They will be studied."

"Mers? Wing or land shifters?"

"Killed or studied." Her response flat, her hands clenched.

"Arie? You?"

"Arie... Arie would be taken and made into a pampered slave as a powerful Necromancer. A pawn that will be bred for necro children or killed as being too strong. Me. I will be shot within a few weeks if not days."

"Why?"

Lauranya raised her hand and let the hand shift up to the shoulder into that of a Whiskered Cat paw.

Illig's jaw dropped. "You're not born, or infected... how the space are you shifting?"

A ghost of a smile crossed Lauranya's lips. "Wrong place and wrong time. Somewhere the virus got loose into the wild and found me."

Arie stood from the back wall, creeping up to her mother, slipping arms around her waist, laying her head on her mother's shoulder for comfort. Tears flowing freely down the young woman's face.

"What are we going to do?" Arie asked, in a choking whisper.

"We need to get Illig healed up enough to leave. He and the other mers might be safe. I have never seen or heard of a water race before. You and I will have to accept Yemoja's will." Lauranya said, with a heavy sigh.

"No! I won't accept that there isn't anything to do!" Illig growled, pounding the wood floor with a rhythm that set a beat through the room.

"Can you fight men and women trained to work as a unit, driven by the fear of how, not if, they will die?"

"How can you just stand by and let them take Arie?!"

Lauranya looked at the floor, then looked up bleakly. "They would have taken her after her first assessment." She touched Arie's cheek with her hand. "These years have been a blessing from the gods."

Lauranya took a deep, shuddering breath, she spoke to her daughter. "Arie, I am going to get my notes in order for when they return. Say your goodbyes to Illig. He needs to leave in the next day or two." Lauranya turned, leaving the room with a firm step and bent shoulders.

Arie stared after her mother, turning to Illig then back to her mother's retreating back.

"Arie?" Illig splashed her to get Arie to turn towards him. "What did she say?"

"She's putting her notes together so her work won't be lost."

Illig gritted his teeth. "What is….How is she going to get me out of here?"

"Through the shaft. It goes down to the bottom floor where the undead guards are." Illig looked at her thoughtfully for a moment. "It's 100 feet down?"

"130 I think."

"I need to test my legs." Illig said abruptly, pulling himself out of the pool.

"Legs?" Arie asked dumbly, her eyes on his tail.

"I need to shift. I need to see if I can or if the damage is too deep."

"How will you know?"

"I'll bounce back into tail form." He said, with a grin. "Okay, I'll turn back to a mer screaming in pain because I'll have ripped something serious."

"Should you be doing this?"

"Yep!" He swung his tail over and laid on the edge of the pool. Arie knelt beside him.

"Is there anything I can do?"

"Nope...just, stay beside me?"

"I can do that."

"Well, one more thing?"

"Of course?" She bounced to her feet ready to get towels for his gills. When he reached a hand to hers pulling her back down. "No towels?" Confused.

"No, no towels this time." He pulled her gently close to him, touching his lips to hers. "For luck."

Arie pulled back slowly with a quirking lip and a questioning look. Illig to a deep breath and started his shift. The pain was.manageable as his leg separated bone, muscle, and skin, rebuilding to legs.

He lay on his back for a moment more, gasping. Arie tilted her head looking at his muscular body. "That was amazing. Is your clitoris supposed to be that big?"

"My what?!" Illig tried to say calmly but came out more of a rumbled huff of grunted air.

"Your clit." Arie pointed at his lower region.

"That's not a clitoris! It's a penis."

"Oh. What does it do?"

"Umm…" Illig had to stop speaking for a moment. He knew it was just Arie and Lauranya, but he hadn't expected a discussion on anatomy so soon after switching back to his land form. "Tell you what, help me get to the roof, and I'll explain on the way up."

It was Arie's turn to stare. "You're leaving us." She shook her head, swiping at her eyes surreptitiously.

"Your mom is waiting for me to heal and shift. I'm healed and shifted. The sooner I hit the water, the safer you are." He rolled to his side, sitting on his knees to look at Arie. "I don't want to get either of you killed." His mouth was a firm line. "However, I could use a hand." He held a hand up for help standing. "Haven't used the legs in a while. Not used to this no swimming thing you call walking."

The fluttering in her stomach making her blush and giving him a confused smile. She reached a hand to help him up. She noticed for the first time how warm and muscular his hands were as they covered her smaller hand.

Illig staggered up, leaning heavily on Arie, his knees wobbled. His muscles had atrophied slightly, with the lack of exercise, in the weeks he had been healing. Arie wrapped an arm around his waist, bracing him against her as he took his first cautious step.

"Only a few hundred more to go, eh?" Illig tried for levity.

"We only have one set of stairs to climb to get to the roof and the window lift." Arie chirped.

"Only one? Void, my tail or legs will never speak to me again." Illig theatrically grumped. His leg muscles were protesting. He didn't want Arie to see the pain he was in. She wouldn't have helped him to the water and his plan would be for naught.

"At least not without a lot of screaming?" Arie shot him a sly smile.

"Keep laughing it up, blondie!"

Arie giggled as Illig shuffled forward, one slow step at a time.

The roof was achieved. Illig was out of breath, panting, leaning on the wall as Arie pushed the door open a crack. She listened for the transport. Nothing. The wind and water the only things she heard. The door opened without protest, letting in a warm wet breeze in with a hint of fish.

"Just a little further." Arie's encouragement made Illig smile slightly. He reached out an arm to wrap around her shoulders.

"Is there nothing that you can't find the good in?" Lines of pain mixed with his smile, at her enthusiasm. She took his weight again as they made their way to the window lift. The limping made the pair look like a couple of sailors after an 8-hour drinking binge, walking towards their berth over rocky ground.

"Most things are good!" Arie insisted. The breeze danced merrily through her shoulder length hair, tickling Illig's nose.

"Pfft, woman, you need to braid your hair!" He waved his hand across his face as her hair mocked him.

"I'll get right on that." She quipped back, with a roll of her eyes.

"Yep, yep. Should listen to your elders." Illig said snarkily, before letting out a gasp of pain, trying to bend while standing, grabbing for his calf. "Oww...stupid calf muscle! It's terrible getting old and creaky!" Illig moaned, only partially feigning crippling pain.

"You're not that much older than me." Arie snickered, catching him as the calf muscles cramped hard enough to buckle the leg.

"Oww. Space. This swim is going to suck meteorite dust." Illig swore. He hopped on his other leg the last few feet to the balustrade. Luckily the window lift was within a foot of his resting spot.

Arie tested the chain, held on then jumped down with a controlled drop onto the twisted metal frame. The metal only shivered but did not sway.

Illig looked over the side at what she was doing. "The lift get twisted in the storm?"

"What?" Arie looked down at the lift. "No, something tried to eat mom when she decided to try and do skein netting from the lift at the water edge. It got the frame instead."

"Your mom is lucky! Lots of things find us tasty."

"Yeah. She jumped 10 feet straight up in the air." Arie looked down the stone wall. "If you look you can see where her claws dug into the rock to hold her up as the thing let go of the metal and tried for her instead!"

"Was that recent?" Illig looked into the dark blue waters a little worriedly.

"That, no. The waters were only at the 7th floor. That was...right after we had to kill all our rabbits and needed more protein." Arie tugged on a chain, the muscles in her arms cording. Illig watched her arms and chest. He had to look to the side into the water as parts of him approved of her almost island dressing or lack of.

"The guards take care of any flat heads or anything else big that comes around now. Not just those things that come to the windows of the building." Arie continued pulling the lift within a couple of feet from the top so Illig wouldn't have to jump down.

"Okay, on you go. Just pull the chain and it'll lower you to the water." Arie scrambled over the sidewall, straddling the rough surface. A couple of scrapes showing pale against her slightly sun-kissed skin.

Illig hobbled over the last foot or three to her. He got one leg onto the balustrade, almost tipping over as he tried to pull the other leg over. He blushed, refusing to look Arie in the eye.

Arie nodded. "Right." Was all she said as she got back onto the metal frame. Her hips level with the balustrade and him. She helped him down the sidewall.

"I...I need help." Was all he said as his hands wrapped around the metal chains, white-knuckled.

Arie gave him a quick hug. "I can do that!" She moved to the other side. Her bare feet, steady on the twisted surface. Arie began pulling the chain down slowly. Illig had to release the chain he was holding; the chain pulled his hands down into a pulley.

Illig held on to a non-moving chain while Arie lowered them to the water. He saw a couple of the divots Lauranya had clawed into the granite with her nails. His fingers traced them, as they moved downward.

"Your mom is really strong."

"She is." Arie puffed out her chest, with a smile. "She's amazing." Her face darkened as Arie remembered the morning conversations. "I don't want her to die." She whispered.

Illig saw a tear fall down her cheek. He reached out to touch her cheek, stopping the trailing tear.

"Hey. We're going to do something about that." A low ripple from the building broke across the lift, getting his feet damp.

"I'll wait until you've changed and are in the water

before heading back up," Arie said, with a tremulous smile. "I'll miss you."

She leaned over to kiss him on the cheek. Illig wrapped his arms around her pulling her close.

"Forgive me." Was all he said, before diving into the water with her glued to him.

Lauranya spent the next few hours poring over old records. She collated all the dated work, picking out the best research she had done, stopping to clean up a phrase or paragraph here and there. The data was impressive. The width and breadth of her research covered a span of 14 ship years. She smiled fondly at each bit of art, seeing Arie's talent grow as the years progressed. She bent her head as she backed up her work both on the computer, in paper and on a memory insert. The reflection of those years, as Arie's wording or inserted sketch caused the occasional tear.

"Esu! Woman, you knew this would happen." She whispered, running a hand across her cheek. "Perhaps Ori will take pity and send me somewhere as good as the years in the tower have been."

Jacks appeared next to her, faded even for a ghost. "He took Arie!" then dissipated.

"What?! Jacks? Jacks!" Jacks ghost grew a little stronger, but the spirit and the voice were mere whispers.

"He's taking Arie to the west."

"Who? Arie!" Lauranya jumped from her set, her feet hitting the wood floor with a thump. She ran pell-mell to the pool room. Calling for Arie with every breath. The room was empty of Illig or Arie.

"Topside." Jacks whispered, so pale he was barely an outline anymore. Lauranya's meager necro gift, summoning Jacks on a fraction of the gift Arie held.

Lauranya spun on her toes, running for the rooftop. Usually, the hallway was dark, but the door was still open, filling it with glowing summer light. The wind was fresh and playful blowing down the hallway.

Lauranya made the rooftop, looking frantically for her child, her voice going hoarse as she continued to call out.

"Window lift." Jacks said with a voice softer than a sigh.

The metal lift was to the water...and empty. Lauranya collapsed on the stone floor. "I have lost my child!" She wailed to the bright sky. The sun was still moving over the blue sky without a care for a mother's loss.

About the Author

My interests are widely varied, so much so that when discussing different types of genres and subcultures; I keep being asked which lane I'm driving in. All I can say is that my lane is usually all over the map! My stories are never just short stories. I think I have one, maybe two that I can/will call short, but even then they will end up being close to 75 page novellas. I keep a dream journal and a notebook just for one liners/off the cuff remarks because anything can and will be used! An SCA enthusiast with a wide range of friends and interest including but not limited to fencing, dancing, cooking and reading anything not being sat on by a cat.